He Was Endlessly Patient with Her. . . .

They sat together on the couch where they would soon lie, sipping wine, not speaking, just touching—fingers, hands, arms, faces, throat. "Your skin is so beautiful, so soft." How many times did he say it? She saw the tenderness in his eyes and knew it was love, heard the huskiness in his voice and knew it was desire, sensed the wonder in him as he surveyed her body and knew her own pleasure at his arousal.

Oh, how he enflamed her! She trembled at his touch and shuddered as she pressed her body against his, his kisses making her mouth a conduit of sensations that seemed to sweep her whole body. The things he knew. . . .

She sensed how much he wanted her; yet he took his time. When she could stand it no longer, she whispered, "Now, Morgan, please, *now.*"

"Yes," he answered, his voice husky with passion. . . .

Desire's Legacy

ELIZABETH BRIGHT

A RIVER BOOK

Published by:
River Publishing Co., Inc.
149 Fifth Avenue - Suite 1301
New York, NY 10010

Printed in the United States of America.

ISBN: 1-55547-326-1

First Printing July 1994

PART I

Cassie

Chapter 1

For Cassie Brown, the kiss just happened, naturally, perhaps inevitably. She was being rowed down the river by Morgan Kingston, when he pulled to shore, wanting to show her a beauty spot nearby. He stepped to the bank and reached out his hand to assist her. But, as she stepped out of the boat, her skirt caught momentarily on the oarlock and she fell forward against him. Suddenly, his mouth was on hers, his lips hungry, devouring, yet gentle. Cassie was just eighteen; this was her first real kiss, and she felt elated by its sweetness, weakened by its passion.

It seemed to her to go on the longest time—and the shortest. Involuntarily, her body seemed to relax, melt, flow into his, her softness yielding to his hardness as she leaned against him, and his arms came tightly around her waist. She had dreamed of being kissed, but no dream had prepared her for this. Her right hand still clutched the brim of the yellow-straw picture hat atop her head, but the rest of her had yielded completely to Morgan's touch.

Then he was standing before her, his hands on her shoulders. Without willing the action, she released her hat and brought her fingertips to her lips, touching the place where she had felt such pleasure. Her eyes were wide with wonder. He was smiling, his brown eyes soft and warm. "I've wanted to do that for a long time, Cassie."

She thought he was going to kiss her again—and she wanted him to—but he didn't, not then. He took her hand and led her up the bank and along a path beside the river. She followed numbly, unable to keep up with his pace. He led her through a copse of trees. "Isn't this beautiful, Cassie? It's my favorite spot at Aurial."

It was beautiful. The hazy July sunlight, filtered by the moving leaves of birch, aspen and acacia trees, seemed to shimmer. He led her a few steps further, their shoes making crackling sounds on the dead leaves of the previous autumn, then he stopped, turned her to her left, his arm around her waist, and pointed. "This is the only place you can get this view." A few hundred yards ahead of her, atop rising ground, lay the great house of Aurial, the Morgan-Kingston estate on the Patuxent River in Maryland. The stone house, painted white, was in profile now, the majestic wooden columns of the portico guarding the veranda and the green expanse of lawn that led down to the point of land where Short Creek joined the Patuxent.

"It's lovely, Morgan."

Again, he turned her. She saw the river flowing below, their rowboat bobbing at the edge; then, in the opposite direction from Aurial, another great house, squarer, of painted white wood, with black shutters. "That's Kingston," he said, "the home of my grandfather Kingston. All his life, he coveted Aurial. It stood on higher ground and had a better location at the point. He hated my grandfather Morgan for owning it." He turned Cassie back to look at Aurial. "I've always imagined my grandfather Kingston standing here, looking at Aurial, wanting it so badly. He got it, but he died soon afterwards and never enjoyed it. Not until my father, Ned Kingston, married my mother, Moira Morgan, were the two estates truly joined."

He turned to her. "Did you know that story?"

She smiled. "I think so, but I'm glad to hear it

again—from you. And I'm glad you brought me here, to see this view."

"Yes, I wanted you to see it." He smiled. "It's the second most beautiful view I know."

"Second?"

"Yes." Slowly, his smile fading as his head lowered to hers, he kissed her again, a brief, electric touching of the lips. "You're the first."

"Morgan, I—"

"Was that your first kiss a moment ago?"

"Yes, I—"

"I wish it had been my first—but it was certainly the best. What a mouth you have!"

Then he was truly kissing her, longer, deeper than before, and again she felt overcome by sweetness and desire. Her mouth was open, his tongue slipped gently inside, and she felt her lips close over it, felt wondrous sensations as his tongue thrust deeper into her mouth and his hands traced delicate circles on her back. She gave a small moan, releasing his tongue, and then his lips were everywhere—at her eyes, her cheeks, her throat, even her ears—smothering her with tiny, butterfly kisses amid expressions of wonder and delight. Her hat fell away, but she was powerless to retrieve it; her whole body trembled with a delicious weakness, and she soon forgot the hat completely, as his tongue again entered her mouth and began to explore, searchingly, tenderly, sliding over her teeth, her gums, the sides of her mouth, then meeting her own tongue and curling sensuously around it. She felt herself on the brink of an abyss and, wrenching her mouth from his, took in a deep breath of air.

"Oh, God . . . Morgan. I . . . can't . . . stand it."

But she did, her lips again finding his. She knew she must stop him before it was too late. Twisting her mouth from him, she gasped, "We can't . . . we mustn't. . . ."

"Why?" He tried to kiss her anew, but she swung her head away and pushed against him. He saw her looking around frantically. "There's no one to see us here, Cassie."

Again, she pushed at him, her hands against his chest. "I can't . . . we shouldn't."

"You know I care about you, Cassie. I didn't bring you here to do this. It just happened. We're two people who . . . who care about each other."

"I know, Morgan, but still—"

"So we kissed. What's wrong with that?"

She stared at him, mouth open a little, disbelieving his question. "You know."

"I know what?"

She reached out and touched his cheek with her hand. "This."

He seemed perplexed. "What're you talking about?" He reached up, clasped her fingers and held them against his cheek.

Then she realized he couldn't see what she saw against his face. Slowly, turning her hand, taking his fingers, she brought his hand down until it was between them, their fingers intertwined. She waited until he looked down at their hands, then she said a single word: "That."

She watched as recognition, then understanding, came to his face, followed quickly by consternation. There was a hint of anger in his voice as he said, "Oh, Cassie, you can't believe I care about that."

"If you don't, you should." Her voice was little above a whisper.

"Cassie, *don't.* Don't even think it. You're the most beautiful and desirable woman I know."

All things considered, it was quite a compliment, for Morgan Kingston had spent all his nearly twenty-four years surrounded by four celebrated beauties. Most famous of all was his grandmother. Born Glenna O'Reilly, she had become Glenna Morgan, the name most people still knew her by. Now the wife of New York banker Franklin Fairchild, she remained, even at age sixty-five, a handsome, silver-haired woman, a living legend. His mother, Moira Morgan Kingston, now the wife of attorney Lawrence Hodges, was a stunning, sensuous woman of forty-four, her beacon of flaming hair still her trademark. His sister, Danielle Kingston Summers, was to many men the most delicately beautiful woman they had ever seen. And his stepsister, Miriam Hodges, her sensitive features framed by a platinum halo of hair, already promised to become another of the family beauties. For Morgan to call Cassie Brown the most beautiful woman he knew was either flattery—or the statement of a man very much in love.

Yet, Cassie Brown *was* beautiful, by any standards. Her ebony-black hair fell in soft waves to her shoulders, the ends turning out naturally and bouncing as she walked; her warm, bright eyes of rich, dark hazel were set wide apart in an almond face, and that luscious mouth, which Morgan had so wanted to kiss, was wide and generous, with full lips turned out sensuously. But what made her such a remarkable beauty was what she now commanded Morgan to see, for the skin of her fingers intertwined with his was a soft, warm, luminescent brown, the color of cocoa.

Cassandra "Cassie" Brown was born a slave in 1857, although she had no memory of slavery. Neither did she recall her father, a fugitive slave who had no knowledge he had conceived a child, nor her mother, who had died giving birth to her. Cassie was raised on a plantation near Charleston, South Carolina. She had only the dimmest memories of the place, and of the people who had looked after her there. On February 17, 1865, Union forces, under General William Tecumseh Sherman, occupied Charleston, and at age seven, Cassie, an orphan, became a sort of mascot to Northern troops, waiting on tables in the barracks, shining shoes, running errands. Touched by her waif-like air, they were good to her. For the first time in her life, she had enough to eat, a warm place to sleep. She was not afraid of the blue coats.

Even at that young age, her beauty was apparent, for as happened with so many slaves by the middle of the nineteenth century, a diversity of genes had combined in her blood, African and white and a pronounced streak of West Indian. The result of this mixed blood was certainly alluring: the hazel of her remarkable eyes, the delicacy of her features, the fine nose, perhaps too small for her face, the wide, tantalizing mouth. Union troops called her a "chocolate white girl." She remembered that, but for a long time she didn't understand.

Cassie was saved from the fate of most beautiful colored girls in the South, first by a kindly troop commander, then by Danielle Kingston Summers, Morgan's sister. When Cassie was thirteen and just blossoming into tall, statuesque womanhood, the troop commander recommended her to Danielle, a Yankee woman who had just come to live near Charleston with her husband, Walter Summers, a former Confederate officer and spy. Danielle took Cassie into her home, protected her, and trained her to be a maid and nurse for her children. In the process, Cassie Brown, only seven years younger than Danielle, became both friend and confidante of her "mistress."

Cassie, now standing in the lovely copse of trees at Aurial, trying to explain to Morgan Kingston the difference between them by clasping his hand so he could see the contrasting color of their skin, was far removed from her slave origins. The kindness of Union troops and the friendship of Danielle Summers had obliterated any vestigial fear of white people, all sense of inferiority. Even her speech, accent and manners had become refined under Danielle's tutelage. Oh, Cassie knew her place as a servant—around Walter Summers especially—but she was never obsequious. Rather, she possessed a natural reserve, a quiet dignity that more than a few people found disturbing. This demeanor stood her in good stead, however, for it often masked the anxieties, uncertainties and confusion any girl of eighteen would have. Never did she need it more than now, as she tried to fend off the impassioned advances of Morgan Kingston.

"Cassie, I love you. I wanted to say it when I visited you in Charleston last year, but I felt I had no right. You were too young. But, now, I must say it, Cassie. I have to. I love you."

"Please, Morgan. It isn't possible. You must know that."

It was an agonizing moment for her; her mind, her good sense, both fighting a valiant rearguard action against her nearly overwhelming desire. Morgan Kingston was the most appealing man she had ever known, and to have him kiss her so and declare his love for her created immense temptations. He was extremely handsome: tall, muscular, with jet-black hair, a rugged, manly face, deepest brown eyes, a wide mouth with a full, protruding lower lip, and a pronounced chin. In the center of the chin was a deep cleft. From Danielle, Cassie knew about the origins of that cleft, indeed all about Morgan Kingston. He had inherited the cleft and his intriguing good looks from his uncle, Bradford "King" Kingston, the family rake and gambler. But Morgan had the personality of his father, Nathaniel "Ned" Kingston. Son, like father, was serious, trustworthy, essentially decent, a farmer, a man of the land. As the scion of Aurial, the huge Morgan-Kingston estate—in addition to his considerable personal attractions—he was irresistible to many women. Yet, Morgan was not a womanizer. As Danielle had said to Cassie, "Morgan is a one-woman man like daddy was, but it's going to take a remarkable woman to get him."

And now, her hands were clasped in his, her long, brown fingers interlocked with his strong, calloused farmer's hands, while his declaration of love for her hung in the air between them. For Cassie, it was a moment etched in time.

"Cassie, I'm not blind. I know what color your skin is—the loveliest color I have ever seen, the loveliest skin. God, how my hands ache to touch it."

"Please, Morgan, I—"

"Let me finish. I also know what it means—that I am white and you are colored. I know what people

will think and say. But I don't care. Please believe it
doesn't matter to me. I was raised in England—Danielle, too. Neither of us was born with notions that skin
color matters. It's what a person is that counts, and
you are the dearest, sweetest, most decent girl I know.
Can you believe that?"

Slowly, she nodded her head, unable even to blink
under the intensity and earnestness of his gaze. She did
know that Morgan Kingston and his sister were without racial prejudice. The whole family seemed to accept her. The Morgans, if not the Kingstons, had always
run a free plantation. Morgan and Danielle, as well as
their mother Moira, had been virtually raised by black-
skinned Joe and Jessie, longtime servants to Glenna
Morgan. They were practically members of the family.
Hatred of Negroes was simply unknown to Morgan,
and for Danielle, life in South Carolina, with its Deep
South prejudices and tensions, was often a nightmare.

All this Cassie knew, yet it did not alter the instruc-
tions of her mind that any sexual liaison with Morgan
Kingston was impossible.

"Say you believe me?"

She sighed. "Yes, Morgan, I believe you. But—"

He waited for her to continue, but she did not. "But
what?"

She sighed more deeply now and shook her head
forlornly, unable to think clearly.

He misunderstood. "You can't think that." He
gripped her fingers more tightly. "You can't believe
I'd do that."

She sensed his rising anger. "Do what?"

"Take advantage of you. You can't think I'm just
another white man trying to . . . to . . . abuse a beautiful colored girl."

She understood then, and emotion rose in her
breast. "No, I never thought that. You couldn't . . . I
wouldn't—"

Her protests were lost as he again swept her into
his arms. Her mouth. He'd said it was beautiful, but

she had never known its potential, the sensations now created, spreading like fire, melting her. She felt herself surrendering to the sweetness of the kiss, the passion of her body pressed against his. She was sinking into a warm, dark abyss of longing—and danger.

She broke away, her head against his chest, clinging to him, trying to breathe, orient her thoughts. She must be sensible about this—she *must*.

He gave her no time. "I love you, Cassie. I want you."

He turned her face toward his, and she could offer no resistance. Strange words came from her mouth, "Yes, yes," just before his lips, scalding now, more open, created greater and deeper hungers within her.

It was he who broke away. His breath shortened, he said, "I knew it would be like this . . . with you . . . with us."

"Yes." She knew no other word.

"Can it be so wrong . . . for us, you and I—" He kissed her again. "I must, Cassie . . . I must—" Again, his moist lips were on hers, again she melted at his touch. "Tonight. I know a place . . . we can be alone. . . ."

Again, his mouth tormented her, but she fought him, shaking her head gently even as his kiss thrilled through her.

"You must . . . please. . . ."

Now she pushed him away, stepping back, looking at him, eyes wide with passion and confusion. "I don't know, Morgan. I—"

"Please. You know you want to."

She looked around, searching for distraction, something to do. Her straw hat, fallen to the ground. She bent, picked it up and refastened it to her hair. The action helped to calm her.

"Don't you want me, Cassie?"

She lowered her arms. "You know I do."

"Well then?"

"Let me think. I can't with you near." She managed

a sort of smile. "I'll think about it. Will that do for now?"

He smiled back. "I guess it will have to."

Her smile was brilliant. "At least that's some progress." She glanced at Aurial in the distance. "Hadn't we better get back now?"

Chapter 2

The length of their absence was noted at Aurial. Morgan's mother, Moira Kingston Hodges, was sitting in the gazebo overlooking the river, and absently glanced at the water. It was time Morgan and Cassie returned. The thought hardly registered on her consciousness. If she had been aware of it, she would have scolded herself for worrying.

Moira did worry inordinately about her children, always had, and couldn't seem to help it. But over the years, far less of her worry had been over her strong, handsome son than over her daughter, who now sat opposite her in the swing in the middle of the gazebo.

Danielle Kingston Summers and her children had arrived along with Cassie yesterday, and the whole evening had been taken up by the reunion with Glenna and Morgan, Joe and Jessie. Aurial had rung with squeals of joy and happy laughter now that the whole family, or much of it, was united again. It had been two years since Danielle's last visit, and everyone had talked at once about her and her children. Stephanie, five, and Andrew, four, had been fussed over and hugged and hugged. A happy, boisterous time it was.

This afternoon in the gazebo was the first opportunity Moira had to be alone with Danielle. Cassie had put the children to bed for their naps, and Glenna had lain down for a rest. Morgan had suggested taking Cassie for a row, leaving Moira alone, at last, with her daughter.

She glanced at her. Danielle was looking away at the river, a slight smile spreading her lips, and once again Moira registered how extraordinarily beautiful she was. Danielle had the girlhood coloring of her grandmother Glenna, black hair like polished onyx, large, sapphire eyes under dark, double lashes, and the fairest skin, the color of new-fallen snow. It was, as Glenna always said, the Irish coloring. It seemed to Moira that Danielle had become more beautiful since she had last seen her, taking on maturity, slightly more definition to her features, a greater poise and self-assurance. As a girl of nineteen, Danielle's courage had been tested when she was kidnapped out West. She had not been found wanting, and these adventures, plus love and motherhood, the demands made on all women, had added character to her features, enhancing her beauty. Yet, Danielle retained her remarkable petiteness and delicacy. No matter what, she was always a lady, quiet, controlled, seemingly content within herself.

Moira glanced at the bodice of Danielle's summer frock, light blue in color, seeing her modest décolletage. Oh, how she had worried about Danielle, so young and—with that womanly figure—so terribly vulnerable. And when she had learned that beneath that cool, snowy exterior, Danielle possessed her own internal fires, her own fierce passions, she had been sick with apprehension. Only with Danielle's marriage to Walter Summers had she been able to relax—and even then, not completely.

"Two children and you haven't gained an ounce. How do you do it, Danny?"

Daughter glanced at mother and smiled. "Look who's talking."

Moira's head went back in her full-throated laugh. "If only it were true. I fear the years take their toll on slenderness."

"I only hope I pay so little toll when I'm forty-four. I think you're as beautiful as ever, mother."

Danielle spoke the truth. Moira Hodges's mane of red hair had lost none of its dramatic hue, and her rosy skin—it seemed as if some of the color had been washed out of her hair to tint her complexion—was still luscious. Oh, it had softened with the years and taken on a few lines, but this only added character. Her waist had thickened slightly and her breasts filled out, but Moira still gave the appearance of wild, impetuous sensuality. She had bemoaned that fact all her life, but knew her appearance merely revealed her true nature.

Moira laughed a moment longer, then grew serious. "It's so good to see you, Danny. Are you happy?"

Danielle was startled by the directness of the question. "Of course. Don't I look it?"

"Yes—now. But I—oh, I don't know. There's something about you." She smiled. "Tell me I'm a meddling old mother."

Danielle smiled. "You *are* a meddling old mother— whom I never could fool."

"Want to talk about it?" She waited, watching as Danielle looked away from her, down at the lazy river below. When no answer came, Moira prompted her. "Are you and Walt having problems?" When, again, no answer came, she said, "I really don't mean to pry, Danny. If I—"

"No, it's all right, mother." She turned to look at her. "It's just that I don't know what to tell you. I'm not sure I understand myself."

"Do you love Walt?"

"Yes, I love him. It's just. . . ."

When Danielle again drifted into silence, Moira took

a calculated risk. "Are you and he having troubles, you know . . . in bed?"

"No, that part is all right. Sometimes, I think that's all that is." She hesitated, looking down at her hands, weighing her words. "I really don't think there's anything wrong between Walt and me. It's just where we live. Charleston—all of South Carolina—is impossible, mother. It seethes with hatred. Negroes and whites are at each other constantly, there are nightriders and mobs. Everyone is shooting and burning and lynching. You can see flames at night and hear gunfire. It's a nightmare."

Moira reached out to clasp her daughter's hands in hers. "But aren't there federal troops there? Can't they keep order?"

"They try, but it's hopeless. They can't be everywhere."

"But, surely, you and Walt can . . . can isolate yourself at Seasons." She and Morgan had visited Danielle and her family the previous spring. She had a mental image of the Summers plantation, the big house, the splendid trees lining the drive. It had seemed so secure and isolated to her. "You aren't in danger, are you—or the children?"

"No, Walt sees to that." She shook her head, a gesture of frustration. "That's just it, mother—the guns, the need for protection. I can only hope things will quiet down soon, after the election, perhaps."

"I'm sure they will, Danny. Larry says South Carolina is very close. It can go either way." She was referring to the Presidential election of 1876, with Republican candidate Rutherford B. Hayes pitted against Democrat Samuel J. Tilden. Lawrence Hodges was special assistant to Tilden, long his close associate. Even now, he was away on a swing of western states to garner support for Tilden.

"I hope so, mother. I do hope so."

"Is that what you're unhappy about, the pre-election turmoil?"

Danielle pursed her lips. "I don't know. I suppose."

She sighed. "No, that's not it. It's more than the election. Mother, I have no racial prejudices. You must know that."

"Yes, I know."

"Living in the South—well, it's very difficult for me, the antagonism, the segregation. When I see how the Negroes live, I can't bear it. Mother, slavery never ended. If anything, the Negroes are worse off than when they were slaves—the hunger, the terrible housing. Many have no homes. They just wander around, living off the land, sleeping where they can. I never dreamed it would be so bad when I went there."

"Surely, it will improve, Danny. The government is—"

"Mother, the government can't change attitudes. There's so much hatred. The colored people will not be accepted as equals, and the Yankees are hated for winning the war. Mother, I'm a Yankee, a *Damnyankee*. They say it all as one word."

"But, surely, you and Walt are—"

"Walt is a Southerner, mother. He was a Confederate officer. He spied for the South in Washington."

"Of course, Danny, I know that, but—"

"Mother, Walt loves me. He loves me very much. We speak of all this as little as possible. He does everything he can to shield me from it. But he is a Southerner and his loyalties are with the South—the *white* South. He's doing all he can to see that Tilden wins and the Democrats gain control of the state government. He says *Democrats,* mother, but what he really means is *white*. It's called white supremacy—a return to slavery."

"Surely not, Danny. The Constitution has been amended. Slavery is forbidden."

"Oh, yes, I know. It won't be *called* slavery, but it will have the same purpose." She made a gesture, her fingers curled into a fist, her extended thumb hard against the arm of the swing. "Blacks will be under the thumb of white supremists, mother. I fear for them if the federal troops leave." She saw her mother sit back, deep in thought. "Walt wants this, mother. He believes it will be best for the South—solve all the problems."

"You're saying he is a white supremist?"

"Yes."

"And you can't accept that?"

Danielle sighed in resignation. "I don't have much choice, do I?"

"No."

Danielle forced a smile. "I'm just glad to be here with you, away from it for a while. Hopefully, it will be easier when I go back."

Moira returned the smile, trying to be reassuring. "I'm sure it will, darling. You say you and Walt are in love. When two people are in love, they can—"

"—surmount anything. I believe that, too, mother. So don't worry. Everything will be fine—or at least better. I'm sure of it." She reached out and patted her mother's hand. "Let's talk about happier things—" she laughed, "—like you and Larry."

"Yes, I am happy, Danny."

"You don't have to say it. That grin on your face says it all."

"No, it doesn't. I simply never believed, after your father was killed, I would ever be happy again. I look back on those years of widowhood. Such a waste. I just hope my unhappiness didn't affect you and Morgan too much."

"It didn't, mother, not at all. We were just wishing you'd find someone to make you happy."

They sat a moment smiling at each other, both their minds dwelling on the same memories. It had been Danielle who had inadvertently brought Larry and Moira together through her insane affair with Hamilton Garth six years before. Moira had gone to Hodges to seek help in restraining Danielle from running away with Garth. Danielle had gone off with him, anyway, and been stranded out West, but the romance between Moira and Hodges had been kindled.

The memories of Garth, painful and unpleasant,

were only fleeting, as Danielle's thoughts returned to the present. "And Miriam? Are you and she . . . ?"

Moira sighed deeply. "I'm afraid not, Danny. I've tried everything I know to get close to her, but she just will not accept me."

With her marriage to Lawrence Hodges, Moira had become stepmother to his children by his previous marriage to Priscilla Prentiss Hodges, who had died. The youngest child, Thomas Hodges, now seventeen, had quickly come to accept Moira and a bond had grown between them. But the daughter, Miriam Hodges, now nineteen, had for six years remained hostile to Moira.

"Have you talked to Larry about her?"

"No, and I will not. It's exactly what she wants me to do—in the hope that it will create a wedge between Larry and me. I simply will not permit that to happen."

"And Larry still doesn't realize how beastly she is to you?"

Moira shrugged. "I don't think he does. In front of him, Miriam is all sweetness and light, calling me 'MaMa' in the French manner, as you used to do. She virtually drips consideration for me. When her father is not there, 'MaMa' is a word of derision. She's disdainful, contemptuous."

"How awful for you."

Moira gave a wan smile. "Oh, it's not so bad. We've become like two ships passing in the night—unfriendly ships doing their best to ignore each other's existence. I'm just glad she's in New York right now, and not here to spoil our good times. Is that too terrible to say?"

Danielle smiled. "I was about to say the same thing. She makes me uncomfortable."

"She resents your beauty, Danny."

"But she's very pretty herself, mother, beautiful really."

"Yes, but she's insecure. Part of her feels we don't really accept her, don't care for her. After all, she's not blood-kin, doesn't really belong to us—that's what she tells herself. And it's that—that insecurity, that vulnerability—that keeps me from judging her, from giving up. I can understand what she must feel—her own mother dead, me a usurper, with a daughter of my own, a beautiful, loving daughter. . . ."

"I think you exaggerate."

"Perhaps, but there is also the matter of Morgan. She sees how fond he is of you and—" Moira laughed. "Need I finish?"

"She has set her cap for him?"

"Oh, I don't know. I can't tell if she's really fond of him or just trying to get at me by ensnaring my son." Again, Moira laughed. "In any event, it isn't working. Miriam is just a kid sister to him."

"I wouldn't be too sure, mother."

Moira's laugh deepened. "I fear the more she flirts with him, the more she reminds him of Melissa Carder. Remember her?"

"Of course. His one great love." Danielle smiled. "Only she was just using him to try to hold onto Aurial for her father."

"Exactly. I'm happy to report Morgan is now rather wary of flirtatious, forward young women."

"Particularly if they are blonde, like Miriam?"

"Yes." Suddenly, Moira stopped smiling. "Aren't we terrible, Danny, sitting here gossiping like a pair of old hens about a young girl who can't defend herself? The truth is, I want to be friends with Miriam. Oh, I know. On the surface, she seems vain, frivolous, cold. But on occasion, Danny, I've had a glimpse of the sensitive girl beneath that hard exterior. Once—it must have been about five years ago—I came across her weeping, out in the copse. She'd been reading a book, and when I asked her what was wrong, she said, 'nothing,' and hurled the book away from her, ran away. I picked it up—the book—and what do you suppose it was? *Little Women*—you know, the novel by Mr. Alcott's daughter? I found the tear-stained page—she'd been crying over the death of poor Beth March. I'd cried over that place, myself, a grown woman. Oh, Danny, how my heart reached out to Miriam then. Surely, the girl has feeling."

"I wouldn't trust her, mother," Danielle said dryly.

"It's she who doesn't trust me," Moira answered forlornly. "I've tried." She sighed. "God, how I've tried. But I suppose she's read all the fairy tales about wicked stepmothers, and can't believe I wish her well. Still, I know she longs for a mother. I've peeked in on her sleeping, and seen her lying with her rosary beads clutched in her hand. She'd fallen asleep praying to the Blessed Mother, poor child. Oh, Danielle, I know that Miriam has a good heart. It's her grandmother, that proud Mrs. Prentiss, who fills her head with nonsense. Makes her feel she doesn't belong to us, that we can't love her as her own kin does. Well, I suppose the old woman wants Miriam all to herself—she has no one else. And then there's the economic factor—she's bound and determined that somehow Miriam will restore the Prentiss fortunes."

"They have fallen on hard times?"

"I don't know how hard, but Larry says most of the Prentiss money is gone, squandered by that old woman."

Miriam Hodges was at that moment in New York City, in raptures over a new dress provided by "that old woman," Edith Prentiss.

"You like it, don't you, dear?"

"Oh, yes, grandmama, I love it." Her delight showed in the image in the mirror. Her delphinium-blue eyes had never seemed larger or more shining, the smile on her oval-shaped face wider or more brilliant. But Miriam's glimpse of her face was brief, for her attention was focused on her new gown. It was made of yards and yards of shimmering white satin, scintillating with rhinestones set into the bodice. As she twisted her torso before the mirror, the gems caught the gaslight and reflected brilliantly.

But it was not the gown so much as the lack of it that enraptured Miriam. Never had she worn such a daring dress. The fitted bodice had tiny cap sleeves just below her shoulders and was so deeply cut, the sight of it almost took her breath away. Her breasts, pushed up and together by whalebone, were almost entirely exposed. Her gaze fastened on the deep valley between her breasts. She hadn't realized she possessed so much cleavage. She laughed, her voice musical with delight. Wait till Morgan Kingston saw her in this gown! He wouldn't think of her as his little sister anymore. Again, she laughed. Little sister had become big sister. Hands on hips, she again twisted her upper body, her eyes fixed on the movement of her décolletage. Yes, Danielle Kingston had nothing on her. All her years of growing up, Miriam had envied her stepsister and stepmother. At times, all she could see were their breasts and the daring gowns they wore, while she remained a stick for what seemed forever. Then, at last, after all the other girls she knew were formed, she had begun to develop. But the scars of envy were there. She could never compete with Danielle and the hated Moira. Morgan would never notice her, when he had his sister and mother to compare her to. Now, in delight, she felt she could compete. Morgan Kingston would no longer find her wanting.

"I'm glad you like the gown, my dear. I so wanted you to."

"Oh, yes, grandmama. I'm just thrilled."

Edith Prentiss laughed, dryly and cautiously so as not to start a bout of coughing. "Does it seem familiar to you?"

Miriam turned from her image to look at her. "No, should it?"

"Yes, very much so." She extended a gnarled hand. "Come, I'll show you."

With effort, Edith Prentiss led her granddaughter, her hope for the future, out of the bedroom and down the stairs to the drawing room of the big house on East Seventeenth Street. At age sixty-eight, Edith Prentiss suffered from painful gout in her left foot, which made walking difficult even without the rheumatism in her joints. She used a wheelchair as often as possible, but now, pain or no pain, she was extending herself. Her plans were near fruition. This girl beside her, now a stunning young woman, was going to recoup the Prentiss fortune.

Miriam came down the stairs in silence, walking slowly to accommodate her grandmother, but also imagining she was making a grand entrance to a group of astonished admirers below. She looked down, although she knew she wouldn't if she were really making an entrance. What she saw did not disappoint her. Indeed, she was fascinated by the jiggle of her breasts as she descended each step.

In the drawing room, Edith Prentiss turned up the lights and pointed. "There."

Above the mantel of the fireplace was the portrait of Priscilla Prentiss, Miriam's mother. She had seen it so many times, she hardly noticed it anymore. And how many times had she heard how much she resembled her mother? She really couldn't see it. She had the same color hair, so blonde it was nearly platinum, similar blue eyes. The shape of their faces was similar, too, but beyond that everything was different. Miriam felt her own lips were fuller than those painted in the portrait, and the nose was very different, more retroussé. She had never felt she looked very much like the woman in the portrait.

"See it?"

"Yes, I see mother."

"Not her, Miriam, her dress."

With shock, Miriam realized she was wearing the same gown as her mother.

"She was so lovely in it. Oh, how the men admired her. Couldn't take their eyes off her. Wasn't she a beautiful woman?"

Miriam stared at the painting in dismay. Her mother's dress? It couldn't be!

"I've kept it all these years, waiting for you to grow up." The gnarled fingers touched Miriam's arm. "And you're every bit as beautiful as she was."

"The same dress?" She still couldn't believe it.

Edith Prentiss's dry laugh was so full, she almost began to cough, barely restraining herself in time. "Oh, it's not exactly the same, dear. I knew it was out of style, so I had a dressmaker alter it. He refashioned the skirt, moving the fullness from the front to the back and attaching the bustle. Other than that, everything is the same. The bodice fits you perfectly. You are exactly like your mother."

Miriam knew it wasn't so. She glanced at the portrait. She was more developed, probably taller than her mother. That's why the dress had so much more décolletage on her. Her delight in the gown was suddenly gone. It wasn't a new dress. It was a hand-me-down, fixed up to save money and make do.

"I'm so pleased you like the dress, Miriam. I knew you would."

"Yes, grandmama. Thank you."

Edith Prentiss was not without empathy, quickly detecting the change in Miriam's mood. "Is something wrong?"

"No, everything's fine." She looked at her grandmother, seeing disappointment rising in her face. Miriam couldn't hurt her. Except for her father and stuffy Thomas, she was the only real relative she had in the world. She forced a smile, letting it widen in radiance before she bent to kiss the old woman's cheek. "I just love the dress, grandmama."

Edith Prentiss smiled, revealing yellowing teeth. "I knew you would, dear. She was so lovely in it. You are, too."

Her effort to be kind to her grandmother brightened Miriam's spirits. With real feeling, she said, "I do so want to be like her."

Edith Prentiss patted her cheek. "And you are, Miriam. You will excel her—in every way." Again, she smiled. "I have another surprise for you. Someone is coming to dinner tonight—someone who is dying to meet you."

"Who is that, grandmama?"

"His name is Peter Blakeley, and he is one of the richest, most eligible bachelors in New York."

Not very interested in having her companions selected by her grandmother, Miriam said, "Really, grandmama? How do you know him?"

The hesitation was brief. "Oh, I've had some business dealings with him. I told him about you, and he is *so* eager to meet you." Another dry cackle. "When he sees you in that gown, I'm sure he'll be quite smitten."

The idea did not please Miriam. "Really, grandmama, I don't think—"

"I doubt if you'll have to do much in the way of encouragement."

"What is it you expect of me?"

Edith Prentiss took her arm and began to lead her away from the fireplace and back upstairs. "Nothing, my dear. Just be your usual sweet self."

Miriam remained puzzled, but dutifully said no more.

Back at the gazebo at Aurial, Danielle and Moira were soon joined by others. The first to arrive was Glenna, Danielle's children clinging to each of her hands. Glenna O'Reilly Morgan MacDoul Fairchild was now sixty-five, matriarch of the family. Silver-haired, fuller-waisted, somewhat slower of step, she was still a handsome woman. The beauty that had marked her as a girl and young woman was evident in her fine facial bones and splendid complexion. Time had softened her skin and added the markings of a full life, but her intelligence, courage and wisdom showed in the lines of her face. Orphaned in Ireland in 1829, she had been captured by Barbary pirates. To escape slavery, she became the first European woman to cross the Sahara Desert. Rescued by her true love, Daniel Morgan, she had wed and come to live with him at Aurial. With his death, she had married Daniel's friend, Captain Ian MacDoul, a hearty Scotsman, and traveled the world with him in his clipper ship named for her. Widowed a second time, she had married investment banker Franklin Fairchild, with whom she now lived in New York. As she crossed the lawn with her great-grandchildren, Glenna was smiling happily, for she was back at Aurial, her family around her.

"Look who I found just getting up from their naps," she called, nodding benevolently from one child to the other.

Moira and Danielle both rose, Moira speaking first. "My goodness, what a splendid picture they make, mother and those two darling children."

Beaming, Danielle said, "Yes."

Both women went to meet the trio, and Moira knelt before Stephanie Summers. "Did you have a nice nap, darling?"

"Yes, grandma."

"And such a pretty dress." It was a white pinafore.

"GlennaMa helped me pick it out."

Danielle smiled. GlennaMa was her pet name for her grandmother since childhood. Now her own child had picked it up.

It was "GlennaMa" who now spoke. "I've never seen such hair as Stephanie has, Danielle. Where on earth did she get it?"

Danielle smiled and shook her head. "Walt says Nature couldn't decide whether to give her red hair after her grandmother or blonde hair like her father, so she did both."

It was as good an explanation as any, for Stephanie Summers had truly astonishing hair—long, luxuriantly thick, hanging in curls halfway down her back. It was a mixture of brilliant red and straw blonde, as though the colors had been alternated by strands to create a reddish-gold color. In sunlight such as now, the red was enhanced. By gaslight, the blondeness prevailed— a deep, burning gold.

"All I can say is, I pity the young men when she grows up."

Danielle laughed at her grandmother. "I think maybe you should pity her mother. She'll have to do all the worrying."

Moira, having moved a step, was hugging Danielle's son, holding him in her arms, talking to him. When she looked at Danielle, her eyes were moist. "When you named him Andrew Morgan, did you know he was going to look like his namesake?"

"Does he, mother?"

"Oh, yes, more each time I see him." She looked at Glenna for agreement. She was nodding.

Andrew Morgan was Moira's brother, Glenna's only son. In a short, tragic life, he had lost Aurial gambling, then gone to California in search of gold to buy it back. He found the gold and re-established the Morgan fortune, but at the cost of his life.

"I think, Moira," Glenna said, "you and I are going to have to stop breaking into tears every time we look at him, though."

Moira smiled. "Mine are tears of happiness."

"Miss Danny, I'm sorry. The children."

Danielle turned to see Cassie Brown climbing the steps from the boat landing, Morgan just behind her. She seemed distressed and was making an excuse for being gone so long. Danielle smiled. "Don't be silly, Cassie. We have no shortage of grandmothers and great-grandmothers to look after the children. I think they're going to come to blows over who can spoil them the most. So you might as well enjoy your vacation. Did you have a nice row?"

Cassie smiled a bit nervously, suddenly wondering how she looked. Could they tell? "Yes. It's very beautiful."

"I took her down to the copse of aspens," Morgan said, "to show her the views of both Aurial and Kingston."

"It is lovely, isn't it?"

"Yes," Cassie said, "a very special place." She could not bring herself to look at Morgan.

Chapter 3

That afternoon and evening, Cassie Brown was sure of only one thing—Morgan Kingston was a tremendous temptation to her. His kisses lingered on her lips, the sensations and sweetness returning periodically to arouse and tempt her. More than a few times, she glanced at herself in a mirror, seeking reassurance she was unchanged.

Her mind stubbornly fought the temptation, but her will was weak and vacillating. Worse, events conspired to make resolve difficult.

In the early evening, for example, as she was brushing Danielle's hair as she sat at her vanity, Danielle reiterated, "I meant what I said, Cassie. This is your vacation, too. I want you to have a good time."

"Yes, Danny." It had been difficult at first for Cassie to use the familiar first name. But Danielle had insisted on it. They were friends, not mistress and servant. Oh, it was perhaps wise to call her "Miss" in front of others, Mr. Summers especially, but when they were alone, she never wanted to hear the word. "I am enjoying myself. It's so lovely here."

"Yes."

Cassie smiled at the reflection in the mirror. "And you seem happier, too, Danny."

"Oh, yes, it's so good to see mother and GlennaMa

27

—Morgan, too—and to be away from . . . from all the—well, you know what I mean."

"Yes." And she did. Aurial seemed an island of tranquility after the turmoil of Charleston, and she felt completely accepted by this warm, loving family. But, she realized, one tension had been replaced by another.

"What are you doing this evening?"

"Tonight?" The question surprised Cassie.

"Yes. I won't have you sitting around here sucking your thumb."

"Oh, I'm not sure. Mr. Kingston has—"

She was interrupted by Danielle's musical laugh. "Mr. Kingston! Good heavens, Cassie, call him Morgan. Has he invited you somewhere?"

Cassie felt trapped. "Yes, sort of. He—he suggested a . . . walk—to show me Aurial by moonlight."

Danielle smiled at her. "That'll be lovely, Cassie. You're going, of course?"

She bit at the inner surfaces of her lips. "I—I don't know. I'm not sure."

"Don't be a ninny. Morgan won't harm you."

"I didn't mean that, it's just—"

"Then go for a moonlight stroll." She paused, looking at Cassie's reflection in the mirror, seeing the seriousness on the beautiful brown face. "Cassie, Morgan is very lonely. I can't blame him for finding you attractive—for wanting you as a friend."

"Lonely?"

"Oh, I know, he's the handsomest thing around. But all the same, I can't remember when he last went out with a girl. And I know why. Did I ever tell you about Melissa Carder?"

"I don't believe so."

"It's not too long a story. While we were all living in London after the war, a man named Dodd Carder took over Aurial, claiming ownership. It was all fraudulent, of course, and when Morgan showed up to claim the family property, Carder knew his only chance of holding onto Aurial was to marry his daughter Melissa to Morgan. Well, she was a little older than Morgan

and vastly more sophisticated. He was only seventeen
at the time and she easily ensnared him. He fell in love,
or thought he did, and planned to marry her. Of
course, eventually, he realized he was being exploited
and got rid of her. But ever since, he's been extremely
wary of women—much too wary if you ask me—particularly of blue-eyed blondes." Danielle turned on the
bench to face Cassie directly. "I'm so pleased Morgan
is paying attention to you. It will be good for him, you
know. Have a nice walk." She smiled. "I understand
the moon is full tonight."

Cassie never got a chance to reply before Jessie entered, insisting on brushing and arranging Danielle's
hair. "I don't get to do this very often, and you're with
her all the time," she said to Cassie.

As Cassie turned over the brush, she felt Jessie's
arm snug around her shoulder and heard her say, "Miss
Danielle, where on earth did you find this beautiful
child?"

Danielle grinned at them both. "Some people just
have all the luck."

Jessie, now past sixty and seeming to grow more
corpulent with each passing year, had been servant to
Glenna Morgan since she was in her teens. She had
practically raised Moira, Danielle and Morgan, and
had participated in, or suffered through, all the family
adventures and travails. She was indeed family, along
with her husband Joe. He had been at Glenna's side
even longer than Jessie, having rescued her from the
African jungles when she was eighteen. Utterly devoted
to Glenna, Joe had even taken her maiden name as his
own, however incongruous the name Joe O'Reilly
might be in a man as black as coal.

"I can't tell you what a relief it is to have this
child here." Jessie hugged Cassie even tighter.

"Relief?"

"Yes, Miss Danielle. I'm getting old and slow, and
I been wondering who was going to take over raising
this family."

Smiling at her, Danielle shook her head. "Don't be

silly, Jessie. You've always been here, and you always will be."

"Don't I wish, but it's nice to know you got this wonderful girl to look after you down in that godforsaken place you live."

"I can't disagree with that."

Cassie felt Jessie release her to begin brushing Danielle's already shining hair with quick, expert strokes, the ample flesh of her brown upper arms shaking with each stroke. For her part, Cassie stepped back, listening to the two women.

"You've done a simply grand job training Cassie. She's gonna be a good one."

Danielle became serious. "Train is not the word, Jessie. Cassie's my dear friend, not my servant. She's no more a servant than you are—or Joe."

"I know, Miss Danielle. I thank my lucky stars for the day I came to work at Aurial when old Mr. Morgan, Dan'l's father, was still alive. I couldn't have been more than ten or twelve. But I was trained as a servant. I know my place."

"A place of honor and affection."

Cassie watched as the older woman's hands stopped in midmotion. She blinked back tears, then bent to squeeze Danielle's shoulders and kiss her cheek. A white hand came to the round, brown face, holding it. White on brown, again, thought Cassie, and winced inwardly.

Words were whispered that Cassie couldn't hear, then Jessie resumed her brushing. Danielle spoke. "I want it to be the same with Cassie. I won't have her wearing a uniform, eating in the kitchen. I want her to find love, get married like you and Joe, have children. If this means I lose her and she makes her own home, then—" She laughed. "—I'll visit her often. Right, Cassie?"

She had to say something. "Just don't marry me off too soon."

Jessie turned to her. "The way you look, child, it won't be hard to find a man." To Danielle, she said,

"You just look after her. Keep those rascals and scalawags away from her."

"With a whip, Jessie, with a whip."

The family dinner was served buffet-style, with everyone dining on the veranda to enjoy the spectacular sunset and twilight. Cassie took refuge beside Joe and Jessie, but it didn't last long. Morgan came to sit beside her. He seemed a little nervous, talking a bit more animatedly about Aurial and family memories.

When he was alone with her, he said, "Tonight?"

She looked at him, biting at her lips. "I'm so afraid, Morgan."

"Nothing will happen that you don't want to."

Despite herself, she smiled. "That's what I'm afraid of," she whispered.

He had urged her to walk out the front door with him, be open about going out together. But when she hesitated, he suggested an alternative. Now he stood in the deep shadow of the stables, his gaze fixed on the kitchen door of the great house, his stomach churning with anticipation of her coming, and fear that she would not.

Morgan Kingston welcomed his unaccustomed feeling of excitement. Not since Melissa Carder had he felt it, the eager clamor of his nerves, the wild wanting, the heightening of all his senses. Even now, the odor of honeysuckle assaulted him. He could hear every lap of the river against its banks, and feel the warm breeze as a caress against his face. Never had moonlight been so radiant. Yes, it was time. He had been too long without a woman, without love. Like an old, seldom-seen friend, he embraced it.

Morgan was not blind to the situation. Cassie was a Negro. He knew the pitfalls, the hatred and talk that would surely come, but none of it mattered. Some time ago, he had accepted his captivation. There was something about her brown, luminous skin, gazellelike eyes and vulnerable, inviting lips that excited him more than any woman he had ever known. As an innocent boy, he

had thought Melissa Carder the apex of desirability. But
Cassie Brown aroused him far more. For over a year,
lying in his bed at night, he had thought of her, wanting those lips, the feel of her skin, the spread of her
thighs beneath him.

Over and over, a thousand times over, he had asked
himself why. He had first seen her when she was four-
teen, accompanying Danielle and Walter Summers on
a visit to Aurial. She had seemed so young and innocent, all eyes, so timid and bashful, that he had reached
out to her, talking with her, drawing her out, making
her feel welcome. Then, the previous spring, he and
Moira had visited Seasons. Walter had wanted his advice on rejuvenating the depleted soil of his plantation.
Morgan had stayed for nearly three months, delaying
and delaying his return to Maryland because of his
infatuation with Cassie. She had grown so tall and
lithe, so womanly. Her beauty, natural grace and quiet
reserve had enflamed him, but he had not so much as
touched her, although he was alone with her some part
of every day. He had been in a state of restless anticipation for weeks, ever since he knew she was coming
to Aurial. His kissing her today had been planned
deliberately and the subject of countless fantasies. He
had to know if she responded to him. Her arousal, as
she sagged weakly against him for support, had impassioned him even more than the deliciousness of her
lips.

The door opened and she stepped out into the moonlight. Heart pounding, he strode from the shadows toward her. He saw her eyes widen as he put his arm
around her waist.

She jumped free of him. "No! If anyone is watching,
we are only going for a walk.'"

Smiling, he tried to take her hand.

"No, not even that."

Thus, side by side, they walked through the garden,
across the lawn and along the mail road beside Short
Creek. She looked up at the sky and moon, then down
at the flowers and shrubs, pearly in the moonlight,

frequently gulping in the sweet air in a vain effort to calm herself. Her consent to come out, her presence here now were, she knew, tantamount to surrender. She had given up the battle. She wanted this man—this night at least. She wanted an end to the longing, a revelation of the mysteries of her body. She could fight it no longer. When he stopped in deep shadows along the road and kissed her, it was even more wondrous than in the afternoon, their mouths more urgent, their longing more frenzied.

He took her to his hideaway at Kingston, a small study smelling of books and old, leather furniture, with a separate entrance from the garden. It had been his grandfather Kingston's study, kept pretty much as it had always been. With Larry Hodges at Aurial so often, Morgan had surrendered his father's and grandfather's study to him and moved his office to Kingston, now used mostly as a guest house. It was more private at Kingston, a good place for a man to be alone. What he didn't know was that in this very room, on this same couch, his mother had given herself to his uncle "King" Kingston in the same sort of reckless passion he now felt. But Morgan had wondered why his mother seldom came to this room and felt so ill at ease when she did.

In her innocence, Cassie was completely unaware of Morgan's nervousness. Indeed, he seemed incredibly calm, unbelievably relaxed, as he admired her dress, a cool, green cotton with a white design that Danielle had insisted she borrow for the evening, then keep. He poured them both wine and showed her around the study, pointing out mementoes of his grandfather. He embraced her often, telling her there were no lips like hers. Once, when she looked around fearfully, he told her the doors were locked, the drapes closed. No one would come.

He was endlessly patient with her—himself, too. They sat together on the couch where they would soon lie, sipping wine, not speaking, just touching, fingers, hands, arms, faces, throat. "Your skin is so beautiful,

so soft." How many times did he say it? She saw the
tenderness in his eyes and knew it was love, heard the
huskiness in his voice and knew it was desire, sensed
the wonder in him as he surveyed her body and knew
her own pleasure at his arousal.

Oh, how he enflamed her! She trembled at his touch
and shuddered as she pressed her body against his, his
kisses making her mouth a conduit of sensations that
seemed to sweep her whole body. The things he
knew. . . .

She sensed how much he wanted her, yet he took
his time. His lips moved slowly from her mouth to her
breasts, licking her neck and the well of her cleavage
on the downward journey. Tenderly, almost reverently,
he undid the buttons of her dress, removed her corset,
and then his lips were on one nipple, sucking, licking,
nuzzling, while a cool hand fondled the other nipple
into an equal state of arousal. Then she felt his other
hand on her thigh, then both hands, and her desire
traveled quickly from her breasts to her womanly
center. As his long fingers caressed the warm skin
of her inner thighs, lightly, lovingly, she felt her legs
spreading of their own volition, and then she felt his
fingers *there,* and was stunned by both the pleasure and
her own readiness. She was ready, more than ready, and
with a small groan she reached for him, felt his manhood hard and straining against his trousers. And then
there were no trousers, only bare flesh, white against
brown, and again his fingers, tickling, caressing, gently
prodding. . . .

It seemed to Cassie she was all dampness and desire.
When she could stand it no longer, she whispered,
"Now, Morgan, please, *now.*"

"Yes," he answered, his voice husky with passion,
as he carefully positioned his body over hers. Finally,
she felt him enter her, tentatively, solicitously. Then
she felt him thrusting, gently at first, but with ever-
increasing passion, and she marveled at the knowledge
in her own body, which seemed to meet his every
movement with an answering thrust, seemed to draw

him ever deeper inside her. Just as the tension became unbearable, just as their wave of passion reached the crest, she felt a wonderful shuddering at her center, tiny tingles of pleasure that grew in intensity until her whole body was convulsed with ecstasy. She cried out, and an instant later heard his answering cry, as his body shook with a release she knew must be as rapturous as her own.

Afterwards, they lay in each other's arms on the couch. He wiped away tears she did not remember shedding, whispered endearments that made her blush with delight, and caressed and caressed her. "I can't stop touching you," he said. Nor did she want him to.

"I knew it would be like this—with us."

She raised her head from his shoulder to look at him. "How did you know?"

He touched her cheek, gently pushing her back into the crook of his arm. "Because I love you."

"Oh, Morgan, you can't love me. You just can't."

He laughed softly. "Who says?"

"You can't. It's all so . . . so impossible."

"But it's happened. Don't you believe I love you—after this?"

"Yes, yes, but you can't." In her agitation, she squirmed away from him. There wasn't room for her to sit on the couch, so she squatted on her knees, straddling his legs.

He laughed. "If you think that position's going to make me keep my distance, you couldn't be more wrong."

"Be serious. You say you love me. Why? We hardly know each other."

"I know enough."

"Is it because I'm colored, you're white? Is it because we are forbidden to each other? We could both be shot or hung. Is that why you love me?"

She had expected her words to anger him. They did not. "No, that's not the reason. Just now, when we made love, didn't you feel it?"

"That was just flesh, Morgan. There's more to love than flesh and passion."

"Of course there is." He smiled, a tender, indulgent smile. "I guess you didn't see what I saw. We came to each other openly, without sham or shame. There was no hiding, no protests or apologies, just desire admitted and fulfilled. Do you understand now?"

"Understand what?"

"I've made love to a woman before, Cassie. I thought I was in love with her. All the sensations were there, some of them, anyway—" he smiled, "—though hardly as good. What I'm trying to say, Cassie, is, I love you for your honesty. Your mind, your body, the way you let me touch you and responded to me was honest in its innocence, its sense of discovery, its need. Oh, I can't say it very well, Cassie, but you are the truest person I know, the one woman, outside of Danielle and the family, of course, who lets me be myself. There's no pretense in you, no sense of using or being used. Is the word *integrity?* I don't know. I'm comfortable with you, Cassie, I'm in my own country. I love you."

She bit her lip, hard, white teeth digging into pink skin in an effort to hold back tears. "Oh, Morgan."

He pulled her down beside him again, rubbing her back gently. "Oh, I know the problems, darling. I'm not simplistic or naïve. But I've been looking for a girl like you all my life. Nothing else matters." He laughed gently. "And I'm so lucky. To have you be so beautiful, so soft and warm, so exciting. . . ."

Even as he spoke, he was turning from his back to face her, nibbling at her lips, kissing her, arousing her anew. Then the words, so long fought, so frequently denied, were there. "I love you, too, Morgan. I can't help it."

"I knew it. And I'm so very glad." Again, he kissed her, softly, lingeringly. "I want to marry you, Cassie."

Moaning, she clutched at him. "Oh, God, Morgan, what is to become of us?"

Chapter 4

To the extent pride and ambition are part of love, Edith Prentiss loved her granddaughter. She was proud of Miriam's beauty and spirit, and she certainly was ambitious for her. To the old woman's eyes, Miriam was just like her mother—only she would far exceed her.

Priscilla Prentiss Hodges had been a great beauty, no doubt of that, blonde, blue-eyed, with an appealing figure. She was also intelligent, witty, empty and possibly cruel. Even in death, Edith Prentiss could not forgive her daughter for throwing away her talents and opportunity by her marriage to Lawrence Hodges. He was a nobody, a young lawyer of no particular wealth or promise, who had attached himself to the star of that ascetic do-gooder Samuel Tilden. Priscilla Prentiss was a natural coquette. With scarcely more than a movement of her little finger, she could enflame a man. She could have had anyone, but she settled for marriage to that foolish Hodges. Edith Prentiss could not blame her for being unfaithful to him, but what had enraged the old woman was that Priscilla cuckolded her husband to no advantage. She did it for diversion, for conquest, perhaps to humiliate Hodges. She should have made a fortune.

Money was important to Edith Prentiss. Her husband, Barton Prentiss, had squandered much of the family wealth on women and gambling. His death had

mercifully kept him from spending it all. That task had
been left to her. She hadn't spent it so much as lost it
in foolish investments, which she had hoped would
recoup the fortune. All had failed. Now she was nearly
destitute. All that remained was the house. To maintain
it, she had sold off the jewelry and the better antiques
and paintings. She was down to a single, disgruntled
servant. The specter of the poorhouse loomed large
before Edith Prentiss—unless this beautiful child in
the shimmering white dress could save her.

"I'm going downstairs to receive Mr. Blakeley when
he comes." She smiled at Miriam, who was once again
admiring herself in the mirror. "I'm sure you'll want
to wait a few minutes after you hear the doorbell. In
such a gown, one must make a proper entrance."

"Yes, grandmama, I know." There was a strange,
breathy quality to her voice, a reflection of the inner
excitement she now felt. Her disappointment at the
hand-me-down had left her. She was now anticipating
meeting this stranger who was said to have seen and
admired her.

That much was true. Shortly after Miriam had arrived in New York from Maryland, Edith Prentiss had
taken her shopping, although precious little money was
spent. By pre-arrangement, Blakeley had been in the
Lord & Taylor department store to see Edith Prentiss's
granddaughter. A slight nod of his head had sealed the
deal. This evening was thus arranged.

As Edith was waiting in the parlor for Hannah to
bring in Blakeley, she felt a surge of love for her
granddaughter. What she was doing was hardly fair to
a girl so young. But this doubt was fleeting. It was time
Miriam faced up to her duties and responsibilities as
a Prentiss. Edith owed Blakeley money, several thousands. She had no way to pay, except to surrender the
house. Or had she?

"You are unmarried, Mr. Blakeley. You must be
lonely. My granddaughter will be visiting me shortly.
She is quite lovely. I told her about you, of course,

and she has expressed a keen desire to meet you. Do you think you might like to?"

She had seen the amusement in his eyes, the slight shrug of his shoulders.

No words had been said, no hands shaken, no contract signed, but the solitary, nearly imperceptible nod of his head had sealed the bargain. Miriam Hodges, if she cooperated, might be acceptable as recompense for her grandmother's debts

As she waited in the parlor, Edith Prentiss smiled inwardly. Peter Blakeley might have a dreadful reputation, might be a social pariah in New York, but he was as rich as Croesus. Miriam Hodges, her daughter's child, held within her young body the capacity not only to wipe out a troublesome debt, but to strip Peter Blakeley of significantly greater sums. Edith was supremely confident of that. Wait till he saw her in that dress.

The doorbell rang, and in moments Peter Blakeley was brought to her. She received him warmly, acknowledging his bow, and offered refreshments. He asked for whiskey. Fortunately, there was still a half-bottle in the house. At her bidding, he poured his own drink, and a sherry for her.

As he handed her the glass, she said, "My granddaughter will be down in a moment, Mr. Blakeley."

"Of course,"

Edith hesitated, watching him sip his whiskey. "May I speak frankly?"

"By all means."

Again, Edith hesitated, then plunged ahead. "My granddaughter is a young woman of breeding. She has led a sheltered life. Her . . . her virtue is . . . is complete. Do you understand?"

"Of course, Mrs. Prentiss." He rendered a slight smile. "I expected nothing less."

"Miriam has lived much of recent years in the Maryland countryside. This will be her first . . . first experience with . . . sophisticated New York life. I'm sure

you will have proper regard for her . . . her sensi-
bilities."

His bow was most formal. "I understand completely,
Mrs. Prentiss. Rest assured I have a thorough regard
for her innocence. You needn't worry."

With no small excitement, Miriam made her entrance,
full of curiosity about Peter Blakeley. While waiting,
she had tried to tell herself he could not possibly be
as handsome as Morgan Kingston. Morgan was much
on her mind. She wanted him to see her in her dress,
witness his surprise and admiration, sense his desire for
her. No longer would she be just his "kid sister." He
would know her teasing and flirting with him was not
girlish playing, but womanly wiles. Oh, how she would
enflame him in this gown. But first, another man was
to see her, and she was full of speculations about him.
What would he be like, this man her grandmother so
wanted her to meet? Grandmama had evaded most of
her questions about Peter Blakeley, telling Miriam she
would soon be able to judge for herself. Her grandmother's reticence and cryptic smile had added fuel to
Miriam's wildest conjectures. Perhaps, in a different
way, Peter Blakeley would prove as exciting as Morgan
Kingston. No—that was clearly impossible. Nevertheless, she longed to test her charms on some good-
looking man, longed for adventure, romance. Peter
Blakeley might furnish this opportunity.

When she stepped into the parlor and saw him,
Miriam had to steady herself against a chair to keep
from reeling with shock. She was completely unprepared for such a disappointment, such a mockery of all
her girlish fantasies. Could this really be the man her
grandmother was so eager for her to meet? Was grandmama blind, or insensible?

Peter Blakeley was too old. That was Miriam's first
impression. Besieged with queries, grandmama had said
he was "about thirty." That, Miriam now saw, was
optimistic, to say the least. Actually, she could not
guess his age. He was at the time in a man's life when
he could be anywhere between thirty-five and fifty, and

whichever number was correct, he was too old for her. Her second disappointment was in his height—or rather, his lack of height. In her heels, she was almost as tall as he. Morgan towered over her, making her feel dainty and feminine. Moreover, Blakeley projected an image of utter blandness. He had a sallow, glossy complexion, spectacles that made him look owlish, a thin, seemingly lipless mouth, and sandy, nondescript hair, parted in the middle and plastered down with pomade. His most distinct feature was his eyes, pale blue, almost gray. Miriam had never seen such eyes, so cold. There was cruelty in them, and menace—even malice.

"Miriam, my dear, may I present Mr. Peter Blakeley of New York?"

Miriam recovered enough to smile, limply. "How do you do?"

"I am enchanted to meet you, Miss Hodges."

That he was. She saw it in his eyes. They seemed to stab at her face, her half-exposed breasts. Inwardly, Miriam trembled. But from somewhere, she found the inner resources to smile at him, accept a sherry, talk to him about New York, life in Maryland, make various small talk. She tried to tell herself he was an older man, a friend of her grandmother's, someone she had to be dutifully pleasant to. That he had come to meet her, that she was being paired off with him, was an idea she barred from her mind.

When Peter Blakeley said he was enchanted with her, the word was an understatement. More accurately, he was filled with desire. This girl, so young and beautiful, attired in this daring gown, was just what he needed at this time in his life. And she came from a good, if impoverished, family. This comely young woman would lend him respectability by day, carnal delights by night. He sensed he had struck a satisfactory deal with the old hag.

Peter Blakeley had long ago accepted public disapproval of how he made his money. He dealt in hardship, human suffering—reaped enormous profits from

it. He had a large safe in his home, and always there
was a goodly sum of hard cash in it: greenbacks, gold
and silver, if necessary. A man, an occasional woman,
who was in trouble came to him. He had cash, no
questions asked, when it was available from no other
source. If a person needed money, right away, to pay
off a gambling debt, a bit of blackmail, perhaps to feed
the wife and children, Peter Blakeley was always good
for it. Everyone possessed something, a house, a store
or factory, a family heirloom, some trinket. He would
buy them at sacrifice prices, a mere fraction of their
real worth. Protests and tears were meaningless to
him. Virtually every time, a desperate need for cash
parted a man from his possessions. It might not be
banking on Wall Street, but it had made Peter Blakeley
a rich, if exceedingly unpopular, man.

His problem was that the way he made his money
ruined his social life. No respectable New Yorker would
be caught dead with him. And for one of their daughters, even the plainest, least desirable spinster, to go
out in public with him was unthinkable. Blakeley had
been married once in the half-forgotten past to a Boston woman, who had been so eager to rid herself of
him she demanded no settlement. To meet his needs,
he employed prostitutes, but that was expensive and
wholly unsatisfying to him. At age forty-two, what he
wanted was respectability—or so he thought. Actually,
he wanted to tweak the noses of the "better" New
Yorkers by proving he could attract and ensnare one
of their own.

Thus, his interest in Miriam Hodges. He had made
"purchases" from Edith Prentiss. He had even loaned
her money—not his usual practice—figuring to acquire
this fine old house. When she suggested her granddaughter in exchange for the notes, it had amused him.
Artworks, antiques, jewels, yes, but never had he "acquired" a beautiful woman in this way. He had gone
along with what he considered a joke, even going to
Lord & Taylor to have a look at her. That had been

enough to pique his interest. Seeing her now settled the matter.

Blakeley sensed at once this girl might be ideal. She was terribly young. That was a drawback. But why not? She was certainly beautiful enough, and she came from a prominent family that was now impoverished. She was from out-of-state, and wouldn't know his reputation. He could sense the astonished glances, the buzz of voices, when he appeared in public with this girl on his arm. Just thinking of it filled him with glee. He glanced at her bosom. Properly handled, she could do much more. She could be a prize of prizes. Yes, a most satisfactory deal had been made.

"I thought we might dine at Delmonico's, Miss Hodges." The thought of entering New York's poshest restaurant with her excited him. "I hope you will do me the honor of accompanying me."

Miriam was surprised. She turned to her grandmother. "I thought we were dining here."

The old woman's smile masked her discomfort. "There has been a change of plans. Mr. Blakeley thought perhaps—"

"Yes, will you come?" He saw Miriam's hesitation. "I'd be honored to have you join us, Mrs. Prentiss." If the old woman came, the deal was off.

"No, you two young people enjoy yourselves. An old woman needs her rest."

Miriam was thrilled by Delmonico's. She had been there before with her father, brother and Moira, but that had been nothing like this. As they entered, she felt eyes leaping at her. It excited her to know she attracted so much attention. As she sat at the table and the waiter fussed over them, she felt she was all breasts and blonde hair. This knowledge gave her confidence. Peter Blakeley might be too old and not much to look at, but he certainly knew the right places to take a girl.

Aroused, excited, she extended herself. After all, she could practice the wiles she intended to employ on Morgan. She could gauge the extent and effect of her power on Blakeley, if nothing else. So she made eye contact with him, smiling frequently. She admired the famous restaurant, the champagne he ordered, and bent frequently toward him, lowering her cleavage, to speak to him as though she had something intimate to tell him. Laughter came easily to her.

"You have a brother, I believe?"

"Oh, yes, Tom." Stuffy Tom, so like her father. If he could see her now. Perhaps he would not be so hateful to her because she saw their stepmother for the intruder she was. Stubborn, foolish Tom adored Moira. But, then, he was only seventeen. What did he know?

"Is he in New York?"

"Tom? Oh, no, he went off to Atlantic City with some friends."

Dinner was ordered, her champagne glass refilled. She began to feel this funny little man was—well, funny. She laughed often, if not always in amusement. She sensed the effect of laughter on her breasts, which seemed to captivate him. Yes, it was easy, very easy. Here she was, in the smartest restaurant in New York, this man, so very rich, practically at her feet. What would Morgan Kingston say to that? Suddenly, he seemed more distant, extremely young, not as handsome as he had been before. It was strange how Peter Blakeley's looks had improved with each glass of champagne.

"I hope you might let me show you some of the sights of our fair city tomorrow, Miss Hodges."

"Why I'd love that, Mr. Blakeley."

"Peter, please. And may I call you Miriam?"

"As you wish—Peter."

"We have some of the finest shops in the world in New York. I'd like to show them to you. Perhaps you might find some trinket or bauble to fancy."

Trinket? Bauble? Diamonds, furs. This little man was rich, loaded with money. Yes, she might fancy something. "Every girl loves to shop, Peter."

"Then we shall."

She smiled at him, lowering her eyelids as she did

so. "You must be very lonely, Peter, to give so much time to a young girl such as I."

"As a matter of fact, I am lonely."

She looked at him intently. "Are you? I am, too."

"I find that hard to believe, a beautiful young woman like you."

She laughed, lightly, musically. "But it's true. And I know why. You said it yourself—*young*. I fear only younger men are attracted to me. And, to be frank, I find young men so—so young, so juvenile. Would you think me bold if I said I find older men more attractive?"

"I most certainly would not."

"An older man is more worldly, wiser, more settled. These are qualities I fear I lack."

"I'm sure not."

Again, she laughed, leaning toward him. "Oh, yes, I am often unsure of myself, flighty, impulsive. I need the guidance and counsel of an older, more mature individual, who knows the ways of the world, the pitfalls a young girl may encounter."

She saw his quick, furtive glance at her bosom. "Then I shall do my best to live up to your expectations."

Their meal was lavish, far in excess of what she could eat. But the waste did not disturb her. She was enjoying the uses of money, the sense of power that wealth produced. And she was enjoying what seemed to her to be celebrity status. Everyone kept staring at her, marveling. Well, why not? Was she not, after all, a beautiful young woman? And wasn't her escort one of the richest men in New York?

After Delmonico's, Blakeley took her to the Hoffman House, Harry Hill's emporium, dancing at the new Forty-second Street Hotel. Everywhere, she was a sensation, people staring at her. She became quite giddy on successive glasses of champagne, laughing frequently, flirting with Peter, touching his hand or cheek, pressing her breasts against his arm as they walked. She was not so giddy she didn't know what she was doing. She knew the effect she was having on him. He was practically panting for her. What was wrong with that? Why not give a little pleasure to an older man who was lonely? He had certainly been generous to her.

As he took her home in his carriage, he tried to kiss her. She managed to turn her head, just brushing his cheek. "Why, Peter," she said, "you're so impulsive. And here I thought you were going to give me wise counsel." It worked; he did not persist.

For his part, Peter Blakeley was not upset by the rebuff. This girl, so young, beautiful and flirtatious, was all he had expected and more, much more. With her on his arm, he had set New York on its ear. The whole city would be buzzing about him. There was plenty of time. Tomorrow he would take her shopping, and to the carriage parade and promenade in Central Park. More people would see him with her. And she would discover what money could buy.

Chapter 5

During the next few days, Cassie felt like a piece of flotsam on a storm-tossed emotional sea. Grinding fear and guilt were punctuated with moments of ecstatic happiness, despair alternated with feverish hope. Worse, she felt helpless to control any of it. Indeed, she could barely endure.

She had, she discovered, no capacity to resist the impassioned lovemaking of Morgan Kingston. His youth and vigor, released from years of wanting and searching, seemed to flow from him in torrents now that he had found someone to love. Her mouth became a cup from which he was compelled to drink, and her inviting lips became his font, filling him with passion until her slender thighs opened to offer him the receptacle of love. His desire seemed insatiable, her response infinite. Her will was broken, her carefully-nurtured resolve melted within Morgan's muscular arms. She had no power to deny him . . . or herself. This man, so attractive and powerful, so desired and forbidden, became her personal Prometheus, offering fire, creating life from clay. Each day, it seemed to her, she died in his arms and was reborn.

Theirs were stolen moments. She insisted on it, making him swear not to tell anyone, no matter how much he hated the skulking and wanted to declare his love for her. "Not now," she said. "I'm not ready." Several times, they returned to his study at Kingston. Once they made love amid the shimmering light of the aspen copse, another time in a tobacco shed filled with pungent aromas. One night, setting her atremble with fear, he came to her room next to the nursery, and in the darkness they soundlessly told each other of their love. She was no longer as passive as she had been that first time, and was as thrilled by his pleasure at her touch as by her own pleasure at his.

Yet, the physical expression was only a part of their love. She would be drawn to a window and down below would be Morgan looking up at her. It was as though he had willed her to come. That happened often. She would know he had entered a room before she saw him. Always, she could sense when he was looking at her. How many times did she beg him not to? He would speak to his mother, grandmother, Danielle, and she would know what he had been thinking and that he was about to say those exact words. In a room filled with chatter and happy laughter, she heard only his voice.

They talked often and long about what had suddenly become the central problem of her life. "Why must we

hide it, Cassie? Why won't you let me declare our love
and marry you?"

Always, her answer was the same, "Because I love
you." He protested. She was speaking nonsense. "A
Negress, a former slave, as mistress of Aurial? It would
never work."

"It would, Cass, I know it would. You are all beauty
and grace. Aurial would bloom under your touch."

"Perhaps, Morgan, perhaps, but there is more to life
than Aurial. Maybe our love would keep us happy
here, but Aurial is not an island. There are neighbors,
townspeople. We must live with them. There is talk
of your running for Congress one day, perhaps even
for the Senate like your grandfather Morgan. With a
colored wife on your arm? Never, Morgan, never."

"It wouldn't matter, Cassie."

"Oh, but it would. I love you, darling. I cannot bear
to think of you socially ostracized, the butt of jokes
and ridicule, constantly defending your wife's honor
and your own. I care too much for you—and about
you—for that."

He laughed. "You simply don't know the history of
the Morgan and Kingston wives. My grandmother
Glenna, that sweet, refined, whitehaired old lady, has
scandalized people her whole life. When she and my
grandfather were first married, all Washington was agog
with stories about her living in a sultan's harem, being
sold into slavery to a jungle tribe and rescued by old
Joe. He was young then, of course. And I guess the
rumors were only a fraction of the truth. It got so bad
that Andrew Jackson invited her to the White House
and sat her at his right hand as his personal endorse-
ment of her."

"But, Morgan—"

"Hear me out, Cass. It was even said she kept Joe
around just to service her. Nasty things were said, real
nasty. My grandfather just laughed. Indeed, he encouraged her to wear the most scandalous gowns of the
day. The more people talked about her, the more elec-

tions he won, or so I'm told. You'd be setting no precedent, Cassie."

She shook her head. "I'm not your grandmother, Morgan. I never could be."

"My mother has always been talked about, too. She had, I guess, a scandalous affair with my father's brother, the one I'm supposed to look like, before her marriage. Then she traveled west with the Forty-niners, and God knows what happened then. I know she and grandmother ran a saloon called Morgan Manor out in San Francisco. She lived alone here at Aurial during the Civil War. I guess people accused her of sleeping with half the Union army. It wasn't true, but there was talk.

"And Danielle. She was the mistress to one of the worst robber barons in New York. I knew him. Practically a scoundrel. She lived with him openly, even traveled in his railway car. It was wrecked. She was captured by some demented half-wit." He laughed. "My lovely, demure, always ladylike sister has caused more tongues to wag than the worst government scandal. Don't you see, Cassie? If people talk about you, it will be only typical." He leaned down and kissed her gently. "Why, it's practically a tradition. As a Morgan and a Kingston, I expect nothing less in my wife."

Such words had a powerful effect on Cassie. She saw the great house with new eyes. She watched Moira, Glenna, Danielle, too. Yes, she could run this house, fulfill her role as a mistress of Aurial. It would be a challenge, but also an opportunity. She would work, study, improve herself. It appealed immensely to her, the safety, the respectability. A slave child rising to be one of the most important women in Maryland. She wanted it very much. She knew a great marriage could make it happen.

She turned to him, silent tears rolling down her cheeks, and clasped his face, brown against white, making him look at her. "Morgan Kingston, you are the only male heir. You bear the names of two great families. I cannot be a party to making those who bear those names in the future brown or tan."

"Nonsense. I understand my uncle King married a beautiful colored woman named Lila out in California. They probably have kids by now."

And so it remained, an impasse. She heard his indignant protests. She believed him when he said he didn't care about her color. She was influenced, greatly so, by his insistence that he deserved happiness in life. And deep in her soul, she believed that one day she would give in, surrender to her own wanting and his. But not now. And so their clandestine affair continued. Neither could muster the courage to stop it. She could only hope that it remained unknown, numb with fear that they might be discovered.

A few times, she thought of telling Danielle, going on her knees, begging forgiveness, asking her to help her. It almost happened the morning after her first evening with Morgan.

"Did you and Morgan have a nice time last night?"

Cassie had stared at Danielle's reflection in the mirror. She couldn't speak.

"That moonlight would have enchanted the devil himself." She smiled. "I must confess, I spied. Watching you two walk off, I envied you."

Words of confession were filling Cassie's mouth, ready to be blurted out.

"Do you think I should wear that new blue gown or save it? GlennaMa says Mr. Fairchild is coming this weekend. We're going to have a party."

The opportunity seemed lost. Cassie swallowed. "I think you're lovely in whatever you wear."

The worst turmoil for Cassie came, not when she was with Morgan, but when she was not with him. Her thoughts became an incantation of promises to break off with him, this very night, end this madness before both of them, the whole family, were consumed by it. Then, each day, having failed, guilt eroded her insides, like an acid. The one night she found the courage not to see him, he came to her room. She was consumed by fear of discovery, but the fear, the silence, the darkness only made her want and need him the more.

Her greatest anguish came from a single question: Did they know? They must. They must see it in the way he looked at her, the lingering of his hand when it touched hers in passing a plate, accepting a glass. Surely, Danielle, of all people, must realize what was happening. But if she did, she didn't care, no one did. Always, they were thrown together. "Cassie, do you mind fetching some more wine from the cellar? Morgan will show you where it is." *Oh, God!* "Are you going into town today, Morgan? I've given Cassie a shopping list." *Holy Mary, Mother of God, help me.* "Another row on the river? You two are turning into sailors." *Didn't they know? Were they blind?* "I've never seen Morgan so happy. I think he's spending these evenings at some mischief. At least I hope so." Years before, Danielle had converted Cassie to the family's faith, Roman Catholicism, and taught her the beautiful prayer of petition, the *Memorare*. Now Cassie found herself saying it frequently. *O, Mother of the Word Incarnate, despise not my petitions, but in your mercy, hear and answer me.*

Franklin Fairchild came down to Aurial for the weekend. Now in his seventies and nominally retired from the powerful Fairchild and Son bank of Wall Street, he nonetheless remained active in the business. One of the reasons was at his side as he arrived at Aurial, his grandson, Benjamin Fairchild. Not yet thirty, Benjamin had become an increasingly powerful factor in the bank. In part to combat the depression that had begun in 1873 and still continued, the elder Fairchild had decided the bank needed to invest in new, innovative industries with a potential for growth. He chose his grandson for this task, leaving his son, Dexter Fairchild, in charge of more conventional bank activities. However, because of Benjamin's youth, the elder Fairchild supervised his investments and exercised a veto power over them. He was, nevertheless, exceedingly proud of the young banker's accomplishments. A couple of real estate investments had paid off handsomely. He had placed some bank funds in the new, fledgling oil industry, citing its potential for growth. Franklin Fairchild was still dubious, but he had wanted a younger man with the courage to take risks. Might as well allow him a modest plunge or two.

Benjamin came along supposedly to look after his grandfather, whose step was not as firm as it used to be. The real reason he came was to see Danielle Summers, for whom he had carried a torch all these years. Fresh from college, he had met Danielle when she and her family first arrived from London in 1870, staying at Franklin Fairchild's home in New York. Benjamin had taken Danielle out on her first date in the city—actually, her first date of any kind. He had been enthralled by her, even as the date turned into a disaster. They were dining at Delmonico's when Hamilton Garth bought them champagne and came to the table. Danielle's obsession with Garth had begun at that moment. How many times Benjamin had wished he had refused the champagne.

Six years had elapsed. Danielle had wed Walter Summers, who had rescued her from her captivity out West. She lived in South Carolina and was the mother of two. Benjamin hoped that seeing her again would somehow cure his affliction. She might have grown fat, or might not be as beautiful or as charming as he remembered. Then, perhaps, he would be released from his infatuation. She would no longer be the standard to which he compared all other women. He would then be able to propose to one of the many young women he knew wished to be his wife. To the extent he hoped Danielle would no longer be appealing, he was disappointed. She had simply grown more beautiful, more captivating. The sight of her, greeting them on the veranda as their carriage arrived, wounded him. He was in deep trouble, and he knew it.

Danielle was surprised to see Benjamin, and at once delighted. She remembered him, of course. When she was eighteen and he was twenty-two, she had thought him terribly young, not very handsome, disconcertingly unsure of himself. She remembered he seemed to have a great need to talk, filling every awkward moment with chatter. She saw now that he had changed. He seemed taller than she remembered, perhaps because he was slenderer. His boyish, freckled face had assumed greater maturity, and his whole bearing exuded greater confidence and, yes, an aura of power. GlennaMa had said Benjamin was becoming an important member of the bank.

"Good heavens, Benjamin, such a surprise. It's so good to see you again." Smiling, she extended both her hands in greeting and, as he bent toward her, offered her cheek for his kiss.

He was beaming. "Danielle, it isn't possible. You are more beautiful than I remembered."

She laughed. "You suave New Yorkers. I refuse to believe a word of it."

"It's true, Danielle."

She had seen it in his eyes, admiration certainly, but also something more. The simple sincerity of those two words, "It's true," confirmed what she already knew. Benjamin cared for her. She guessed he always had, and she felt a momentary guilt for never having given him a particle of a chance. "Then I thank you." She smiled at him, squeezing his fingers, which held hers. "It's good to see you again. I'm glad you came." She turned from him to greet his grandfather, and they all went inside to begin the weekend activities.

She and Benjamin were together a great deal, at meals, horseback-riding, croquet, a row on the river. For the most part, his conduct was entirely proper. He was an old friend, grandson of her grandmother's husband. They had a lot of catching up to do in the accounting of their lives. If he was perhaps a trifle intimate in some of his questions, it was understandable. He was a friend.

"GlennaMa tells me you have become quite an important banker."

"I don't know how important—" he smiled, "—but family connections haven't hurt."

"Aren't you in charge of new accounts, or something like that?"

"Yes. Grandfather has given me my chance to do what I've always wanted to do."

"And what is that?"

"Don't you remember?" He watched her shake her head. "When we were at Delmonico's that night and . . . may I speak of it, Danielle? Garth, I mean."

The name hurt her, but she smiled. "You already have."

"When I was telling you about him, I mentioned that I hoped one day I'd get a chance to exhibit some of the daring and risk-taking men like him make a fortune on. I've been given my chance, and I'm enjoying it."

"What sort of risks?"

She listened as he told her of encouraging investment in the new bridge to Brooklyn, and of his interest in plans for a railroad to run under the streets of New York. He had already invested in the petroleum industry. For a few minutes, he described to her how it would one day be an important industry.

"Actually, Danielle, you and I live in an exciting time. Big things are happening. In March, on the tenth to be exact, a fellow named Bell, Alexander Graham Bell, actually made his voice travel over a wire. He spoke to his assistant, saying, 'Watson, come here; I want you,' and his voice was heard clearly."

"I find that hard to believe."

"It's true, however. Two months later, this fellow Bell demonstrated his invention before a group of scientists in Boston, and they were impressed. I am, too. Think of the possibilities. People will be able to speak to each other over long distances. A company—they're calling it a telephone company—is being organized. I want the bank to invest in it."

She smiled. "What an exciting life you lead, Benjamin."

"There's more, Danielle, much more. There's a fellow named Edison in New Jersey. Very clever inventor. He's already invented something he calls a microphone. He believes very shortly he will perfect some kind of a box that actually plays music in your own home. A phonograph, he calls it. And I know he's working on a new type of light fixture. It will run on electricity, not gas. Think of that! I'm watching his work carefully. I feel a lot of good will come of it."

Again, she smiled at him. "I won't pretend to understand all this, but I can understand that you're enjoying what you're doing. I'm glad to see you so happy."

He looked at her, suddenly serious. "I'm not completely happy, Danielle. Something is missing, something I wanted very badly and didn't get."

Her smile faded as she looked at him. There seemed to be nothing to say. Nor did she have to, as she heard him ask, "Are you happy, Danielle?"

"Me? Yes, of course. The children keep me busy and—"

"Stephanie is lovely—Andrew, too. With you as their mother, how could they not be?"

She laughed. "Thank you, Benjamin, but I rather think they favor their father."

He winced. "And he . . . your husband . . . how is he?"

"Walter's in Charleston. He couldn't get away."

"I know that. I just wondered if you and he are happy in your marriage."

It was too intimate a question, and Danielle was grateful when Moira called to them that dinner was served.

But he would not let it go. Later that evening, he said, "You must know I care about you, Danielle. Is it so wrong of me to want your happiness?"

"Of course not." She smiled at him. "And it's sweet of you to think of me. But you shouldn't worry. I'm happy in my marriage, Benjamin. Walter and I are very much in love."

He laughed. "I was hoping he beat you regularly and ran around with other women."

"I'm afraid not." Her smile was dazzling. Why was it such an effort, though?

"Forgive me, Danielle. Something is wrong. I can feel it."

She bristled a little. "When did you become so perceptive, Benjamin?"

"Have I gone too far?"

"Almost." She sighed. "All right, you are perceptive. I am not happy in Charleston. Just now, it is—well, you must know, the situation between the coloreds and the whites, the violence. I find it difficult."

"I can understand that. Any chance of your moving back up North—" he smiled, "—where I can see you more often?"

"I'm afraid not. My husband is a Southerner. Seasons is his home. He loves it there. I'm sure I will come to also."

"No doubt you will, Danielle." He sighed.

From across the room, the voice of Franklin Fairchild boomed. "I almost forgot. Have you heard the news? General Custer had his whole command massacred at some place called Little Big Horn. The news just reached New York."

Discussion of that news brought Danielle welcome relief from Benjamin's probing questions.

Chapter 6

Moira had planned for the party honoring her mother and Franklin Fairchild to be small and casual, just a few friends and neighbors. It didn't work out that way. Glenna suggested a few people from the Grant administration, including the President, Fairchild's good friend, who ought to be invited. Since this was an election year and her husband was a close associate of Samuel Tilden, Moira had to invite others for political balance. Until the last, she hoped that Larry might get back to be host. When he did not, she did her best to make good use of any political opportunities that arose.

Inevitably, the party grew in size to more than a hundred guests. Nonetheless, Moira tried to keep it casual and summery, opening up the house, serving a light buffet. At the last moment, she hired a small orchestra for dancing. The Morgans and Kingstons had a reputation as party-givers to uphold. Aurial had witnessed many a grand fête.

Cassie was extremely busy that Saturday, for which she was grateful, helping to arrange the flowers, polishing silver and setting the buffet. She had the children to look after, too, then dress them for their ceremonial appearance. Finally, she did Danielle's hair. There was scant time to think of Morgan and her problem.

Cassie had hoped not to attend the party or, at the most, appear with the children, then take them off to bed. Danielle would not hear of it. She expected Cassie to attend and have a splendid time. Thus, at Danielle's insistence, she was beautifully-gowned as she stood behind Danielle fixing her hair. Cassie's gown, purchased for her in Washington especially for this party, was an unusual *café au lait* color, worn off the shoulder, with a heart-shaped cleavage. The shade greatly enriched her complexion, deepening her luminous cocoa coloring.

"You look just lovely, Cassie," Danielle assured her.

"I still don't think I should go to the party."

"Nonsense."

"I feel overdressed and extremely uncomfortable." It was a reference to the décolletage of her gown. Never had she worn anything so revealing; her breasts rose from the bodice, creating a deep mahogany well of mystery. Only it wasn't a mystery anymore, was it? At least, not to one man.

Danielle laughed lightly. "I fear the women of this household have a certain tradition to uphold." It had begun with Glenna, at Daniel Morgan's insistence. She was celebrated for her daring gowns, wearing them even at the White House and charming Andrew Jackson in the process. Moira was long accustomed to display of her remarkable figure, and Danielle—well, she had just grown up with it. She had scandalized New York when she was mistress to Hamilton Garth, but even before, when she was so shy, she had worn an utterly shocking gown to a royal ball in London. She smiled. That was where she had met Walter Summers. She was certain that this night her mother and GlennaMa, too, would be gowned to reveal their womanliness. Nothing less was expected of her.

Still, Danielle had misgivings. She was a young mother, away on holiday from her husband. There was no call for such a gown as her own. It was of cool, thin muslin, beautifully draped, and of a shade of blue she favored because it deepened and magnified her eyes. There were little puffed sleeves at her shoulders, but this effort at demureness seemed only to accentuate the rise of her snowy breasts from the deeply-cut bodice. She had worn the dress once before, and it had pleased Walter. But, now, Walter wasn't here. Someone else was.

"Besides, if I can wear this gown, you can wear yours."

Cassie made a face at her in the mirror. "Whatever you say, ma'am."

Danielle was certain of the effect the gown would have on Benjamin. She didn't want it. Or did she? She had been unsettled by his coming. His attentions, his dark, burning eyes, the intimate way he spoke to her, unnerved her, brought back memories she had long forgotten, or at least closed out of her mind. She knew well her own passions, their cursed ability to flare and consume her even with a man like Garth, whom she had not even liked. She had thought all this was behind her. Her husband knew what lay beneath her cool exterior, and he had the ability both to fuel and to quench her fires. She should have insisted that he come with her. Benjamin Fairchild, now older, distinguished, self-assured, was . . . he was nothing, just an old friend. But this dress? She shouldn't encourage him. Was it too late to change?

"I suspect *one* gentleman will admire your gown."

Danielle looked wide-eyed at her friend's reflection in the mirror. "God, Cassie, do you read minds? I was just thinking, I—"

"I know. I saw it." She smiled. "There can be nothing wrong in enjoying the admiration of an old beau."

And now, Danielle smiled, too. "It is flattering, I must say. But he is . . . or was . . . hardly a beau. I treated him terribly. I couldn't see him at all."

"Obviously, he was more observant of you."

Danielle joined her laughter. "Does it show that much?"

Cassie hesitated, and in that instant reached out to Danielle for help. "Doesn't love always show in the eyes?"

"So I've heard."

At that moment, Stephanie and Andrew burst into the room. If there was more to be said between the two women, it was lost in the excited voices of the children.

The Aurial gala was a huge success. Cassie did her best to hide, remaining in the background, staying with the children, which she felt was her role in the household. Morgan came to her, whispering, "God, but you're beautiful. Tell me now you're not to be mistress of Aurial."

"Please, Morgan. Not tonight." Her whisper was plaintive.

Smiling, his voice normal, he bowed and said, "My dear Miss Brown, will you do me the honor of this dance?"

She hissed through clenched teeth. "No, I won't. Just let me be tonight."

The children were allowed to stay up later, and how she wished they weren't! Eagerly, she counted the minutes until she could take them up and put them to bed. She would not come back down. But this plan came to naught. Jessie appeared, insisting on tucking in her "little darlings." They didn't know what real bedtime stories were until they heard hers. Cassie appealed to Danielle with her eyes, but got only laughter in return.

Danielle did more. "Would you do me a favor, Benjamin? Cassie is acting like a stick. Will you dance with her? Morgan can't get her out on the floor."

He smiled. "All favors should be so easy. She's a beautiful young woman."

Cassie could not refuse one of the honored guests. Stiff but obedient, she accompanied Benjamin to the floor, moving into a waltz. When Morgan cut in, she was in his arms, unable to help herself.

"Finally," he said. "I was beginning to think you didn't dance."

"I wish I didn't." When he laughed, pulling her closer to him, she said, "Oh, Morgan, I'm so afraid."

"Of what?"

"Of you, of myself, of everyone seeing, knowing, discovering us."

"Then let them. It's all I can do to keep from stopping the orchestra and making a big announcement."

"You wouldn't dare!"

"I would—unless my girl has every dance with me."

Once again, he worked his physical effect on her. Near him, in his arms, hearing his whispered endearments, she felt her resistance to him weakening. Always, it was so. But she was determined to do nothing in public to bring on trouble. She begged him to behave.

"What's wrong with the garden in the moonlight?"

"You know very well what's wrong."

"Oh, Cassie, I'm dying to kiss you. Sweetheart, please?"

Several times, she refused him, but finally, to stop his teasing, she relented. They would just stand on the terrace and take some air.

His knowing laughter swept over her. "Of course. What else did you think I had in mind?"

It was no use. She felt powerless as he led her into the garden. She could only insist they go far from the house, where no one could see them. Even then, she looked around furtively, as he swept her into his arms.

"Oh Morgan, if anyone sees us."

"I hope they do. Besides, the moon's behind a cloud."

At last, she surrendered to her longing, yielding her lips, her tongue, pressing her soft, warm breasts against his hard, male chest. Once, she broke away for a moment, looking around to see if they were alone. There was no one, and she yielded again, moaning softly as his eager hand slipped into her bodice and gently stroked her bud-hard nipple. She could feel his manhood against her thigh, and then at her center, and she groaned as she felt herself weaken, melt.

If the cloud, swept by an unknown wind of heaven, had not moved, they might have gone undetected. In their passion, neither Cassie nor Morgan was aware of the light from a waning, three-quarter moon drenching them. A figure at an upstairs window saw them, then gasped in astonishment and fright.

"Tonight, later. I'll come to your room."

Cassie's words denied him, "No, please," but her body, straining against his, through her dress, beckoned.

There was another pairing in the moonlight that evening. Danielle, a trifle giddy from wine, went willingly, eager for a breath of air. Benjamin's decorous conduct had helped her relax with him and enjoy the party. And Cassie's remark helped, too. There was no harm in enjoying the admiration of an old beau.

"There's something about a beautiful woman in the moonlight, which brings out the worst in men."

She smiled. "Not in your case, I trust."

"I fear so. All the poetic words have been uttered and written. If a man says anything, he sounds like a dull, uninspired clod."

She laughed. "That wasn't too bad in itself."

"I guess it wasn't." His laughter waned along with hers, and they stood facing each other in the moonlight. Both felt the awkwardness. Then he raised his stemmed wine glass in a toast. "To my folly." His voice was extremely husky.

"Folly, Benjamin?"

"Yes. When I heard you were here, I confess I insisted on coming along—" he smiled, "—to look after grandfather, of course." He saw her answering smile. "I wanted to see you. I hoped you'd grown fat and ugly, somehow become dull, perhaps tedious."

She laughed. "You didn't really think that?"

"I did. I hoped that when I saw you, I would be released from my . . . my infatuation, and thus come to find another—any other—suitably attractive." He looked at her, tried in vain to smile, then in one jerky, convulsive movement raised his glass and drained it. "I fear I have committed a great folly."

She was suddenly touched, and could feel her eyes moistening. "Oh, Benjamin, if it were within my power, I would release you. I want only your happiness."

He nodded, firming his mouth as he did so. "I know. But you don't have the power." They seemed suspended in time and place for a moment. He was unaware of having consciously willed it, but he was slowly bending toward her. "Forgive me," he said softly, just before he kissed her. He did not embrace her. He merely bent his face to hers, brushing her lips gently, tenderly. In appearance, it was just a gesture of affection between old friends, but in its effect on both, unspoken, it was a great deal more. "Again, forgive me, Danny. If I am never to have you, at least I will have kissed you once in the moonlight."

Lips still tingling, she managed a smile. "There is nothing to forgive." She saw him moving toward her again and turned away. "But there would be a second time, Benjamin."

Immediately, he moved back, laughing softly. "Ah, the impulsive male. But you're right. Once should be enough. I'll treasure it always—and mark it in my memory by never again kissing a woman in the moonlight."

"Didn't you say you weren't poetic?" She saw him turning up his empty glass, nervously seeking more wine. "Here, take mine." She watched him take it and sip. "I really am unworthy of you, Benjamin. I know you'll find someone to love—and soon."

He smiled. "It is my parents' most fervent wish."

"And half the maidens' in New York, I imagine.'"

"There might be one or two, I wouldn't know."

"I'll bet."

Again, laughter, dissolved into awkwardness, broken by him. "If you belong to another, and I know you do, may I still hope for your happiness?"

"Yes, and thank you."

"And may I hope that if, God forbid, something should go wrong and you have occasion to think of another, it might be me?" He saw her just standing there, all eyes in the silvery light. "I'll still be waiting, Danny. I think I'll always be waiting."

She continued to stand there, staring as though seeing him for the first time. He saw her blink, once, twice, then she was coming up toward him. He heard words: "And now you forgive me." Her kiss was not

of affection. It was too open, deep and long for that,
and for just an instant he felt her body pressed against
his. Then she was gone, back into the house. And in
his loins, he knew what he had to forgive her for.

The party lasted late. It was after one in the morning
when the last of the guests departed. Glenna and Franklin Fairchild were sent off to bed, a tired Joe and Jessie,
too, and the others worked hard to perform the necessary tidying up. It was past two-thirty when the last of
the downstairs lights were out, and all went to their
separate rooms.

Cassie crawled into her bed in the room next to the
nursery, exhausted both physically and emotionally. It
was too late for Morgan to come. So sure was she that
he wasn't coming, she donned her nightgown. Yet, she
lay there a time listening to the creaks and night sounds
of the house. No, he wasn't coming. With relief, she let
herself slide into sleep.

It might have been better not to sleep. She never
did quite awaken, despite his coming into bed with her,
despite his impassioned kisses, despite her nightgown
being slipped over her head. Never had it been like
this, sleep tugging langorously at her mind, while her
body was highly sensitized. Never had he been so passionate, so demanding, never had her skin felt so electri-
fied by his touch. There, in the darkness, his mouth
devoured hers, her breasts leaped to his hands, and
when her thighs opened for him, never had she known
such eagerness. Half-drugged with sleep, it was as
though her body, separated from her mind and possessed of a will of its own, was transporting her to a
new height of pleasure.

She had heard no sound, no telltale rustle of slipper,
no creak of board, no turn of latch. There was only
light, blinding though just a single candle, and etched
in her mind was the horrified face above it and, in-
delibly, awareness of what the face saw, she on her
back, thighs spread, Morgan's body above her, her
fingers encircling, guiding. There were three words,
"God forgive me!" Then the light went out.

Chapter 7

Jessie would never have gone to Cassie's room if she had suspected Morgan was there. She was astonished, horrified by what she saw. It was all a series of errors.

Jessie had not wanted to see them in the garden, either. She had been standing in the darkened nursery, remaining with the children until they were asleep. The embrace she saw down below would have been unremarkable—she might have smiled, knowing young love was in bloom in the moonlight—had she not recognized the dress, the dark skin at the shoulders, as Cassie Brown. Who was young Cassie kissing? she wondered, with amused curiosity. But it went on so long. Even from so far away, Jessie could sense their passion. This was no romantic kiss in the moonlight, but two. . . . She tried to close her eyes, turn away. She almost did. But when they separated, came toward the house, she watched, revolted by her own spying. Mother of God, it was Morgan.

For the rest of the evening, Jessie was in turmoil. Long after she feigned a weariness she did not feel, and went to bed to escape lest her face reveal her knowledge, she lay abed beside the softly snoring Joe, her mind a whirlpool of worry. Later, she would wish mightily she had awakened Joe and told him. He would have scolded her, said, "Old woman, roll over and go to sleep." Later, when he learned what she had done, he upbraided her unmercifully.

Lying in bed, Jessie felt a thousand years old. There had been so many crises in rearing this family. Such beautiful women. What a curse beauty was! Wearily, she remembered: Glenna captured by the evil Winslow, Moira throwing herself at that rascal King Kingston, Andrew losing Aurial because of that no-good colored hussy Lila, Moira lost in the West—Danielle, too. Yes, Danielle, so lovely and delicate, abducted and raped in London, throwing herself at that scoundrel Garth, she and Moira kidnapped. Lord, it was too much for one tired body to withstand. And now, Morgan, passionately embracing a beautiful colored girl. Too much, she couldn't take more.

But she had to. Glenna must never know. She had endured too much already. Nor Moira. Jessie must find a way to cope with this herself. Cassie was colored. She must know. Any white man, Mr. Morgan above all others, was forbidden to her. Yes, she would talk to Cassie. A sweet child, but so beautiful—oh, the curse of beauty among Negro girls—and so young! Yes, she would bring Cassie to her senses.

What if you are wrong, old woman? What if it meant nothing? Your eyes are old. What if you saw wrong? Let it be. No, I saw. Maybe it was just wine and moonlight, two young people carried away. Still, it's wrong. Cassie must never—not with Morgan, Moira's child. I'll find out. I'll talk to Cassie. She'll tell me. In the morning. No, now, when the house is quiet, and there is no one to hear.

Dearest Mother of God, why hadn't she stayed in bed?

"God, Morgan, that was Jessie."

"I know." He tumbled off her, out of bed. In the darkness, she sensed him pulling on his trousers, buttoning his shirt. "You stay here. I'll take care of it."

"What are you going to do?"

"What I must. What I should have done a long time

ago." She sensed him bending over her, felt him searching out, then finding, her lips for a quick embrace. "It's better this way, Cassie, believe me. I'm actually relieved."

She wanted to protest, to scream after him, but she knew that not even that would help.

Moira was awakened by the insistent tapping at her door. Quickly, she squirmed to the edge of the bed, turned up the kerosene nightlight and, donning her robe, went to the door. "Morgan?"

"I have to talk to you."

"Now?"

"Yes."

She shrugged and opened the door for him to enter. "Do you realize what time it is, Morgan? Are you drunk?" She had never seen her son drunk, but there was a first time for everything.

"You know I hardly drink." He motioned toward a chair. "Please sit down, mother. I have to talk to you."

Resigned, but hardly amused, Moira sat on the edge of the bed. "All right, Morgan. You've got me awake now. What is so earthshaking at this time of night?"

"I should have told you days ago, no, weeks ago, even months, when I first knew."

Now her amusement did rise. How like his father he was, so direct, so earnest. If only he didn't look so much like his uncle. "Knew what, Morgan?"

"I'm in love, mother, deeply, hopelessly in love, and I want to be married."

She wanted to laugh. It was uproariously funny, her son, so serious and somber, waking her up in the dead of night to tell her he was in love. But, not wanting to hurt him, she managed to restrict her humor to a smile. "Fine, Morgan. May I know who the lucky girl is?"

"Cassie Brown."

The name stabbed at her, but for a moment she disbelieved. "You're not serious?"

"I am, mother. I've never been more serious in my life."

Humor doused, she looked at him, blinking, pursing her lips. "I see." She didn't know what else to say. Then she looked away, down at her hands.

"No, you don't see. Cassie and I are lovers. I was . . . with her . . . in her room. Jessie came in . . . found us."

Moira's eyes were burning. The tears would come. She didn't want them.

"It will be all over the house by morning. I don't want you to hear it that way. I came straight here . . . to tell you. I should have done it days ago. It would have been better than this."

Wearily, Moira arose from the bed and walked away from him to her vanity. She picked up her puff and dabbed at her face. Then she realized what she was doing. How silly. Powdering one's face in the middle of the night. She dropped the puff, sighing deeply. She was so tired. She had no strength to cope with this.

"I want your blessing, but I'll marry her even without it."

The sound of his voice, more than his words, aroused her. "I know."

"I mean it, mother."

Yes, he meant it. He was a strong-willed man, not to be denied. Again, she sighed, deeply, her chest rising and falling from the effort. "Morgan, I'm too tired to even try to think. You must be, too. Let's go to bed. Everything will be clearer in the morning."

"No. Jessie will—"

"Jessie will say nothing. I'll see to that." Energy came from somewhere, and her voice took on firmness. "Nor will you say anything. After Mr. Fairchild and Benjamin leave tomorrow, we will discuss this—not before. Do you understand?"

"I'm going to marry Cassie, mother. I mean it."

She saw his determination. "Yes, Morgan, I believe you mean it. Now goodnight.'"

After he had gone, she took a candle and went to

Joe and Jessie's room. The door opened without her rapping; apparently, the light from her candle had signaled her arrival through a crack beneath the door. Jessie stood in the doorway, and the two women, so long devoted to each other, exchanged looks. Eyes, not words, said everything. Then Jessie, agony etched on her tearstained face, nodded wordlessly. Moira returned to bed. It was dawn before she could sleep.

Cassie did not obey Morgan. For a time, she lay there in the darkness in fetal position, knees to her chin, clutching her stomach, filled with misery and guilt. She said the *Memorare,* and the *Salve Regina.* Then, slowly, she got up, put on her nightgown and robe. She had to be ready. For what, she didn't know. Perhaps she expected screams, shouts, recriminations, confrontations. But, straining her hearing, she detected only the wind, aged boards, the lap of water at ancient banks. This surprised her.

In time, she went to the nursery, crossed it while glancing at the sleeping forms, then opened the door on the other side.

Danielle awoke at once and saw Cassie. "The children?"

"No, they're all right."

Danielle kept a small nightlight in case she had to go to the children, or one came to her in a house strange to them. In its meager light, she saw Cassie's distorted face, even as she heard the anguish in her voice. "What's wrong, Cassie?" The reply was a low, agonized moan. At once, Danielle went to her, and felt Cassie's delicate shoulders shaking within her arms. "Oh, my darling, what's wrong?" Cassie's sobbing only augmented, and Danielle led her to the bed. She sat beside her, holding her tightly, as though trying to keep the sobs from tearing her friend apart.

Danielle was a long time getting the story. But, at last, key words, forced out, disclosed the truth. "Morgan and I . . . in love . . . Jessie came . . ." Danielle guessed at the rest.

For a time, Danielle, desperate to comfort her
friend, said, "It's all right, Cassie." But this seemed to
produce vehement shakes of the head, gasped denials
and even more sobbing. So, she reverted to, "Everything will be all right." This hardly seemed more
helpful, but in time Cassie managed at least a little
coherence.

"I—I . . . wanted to . . . tell you. I . . . I . . . thought
. . . you knew."

"I guess I did, darling. I'm sure I did. I just didn't
think about it."

"Oh, God . . . it's . . . so awful . . . I'm . . . so . . .
sorry."

"Don't be sorry, darling. It couldn't be helped."
Smiling, she lifted Cassie's head up, making her look
at her. "You should be happy. Morgan's in love with
you, isn't he?'"

Cassie's face again became contorted. She nodded
her head violently; then, to silence her wails, buried
her head in Danielle's shoulder, sobbing. Friend held
friend for a time, patting her back, making cooing,
comforting sounds, as though she were a child. Finally,
Danielle laid Cassie down on her bed, covered her and
crawled in beside her, holding her close, gently rubbing
her back. In time, she heard her breathing become
more regular, although there was still an occasional
sob, long after Cassie was asleep.

Danielle lay awake for some time, trying to think.
Cassie and Morgan. She said the names to herself several times, linking them in her mind. Cassie and Morgan. She realized now she had seen it, even encouraged
them. Cassie and her brother. Why not? She could
sense the appeal this quiet girl would have for him.
Why not? What was wrong with it? She knew, of
course, and at once sensed there might be opposition.
She would be no part of it. Never, she couldn't. She
would give Cassie wholehearted support—Morgan, too.
This she promised herself.

Before she fell asleep, Danielle's mind reverted to
her impulsive embrace of Benjamin Fairchild. She

smiled at the memory. Very nice. Nor did she scold herself. Wine, moonlight, an attractive man saying romantic things. It had meant nothing, really. Yet, there was danger. She had no fear of an affair with Benjamin. He was off to New York tomorrow, and she would be going back to Charleston before too long. It might be years before she ever saw him again. The danger was in knowing someone in the world loved her and was waiting for her, for something to happen to her and Walt. Yes, that was dangerous. She didn't want it. She should not have encouraged Benjamin.

Danielle awoke first in the morning, got up and splashed water onto her face. She was applying a face cream, when she saw Cassie was awake, lying abed, looking at her. Danielle brought her a glass of water, then asked if she felt better. Cassie lay back, sipping the water, and nodded. "Do you want to tell me what happened? I can guess, but I ought to be sure."

Cassie found the words hard to say. Twice, she opened her mouth and nothing came out. Finally, "Morgan was in my room. We were . . . we were . . ."

"You needn't say what you were doing."

"Jessie came in . . . saw us." She felt the tears coming and, to stop them, she covered her face with her hands. Words, muffled by fingers, were heard. "Oh, Danny, it was so awful!"

"Jessie wouldn't spy, Cass. There has to be some explanation. Maybe it was an accident. Jessie's getting old. Perhaps she thought she heard the children, opened the wrong door. I'm sure she feels as badly as you do."

"But I'm so *ashamed,* Danny."

Danielle smiled. "Ashamed of being with Morgan— or ashamed of being seen?"

"*Both.*" The word was half-sob.

"Aren't you in love with Morgan; he with you?"

"Yes." Again, the strange, constrained voice.

"Then I don't think shame has any place in it. Some things just happen. We do not will them." She saw Cassie remove her hands from her face, looking at her. "What happened after Jessie came in?"

"She said something. She was sorry. No, 'forgive me,' she said, then she left. It was only a second—but it was long enough.

"Then what happened?"

"Morgan got up, dressed and left."

"Where'd he go?"

"I'm not sure."

"What did he say?"

"He said he was going to do what he should have a long time ago."

Danielle sensed what it meant, but asked anyway. "Do you know what he meant?"

"Yes. Oh, Danny, it's so awful. He wants to marry me. For days, ever since we came, he's wanted to tell everyone. I begged him not to, pleaded with him. I'm the one who wanted it kept secret."

"Why?"

"Oh, Danny, you must *know*. I'm colored. I can't marry Morgan, have his—"

"It seems to me that's his decision, too."

Cassie stared at her a long moment, those words sinking in. "Oh, Danny, I'm so mixed up. I don't know what to think."

Again, Danielle smiled. "I can see that."

"I wanted to tell you, talk to you. I tried, but every time, something came up. I never could get it said."

Danielle reached out and caressed the dark face, wiping away tears. "I'm sorry I wasn't more help to you. I realize now I did see, or should have . . . you and Morgan . . . what was happening. But it wouldn't have mattered if I had. Can you believe that?" She smiled. "You're perfect for him, Cassie. I can see why he loves you. I wouldn't interfere in that. Not for the whole, wide world."

Cassie clasped the white hand against her cheek, turning, kissing it.

"Do you feel better now?"

"No. What's going to happen?"

"I don't know. Nothing, probably. I imagine Morgan went to mother last night and told her."

"She must hate me."

Danielle laughed lightly. "I doubt that. Mother will. . . ." She hesitated. Moira Hodges could be tempestuous and unpredictable. "We'll just have to see what mother says and does. You needn't be afraid."

"But I am. I'm shaking with fear."

"Then don't. You are my dearest friend. Whatever happens or doesn't happen, you have my support. I'm on your side. All right?" She saw Cassie slowly nod her head. "I only want to know one thing. You and Morgan . . . are you sure?"

"Ohhh." The sound was mostly wail. "I'm not sure of anything. I just know when I'm with him, I—"

Danielle laughed. "That's a pretty good sign."

Chapter 8

As often occurs in warm, close-knit families, a magical form of communication took place that Sunday. Everyone was told what they needed to know in as few words as possible, sometimes none at all.

In a perhaps typical conversation, Moira said to Danielle, "Morgan came to me last night, he—"

"I know. I've talked to Cassie."

No other words were spoken about it. Moira gave a fuller report to Glenna, who had been asleep. But even that discussion was a marvel of brevity. Moira: "Morgan loves Cassie, wants to marry her. Jessie discovered them together last night. Do you want to tell Franklin?"

"Not today. I will later."

The words were insignificant. It was eyes and hands that spoke, expressing surprise, dismay, heightened sense of family, awareness of crisis, a tinge of sorrow, knowledge of the need for special comfort and care. If an observer knew them well, the specialness of the greeting between Danielle and Morgan in the upstairs hall might have been noticed, the length of the eye contact, the unusual wanness of the smiles, the tender inflection to the mutual "good morning." When Morgan kissed his grandmother at breakfast, she reached up and patted his cheek. She didn't usually do that. Voices at the table were a shade brighter, the conversation more animated and attended to. Jessie was more noticed and spoken to than normally. In this way, the family cared for one another, and salved wounds to prevent infection. The children, fussed over as distractions, did not notice, nor did the Fairchilds. Cassie, though new to the family, was aware of every nuance.

The only real emotion came in the kitchen, when Jessie greeted Cassie. Weeping softly, she embraced her, saying, "Child, child, I'm so sorry." She longed to say more, to explain, to somehow make everything right, but after last night, she could only be silent.

They all went to Mass at the village parish; then, refusing lunch, the Fairchilds departed for New York in the early afternoon. Danielle's farewell to Benjamin was gracious but conventional, a simple handshake, a proffered cheek for the ceremonial kissing of air. Against his ear, she whispered, "It was only the moonlight, Benjamin."

He leaned back from her, smiling. There was warmth, yet also measured distance in his eyes. "You needn't explain. It's dangerous stuff. Gotta watch it."

She smiled at him. "I believe that's why they speak of lunacy."

"Yes." He held her hand a fraction longer, then turned to go. "I'll see you, Danny—sometime."

She wished he hadn't said that. She said nothing in reply.

The carriage bearing the Fairchilds was hardly gone from view, when Morgan announced, "I'm taking Cassie for a walk."

It sounded strange, a trifle too loud, too pregnant. It needn't have been said at all, he could have just done it. But everyone understood. It was a declaration of independence, a statement of the new openness of his relationship with Cassie. There was another meaning, too. If his mother, grandmother and sister were going to hash over Cassie and him, they had better do it now.

Trembling, Cassie went with him. The three women stood on the veranda watching them walk away, saw Morgan deliberately put his arm around Cassie's waist. None of the three said a word. Each, in turn, went into the house, seeking the solace of solitude. They were not yet ready to talk.

It seemed to Cassie that they walked a long time in silence, along Short Creek, past Kingston. Momentarily, she feared he intended to go to the study. He did not. She should have known better. Past the house they walked, along the white fence, beside the meadow where the horses grazed, raised their heads, snorted, whinnied, ran. It was a pleasant sight. Cassie hardly noticed.

"I love you, Cassie."

Of all the words he might have uttered, none were better, more important. "Yes, I know you do."

"Jessie was looking out an upstairs window, saw us in the garden. She was upset, uncertain. She wanted to talk to you. She had no idea I would be there."

"Who told you?"

"Mother, this morning. Don't hate Jessie. It was an accident."

"I don't hate her—or anyone."

The meadow gave way to a stile; then, beyond, a small stand of trees, maples, hickories mostly, a tall beech providing shade along the path.

"It's going to be all right, Cassie."

"No." Of all the exchanges of that morning, the

smoothing over, the reaching out, the acceptance of
her, the comforting of Jessie, one had failed. It was the
one that mattered the most. Moira's eyes, green-hazel,
luminous, trying, wanting to succeed, failing. What had
been there? Coldness? No. Anger? No. Cassie knew.
Fear. No kiss on the cheek, no pleasant words that
would make it go away. *His mother was afraid.*

"No, it isn't, Morgan."

"Yes, it is. Everything will be fine. Trust me."

"Morgan, your mother will not accept me—us."

He sighed. "Mother is mother. Mother is all mothers.
My announcement was too sudden. She wasn't prepared. She would have reacted the same regardless of
whom I said I was marrying. It had nothing to do
with you."

"You're wrong, Morgan."

The woods gave way to another stile and fence,
then a proud field of half-grown tobacco plants, healthy,
strong, nodding in the breeze. Ahead in the distance
was a tobacco shed, where by fall these leaves would
nestle.

"If I'm wrong, Cassie, it still won't matter. I love
you. I'm going to marry you, no matter what."

She stopped on the path and turned within his arm
to look at him. "Morgan, I will not cause a rift in your
family."

"There'll be no rift. But if there is, you won't be the
one who causes it."

Late that afternoon, at what would normally have
been a pleasant time for talk before dinner, Morgan
said, "Have you ladies had your little chat?"

There was derision, antagonism in his voice, in his
use of the word "ladies." Moira ignored it. "No," she
said.

He was standing by the mantel, a glass of whiskey
in his hand. He didn't usually drink whiskey, but now
he needed it. "Good, then you won't have to bother.
Nothing you say or do will alter a single fact. I'm
going to marry Cassie."

Moira met his gaze, saw petulance, stubbornness, pride. "I understand that. We still need to talk."

"Why, mother? I don't remember a family conference when Danielle married Walt. I don't believe grandmother had to explain her marriage to Mr. Fairchild. And I know for a fact that my opinion was not solicited before you and Larry wed."

"That's unkind, Morgan." Moira's voice trembled with anguish.

"Is it? It seems to me it is you—all of you—who are unkind to the girl I intend to marry. It's my choice, not yours."

"Of course. It's just—"

"There are no 'justs,' mother. It's a fact. Accept it."

"Morgan, please." It was Cassie's voice. She saw him turn to her, and she appealed to him with her eyes, liquid, near tears. "Please, don't be so angry."

"She's right, Morgan." Moira made her voice as calm as she could, somehow finding a place to bury all her pain from this confrontation. "You asked me to accept Cassie, your marriage. Is it too much to ask for a chance to do it?"

Sharp words lay on his tongue. *Why is it so hard for you to accept her?* He bit them back. "All right. I'm taking Cassie out to dinner in Washington. Perhaps tomorrow you will have. . . ."

Cassie saw him look at her, heard his words, "You were lovely in that dress last night. Would you wear it again?"

Danielle stood up. "I'll help you dress, Cassie."

After the children were in bed, the conference was held in Moira's bedroom, the largest in the house. Glenna and Danielle sat in two matching stuffed chairs, Moira on the edge of her bed. They were three beautiful, courageous women of as many generations, representing two-thirds of a century of wisdom.

Glenna contrived to speak first. She knew Moira's attitude, sensed that Danielle would defend Cassie. She wanted to defuse the tensions. Part of her plan was to appear outwardly calm, as though she attached no undue significance to this meeting. To this end, she brought her emery board, to work on her nails. From long experience, she knew the value of busywork for the hands to free the mind. She also hoped to convey the impression her manicure was of at least equal importance to this discussion.

"I fear I must agree with Morgan. There is little point in our talking about it. He seems determined to marry Cassie. It seems to me we have no choice but to accept it—and continue to love Morgan and the woman he has chosen."

It was a characteristic attitude on Glenna's part. She had helped Moira, then Danielle, weather their follies by offering them unconditional love and support while they came to their senses. It was to her a far more useful method than any advice or interference. Both her daughter and granddaughter were aware of her technique. Now Danielle quickly endorsed it. "I quite agree with GlennaMa. There is nothing to do but accept." She looked at her mother. "I think far too much has been said already."

"He is your grandson, your brother. You both love him. But he is my son, my only son. I plead a special relationship, a special concern." Indeed, Moira's voice bore a supplicating tone.

"Concern that he is marrying Cassie?"

Moira firmed her mouth against her inner trembling. The hateful, horrid words were coming, and there was nothing she could do about it. For sleepless hours, she had known they would be said. They had filled her mind this whole, endless day. Her nerves were rubbed raw by fear of them. And she knew she was in a poor state to withstand them. Larry had been away for over two weeks. She was tense, irritable, explosive. She wished Larry were here, to relieve her, talk to her, calm her down. But she was alone.

"Yes." She made herself say the word firmly, levelly.

"Because she is colored." It was no question, but a statement.

"Yes."

Moira heard her daughter suck in air, then exhale amid hated, anticipated words, *"Mother, how could you?"*

Trembling visibly now, Moira looked at Danielle squarely. "I am not a bigot, Danielle."

"I don't know what *you* call it."

Anger flared in Moira. She didn't want it, but was powerless against her own nature. "It is called being a mother, loving my son, wanting his happiness."

Danielle's laughter was mocking. "At least, that's a new word for it."

Moira came to her feet, fury raging within her. "You are impertinent. You will *not* speak to me this way."

"Stop it, I say!" Glenna's voice was sharp. "Moira, you will calm yourself. Danielle, you will learn not to say things you will regret."

At once, Moira turned, went around the bed and stood looking out a window at the dusk, her back to them, visibly gaining control of herself. Danielle looked down at her hands, sighing. "I'm sorry, mother."

"I'm sorry, too." Moira turned to look at her daughter. "Have we ever fought before, Danny?" Her eyes were moist.

"I don't think so. I can't remember it." Her voice broke.

Tears were flowing openly down Moira's cheeks now. "I can't bear to have you think me a bigot, let alone say it. It . . . it hurts terribly. You must know . . . how much I love Jessie, and Joe. You must know

"Oh, God, no, Danny. Don't think that of me!"

Danielle wrestled with her own emotions but, as the accuser, it was easier for her. "Mother, I wouldn't hurt you for anything, you know that. But I must speak the truth. You can love Jessie and Joe as servants. But Cassie would be your daughter-in-law, the mistress of Aurial, your equal. Isn't that what you cannot bear?"

"Oh, God, no, Danny. Don't think that of me!"

Danielle had to swallow hard, couldn't help it, but

her voice was still calm as she said, "Then what is it, mother? Tell me."

Moira looked at her mother for help, but there was none there. Glenna's left-hand index finger was suddenly of monstrous importance to her. Left alone, Moira went to a dresser drawer, extracted a handkerchief, wiped her eyes and blew her nose.

"All right, I'll explain. Your grandmother was born and raised in Ireland, County Cork. I doubt if there is a colored person in the whole county."

"We have the black Irish." Glenna smiled.

"Don't be facetious, mother. They're just descendants of the Spaniards from the days of the Armada. Their hair and eyes may be black, but their skin is white."

Grateful for a chance to lighten this discussion, Glenna said, "I'm glad to see you haven't forgotten everything I taught you."

"Danny, what I'm trying to say, despite your grandmother, is that she has no inborn racial prejudice."

"I certainly hated the English for a long time."

"Be serious, mother! I'm trying to tell Danielle that prejudice is not natural to this family. And yet, it could have been. Tell her about Joe in the jungle."

"Must I?"

"I think it would help."

Glenna sighed. "I think she knows."

"I would like to hear it, GlennaMa."

Another deep sigh came from Glenna. "When I was taken south across the Sahara, I was sold to a jungle tribe. They were a primitive, superstitious people, who believed my white skin would protect them from the bullets of white slavegrabbers. All the men, the warriors, the youths—" she stopped, looking at Moira in appeal, "—they all had me, Danielle. They planned to kill me, make my skin into a potion."

Danielle had heard it before, but she was still horrified. "How awful, GlennaMa."

"Yes, it was. I passed out, as you can imagine. When I came to, Joe—he was just a boy then—was rescuing me, cutting me loose. He got me to a canoe. We floated downriver to safety. I owe my life to Joe." Again, she looked at Moira, appealing for help that did not come. "Joe told me he had . . . to be . . . one of them . . . to save me. I had no memory of it. My body had gone into shock, my mind forgot. I've never held it against him."

Moved by her grandmother's painful confession, Danielle went to her, kissing her cheek tenderly.

"The point is, Danny, your grandmother could have hated all black men for what those natives did, but she didn't."

"How could I? I hated them for what they did to me, but not because they were of a different color. There were white men who were no better—worse, because they were deliberately cruel." She sighed. "And I refuse, Moira, to discuss any more of this."

"All right, mother. And Danny, please sit down, let me finish. I didn't learn to hate colored people from my mother—or my father. Aurial was always a free plantation. We never owned a slave. Jessie practically raised me, when mother mourned my father so long. I didn't imbibe the local hatreds as a child. Neither did you—or Morgan. I sent you and him to London with Glenna, when you were young. You lived there till you were almost eighteen, Morgan seventeen. I understand your attitudes, believe me, I do."

"Then what are you trying to say, mother?"

"I'm saying there is a difference between you and me, between your grandmother and me. I lived here before the war, when you hardly remember, when mother was off sailing with Cap'n Mac. I lived here during the cursed war, while you were in London. I know. I know these people, the attitudes, the hatred, the—"

Danielle's anger suddenly burst. "Don't tell me about hatred, mother. I live in the South, remember? White feelings against the colored folk here in Maryland is a Sunday afternoon picnic in the park compared to Charleston."

Faced with her daughter's renewed anger, Moira suddenly felt terribly weary. "Yes. Then you understand, Danny. Those attitudes will destroy Morgan and Cassie."

"Not if their love is strong enough."

"She will be hated, snubbed, ostracized. He will spend his whole life defending the honor of his wife. He will break off with old friends, quarrel with neighbors. He will become irritable, angry, defensive. Cassie will see what is happening to him, blame herself. The quarrels with outsiders will become their quarrels. Their love will not survive it."

"It will if they love each other enough."

Her jaw trembling with fatigue, Moira managed to say, "That is ... exactly ... my point."

Danielle, anger still within her, looked at her mother. She understood, but she didn't want to believe it. She turned to Glenna, searching for support, but her grandmother kept finding a rough spot on the nail of her ring finger, right hand. Danielle turned back to her mother. "You think they don't love each other enough?"

"Danny, you came here with Cassie a few days ago, not much over a week. They went for a row on the river. You and I watched them paddle off. Now they want to marry."

"Morgan came to Charleston. You were with him. It began then." She spoke defensively, true to her promise to defend Cassie.

Moira, near exhaustion, could say nothing.

For what seemed endless time, Danielle stared at her. "What is it you want, mother?"

One by one, Moira's nerves, frayed by fatigue, worry and emotional exhaustion, began to snap. She managed a few words, "I only ... want ... their happiness." Then she began to sob uncontrollably.

Danielle had risen to go to her, when she heard a single word from Glenna. "Danielle." She turned, saw her grandmother shaking her head. "She wants time, Danielle, for them to be sure."

Near tears herself, her fingers at her lips, Danielle said, "Do you believe that's wise, GlennaMa?"

The silver-haired woman smiled. "Age is supposed to bring wisdom, but it doesn't. Morgan will never listen to any of this."

Danielle knew. "You want me to ask Cassie to do what Morgan will not?"

The words just lay there. Then, from somewhere, Moira found voice amid her tears. "Just . . . ask her . . . if—if she is . . . certain."

Danielle went to her mother then, putting her arms around her, holding her, cradling her bent, trembling head against her shoulder. "If she says yes, then will you accept her, give your blessing, love her?"

From her mother's head against her shoulder, from her body racked with sobs, Danielle felt the affirmative answer.

Chapter 9

Miriam Hodges knew she was hanging between Scylla and Charybdis. With a skill she had not known she possessed, she had somehow avoided Peter Blakeley's bed. This Sunday evening at his home, she was anything but sure how she would do it again.

They were at dinner, a private tête-à-tête. He was in his evening suit and she was dressed, or maybe undressed, to the nines. In ten whirlwind days, she had

created a sensation in New York. She was almost
dizzied by it. It had all happened so quickly.

True to his word, Blakeley had taken her shopping.
And such shopping! He had taken her to the Fifth
Avenue salon of Pierre Chambeau, the most expensive,
creative, controversial couturier in New York, famed
for the elegance and exotic daring of his gowns. He
dressed only the most beautiful women. Nor was beauty
enough. They must have the figures to wear his demanding fashions. Simply to be accepted as his client
was a privilege. Breathlessly, she saw the effeminate
Frenchman look at her, then take measurements. When
he brought out a bolt of cloth and began to drape it
around her, she was thrilled. And, wearing the gowns
he created for her, all purchased by a willing Peter
Blakeley, she became a sensation. What she didn't
know was that Pierre Chambeau had begun his career
six years previously by dressing Danielle Kingston, who
was his standard for feminine beauty. Nor did he
know Miriam Hodges was stepsister to the one woman
he truly admired.

The gown of marine-blue satin she now wore at
Blakeley's request was the first Pierre had made for
her. If Miriam had thought the renovated gown of her
mother's bold, she had no words to describe this one.
There were no sleeves at all, and the bodice was as
nothing, just decorated wells, in which her breasts
nestled. She was not sure how the dress stayed up, and
when she first wore it she was not at all certain it
would. She supposed it had to do with the bits of
whalebone that cupped her breasts and the fact the
satin was utterly fitted to her waist and over her hips,
the skirt falling narrowly to her shoetops. There was a
short train behind. The bustle was merely a token.
Worn with long, matching gloves rising above her el-
bows, it was a shocking garment, for her upper back,
shoulders and the tops of her breasts were bare. It had
taken all her nerve and aplomb to wear it the first time.
Even now, Blakeley's hot eyes on her, she was ill at
ease and desperate not to show it.

"May I say you enchant me, my dear?"

He used the word a lot, too much. "Thank you, Peter." She knew she should say something witty, flirtatious. On other occasions, she had. But she couldn't think of anything just now.

"Is something wrong, my darling? You seem pensive."

Yes, there was. This dress was terribly wrong. She had worn it in public, proud of her figure and the attention she was garnering. She had been greatly stimulated by the knowledge that all eyes were upon her. But now, only two eyes looked at her. She was half-naked and alone with him. Her stomach churned with apprehension. She forced herself to look at him and render a half-smile. "You have kept me on such a whirl these past days, Peter. I think I'm just tired."

"I quite understand. That's why I thought you might enjoy a quiet evening together."

She forced her smile wider. "I am enjoying it, Peter —truly." She tried to eat then, hoping food would quiet her stomach.

Her feeling of being in a cage, trapped, had been increasing for days. She had accepted gifts, elegant clothes, jewelry, even a fur wrap because she had been chilly one evening, from a man she hardly knew and really didn't like. She had been thrilled, naturally. They were gowns she had only dreamed of. She often felt she ought to pinch herself to make sure it was really happening to her. He took her to the finest places, the opera, summer concerts, the carriage parade and promenade at Central Park Mall, the poshest restaurants, the best clubs. Her name had even appeared in the newspapers as companion to Mr. Peter Blakeley. It was heady stuff.

But more was required of her, she knew. At first, she believed—hoped anyway—that being beautiful and daringly-attired was enough. He seemed to want it so. She could see the pride in his eyes. He almost seemed to become taller when he was with her. Certainly, he was more affable, more communicative. She did not

want for attention, but only from him. Few people
even spoke to him. Hardly anyone came up to be introduced to her. This seemed strange to her. She felt
at times like an island, elegant and beautiful, in a social sea.

She allowed him to kiss her on the third evening.
His mouth had been hard, cold, his breath smelling of
stale tobacco and brandy. She had felt nothing, only
the need to endure. Since then, the kisses had become
more frequent, longer, deeper, more impassioned, and
she had learned to feign response. She knew she was
inexorably losing her virtue with him, the mouth-filling
kisses, the caresses to her throat and shoulders, the
fondling of her breasts, the bending of his head in the
darkened carriage, the sensation shooting from her
nipples. She liked it, even wanted it, but not with him.

The truth was—and Miriam was very slowly coming to recognize it, could not yet admit it to herself—
that she had a deep, physical aversion to Peter Blakeley.
It was more than physical, it was moral, too—something in her innermost depths cried out against this
man even as he squired her hither, thither and yon,
against the coldness and hardness she sensed at the
center of him, despite his superficial charm and graciousness. There was something inhuman about Peter
Blakeley. Something that negated her, the best part of
her; he saw her only as a beautiful *thing,* a precious
curio to add to his collection of curios purchased at
the price of human pain. And this detached, calculating
aspect of him scared her to death. Every night, she
thanked God that she had escaped his clutches once
again; in the still of the night, in her loneliness and
fear, she clasped her rosary beads and said a fervent
decade of thanks to the Virgin Mother for sparing her
thus far. But she knew she couldn't go on like this,
enjoying the benefits of his wealth and yet, each time,
contriving to avoid paying the piper. She would have
to pay, eventually . . . and dearly.

She had used every ruse, emphasizing her innocence
and fear. Such silly phrases as, "You wouldn't take ad-

vantage of a young girl, now would you?" had worn
thin, along with faked giggles and playful tickling of
him. She had pleaded fatigue, the lateness of the hour,
a headache, and made promises, promises. Yes, she
would say, she wanted him, but tomorrow would be
better. Twice she had seen the cold fury in his eyes
and it had frightened her. But he had gone along. How
much longer? Would he tonight?

Miriam's seduction was not so much accomplished
by Peter Blakeley as by Edith Prentiss. The old woman
was ecstatic over her granddaughter's success, squealing with delight at the gifts she received, hugging her
in joy at her transformed appearance. "My dear child,
I thought your mother a great beauty. But you exceed
her in all ways, a thousand times over. How elegant
you are! How grand! All New York must envy you. I
am so proud, I could weep."

Each day, the old woman demanded a full report:
where had they gone, what had they done, whom had
she met, what had been said. To think, her granddaughter dining at Delmonico's with the wealthiest
bachelor in New York. He was at her feet. All of New
York was at her feet. Had he kissed her? Yes. Had
he . . . ? Miriam stared at her in disbelief. No, it wasn't
that kind of relationship. Don't be silly, child. Men are
always men. She did care for him, didn't she? He might
not be the handsomest of men, but he really was a
dear, and so rich! Look at the necklace he had given
her. And imagine! Gowns by Pierre Chambeau.

"What do you mean, you don't want to go out with
him again?"

"I mean just that, grandmama. I really don't care
for him."

"Don't be silly, of course you do. He's adorable."

Miriam sighed. "Not to me, grandmama. I know
what he wants—and I can't. I don't want to." She saw
distress rising in the old woman's face and completely
misread its meaning. "I knew you'd understand, grandmama. We have both made a terrible mistake. I'm
going to return all the things he's given me. I'll write

a nice note. I'll say he is very sweet and dear, but it's not fair of me to lead him on. I'll find some way to phrase it nicely." Miriam's panic was evident in her voice, but Edith ignored it.

"You'll do no such thing! You'll get into that new gown and go out with him tonight. You will put such foolishness out of your mind."

"But, grandmama, he wants me to . . . to go to bed with him. He wants to—"

"All men want that. They think it their right."

Miriam stared at her in disbelief. "You mean you *want* me to?"

The old woman felt a pang of guilt, but did not waver in her resolve. "If it is necessary."

"It *is* necessary—if I go out with him again."

"Then so be it."

Still, Miriam stared at her. "Grandmama, you can't mean that."

"Oh, yes, I do." The words were firm, the voice cold. Then she tried to soften it, putting her hand on Miriam's shoulder. "Oh, I know, you are young, afraid. I was, too. All women are afraid—the first time. But it's not so bad, believe me. You may even find it—well, pleasant, in a way."

Miriam tried to laugh. "You're not serious, grandmama. You can't mean it?'"

"I am extremely serious, child."

"But he's so awful. I don't care for him. You can't ask me—".

"I can and I will. You are being young and silly. It is time you grew up and assumed your responsibilities."

"What do you mean? What responsibilities?"

"As a Prentiss, child. Prentiss women have always been beautiful, witty, charming, able to make an important marriage."

"With Peter Blakeley?" The ridicule was barely concealed in her voice.

"Yes, with Peter Blakeley. He is rich. He will solve our problems."

Miriam looked at her quizzically. "What problems?"

"You cannot be blind, child. The Prentiss money is gone, wasted, squandered by your grandfather. I am down to a single servant, Hannah, and she is next to worthless. I can barely hold onto this house." She saw Miriam's eyes widen. "Didn't you know all this?"

"No, I never knew." Her voice was barely audible.

"Then it's time you did. I cannot afford to give you a proper coming out—and your stupid father doesn't care about society, and will not. You must make your own way. You must provide for yourself, your future."

"And for you, grandmama?"

Touched by the question, Edith Prentiss impulsively hugged her. "Yes, if you will. We must not lose this house. We must rebuild the Prentiss fortune, you and I. Peter Blakeley is the way. So he is not the handsomest of men. So you do not really care for him. It is not important, believe me, Miriam. All that matters is that he is rich, generous and cares for you."

The words uttered so vehemently by her grandmother buttressed Miriam's resolve for an evening. But when she was alone in her bed, all she could remember was Blakeley's hands upon her. She shivered, and tears welled in her eyes. Why couldn't it have been Morgan Kingston's hands, his mouth, his lips? Because he was her brother? No, he was her stepbrother. There was no blood relation. Her father had stupidly married his mother for her titian hair and alluring body. Moira had taken advantage of father, using him to further herself. Miriam's jealousy of her stepmother, so long nurtured, flowered once more. She would get even. She would steal her son from her. Why not? She had enflamed an older, more sophisticated, far richer man. Morgan Kingston would be much easier. And he was handsome, greatly more desirable. If he wasn't as rich as Peter Blakeley, he still owned, or soon would inherit, a great estate. Surely, that would satisfy grandmama. Surely, it would reestablish the Prentiss fortune.

But even as these thoughts came to her, she recognized their hopelessness. Morgan Kingston couldn't see her for the dirt he was always digging in. God knew,

she had tried. She had even gone out and helped him
with his stupid tobacco plants. She had worked in the
fields till she had nearly ruined her complexion. The
closest she ever got to him was to fake a sprained
ankle. He had carried her to the house. It felt wonderful, being in his arms. Then he'd turned her over to
his blasted mother.

"What are you thinking, my dear? You seem far
away."

Blakeley's voice from across the table startled her.
She smiled. "I was thinking of all the beautiful gowns
you've bought me." It was the wrong thing to say. She
knew it instantly.

"My pleasure. You are inexpressibly lovely in them."

The consequences of her error came quickly. He rose
from his chair and came around the table to stand behind her. His hands on her bare upper arms, he bent
to kiss her neck, her shoulders. His breath was hot on
her skin.

"You are so beautiful, Miriam, so lovely, so utterly
feminine." His hands moved down over the tops of
her breasts, into the valley between. "Everyone looks
at you, wants you." She felt trapped. "You must know
the pleasure you bring me."

She had to speak. "I hope so, Peter."

"You do, yes. And now I want to bring you pleasure,
too."

She felt she was fighting for her life. "You have,
Peter, this gown, all the things you've bought me, all
the places—"

"It is nothing, my darling." His fingers were sliding
down over her breasts. "I mean the real pleasure a
woman can feel." Then her breasts were lifted free
from the restraint of fabric. "It is time you became a
woman, my darling." His fingers were at her nipples,
thumb and forefinger roughly massaging the hard, pink
tips. "I want it to be my greatest gift to you."

Shivers shot through her, but of fear, not pleasure.
She looked down at his hands, and seeing what he was
doing somehow magnified her revulsion. His fingers

were long, tapering, manicured, almost like a girl's hands. Morgan's hands would not be like that. His were large, tanned from the sun, rough from hard work, yet she knew his touch would be gentle, tender. Oh, what sensations it would cause.

"Yes, my dearest, it is time you became a woman. And what a magnificent woman you will be."

She felt the pressure of his fingers, harder now against her risen ends, as an intrusion, and she closed her eyes against it. Why must this be? She wanted a man, she knew, but not this man, with his pale, thin hands. Morgan. Why not Morgan, a real man, so handsome, so desirable? Why must it be with a man she didn't like? *You must make your own way. You must provide for yourself, your future.* Was this the future?

"Come, my darling."

She felt upward pressure against her breasts. He was guiding her out of her chair.

"Please, Peter, I—"

"I know, darling, you are afraid, but you needn't be. I am the gentlest of men."

Her mind raced desperately. She saw her plate of food. She hadn't finished eating. *You impetuous man, Peter. Let me at least finish my dinner.* She looked around. He had servants, a butler, footmen, both big, burly men. *Later, Peter, when the servants have retired.* Somehow, she could say none of it.

"Yes, Peter, I am afraid."

"You are in the safest, most skilled of hands, my darling."

She felt his fingers making tiny circles, rolling her nipples, creating sensations she didn't want, not with him. "I can't, Peter. Not tonight. I'm sorry." There, it was said.

The movement of his fingers stopped. She could feel a chill from him even before she winced at the hard squeeze of her nipples.

"Miriam, you must. I have humored your girlishness long enough. I have indulged your flirtations and

whims. Enough is enough." He punctuated the word
with a particularly cruel pinch.

"You're hurting me, Peter."

His fingers relaxed. "I'm sorry for that, but I dislike
being made a fool of." His voice was frigid.

"I am not making a fool of you, Peter." She turned
in her chair to look at him. Rage glinted in his eyes.
"I know what you want, Peter, and I want it, too. I—I
just ask you to . . . to understand."

"Understand what?"

"I'm too upset, Peter. I couldn't give myself to you
the way I should—and want to."

"Upset about what?" His voice was wary, disbelieving.

"I received a telegram this afternoon."

"On Sunday?"

"Yes, it was an emergency. My stepmother is grave-
ly ill in Maryland. I love her so, and I'm terribly
worried."

He removed his hands from her and folded his arms
across his chest. "I don't believe you."

Quickly, she stuffed her breasts back into her bodice
and stood up. "It's true, Peter. I wouldn't lie to you—
not about a thing like this."

"It's another of your silly excuses. I won't have it."
He looked at her sternly; she felt like a prisoner at the
bar—before a hanging judge.

Tears came to her eyes. "Please, Peter, don't be this
way. I'm so worried. I must go to Maryland immediately, tomorrow."

"You lie!" His voice rose sharply. "Why didn't you
tell me this before?"

Her tears flowed easily, for she was very afraid of
him. "I didn't want to spoil our evening, Peter. That's
all, believe me." His eyes were pale blue ice. She
sensed his inner struggle to keep from hitting her.
"Please, Peter. Just let me go to Maryland, be sure my
stepmother is all right. Then I'll return to you. I'll—I'll
be . . . do what you want me to."

For a long moment, he stared at her. He seemed to

teeter on the edge of an inner explosion. It did not come. With dignity, he turned and walked around the table, standing behind his chair, facing her. "I do not believe you for a second, Miriam. But, once again, I will indulge you. By all means, go, do what you want to. If you do not return, which I suspect will be the case, I will chalk it up to experience." He forced a lipless smile and bowed slightly. "A most enjoyable experience."

"I'll return, Peter, I promise." She still felt the need to placate him.

He hesitated, then in a cold voice said, "If you do return, then I will have no more of this . . . this foolishness. Do you understand?"

Shivering a little, she said, "Yes, Peter, I understand."

Chapter 10

Danielle waited nervously for Cassie to return from her evening in Washington. To pass the time, Danielle bathed and shampooed her hair, then cut her toenails and fingernails. This prolonged session of pampering occupied her hands, while freeing her mind.

Any chat with Cassie about Morgan had to be difficult and unpleasant. Just broaching the subject implied a lack of faith in Cassie, doubt about her marriage to Morgan. Danielle had never once scolded or disapproved of Cassie. How could she now? How could she suggest there was even a shred of concern about her marriage to Morgan? Yet, mother had a point. It was all happening too rapidly. Was it wrong for a mother, loving her son, to suggest delay, the passage of time before marriage, any marriage, not just *this* marriage? Mother wanted to know if Cassie was absolutely sure of herself and the marriage. Was it too much to ask? Danielle shook her head. It was not. But, oh, how she hated the thought of asking!

Cassie was later getting home than Danielle had expected, and she began to wonder where she was. But in her heart, Danielle suspected where they might be and what was delaying them.

Cassie had not wanted to stop at the study. Somehow, amid her worry and tension, it did not seem right or possible to her. But Morgan insisted, and to her surprise their lovemaking was tender and prolonged, ecstatic and fulfilling. It was as though Morgan were attempting to prove his love for her, drive into her his commitment to their love and life together. When she thought it was over, he still wanted to kiss her, caress her, tell her how lovely she was and how much he loved her, his hands at her breasts, then stroking her thighs. . . . It was not over, not then, not yet.

On her return to Aurial, Cassie went directly to Danielle's room, sitting on the edge of her bed, head down, her body and mind weary.

Danielle looked at her with compassion, sensing what must have happened. She didn't know what to say, but spoke anyway. "Is something wrong, Cassie?"

Cassie gave a deep sigh. "No, I'm all right, Miss Danny."

Danielle winced inwardly. It had taken a long time to get Cassie to stop calling her "Miss." Now it was back. At that instant, Danielle decided she simply could not speak to her friend as her mother wanted. Cassie was already suffering so much. She could not badger her more, asking her to decide what Morgan would not.

"The children are asleep and I don't really need any

help. Why don't you go to bed?" She saw Cassie nod her head, slowly, as though it were a great weight. "Or do you want to talk?"

Danielle thought Cassie was never going to reply, then she heard a whispered, "Yes." Quickly, Danielle went to her friend, stood over her, her arms around her shoulders, Cassie's forehead against her breast.

"It doesn't seem possible. A few days ago . . . I was so content . . . with you and the children. I . . . I knew my place, what I wanted. Now, everything is . . . is . . . turned upside down."

Tenderly, Danielle said, "Yes, I know. Life is like that somethimes." She continued to hold Cassie, rocking her a little, waiting for her to speak. When she did not, she prompted her. "Your evening did not go well?" As a measure of Cassie's confusion, Danielle felt her both nodding and shaking her head against her breast. Danielle smiled. "A bit of both, right?" When she felt the nod, she said, "It's always best to talk about the good things."

"Oh, Danny, I love him so." The words came slowly, painfully. "I know I shouldn't, but when he touches me . . . things happen. I—I can't . . . resist him."

"I know, darling."

Cassie raised her head, looking at Danielle questioningly. "Do you really know?"

Danielle smiled. "Of course. I'm married. And my— my husband was . . . not the first."

"Is it like that always—with men?"

"Not always, but when there's love."

Cassie again lowered her head and Danielle had a moment to think. Morgan, her little brother, would be a passionate lover. Yes, he would, romantic, tender, not so much demanding as compelling a girl like Cassie to respond. It must be difficult for her.

"If you love him, Cassie, and you both wanted, enjoyed, I . . . I don't thing it was too wrong. You shouldn't feel guilty for . . . for what couldn't be helped." Danielle was far from sure she believed those words, but she wanted to comfort this girl she held in her arms. "Did you go to Washington?"

"Yes, it happened afterwards."

"How was that part of the evening?" Again, she felt Cassie slowly shaking her head against her breast. "It didn't go well?"

Cassie raised her head to look at her. "Oh, Danny, I didn't belong. Everyone. . . ."

When words didn't come, Danielle said, "People weren't nice to you?"

"People were . . . oh, I don't know. They weren't nice—or unnice." She pursed her lips into a hard line. "I was ignored, Danny. I didn't belong. No one said or did anything, but I knew they were looking at me . . . hating me."

"I'm sure not, Cassie."

"Yes, Danny, yes. I saw their quick glances. I—I don't know the word, but . . . they didn't want me to see them looking."

"Furtive?"

Cassie looked down at her hands, her body seeming to sag as though very heavy. "I guess so."

Danielle moved her hands from Cassie's back to her shoulders, squeezing with her fingers, as though trying to instill vigor and resolve into her. "Cassie, you're a beautiful girl in a lovely gown. People always stare. Believe me, I know. You get used to it, accept it."

"No, Danny. I was a colored girl out with a white man."

"Perhaps some people cared about that, Cassie, but not everyone."

"It wasn't just white people, Danny. When we were walking on the street, entering the hotel, there were colored men, a footman, porter, bellhops, the young men who clear the tables in the dining room."

"Busboys."

"I saw how they looked at Morgan. They hated him."

Danielle had never thought of it, but yes, Negro men would hate a white man for going out with a beautiful colored girl. And why shouldn't they? But, God, all this was so awful. She sighed. "Cassie, I don't know what to say."

Cassie nodded. "I know."

"It'll change. The war is over, ten years over. Slavery has ended. People will come to accept—"

"No, Danny."

"Yes, Cassie, they will, they must."

"Not in my lifetime."

Danielle bit hard at her lip, not wanting to hear this, not wanting to believe. "If you and Morgan are to . . . to be together, then you're going to have to learn to ignore it, live with it, accept what you cannot change." She waited in vain for Cassie to speak. "Do you understand?"

Cassie's body seemed to slump more. "When we were in the hotel, the dining room, I was so sure, Danny. I knew it would never work—Morgan and I. I would never be able to bear it, the hostility, the hatred, knowing I was the cause, knowing what I was doing to Morgan. I was going to tell him."

"Did you?"

Danielle waited expectantly for a reply, which did not come for a long time. Finally, she heard a deep and prolonged sigh. "I couldn't. When I'm with him . . . alone . . . and he kisses me, touches me. . . ." She sighed again. "I said all that, didn't I?"

"Yes." She waited. "And now? What do you feel now?" The answer came so quickly, it surprised her.

"Love. I love him, Danny. I want him."

Quickly, Danielle's eyes filled with tears. "Then have him, Cassie. By all means, have him."

Cassie responded with another deep sigh. Then came words. "You said I should go to bed. Do you mind if I do?"

Danielle put her arm around her and led her through the nursery to her room. She remained to help her out of her gown and tuck her in bed. Smiling, she kissed her cheek. "This is the best idea. Everything is always better in the morning."

Danielle lay in her own bed, thinking, wondering. She had not done as her mother wished. She couldn't. It was impossible—for her, anyway. To Danielle's surprise, she fell asleep quickly.

The next morning might have been any other. Cassie appeared with the children, both dressed for the day. They climbed on Danielle's bed, awakening her with kisses and happy laughter, then went downstairs to find grandma and GlennaMa. Danielle arose, then submitted to Cassie's ministrations to her hair. They spoke of other things before Cassie said, "You were right about mornings, Danny. I've made up my mind."

In the mirror a pair of bright, sapphire eyes met rich, hazel ones. Danielle did not speak, just looked at her expectantly.

"I know what I want, but I can't do it without you."

Still, Danielle did not speak.

"I want time, Danny. As much as I don't really want to, I know I must get away from him—if only for a little while. I must think. I can't around him. Do you understand?"

Her gaze still fixed on Cassie, Danielle nodded.

"If I am away from him for a while, then I'll know, be sure of myself. I'll be able to accept what must be done."

"You mean not marry Morgan?"

"No, I don't mean that. I love him, want him. But I need time to accept him, our life together. Do you understand?"

"Yes, of course." Danielle looked away from her, almost hating to say her next words. "Then you want to return to Charleston?"

"Yes, do you mind?"

"Of course not. My husband is there. We'll go at once."

"Do you mind, Danny? Am I . . . ?"

Danielle's smile was a trifle forced. "We'd be going in a few days, in any event. A little sooner won't matter." To avoid Cassie's eyes, Danielle rose from the vanity, went to the bed and, stripping off her dressing gown, began putting on her dress over her chemise.

As Cassie buttoned the back, she said, "Morgan won't like it, Danny."

"I know, but he'll accept it. Just don't say anything to the others till I've had a chance to talk to him."

Cassie was surprised at her calmness as she went to the hideaway study that evening with Morgan. There was something about making a decision, even a painful one, she supposed, which restores order to a person. She knew only that she must have the courage to act upon her decision. Strangely, she was confident she would be able to.

At once, as though he had been longing to do it all day, he swept her into his arms, devouring her lips with sweet kisses. Once again, she felt the sharp rise of passion. How could he do this to her?

"You seem happy today, Cassie."

"Yes."

"I was afraid . . . after last night, you might be. . . . You seemed so nervous, ill at ease."

"I was." She smiled. "But I liked what happened afterwards."

"Oh, God, yes." The words were superfluous—his mouth on hers, the pressure of his body against hers spoke volumes. Oh, how she loved his kisses. They seemed to melt her.

"You'll get over being nervous, Cass. You'll get used to it."

"I know. I want to."

She gave herself to him in a way she never had before, naturally, tenderly, yet with a quality of urgency, as though she were a squirrel provisioning herself for a winter of discontent. Never had her skin seemed so sensitized, his hands on her so thrilling. Never had he seemed so strong, so powerful. Never had he filled her so completely, probed so deeply or completed her so devastatingly.

"I love you so much, Cassie."

She lay in what was now a familiar position, back to the couch, her head cradled in the crook of his arm, her leg crooked over his, her left arm embracing his chest. "And I love you, my darling."

"Let's get married right away."

"Yes, we will—soon."

"How soon?"

"When I return." There. It was said, casually, almost without effort. Why had she worried so?

"Return? Where are you going?"

"Danny and I are returning to Charleston."

He tried to get up, but she restrained him with her arm, her leg. "You'll do no such thing," he said. "If she wants to go home, she can go without you."

"I asked her to go, to take me. We're leaving tomorrow."

He struggled harder to rise, but with surprising strength she held him down. "I won't hear of such a thing."

"Yes, Morgan, I want to. I must."

Anger rose in his voice. "Damn them, they put you up to this. Mother, Danielle talked to you. They—"

"No one said anything to me, Morgan. I decided myself, last night, this morning, really. I need to go away for a while."

"But *why?*"

"When I'm with you, like this, I can't think. I need to."

"Think, my eye." Her restraint was too weak now, and he forced her away, sitting on the edge of the couch. "You don't love me."

"But I do, darling. That's why I must go away."

"You don't want to marry me."

"But I do. And that, too, is why I must go away."

He looked at her, an expression of bewilderment and pain on his face. She reached her arms out to him, bidding him back to her, but he would not come.

"I don't understand this at all."

"Darling, I love you, I want you in all ways. I want

to be your wife. All I ask is a little time for us to be apart, for us to think."

"What is there to think about?"

"Many things."

He stood up, angrily turning his back to her. He went to the chair and began to pull on his under-drawers. "You say you love me, yet you have to think about it. You say you want to marry me, yet you have to think about it. Nonsense, all nonsense."

Now she sat up, urgency filling her voice. "Morgan, look at me, listen to me." It was as if she willed him to turn around. "Darling, I have no doubt of our love. But I do have doubts of our marriage." Her face screwed up. "No, I don't, either. I'm sure. It's just . . . just that I have to think, about us, my role here, what life will be like for me, what I must do, what I must accept, how I must respond to hatred and hostility, how I can combat it. You must understand that."

He was buttoning his trousers now. His fingers stopped their movement as he looked at her. "You mean that? Is that really why you want to go?"

"Yes, darling, yes. Oh, Morgan, I wouldn't lie to you."

"But you lie to yourself. It's nonsense. You don't need to go away for all that. We"ll wait a few days, even a couple of weeks, for the wedding. You can have all the time you want to think. I'll help you. We'll talk about it. We'll plan together."

She covered her face with her hands. It wasn't going well. It was all falling apart. "Oh, please, Morgan, don't. Please, if you love me." She heard no reply. Then she moved her hands and saw him. He was look-ing at her intently, but with tenderness in his eyes.

"You really mean it? You really want this?"

"No, Morgan, I don't want it—not at all. But I must, simply must, because I love you, because I want us both to be happy."

"You'll come back?"

"Oh, yes, darling. I'll die a little every second I'm away."

"You'll come back. Promise me you'll come back."

"Yes, I promise—" she held out her arms to him, "—if you'll just come here and hold me close."

He came to her, kneeling on the couch, taking her in his arms, cradling her bare flesh against his.

"I promise, Morgan. I promise, I promise, I promise."

"How long will you be gone?"

"Not long. A few days. No, a month. Not over a month. I'll be back in a month."

"You'll marry me then?"

"Yes, yes, willingly. I'll be half-dead from wanting, waiting."

The summer idyll ended abruptly on Tuesday. Danielle, Cassie and the children, packing hurriedly, departed for Charleston by train. Mother and grandmother, unable to bear Morgan's angry silences, the pained look in his eyes, departed, too. Glenna went back to New York. Moira, having received a telegram from her husband, went to Chicago to meet him. She felt a great need for the comfort of his arms.

Chapter 11

Miriam Hodges's lie to Peter Blakeley was reasonably successful, but confronting her grandmother was quite another matter. Miriam knew she would have to do a great deal better if she was to convince Edith Prentiss of the necessity of her return to Maryland.

Nothing if not ingenious, Miriam quickly hit upon a plan and immediately went out to execute it, sending herself a fake telegram. Thus, not too long after she returned home, she was reading, then showing the telegram to her grandmother.

MOIRA SERIOUSLY ILL. YOU AND
THOMAS RETURN HOME AT ONCE. FATHER.

"What is she sick of?"

"I don't know, grandmama."

"Has she been ill?"

"Not that I know of. She seemed fine when I left."

Edith Prentiss made a harrumphing sound. "Very strange, if you ask me."

"Yes, isn't it, grandmama?"

Edith was sorely put out. This had to come up just when things were going so smoothly between Miriam and Peter Blakeley. It couldn't happen. She wouldn't allow it. "I see no reason for you to return, Miriam."

"But father. He wants me to." She waved the telegram. "Return at once. He's practically commanding it."

"I know that. But he's just upset that his precious wife has the sniffles, or something. It is no reason for you to return."

"But, grandmama—"

"There is nothing you could do, anyway. There are doctors, hospitals, if need be. You'll just be in the way. Thomas, too."

Miriam seized at the straw. "I'd better go and wire Tom. Father doesn't know he's not here."

"You'll do no such thing. Let him enjoy his holiday. This is all just a silly fuss over nothing. I know it."

"But, grandmama, father said—"

"I know what he said." Exasperation mingled with desperation in her voice. "You're a grown woman, Miriam. Your father has no right to order you about like a child. You have duties, obligations. You can't just pick up and walk off after Mr. Blakeley has—"

"Oh, yes, Peter, of course. I'll talk to him at once."

There was a good bit more wrangling between the two women, but Miriam remained adamant, finally leaving the house to "wire Tom" and "speak to Peter." Actually, she wandered around the stores and had a pot of tea, killing what she hoped was sufficient time before returning home.

"Peter was most understanding, grandmama, such a dear, really. He said I should by all means go at once to Moira."

"Humph."

A complication arose. It was too late in the day for Miriam to leave on Monday. It would be after dark by the time she arrived in either Baltimore or Washington, and there was no way Edith Prentiss was going to let her be alone after dark in those "wicked" places.

Thus, it was midday Tuesday before Miriam could leave for Aurial. Even then, she had to make repeated promises to return in a "couple of days," as soon as she knew her stepmother was recovering. To prove her commitment, Miriam pointed out that she was taking only a single suitcase, leaving most of her things behind.

As she rode south in the Pullman daycoach, looking quite fetching, she thought, in a stylish blue gown that Blakeley had bought her, Miriam had second thoughts. Why was she going? Oh, she knew why, to escape the demands of Peter Blakeley. Her lie had been pure desperation, to escape a trap. She could still feel his soft, smooth hands on her breasts, rubbing her nipples. She shuddered at the memory. Yes, all these lies were necessary, but what was she going to do at Aurial? Stay there and rot? Hide out to escape a man she really didn't care about—had a downright antipathy toward? For the first time, she felt a pang of guilt about her grandmother. Grandmama was counting on her to enflame Peter Blakeley, get him to give her things, loan grandmama money or something, so she wouldn't lose

the house. Miriam knew she was confused by all this
talk about the Prentiss fortune. What could she do
about it? Marry Peter Blakeley? Yes, that was what her
grandmother wanted. Miriam sighed. Grandmama made
it sound so easy. But she didn't know. She wasn't the
one doing the marrying.

Miriam forced herself to think of happier subjects.
Morgan Kingston. Was he ever in for a surprise! She
knew she was changed, older, more sophisticated, more
beautiful. She already knew the uses of her body—
some of them, anyway. And if she was going to have
to surrender it to ensure her "future," then it would
be with someone attractive, desirable. At once, Miriam
knew why she was going to Aurial. She was going to
make love to Morgan Kingston. The realization came
quite cold-bloodedly to her. Come what may, she was
going to bed with Morgan Kingston, going to make
him fall in love with her. If she was to marry money,
it would be his. Because she loved him, really loved
him, and could never love anyone else. And Morgan
was rich, not as rich as Peter Blakeley, but rich enough.

Buoyed by these happy fantasies, Miriam smiled. It
would be great fun. When Moira saw the new Miriam,
she would die of jealousy. And, yes, Danielle would be
there. Miriam could sense the expression in her eyes
as she saw the new gowns. *Where'd you get that,
Miriam? Oh, this? It's just a little thing by Pierre
Chambeau. Ever hear of him?* Yes, this was going to
be a productive trip.

Miriam passed the train bearing Glenna, Joe and
Jessie a little outside of Baltimore. Moira was actually
in Union Station when her stepdaughter arrived in
Washington, but already aboard a westbound train.
They did not meet. Thus, having hired a cab for the
twenty-mile trip to Aurial late that afternoon, Miriam
was surprised to find Aurial all but vacant. Her knock
was answered by Hester, the cook-housekeeper, who
was surprised to see her.

"Why, Miss Miriam, what are you doin' here?"

"I live here, remember? I assume I'm welcome."

Graciousness with servants was an art still lost on Miriam, especially when she was tired and nervous.

The door opened wider. " 'Course, Miss Miriam. I just thought you was in New York, thassall."

Miriam stepped into the foyer. "I was, but I'm here now. Where is everyone?"

"Gone, Miss Miriam, left this afternoon. Miss Moira jus' left a while ago to meet Mr. Hodges—Chicago, I think. Miss Glenna, Joe and Jessie, they went to New York. Miss Danielle and the chillun all left earlier for Charleston."

"They're all gone?"

"Yes, miss. It was sorta suddenlike."

"I should say so. And Morgan? He's gone off, too?"

"No, Miss Miriam, he's here—someplace. Don't know 'zactly where."

Miriam looked around the entrance hall and up the great stairway, sensing the emptiness of the place. "I guess I'll go to my room and freshen up. I *do* still have a room, don't I?"

Her pique was lost on Hester. " 'Course, miss. Jus' as you left it."

"Is there someone to carry my bag?"

Hester bent to pick it up. "I'll tote it, Miss Miriam. All the others is gone for the day. Some was given the evenin' off."

"Very strange, if you ask me." But she marched purposefully up the stairs, Hester lagging behind with the heavy luggage. For just a moment, an extremely fleeting one, Miriam realized how terribly imperious and overbearing she was being, letting an old colored woman carry her bag. But there was something about Aurial that always brought out the worst in her.

"Anything else I can do, Miss Miriam?"

"No, that'll be all." She waved her hand in dismissal. "Oh, yes, you can tell me where Mr. Morgan is."

"I dunno, Miss Miriam. He's around someplace. Actually, I haven't seen him all afternoon. Probably out in the barn or workin' in the fields. He'll be in for his supper later. I'se fixin' it now."

For perhaps half an hour, Miriam busied herself. She unpacked her suitcase, hanging up her gowns, paying special attention to the dark blue satin she had brought along. Then she touched up her hair and redid her makeup. For a moment, she inspected herself in the mirror, approving the result. Actually, she longed to put on the evening gown, but knew it was far too formal to wear in the country, particularly when only Morgan would be eating. Her travel dress was a trifle wrinkled, but she hated to change. She had nothing else for daytime that set off her figure so well. The first thing she was going to do was enlarge her wardrobe. All her silly, ingénue dresses were going into the trashbin.

For a few minutes, she prowled the house, looking for Morgan. She even called his name a couple of times, but was met by silence. Finally, she went outside to the stables. A single stableboy met her. She didn't know his name.

"I ain't seen Mr. Morgan all afternoon, miss."

"He couldn't still be out in the fields?"

"No, miss. I know fer a fact he didn't go out today. And all the hands is gone for the day."

"Where could he be?"

"Maybe in the orfice, miss, workin' on the books, or somethin'."

The office. Morgan's study down at the old Kingston house. She knew of it and had gone there several times to see him. "Harness a small rig for me, will you?" She wasn't about to walk all the way over there.

In the settling twilight, she wheeled down the mail road to Kingston, tethering the horse and marching to the study door. It was locked. No light was visible. He had to be there. Not until the third rap did it open.

"Well, Morgan, aren't you glad to see me?" She gave him her best smile, then realized it was probably too dark for him to see it.

"Mirry? Is that you?"

She hated the nickname, and would not suffer it from anyone but him. "If you'd turn a light on, you'd be able to see for yourself."

Resolutely, she pushed past him and into the study. With a little effort, she found the kerosene lamp, then the matches. In a moment, the study was bathed in light. Again, she smiled her most ravishing at him, but quickly saw it was wasted effort. He was looking at her strangely, not quite comprehending. Something was wrong with him. Good Lord, he was drunk! She glanced at the desk. A half-empty bottle, a glass with amber fluid in it.

"Morgan Kingston, what on earth are you doing, sitting here in the dark drinking whiskey?"

"Brandy."

"All the same—or maybe worse. Morgan, what's wrong with you?"

He turned from her, back to the desk and the glass, lifting and draining it. "I don't wanna talk about it."

She heard the slur in his speech. Yes, he was drunk. Impossible to believe, but Morgan Kingston was drunk. "Talk about what?"

"Wha' I don't wanna talk abouse." He seemed to find himself a little, even standing more erect. "Mirry, I'm glad you're home. But I don't wanna see you now. I don't wanna see nobozzy. I jus' wanna be leff alone. So jus' go, leave me alone."

"I'll do no such thing, Morgan Kingston. You're tipsy. You're a disgrace."

"I'm not either."

She laughed. "Oh, but you are. You need someone to look after you. I'm going to the house, get some food and bring it to you. You're going to eat, sober up. And I'm taking this whiskey or brandy or whatever it is, with me."

Less drunk, his reflexes might have been faster, but he was powerless as she snatched the bottle from the desk and darted quickly out the door.

She raced back to Aurial in the gig in a state of elation. This was going better than she had hoped.

Everyone was gone. She and Morgan were alone and he was down at Kingston. They would be alone in the study. The couch would do just fine. And he was tipsy. Good. She knew the effect of alcohol on men. He would want her this night—would he ever!

She entered through the kitchen, telling Hester to prepare a basket of food for Morgan. She would take it to him. Then she dashed upstairs and, panting a little from her exertions, stripped off her dress, her chemise, and put on the satin ball gown. So quickly did she move that her breasts were still rising and falling after she had snugged them between the whalebone and behind the minuscule restraint of blue satin. The buttons at her back were a time-consuming annoyance, and she wished she had help. But she managed. Then she patted her hair, took mere seconds with her makeup and dabbed herself generously with perfume. Yes. The mirror revealed it. Morgan Kingston was in for the shock of his life. As she started for the door, she stopped. No point in letting that woman in the kitchen see her in this. Quickly, she snatched up a light shawl and draped it over her shoulders. As she tripped down the stairs, she was conscious of her naked hips and thighs against the cool satin. Imagine! What a wicked thing to do. But what did it matter? Pantaloons and stockings would just be coming off. The thought made her giggle.

Not twenty minutes had elapsed before she snatched the food basket from Hester and was back in the carriage, racing back to Kingston. Outside the house she paused, removing the shawl and endeavoring to snug the bodice of her gown even further down on her breasts. As she laid the shawl on the seat, she felt the brandy bottle. Men liked to give women drinks. Supposed to make it easier. Why not? Couldn't hurt. She removed the cork, raised the bottle and swallowed. Holy Mary, Mother of God! Awful! Involuntarily, she shuddered. How could anyone drink it? But she forced herself to raise the bottle and take two long swallows. She was already feeling the effects of the brandy as she opened the door to the study.

"God, Mirry, look at *you!*"

She smiled her most dazzling. "Look at what?"

"You. Your dress. Why, you're bootiful."

She looked down at herself, seeming not to notice her extreme décolletage. "This? Oh, it's something I picked up in New York. You like it?"

"God, Mirry, you're bootiful. I never saw such a dress."

"It's the latest fashion." That was anything but the truth. Quite consciously, she bent over to set the basket of food on a chair, lingering on the movement, aware that her breasts were nearly falling out of her bodice. When she stood up, she saw his eyes, pupils wide, and knew her effort was not wasted. "Why, you naughty boy." He held a glass of brandy in his hand. Turning, she saw a fresh bottle on the desk. "I told you not to drink any more."

"Whass wrong with a lillil drink?"

She smiled. "Nothing—if you share it." She walked over to him, standing very near, and took the glass from his hand, raising it, swallowing. She was so conscious of him. It seemed he was about to reach out and grab her.

"I dint know you drink, Mirry."

She laughed. "I don't, usually. There are a number of things I don't usually do." As she handed him back the glass, she suddenly stood on tiptoes, brushing his lips with hers, flirtatiously, lingering just a moment. "Like that, for instance."

He stared at her in stupefaction, unable to comprehend. Then he reached for her, taking her wrist, bending down to her. She let him kiss her, relishing the sensations at her mouth, the pressure of his body against hers. But only for a moment. Giggling softly, she said, "My goodness, Morgan, liquor does make you bold. That's why I brought you food."

Laughing lightly, she pulled his hands from her and walked across the room, quickly putting the food and plate on top the desk. "All right, young man, you can come and eat now." She saw him, still standing, looking at her hot-eyed. She laughed. "Need coaxing, do you?" She went to him and, taking his hand, led him woodenly to the desk, practically pushing him into the chair.

He just sat there. Bending over his back, pressing her breasts against his shoulder, she reached in front of him, spooning potato salad and baked beans onto his plate. She lifted a leg of fried chicken, handing it to him. "Now you just eat, Morgan."

She moved away from him, turning so she was leaning, partially sitting, on the desk, facing him, her breasts level with his eyes, not two feet away from him. Slowly, she raised her fingers to her mouth and began to lick the chicken grease from them. Then she laughed. "You'd better eat, Morgan—or you won't get any dessert." It seemed to her she was all breasts and he was all eyes for them. Again, she laughed. "So you need help, do you?" She took the chicken leg from his hand, bringing it to his mouth, rubbing it over his lips. Then she quickly bent and began to lick off the grease with her tongue. When his mouth came open, she laughed and shoved the chicken into it. "Now eat." She was darting away from him as he tried to grab her.

From the other side of the desk, she watched him bite and chew the chicken. "Now your fork, Morgan. A bit of potato salad." She watched him eat. "So you like my new dress, do you?"

Through a mouthful of food, he said, "God, Mirry, I never saw sush a dress."

Laughter bubbled out of her. "It's not the dress you like. It's what in it."

"You sure are pretty, Mirry."

"Yes, I'm a new me. I had an idea you might like it." She bent over the desk, as though looking for something, her breasts pendulous before his eyes. "There should be bread or rolls here, someplace." Smiling, she looked at him, saw his eyes devouring her. "Or is there something else you want?"

She saw him start to rise from the chair. Extending her arm across the desk, she pushed him back down into the chair. Then she came around the desk, leaning-sitting as before, facing him. She let his eyes consume her for a moment, then slowly, all her native coquetry coming out, she reached inside her bodice and pulled her breasts up and out. It had happened before. How much better with this man. "Are these what you want?" Her low, husky voice suddenly broke into laughter. "Then you'd better swallow your food first." A moment more, and she was holding his head in her arms, sweeping her breasts over his face, quivering with sensation as his lips, teeth found her nipples, first one, then the other. Her shaking turned to trembling. God, it felt so good. Oh, how she wanted him! She knew it would be this way. Thank God she had come to Aurial.

She pulled away from him. Her voice dark, she whispered, "You go over there on the couch and get ready. I'll be with you in a moment." Standing away from him, she watched him lurch to his feet, bend to kiss her. "In a moment." She laughed. "Give me a moment, you impetuous Morgan, you." She saw him head for the couch as she turned her back to him, coquettishly letting her hair down and removing her gown, understanding she must delay the revelation of her body until the last moment. She half-expected him to grab her at any moment, caress her, smother her body with kisses. Slowly, she turned around, eyes bright with anticipation.

Morgan Kingston lay on the couch on his back, still dressed. She smiled. "So you want me to take off your clothes, do you?" She went to him, bending to unbutton his shirt, expecting him to grab her breasts. He did not. Then she heard deep breathing, a strange noise. "What on earth!" Morgan Kingston was asleep, snoring. In her inexperience, she did not know that to give food to a drunken man is to make him pass out.

She bent deeper, dragging her breasts across his face, feeling his stubble of whiskers against her nipples.

Nothing happened. "Morgan Kingston, you wake up this instant or I'll kill you!"

She shook his head, once, then more violently, even slapping both his cheeks. "Morgan Kingston, you wake up!"

He stirred under her shaking and slapping. His eyes came open a little, glazed, unseeing. He found his voice. "Oh, Cassie, I love you."

"What'd you say?"

"Let's get married now."

She stood up, staring at him in shock. Cassie. He had said he loved Cassie, wanted to marry her. Who was this Cassie?

As fast as she could, Miriam dressed and raced the gig back to Aurial, bursting into the kitchen. Hester was not there. She had gone to her room. Thus, it was not until early the next morning, after a night of anger and frustration, that Miriam was able to confront Hester.

"Do you know someone named Cassie?"

"Cassie, miss? Oh, sure. She's Miss Danielle's maid, takes care of the children, too." She smiled. "Cassie's real nice—and so beautiful."

"Beautiful, is she?" Miriam virtually spat the words. "What does she look like?"

"Cassie? She's real purty, got beautiful black hair and the nicest hazel eyes you ever did see. And her skin is so brown, it seems to shine with an inner light."

Miriam stared at her in horror. It was as though the single word had stabbed her. Morgan Kingston wanted to marry a colored girl. *A colored girl!*

She wheeled and ran upstairs. Within a half-hour, she was on her way to Washington, and within another hour on her way to New York. What a fool she had been. She would never be such a fool again.

It was past noon when Morgan arose from the couch, his head pounding. He looked at the brandy bottle and remembered that he'd got drunk, but the food spread on his desk was a puzzle. Questioning Hester, he learned that Miriam had brought his dinner to him. He had a vague recollection of her rapping on the door, turning on the light, scolding him, taking the brandy bottle. But he could remember nothing else, although a vague, uneasy feeling about the evening persisted. Never in his whole life would he become drunk again.

PART II

Danielle

Chapter 12

Danielle, Cassie and the children did not arrive in Charleston until the next afternoon. Danielle had telegraphed Walter Summers that she was coming, but no one was at the station to meet her. It was of no great concern. She simply hired a rig for the twenty-mile journey to Seasons.

As she rode through the city and out into the country, Danielle was again impressed with the beauty of South Carolina. It was perhaps hotter than a girl reared in London might like, and the mosquitoes could be a plague, yet there was so much here that appealed to her. Charleston was lovely, with its flowers and gardens, splendid wrought-iron balconies and gates—easily as ornate as any in London—charming townhouses and cobblestone streets lined with oaks and magnolias, the beautiful church spires, St. Philip's most of all. She found it the most European of the American cities she knew, far more attractive than New York, Washington or even Baltimore. There was also a pace to Charleston that appealed to her, a leisureliness and courtliness, as though even the busiest of inhabitants, the men invariably in white linen suits in the summer, the ladies in crinolines, had time to smell the flowers. Despite the war and its aftermath, Charleston was still a principal center for art, music and letters. Its denizens had a native charm and innate courtesy that was far more

attractive to her than the rough, grasping, hurrying of
New Yorkers and others in the North.

Yes, she could love life here were it not for the
hatred between the whites and the coloreds. Even this
she understood from her reading and conversations with
informed people. Slavery had been grafted onto the
South by the English when few people had considered
it an evil. And in the beginning, slavery was an economic necessity. Bodies to work the fields were desperately needed, and it didn't matter where they came
from. By the time mass immigration of whites from
Europe began and the nationwide underpopulation
problem was being solved, the South was stuck with its
"peculiar institution," slavery. There were so many
slaves that simply freeing them in a democracy would
lead to rule by uneducated, untrained and long-op-
pressed Negroes. It was unthinkable to the white
minority.

The Civil War was not fought over slavery so much
as over economic issues, the impoverishment of the
South by Northern bankers and shippers. Southerners
had bled the ground red in defense, not so much of
slavery, as of states' rights, economic independence and
freedom to decide one's own affairs. Their link was to
Washington, the Washington of Valley Forge, not the
Washington on the Potomac. That the South had been
overwhelmed by superior numbers of men, guns, supplies and money, did not make their cause wrong.
Theirs, even in surrender and the punishment which
followed, was still a moral victory. Even now, most
especially in this election of 1876, South Carolina was
fighting to end occupation by federal troops, banish
government by carpetbaggers, scalawags and Negroes,
to return South Carolina to the white Carolinians, making the victory not moral, but actual. It was only de-
layed.

All this Danielle understood. And more. Having
lived in both North and South, she understood the different attitudes toward Negroes. The Northerner wants
the Negro to be free and well-treated, but he doesn't

want him living nearby. The Southerner for generations has lived and worked in close proximity to Negroes. He just wants them to know their place. Danielle never could make up her mind which attitude was worse. She hated them equally. Even in this, she was prepared to be wrong. If she had grown up in this environment, learned attitudes as a child, suffered fear and violence, then she might have understood. But she hadn't, and she could do nothing about it. She hated it all. It would within a day blot out all the beauty and grace of Charleston, which she could love.

"What are you thinking, mommy?"

Danielle glanced at Stephanie, all blonde-red curls and dark blue eyes. This lovely child added further fuel to her discontent. She could not bear the thought of her children growing up amid all this, accepting hate and fear into their lives.

She smiled at her daughter. "I was thinking how nice it is to be home." It was something to say.

It was near dusk when they arrived at Seasons. Once again, Danielle was impressed with its beauty. It stood atop a small rise amid the low country of the Charleston area, a large, white-frame, squarish house, fronted with stately columns. The dwelling was reached by going up a driveway—Danielle thought of it as an esplanade—of ancient live-oaks festooned with hanging moss. Yes, perhaps it was good to be home.

Esther, the cook-housekeeper long in the service of the Summers family, greeted them, all surprise, smiles and delight. Walter Summers was not there. He had ridden off within the hour. How sorry he would be to have missed them. No, her telegram had not arrived.

Disappointed not to be greeted by her husband, Danielle nonetheless settled quickly into her routine as mistress of Seasons. Luggage was brought in and unpacked. Travel attire was discarded for more comfortable garments. She was briefed by a voluble Esther on all that had happened, concluding it was not much except that she and the children had been missed. There were repeated hugs from the elderly colored woman, who quickly went to work to prepare a home-coming supper. Mr. Walter had not planned to eat at home tonight.

Except for the absence of husband and father, the homecoming was joyous, with the children running everywhere, squealing as they rediscovered forgotten toys. "You'd think we'd been gone a year," Danielle laughed. They were simmered down enough to eat sup-per and, quite a miracle, to go to bed and finally to sleep. Afterwards, Cassie said she was tired and going to bed.

Danielle looked at her, holding her eyes. "Are you all right?"

Cassie's smile was wan. "As good as can be ex-pected, I guess."

"Are you sorry for your decision?"

The smile broadened. "Yes, terribly."

It was after ten when Danielle, now alone, went downstairs. The excitement and elation of coming home, squandered in the disappointment of Walter's absence, led to an inevitable depression. She refused to give into it. He would come home soon. Some sherry, that's what she needed. There was none, so she settled for a small brandy, realizing it would have a stronger effect than the wine.

She could not sit. Strangely nervous, she prowled the ground floor, observing, inspecting the house—her house, her home. It was a type of house invariably spoken of as grand. And it was, with fine, large rooms and many windows. Great care had gone into the build-ing, with its parquet floors, a splendid staircase, elegant railings and wainscoting of fine oak cut on this very plantation long ago. But the grandeur was now seedy. There were cracks in the plaster in many places, a stain from an old leak in the roof. The carpets and drapes were threadbare and needed replacing. And the furnish-ings were sparse, many of the things stolen or sold. There was a sadness about Seasons, and it lasted all year long.

Danielle didn't mind, except that the genteel dilapidation of his ancestral estate was so terribly debilitating to Walter Summers. He hated it, as he hated so much else that had happened. There was no money for repairs. This house, once full of servants, was now down to Esther and Cassie, both of whom were unpaid except for room, board and clothing.

It was not just Walter who had no money. Nobody did. All the planters, all the farmers, most shopkeepers were in the same straits. With the slaves freed and most of them off the land, supported by the Freedmen's Bureau in Washington, there was no one to work and no money to pay them if they did. South Carolina's economy was largely barter. Farmers, once prosperous, were reduced to sharecropping, giving their land to former slaves to work in exchange for half the profits, if any. Or, they rented their land to tenant farmers. Those like Walter Summers, who insisted on farming their land, were forced to mortgage their crops to banks before planting. Since the risk of crop failure was so great, the banks charged usurious interest rates. Walter was always in hock. Most of the little cash he had went for hired hands. Danielle's household money was a tiny fraction of that spent at Aurial. Unlike most of the former planters and their progeny, Walter Summers worked hard in the fields, determined to somehow restore Seasons to greatness. Danielle worked hard, too, cleaning and, with Cassie, doing all the sewing, canning and preserving. She would have worked beside her husband in the fields, but in his pride he would not hear of it.

All in all, Walter Summers was doing better than most. Danielle had begged and begged, until he finally accepted a small "loan" for seed and horses from her mother and GlennaMa. Her trip to Aurial had been financed by such a gift. He had invited Morgan to come down and had listened to him, learning how to rebuild the wasted, sandy soil. And Morgan had convinced his brother-in-law that it was incessant planting of cotton that impoverished Seasons. Thereafter, just this year, really, Walter had begun to plant some tobacco—a new, experimental variety called Bright Leaf—and a few acres of wheat. Even a peach orchard had been started. Walter was encouraged, even optimistic. Perhaps cotton was not king, after all.

Yet, Danielle knew her husband's inner turmoil and suffered along with him. He had such pride, such terrible pride. Once rich, he was now poor. All he had left was land and a house, now seedy and sad. Danielle did what she could, making do, never asking for money or suggesting needed repairs or replacements. She maintained the garden, and they ate well. She filled the house with flowers and sought to keep the atmosphere cheerful. And in her person, she sought always to be beautiful and elegant and loving. But she knew that it was her very person that caused the greatest anguish to her husband. He had married a rich girl, or one he thought of as rich, a girl born in Maryland, raised in London, who had captured New York with her beauty and elegant gowns. That he could not keep her as she had been, or as he thought she ought to be, was his greatest frustration. And she could never convince him that she did not really care about the appurtenances of wealth, or the life she had led in New York. What she truly cared about was something he either could not or would not do anything to change. He didn't even understand it.

About midnight, now extremely tired, Danielle went upstairs to their bedroom, sure he would be along any minute. Taking plenty of time, she undressed and gave herself a sponge-bath from the basin in the washstand. As she washed and dried her body, she was conscious of her risen, hardened nipples, her slender waist, the taut, narrow hips that even motherhood had not spread, despite a painful labor. Yes, she was still beautiful, her snowy skin soft, her breasts opulent. It was with awareness of her own sensuality, her need, that she dabbed herself from a shrinking hoard of perfume, and donned her best nightgown. It was from her trousseau, worn on her wedding night, all white silk and lace, decorated from within by the bright pink of her nipples. She sat at her vanity, creaming her face to further cleanliness and softness, then ritualistically brushed her hair for a time. Finally, leaving a single candle lit, she went to bed. She was not worried about her husband. Walter Summers could take care of himself. She just wondered what he could be doing out so late. Then she fell asleep, to be awakened a little after four in the morning.

"Oh, Danny, Danny, you're home."

He was leaning over the bed, his face close to hers. "Yes." She smiled. "And now you are, too—finally."

"God, I had no idea you were coming so soon. I would never—"

"I sent a telegram."

"It never got here." He laughed. "What can you expect, the way things are running around here?"

She smiled again, or was it the continuation of the same smile? "I expect something."

His face traversed the short distance that separated them, and he kissed her, she him, in longing. The homecoming was complete.

"Oh, Danny, I've missed you so."

"Yes, you needn't say. I can tell."

Again, he kissed her, then stood up, and she crawled out of the bed to stand before him. He said her name one more time, an expression of his surprise and delight, then she was in his arms, pressed against him, his lips hot, eager. Sleep fully gone now, she responded, breath short, lips devouring his, and when his hand found her breast beneath the thin fabric, she moaned with yearning.

"God, Danny, you look so wonderful."

She laughed. "I wish I could say the same for you. You look like you've been in a bar fight. In fact, I know it. You smell like a bar. Then it must have burned down, 'cause you sure do smell smoky." It was said with laughter, teasingly. She was not scolding.

"Oh, that. I went coon-hunting with some of the fellows. Then we built a fire and swapped yarns. Somebody brought a bottle. If I'd dreamed you were here, I'd—"

"I'll bet." But her eyes were bright as she said it.

"How're the little ones?"

"They're fine—but disappointed not to see their daddy."

"I'll make it up to them."

"And me?"

"Oh, Danny." He started to fondle her again, then stopped. "I really do stink, don't I? Let me take a quick shower. I'll only be a minute."

He ran from the room. She knew where he was going. One of his innovations at Seasons—he took great pride in his ingenuity—was a shower. It was just a barrel filled with rainwater and hooked to a pull-chain and a piece of tin with holes in it. Situated off the kitchen, it did not offer maximum privacy, but they all used it from time to time. She thought it marvelous for doing her hair.

While she waited for him to return, Danielle went to her vanity and completed her toilette, a touch of powder, a dab of perfume, idle brushing of her hair. She was in a highly aroused state. And why not? If it had been a long time for him, so had it been for her. She smiled in anticipation.

Danielle had been bothered for a long time by her own capacity for love. It seemed somehow unnatural to her, foreign to what she believed her true nature. The simple fact was, that properly aroused and with the right man, she seemed unable to stop, climaxing repeatedly, each fulfillment shattering and succeeding quickly upon the previous one. Walter was amazed at her, expressing marvel and wonder. And in the privacy of their bedroom, he had more than once tried to find the end to her. He had—exhaustion. Worried, ashamed, Danielle had years before talked to her mother. She was of no help, saying she was the same way and calling it a curse. But in recent years, Danielle had come to accept and enjoy her nature as something she could not change.

If worries and troubles had entered her marriage to Walter Summers, none of the steam had gone out of their lovelife. He had been her first and best lover. Six years before, she had gone to a masked ball in London, shy and embarrassed by the daring gown that Glenna-Ma had insisted she wear. She had danced with a masked man dressed as a pirate. She had passed out on a drug he had slipped into her punch, then awoke in a garret. Still wearing the mask, he gave her an aphrodisiac that greatly intensified her senses; then, in a night of love, ravished her, teaching her the joys and torments of her capacities. But he had remained masked, telling her he was British and horribly scarred. She didn't even know his name. Right after that, she went to New York with her mother, GlennaMa and Morgan. She took up with the rich, relentless Hamilton Garth. Even now, she shuddered from the memory, not so much from his savage lovemaking as her own response to it. Her ability to give herself so completely to a man she really didn't like still troubled her.

She had lived with Garth as his mistress, even going out West in his private railway car. The train was wrecked and she was held prisoner, until a tall, yellow-haired man with warm, brown eyes, named Walter Patten, rescued her. Later she discovered, quite by accident, he was the man from the garret in London. He was not British, nor scarred. He was Captain Walter Summers, a Confederate spy who fled to London to escape the firing squad. Wearing the mask to hide his identity, he had seen her, drugged and ravished her, but fallen in love and followed her to America at great risk to himself. At the same time that she discovered who he really was, so did army officers. He was arrested and was headed for the firing squad, when President Grant, acting on the request of Franklin Fairchild, pardoned him.

"Lord, but you're beautiful."

He was behind her, hands on her shoulders, wearing a robe, yellow hair damp, smelling of soap and cleanliness. He bent over her, kissing her cheek, her neck. She could already feel herself quivering.

She unbuttoned her gown in front and welcomed his hands, calloused, a little rough, to her breasts, kneading, rubbing, fondling, teasing. In the mirror, she saw her mouth open with desire, felt her breath not coming often enough. Oh, it was so good, so necessary.

"Do you want the potion?"

It had been the one true thing he had said in London. He claimed to have been in India, and he had, learning the exotic ways of love that so thrilled her, and bringing back the aphrodisiac that he had used that first time in the garret. He still had a supply, and twice during their marriage they had reenacted that first night of love.

"I hardly think I need it, do you?"

"It doesn't seem that way."

Danielle could not accomplish the final hurdle to sleep, despite her weariness and delicious satiation. She was smiling inwardly, both from memory of their loving and a thought that had just come to her. She really had not worried if her husband was faithful to her while she was gone, but she now knew for certain he had been. There had been many remarkable nights of love in their marriage, but she could not remember when this night had been surpassed.

She listened a moment to his gentle breathing beside her. She loved him. If she had had doubts about that at Aurial, they had been the result of inner tension, and that was now swept away like ashes in the fiery furnace of their passion. Oh, what a good lover he was! A word entered her mind. A true lover, the truest, giving so generously, measuring himself, spacing his needs for her ultimate fulfillment, her truest fulfillment. Accepting her own nature, she knew she must never lose him. No other could be so right for her as this man she had married. *Go to sleep.* Then, from where she didn't know, came a thought of Benjamin Fairchild, and the kiss in the moonlight. Why think of that now? It was so terribly far away and long ago. *Go to sleep.*

Chapter 13

Someone else lay awake at Seasons. Having gone to bed early, Cassie was awakened when Walter Summers entered the house. Listening intently, she heard him go back downstairs, the sounds of the makeshift shower that was below her room, his tread on the stairs as he returned to the waiting arms of his wife.

Why had she thought of that? Never before had she even considered what transpired at night between Danielle and her husband, and she was shocked at her own awareness. She knew why the thought came to her. She now knew what must be transpiring in the room at the other end of the house. She dwelled on it a moment, then forced it from her mind as voyeurism, although she didn't know that word, by thinking of Morgan, her own true love, remembering, reliving, wondering, her mind a thicket of conflicting thoughts.

Only the second night away from him, and already she missed him so. Lying there in a thin cotton nightgown under a sheet, she was excruciatingly conscious of her body, her breasts he had fondled, her thighs, a little spread as she lay on her back, her womanly

center now aching for his entry. A few days ago, such
thoughts would not have been possible for her. She
hadn't known. Now, her whole body seemed eager, on
fire, her mouth open, ready for his kisses. *Stop it! Stop
it! Holy Mary, Mother of God, pray for us sinners, now
and at the hour of our death.*

She forced herself to think of why she had come, to
be away from him, his kisses, his arms, what he did to
her, to think, discover within herself her own true
nature. Already, she was sorry she had come. The
clicks and clacks of the southbound train had made
a mournful dirge to her, and there had been no joy in
the homecoming to Seasons. Apprehension had come
over her like a shroud, the moment she saw the Summers plantation. She shouldn't have come. It would
have been so easy to stay at Aurial—already in her
mind an island of light and beauty and happiness, so
different from gloomy Seasons. She should have given
in to Morgan. He was right. They could have talked
it out there, solved their problems together. All she
had accomplished by this trip was to risk losing him
forever.

No. She forced herself to remember her fear of discovery, the agony on Jessie's face, the hateful looks of her
people in Washington, the haunted fear in Moira's eyes.
She had come because of that, not to lose Morgan. She
had to bolster her courage, understand her role as mistress of Aurial, come to grips with herself and her new
life to be. Yes, to be. She wanted it now. That she
was sure of. A few weeks at Seasons, feeling like a
servant around Walter Summers, an assistant to Esther,
and she would fly back to the arms of Morgan Kingston. At worst, the life he offered was far better than
this. Then she felt guilt. She was hardly being fair to
Danielle. She loved her, wanted only her happiness
and the children's, and she knew they needed her.
Danny, her mistress, her friend, was the one person who
made all this possible. In bemoaning the life Danielle
had chosen, she was stabbing her friend in the back.
Danny must know joy now, her husband home at last,

locked in his embrace, her thighs spread in welcome reception.

No! Stop it! Quickly, she squirmed out of bed. She couldn't lie there, thinking all this. It was indecent, unbearable. She glanced at the window. Still dark, but dawn couldn't be long in coming. She'd get up, go downstairs quietly, make a pot of tea. It would calm her. And there was always something to do. Yes, work was the cure for her disease.

She slipped on her light, summer robe and in her bare feet silently left her room and padded down the back stairs. The darkness posed no threat to her, nor were her movements hesitant in the familiar house.

There was more light in the kitchen, a faint glow from the banked fire in the cookstove. She leaned over the sink to look out the window. So many stars. Then she saw a faint glow near the horizon. Dawn was coming. No, it couldn't be. The glow was to the west and north. Must be a fire somewhere.

She turned back to the stove, lifted a lid and stirred the embers, dropping in some sticks of wood. The room brightened immediately, until she replaced the lid and placed the teakettle on top of it. The darkness was more pronounced now. She shivered. For the first time, she felt uneasy. She didn't know why. To dispel it, she strode to the table and lit the coal-oil lamp, turning up the wick until the kitchen was fully illuminated. Still, her unease didn't go away. She had a sense of being watched.

There was a noise at the kitchen door, a scratching, almost a rapping. It startled her, but did not alarm her. Probably one of the dogs, wanting in. She picked up the lamp and carried it to the far end of the kitchen to see what was at the door. What she saw almost made her drop the lamp. She put her hand to her mouth to stifle a scream.

Through the glass was a face, a black face, all whites of eyes and teeth screwed up into a grimace. Heart pounding, she saw the eyes, the mouth, beseeching her to open the door, let him in. Fingers still at her mouth, she shook her head violently. No, never. She saw lips form the word "please," and the maroon eyes again beg her, then the expression dissolved into a grimace again. The man was in pain, great pain. Through the glass she heard a low moan.

Compassion overrode fear. She set down the lamp, unbolted and opened the door. At once, the man sagged against the doorjamb. He was doubled over, holding his belly with both arms.

"Are you ill?"

With effort, words came from him, half-whisper, half-groan. "Shot . . . help me."

She looked down, saw wet blood at the side of his blue workshirt, on the sleeves.

"Please . . . you must . . . help . . . me." The last word was barely audible.

"All right." She took his arm and, both lifting and pushing, got him to a chair at the kitchen table. Then she went back, closed the door and rebolted it. Why she did this, she didn't know. Then she returned with the lamp. Holding it over him, she saw he was a man in his late twenties, with nearly coal-black skin and kinky, unstraightened hair. His complexion was clear, and he sported a youthful mustache and chin-whiskers. Even with his grimace of pain, she could tell he must be a handsome man.

"Who shot you?" When there was no answer, she asked, "Why were you shot?"

He reacted to that, raising his head to look at her. The pain in his eyes seemed to give way to anger. He hissed, "Because I'm a nigger—just like you."

She had heard the word, but never used it. She'd never heard any colored person use it. Above all, she'd never felt the word applied to her. Bristling a little, she said, "What do you want from me?" At once, she knew it was a ridiculous question. This man, whoever he was, was badly hurt.

He was bent back over now, rocking gently against his agony. His words came out hoarsely. "Lower your voice, woman."

She obeyed. "You need a doctor."

"No."

"I'll get Mr. Summers. He'll know what to do."

She was already turning away to go upstairs, when his hand shot out and grabbed her wrist. "No!" The single word was hissed with surprising vigor. "Not him. Hide me."

"Hide you? I can't hide you."

"You must."

"You need a doctor."

"No. Hide me." He forced himself to his feet, steadying himself on the edge of the table with his left hand, holding his middle with the other. She saw his wound. He was bleeding so badly he seemed to hold a handful of fresh blood. "You must."

She was horrified by his wound, the first she had ever seen, and the man's obvious agony. Her eyes wide, she whispered, "I can't."

From somewhere, he seemed to find strength, standing more erect, his voice clearer. "The nightriders shot me. If they . . . find me, I'm . . . dead . . . shot, maybe hung."

Nightriders. It had meaning for her, all the killing and burning, terror by night. "I can't." She could find no other words.

He looked at her a moment, disbelief, anger, filtering through the pain in his eyes. "That is brown skin you have—isn't it? You are . . . a woman of color . . . aren't you?" His face screwed up into a grimace. She thought it pain. "Or are you a white man's nigger?"

She shook as though he had hit her or flailed her with a whip.

"Please, you can't let me die." He was begging her again, pleading for his life, and it seemed to take the last of his strength. He sagged weakly into the chair.

She looked at him, horror, fear, compassion warring in her mind. She couldn't seem to think. The words just came out. "I don't know . . . where to hide you."

"The barn . . . help me to the barn." He doubled over more, gripping himself with both hands, weather-

ing a wave of pain. "Summers mustn't . . . find me. No
one . . . must. . . ."

She looked at him, her mind still blanked out by
emotions. "The barn's no good. He goes there all the
time."

He raised his head, begging her with his eyes. "Hide
me, please."

Confused, dazed with fear, she looked around the
kitchen as though it offered some safe refuge. Then,
still unthinking, she spoke. "There's a room in the attic. No one goes there. Can you make it?"

"Yes. Anything." As proof, he pushed himself to his
feet.

She stood there, staring at him through widened eyes.
"Hurry."

She looked around, confused, uncertain what to do.
Up the back stairs. They would need a light. She started
to pick up the lamp, but it was too heavy. A candle.
Yes, a candle. She quickly found one in a drawer and
lit it from the lamp. She went to him, put her arm
around his back. At his first step away from the table,
he almost fell.

"Lean on me." As she felt his left arm come around
her, creating a heavy weight on her shoulders, she
realized what a big man he was. Together, her arm
around his waist, holding the candle in her left hand,
they took a step together, then a second, a third. She
stopped. "You must be very quiet. Not a sound."

"I know. Let's go."

The climb up three flights of stairs seemed to go on
for eternity, an agony of fear. Every sound seemed
magnified, his heavy tread on the steps, the creak of
boards, his labored breathing, her very heartbeat. Surely, someone must hear. They would be discovered. But
they weren't.

At last, they gained the door to the attic room, and
she opened it, helped him inside and closed the door.

"Does it lock?" He saw her nod. "Good."

She looked around the space. It was small, so small
a person could barely stand in the center of it, head

between the rafters. A trunk, wooden crates, forgotten bits of broken furniture were stored there. There was, as she remembered, an old cot. When she first came to live at Seasons, she used to come up here to hide and be alone. Now she led the wounded man to it and helped him to sit, then collapse sideways on it. It seemed to her the springs made a fearful creak. Trembling, she lifted his feet to the bed.

He seemed nearly dead to her, lying there, breathing labored, eyes closed against his pain. "I have to go," she whispered. He nodded his understanding. "It will be fearfully hot up here. It's all I can do." Again, he nodded. She looked at him a moment longer, then picked up the candle to go.

"Gag me."

She turned back to him.

"Gag me. I—I . . . don't want . . . to cry out."

She looked around for something to use. There was nothing. Then she put the candle down and, bending, tore a strip from the bottom of her nightgown. She used part of it to wad into his mouth, the rest to tie a band around his head. It seemed a cruel thing to do, but again his nod assured her.

"I'll—I'll come back . . . when I can." Once more, she watched him nod, saw his eyes open a moment to look at her, then she left him.

In the kitchen, she leaned her back against the sink, shaking uncontrollably, fingers stuffed into her mouth to keep from retching. What had she done? Oh, God, how could she have? So stupid. He would probably die up there—might be dead already. How would she ever get him down? How would she ever explain? She had ruined everything. Why hadn't she thought?

But her fear and desperation were nothing compared to her panic when she opened her eyes. Bloodstains, all over the chair where he'd sat, across the floor from the door to the table, then along the floor toward the stairs. *Godalmighty!* She looked down at herself. Blood on her robe. She nearly screamed.

Frantically, she wet a cloth, then her robe, rubbing

as hard and as fast as she could. She applied more water. Yes, it was coming out. More water, harder rubbing. But the stains would not all come out. It would have to do. She would say she spilled some food. It looked a little like teastains. Wringing out the cloth, she went to the table, the chair, wiping hard. They came clean; it was fresh blood. Hurrying, she got to her knees, carefully clutching up the skirt of her robe, and wiped the floor around the chair, then over to the door, rising frequently to rinse out the cloth. Then across the kitchen, up the stairs, all the way to the attic door. She paused to listen a moment. Nothing. No sound.

Back in the kitchen, consumed with fright, panting, she looked around for more evidence. The basin of water, pink with blood. She threw the water down the sink and rinsed out the basin. Then she wrung the cloth as dry as she could. Pink. Everyone would know. She held it in her hand a moment as though it were a dirty, menacing thing. Then she went to the stove, opened it and threw it into the fire, hearing the sizzle. Again, she turned around, surveying the kitchen for evidence of her folly.

The sound seemed to split her open. She jumped, almost screamed, turned. The teakettle had boiled over, sizzling on the hot stove. She grabbed it, lifting it off, burning her hand as she did so. But she was unmindful of the pain. It was as nothing to her inner pain. What had she done? How could she have been so stupid? *O clement, O loving, O sweet Virgin Mary!*

Chapter 14

Perhaps the last place Miriam Hodges expected to be this night was in her own bed at the Prentiss house. She had been mentally, physically prepared to spend the night with Peter Blakeley. But it had not happened —not yet, anyway. She smiled in the darkened room. Just a couple more days. If she had waited nineteen years for this, a little longer wouldn't matter.

She had been surprised how long her anger at Morgan Kingston had lasted. It still seethed below the surface as cold fury, fueling her determination to begin a new life, a new way of living. To think! She had told a peck of lies, wasted money on the fake telegram, and traveled all the way to Aurial, practically throwing herself at Morgan, wearing her most daring dress —not even any undergarments—kissing him, wantonly licking the grease from his lips, revealing herself, letting him fondle her. And what had he done? Fallen asleep! God, such humiliation—utter degradation! He was drunk. She would never make that mistake again —never, never, never.

But her anger at that shame was nothing compared to her rage at him for loving another. A colored girl! A maid, a servant, *a colored girl!* He wanted to marry her, sire a lot of half-black pickaninnies. *Mother of God!* What a fool she was, wanting him, pining for him, thinking she loved him. She was a fool, nine kinds of a fool. He was a child, a hick, a farmer with dirty fingernails. He had made a fool of her. No, *he* was the fool, to think he could ever aspire to a girl like her. She was so much better than he, than all of them, the mother, the sister, the grandmother. They thought themselves so high and mighty, so superior. She would show them, show them all. Morgan Kingston would spend his whole life regretting, knowing—no, never truly knowing—what he had missed.

This sort of mental harangue consumed perhaps half the train ride back to New York. Then, still fueled by anger and bitterness, she began to think of herself and her future. It was all over between her and Morgan Kingston. She had slammed shut the book, a romantic and childish chapter was completed, now and forever. She was beginning the rest of her life. For another moment, mental images flicked across her mind, she and Morgan, at the desk, his eyes hot, desperate, as he looked at her, grabbed for the delights she offered. There was bitterness in these memories, but not as before. Oh, how she had enflamed him. He was in love with another, yet she, Miriam Hodges, had reduced him to bumbling, incoherent stupidity. That knowledge excited her, for what she had accomplished with one man could be done with others, many if she wished. As the train sped her back to New York, it was in the certain knowledge she was a temptress, a woman capable of maddening men with desire.

As she looked out the train window at the marsh lands of New Jersey, it seemed to her that her future stretched out before her. Never again would she be so foolish as to love a man, or even think she was in love. Of course, she hadn't really loved Morgan Kingston. At most, it was a childish infatuation. No, love would not enter her life again. She would *use* men, offering her beauty and her body in return for what they would give her: money, jewels, furs, fabulous gowns, splendid houses, great estates. Possessions were all that mattered, not love. Money was happiness, poverty a disease. Grandmama was right. She had the capacity to rebuild the Prentiss fortune, restore that name to wealth and prominence. She would even take the name. Miriam Prentiss. How much better it sounded.

It would all begin with Peter Blakeley. Already, she could think of him without recoiling. What a child she had been! But her romantic notions were behind her now. She was a woman of the world—or about to be. So Peter Blakeley was not the handsomest of men, nor the most appealing. But she now knew—did she ever—about handsome men. Handsome is as handsome does.

That made her smile. Peter Blakeley might not be much to look at, but he was a man, equipped with the desires of all men. Already, she had enflamed him, reducing him to barely-controlled rage that she had not given herself to him. Good. He would want her the more. And when he had her, he would pay dearly. After all, he would be the first. That had to be worth something extra. For a moment, her mind dwelled on what it would be like with him. Oh, God, she couldn't, she wouldn't. What was it about his pale blue eyes that chilled her to the bone? *Stop it, Miriam.* She could; she would; she must. It was but a tiny hurdle to be leaped. She remembered her pleasure as she had cradled Morgan's head to her breast. Yes. She would receive pleasure, and give it. It was important, she knew—although she was uncertain where that knowledge came from —to give pleasure to a man. She knew she could. What lay beneath her dress was the instrument of her future. If she had much to learn of its uses, Peter Blakeley would teach her—and pay for his instruction.

All the while she raged and plotted her triumph, somewhere deep in Miriam's heart a part of her mourned. *This isn't what you want,* a small, sad voice cried out within her. *You loved Morgan and he hurt you, but don't turn bad because of it,* the voice of honesty persisted. But she hardened herself against it. Bad? *Bad?* Was it bad to be realistic, to realize that men were cruel, uncaring creatures, that all a woman could do was look out for herself? Still, her conscience was uneasy. After all, why should Peter Blakeley pay for Morgan Kingston's sins? Well, why shouldn't he? Was he any better? No, worse—there was definitely something creepy about that little man. Besides, he would get what he wanted, wouldn't he? She refused to feel guilty—not all the angels and saints in heaven could stay her vengeance, on Morgan, on Peter, on the whole crass world. She would conquer that world, she, Miriam Prentiss Hodges. And never, never, never again, would she shed a single tear over a man.

When she reached New York, she dispensed with her lies to Edith Prentiss. "I should have listened to you, grandmama. Why, it was nothing but the sniffles."

"I told you so."

She hugged the old woman, feeling sincere regard for her. "I promise always to take your advice, grandmama."

Edith was touched by her granddaughter's affection and greatly relieved to have her return so quickly. "What about Mr. Blakeley? Men do not like to be toyed with." Indeed, she was consumed with worry that Blakeley, not having bedded Miriam, would now call in the notes.

"Sometimes they do, grandmama. Trust me. I know what I'm doing. I'll let him know at once that I have returned."

That effort produced a good result. She sent a note to him by the disgruntled Hannah, reading: "I told you I'd return. I'm so *eager* to see you. Miriam." She hesitated a moment over the wording. It was perhaps a trifle direct and bold. But, then, why not? He would want to be reassured of her interest. He had made that most clear.

She was surprised when Blakeley came at once, bringing Hannah in his carriage. Rather breathlessly, after running up the stairs, the servant told Miriam that Blakeley was waiting in the small parlor.

In some excitement—who would expect him to be so eager to see her that he would rush right over?—she patted her hair, powdered her nose, smoothed her dress and went down to receive him.

"My dear Miriam, how can I tell you how happy I am to see you?" He was standing, looking at her, a bright luster to his blue-gray eyes.

"You are a flatterer, Peter. I fear you have me at a disadvantage. I just now arrived on the train. I know I look a fright."

"My dear, you are enchanting, as always."

"Thank you, Peter." She smiled and offered her hand. "May I say how good it is to see you again?"

There was a firmness to his grip that made her quake inside. "I never doubted your return, Miriam."

"I'm only sorry I had to leave."

There came an awkward moment then, as she extricated her hand from his and took a seat, while he sat opposite her, hat on his lap. She offered refreshments, tea, coffee, spirits if he preferred. He refused, saying he couldn't stay long.

They just looked at each other then. There could be no doubt of the happiness in his face. His words confirmed it. "I'm glad you're here, Miriam."

"I am, too, Peter. You must know that." His gaze dropped a moment to her figure, then met hers again. She suddenly felt hot.

"Your stepmother has recovered?"

She was flustered for a moment, then remembered. "My stepmother—oh, yes, she's much improved. Her illness was not as serious as my father thought." She smiled. "Isn't that always the way?"

"Yes, I suppose it is." Another moment of awkwardness came. "Did you enjoy your trip?"

She looked at him, eyes level, direct. "May I speak frankly?"

"Of course."

She hesitated, but not overly long. "I did enjoy it, of course. The scenery is pleasant in Maryland, and it is always good to see family, old friends. But, in truth, I was not rewarded." Again, she hesitated, as though searching for words. "I know now my place is here—in New York. You have changed me, Peter—for the better. I now know here, with you, is where my happiness lies."

He seemed deeply affected. Voice husky, he said, "I only want to . . . to bring you greater happiness, my darling."

She lowered her eyelids, looking at her hands in her lap. "I know you will, Peter. I want you to."

She expected some word from him, some gesture, perhaps his coming to embrace her. Nothing happened. She raised her gaze. There was anguish on his face.

"I am most distressed, my darling—more than I can say."

She saw his hesitation. "Yes?" Could he have met someone else, already? No, impossible. His eyes showed he wanted only her.

"If your servant had been a minute later, she would have missed me. Thank God that didn't happen. You . . . you might have misunderstood."

"Misunderstood what, Peter?"

"My being away. I was just going out the door. I have to leave—very soon, in fact—for Boston. Unavoidable business, goddamit. Had I known you were returning so promptly, I would have made other plans. But I didn't know." He sighed. "I am trapped, my dear. Can you forgive me?"

He seemed so contrite, like a puppy being punished, she had to suppress a smile. "There is nothing to forgive. A man has his business affairs. I was just hoping that . . . tonight, we might . . . see each other." Now she smiled. "There will always be another time."

"Oh, yes, yes. It is but a short trip."

"When will you return?"

He seemed to be mentally calculating. One of the "proper Bostonian" families was in trouble. He expected to acquire valuable antiques—a painting, perhaps even the house—for a song. But now, this girl across from him, he decided to speed the process. They would accept his offer at once. He wouldn't fiddle with them. "Friday, my dear." Then he wavered, his lust battling his greed. "Perhaps I'd better make it Saturday. Yes, Saturday. If I have to, I'll fly to be here with you Saturday night."

She smiled. Imagine anyone flying to be in her arms. "I hope you will not be too lonely, my darling."

Her smile broadened. "Not when I think of you."

"Yes, and I will think of you constantly." He stood up. "I really must go, or I'll miss my train."

She rose. "I wouldn't want to be responsible for that." She stepped toward him, extending her hand in farewell. He took it, held it. She saw it in his eyes. He wanted to kiss her. "I will miss you so, Peter." Then he was embracing her, his thin mouth hot on hers, full of passion. She made every effort to respond. But she felt a chill in her heart.

"I can't bear to go."

"You must." She smiled and patted his cheek. "Work hard. Finish your business quickly."

"I will. Believe me, I will." He kissed her again. It was impulsive, briefer. "What will you do while I'm gone?"

She smiled. "Be lonely, my darling."

"Why don't you go shopping? That always amuses women. Go see that funny Frenchman. What's his name?"

"Pierre Chambeau. But I couldn't, Peter. You've been too generous with me already."

"I insist. You have no idea what pleasure it will bring me."

"I know, Peter, but—"

"I'll not take no for an answer. Order several gowns from him. And tell him I want his best one ready for Saturday night."

She saw excitement in his eyes—and desire. "Since you insist."

"I do. Tell him to make something fetching, something which does justice to—" he glanced down, "—to your charms."

A third hurried time he kissed her, then strode to the door and out of the house. A sigh of relief es-

caped Miriam as she watched him go; then she thought
of Saturday, and gave a different kind of sigh.

Thus, she came to spend an unanticipated night
alone in bed. But she was not disappointed. It had
gone well. And tomorrow she would increase her
wardrobe at the salon of the most famous dressmaker
in New York.

The following day, she was ushered into the studio
of M. Chambeau. As he had the first time, he again
made her feel extremely uncomfortable. She was not
offered a seat, looked at or spoken to, but left to stand
there, while he worked away at a sketch. He might
be the most celebrated and expensive couturier in New
York, being accepted as his client might be a badge
of approval, but he was surely a beastly man, dripping
disdain. He made her feel of no value whatsoever. He
might as well be dressing a cow or a pig, for all her
effect upon him.

After several minutes, he laid aside the sketch and
picked up a piece of paper, a business form, she saw.
It would ultimately be the bill. "Hm, Monsieur Blakeley, I see?"

"Yes."

He turned to look at her now, scorn and indifference in his eyes. "You did not like the gowns I made
before?"

"I loved them. They were wonderful. But I need
more—many others." She saw him glance back at the
bill, reading again the name on it. "I want beautiful
gowns, the boldest, most daring you can make."

Without looking at her, he said, "Then you should
go naked, *chérie*."

She felt as though she had been slapped.

Slowly, he turned to look at her. "I meant no
offense, Mademoiselle Hodges. I quite understand
what you desire. If you will remove your—" his
pause was pregnant with contempt, "—your attire, I
will make the necessary measurements."

She hesitated.

"Come, come. I have no time for this."

She obeyed. And as he brought his tape measure to waist and hips and breasts, she again sensed his lack of interest in her. She might have been made of clay or marble, for all he cared. But his occasional "hm" sounds unsettled her.

"You disapprove of me?"

"I neither approve nor disapprove, Mademoiselle Hodges. I am interested only in how well you can wear my gowns."

"And?"

His shrug was hardly comforting to her.

He produced bolts of cloth and began to drape them over her in various ways. She said nothing, realizing he was working and that concentration was essential to him. Finally, there came what sounded like a particularly significant "hm," and he removed the material from her skin with finality. "You may get dressed now, Mademoiselle Hodges."

As she dressed, he busied himself with notes and quick sketches, entirely uninterested in her. Finally, he said, "You may come in for your fitting next week, Mademoiselle Hodges."

"I need the first gown Saturday."

She saw him glance at her, then at the bill. The price would go up, but she didn't care. "As you wish."

She was nearly dressed, when he spoke again. "Are you and Monsieur Blakeley to be married, or is yours a liaison?"

She felt her face go crimson. The impudence of the man! But then, if she were going to be a woman of the world, she supposed she would have to get used to such incidents. In a voice as lofty and disdainful as his own, she asked, "Does it matter?"

"Not to me, I assure you. But sometimes these matters do influence a designer in his work."

"A liaison." She had never heard the word used in this context, but understood its meaning. She saw his diffident shrug and it was disturbing to her. "You disapprove?"

Again, the shrug.

"You think me too young?"

"I do not think anything, Mademoiselle Hodges."

"I assure you, Mr. Chambeau, I know what I'm doing. I will have many liaisons, as you call them."

"I see. You wish to be a courtesan."

Again, he used a word she was unfamiliar with, but once more she sensed its meaning. "Is there anything wrong with that?"

Another shrug, both delicate and prolonged. "There are courtesans and then there are courtesans, Mademoiselle Hodges."

"And what does that mean?"

"It means a courtesan is a state of mind. I once knew a woman—you asked about your age—she was about your age. I should tell you she was more beautiful than you. She had a far better figure. But she had something else that would have made her a splendid courtesan, one in a century. Do you know what that was?"

"No."

"Reluctance. She didn't want to be." He sighed. "Alas, virtue won out, and she is now a happily-married woman, somewhere."

"Who was she?"

"It doesn't matter. You wouldn't know her."

She was hurt by his remarks, and more than a trifle angry by what she considered his derogation of her. "Think what you will, *monsieur,* but I know what I'm doing."

"I wish you success, *chérie.* It can be a most worthwhile occupation."

She stared at him, but could think of nothing to say. Turning, she went to the door. Hand on the knob, she said, "My dress, I hope it will—"

"You will not be disappointed, I assure you."

Chapter 15

The day began well for Danielle. She slept a little later than usual, but arose well ahead of Walt. She'd had more sleep than he. As she dressed, she looked down at him in his slumber. Yes, he was a good man. She smiled. And a great lover. Lord, but she felt good. Hadn't felt this relaxed in a long time. She smiled again, both at herself and at him. Yes, it was good to be home.

Downstairs, she greeted the children with hugs and kisses, as though they had been away, too, and helped Cassie restrain them from running upstairs to awaken their father. She conversed animatedly with Esther during breakfast, and did her best to cheer up Cassie, who seemed tense, tired and withdrawn. She would have to tell her that if she was going to lie awake all night pining for Morgan, she might as well take the next train back to him.

After eating, she went out to inspect her garden, frowning at this, lamenting that. Oh, well, it could be worse, and it would keep her busy. Lots to do here. On impulse she decided to pick a bouquet for the house. The asters and snaps needed thinning, and the zinnias were almost ready to bloom. This was a lovely time of year.

She was nearly finished with the cutting, when she heard the squeals. She turned, and with an armful of flowers, marched into the house, intending to scold the children for waking their father. But she couldn't. What a picture they made, he standing, a child in each arm, both of them hugging and kissing him at the same time. He winked at her and smiled. "Where did these two little kiss-bugs come from?"

A naughty thought came to her mind. Instead, she said, "They may be kiss-bugs to you. They're little rascals to me for waking you."

"We didn't either. We waited like you told us."

"May I plead for the defense, ma'am? I was already down the stairs—or almost—when these two attacked me." More squeals and hugs greeted his words.

Both sat on his knees, or tried to, as he ate his breakfast, chattering happily at his invitation to tell him all about their trip.

"Uncle Morgan has lots of horses, daddy."

"Really, Andrew? What kind of horses are they?"

The boy looked puzzled, then finally gave an exaggerated shrug of his shoulders. "I dunno."

"I should imagine they are Morgan horses—Uncle Morgan horses." Neither child got the joke, but joined their parents in laughter, anyway.

After eating, Walter Summers took his son and daughter by the hand and led them outside to the barn. They could help him saddle Mask, his favorite stallion, and ride out with him to help check the fields. As Danielle watched them go off, she felt overflowing with happiness. A good man, a great lover, the best of fathers. Husband, family, home. She had everything. What on earth had she been dissatisfied about? Maybe the trip away had been necessary. She could appreciate all this now.

At midafternoon, there was a knock at the front door. Calling to Esther that she was getting it, Danielle arrived just after the second knock, opening the door to a heavyset man of about fifty. He wore black boots with saddle pants tucked in, and a red shirt. Behind him, still mounted in the driveway, were three other men, similarly attired.

"Missus Summers?"

"Yes." Her voice was noncommittal.

The man before her smiled, bowed slightly and doffed his wide-brimmed hat, rather showily, she thought. He had iron-gray hair, an ornate handlebar mustache to match, fine teeth and bright, brown eyes. He spoke with a most definite Southern drawl. "Missus Summers, my name is Walters, Beauregard Walters." She had the feeling he was about to offer a military rank, but refrained at the last moment. He did have a military bearing. "I was wonderin' if it would be possible to speak to Captain—I mean, Mr. Summers. Is he in?"

She smiled. The elaborate Southern courtesy always pleased her and made her want to reciprocate. "Yes, of course, Mr. Walters. But I fear he's out in the fields. It may take him a minute to reach here. If you—" she glanced over his shoulder, "—and the other gentlemen would care to wait inside where it's cooler. . . ."

"Thank you, ma'am, but no." He made an elaborate gesture of looking down at his boots, then smiled. "No sense in trackin' up your nice, clean house, Missus Summers."

"As you wish, sir. I'll go ring the bell to summon my husband."

There was no need. As she turned from the door, she saw Walt stalking across the front lawn toward the men on horseback. He must have been near the house and seen them ride up. As he came near the front, he saw Walters and her at the door, turned and came to them. "Beau, I see you found your way here all right." He was smiling, extending his hand. "Have you met my wife?"

"I have had the honor." Again, the smile, the bow. "I'd heard she was just about the prettiest little lady 'round these parts, makin' all our Southern belles jealous. I see how that can be, now."

Danielle laughed. "You should meet my grandmother, Mr. Walters. She's one hundred percent Irish, and appreciates a touch of blarney even more than I."

"But I reckon she's a lady who recognizes the truth, too."

"That she is." Smiling, she nodded acceptance of being bested in the exchange. "I'll go now. You gentlemen must be thirsty after your ride."

"Don't trouble yourself, ma'am. We're only going to be a minute."

"It's no trouble."

She went into the house, ignoring further protests. Fortunately, there was a pitcher of lemonade already made, and in a minute she had poured six glasses and was returning to the front with a tray. She had expected Walt to invite his friends to sit on the porch at least, but they all stood in a knot out by the horses, deep in conversation.

As she approached with the tray, she heard, "He got clean away, Walt, but I think we winged him. Carley here saw some blood."

"Here you are, gentlemen."

Walt turned to her, surprise registering on his face. He reached for a glass. "Thank you, dear."

Walters was more elaborate. "That sure does look like the cure for a thirst, ma'am. Thank you."

She smiled and offered the tray around to the other men. All accepted and drank. It suddenly seemed an awkward moment to Danielle. The conversation had stopped. Whatever they were talking about, she wasn't to hear. Her smile was a little nervous as she said, "If you gentlemen will excuse me, I'll leave you to your affairs."

Walters again. "I know how it is. Woman's work is never done. But we surely do thank you-all for this delicious lemonade, ma'am."

"My pleasure, sir."

She headed back to the house carrying the tray. She paused only a moment by the doorway, to see if the potted geraniums needed watering. It was long enough to hear three words wafted on the breeze.

"Does she know?"

She returned to the kitchen, setting down the tray.

For a moment, she stood there, gripping the edge of the sink. *Does she know?* The words hurt. Either she hadn't been told something, or there was something she wasn't supposed to know. Their silence when she delivered the lemonade suggested the latter. What wasn't she to know? Walt and she had no secrets, or so she thought. Not true. She hadn't told him about Cassie and Morgan. Then she roused herself. *You are a prying old woman. Why shouldn't a man have his affairs? A wife needn't know everything.*

The self-lecture helped, and she was more relaxed when he came inside a few minutes later, carrying the glasses to place in the sink. "That lemonade sure hit the spot, Danny."

"I'm just sorry your friends wouldn't come inside and sit."

"They only had a minute. Besides, they aren't really friends."

She glanced at him. "What did they want?"

"Oh, just to bend my ear. They belong to a group called the Red Shirts."

She laughed. "I got that impression."

"It's a political organization. The members go 'round talkin' to farmers, tellin' them to be sure to vote Democratic this year."

"For Governor Tilden, you mean." She smiled. "My stepfather will like that."

"Yes, Tilden, but more importantly, Wade Hampton for governor."

"Isn't he the general you told me about?"

"Yes, commanded all General Lee's cavalry in the war. Great man. Make the best governor. We got to get Dan Chamberlain and his band of carpetbaggers and scalawags out of the State House if this state is to survive."

Danielle laughed. "I'm sure they know how you're going to vote."

"Who?"

"The men who were here. The Red Shirts."

"Oh. Yes, I told them to count on me." He hesitated, looked down at his feet, then back at her. "They asked me to ride with them this evening, help spread the word in this area. I told them I would."

The look in his eyes seemed strange to her. "Of course, dear. Will you be here for supper?"

"If we eat early."

"I'll tell Esther."

He smiled. "Well, I'd better get back to work."

She stared after him as he left, pursing her lips, biting at the inner surfaces. Then she turned and leaned over the sink.

Does she know? That must be it. Did she know about his being a Red Shirt, going out tonight? Yes, that had to be it. There was always a simple explanation for everything. That would teach her to be a suspicious wife. Suspicious of what? Of her husband doing a little politicking? How silly. Her grandfather had been a United States senator. Her stepfather was Tilden's right-hand man. He was "out politicking" for weeks at a time, and her mother didn't bat an eye. It was good Walt was involved in politics. Practically a family tradition. She wanted him to be. She was happy he was doing it. But no number of such thoughts would keep her eyes from smarting, her throat from hurting. He was lying. She knew it.

The day was a nightmare for Cassie. It seemed to her that Danielle and Walter Summers must know. In horror, she saw a drop of blood on the stairs that she had missed. Quickly, she used spit and a finger to wipe it up. Surely, someone else had seen it. Even when she became convinced the family was acting normally and did not suspect, she gained no relief from worry. Suppose he cried out, or fell out of bed? They would hear. Never had she realized how quiet the place was, how much each voice or creak of board carried through the the house. But her biggest fear was that he would die up there in the attic. What on earth would she do? Over and over, she railed at herself for her folly. She should never have helped him. She should have sent him on his way or called for help. Anything was better than this.

Late in the morning, when the family was outside, Esther occupied in the kitchen, Cassie crept up the stairs, the key to the attic door a great weight in her pocket. The attic was an oven, shooting out a blast of hot air as she opened the door. When she looked at him, she gasped, certain he was dead. He lay as she had left him, on his back, the macabre gag tied to his mouth, arms lifeless over his chest, his shirt and the mattress around it a mass of brownish, blackish blood.

"Oh, Mother of Mercy, please, *no*."

She wanted to run from the room, but forced herself to creep closer to the cot. It seemed to her she could smell death. Standing over him, she saw his lids were closed over sunken eyes, his face gleaming with sweat. *Sweat!* She studied his chest. It was moving, but almost imperceptibly. Yet, he was alive. Thank God, he was alive. But barely. How much longer?

She returned in the afternoon. He lay as before, except his left knee was bent. He had moved. Again, she studied his chest, detecting its gentle movement. Still alive, but was he asleep or unconscious? She didn't know, and was afraid to touch him to find out. This time, she forced herself to study his wound. His midsection was a mass of black blood. It seemed dried, and she could detect no fresh, red color. Perhaps the bleeding had stopped. Where had he been shot? She still could not bring herself to touch him, but it seemed to her the worst spot was not in the center, but off to the side. Perhaps he had not been shot in the stomach.

For a long moment, she studied him. He was not dead—yet. But he had a terrible wound. He needed a doctor, but that was impossible. If he was to live—oh, God, he had to live!—it was up to her to do something for him. But what? She tried to think. The wound ought to be cleaned, a bandage put on. Yes, she would come when she could, try to clean him, put a makeshift bandage on him. Maybe it would help.

The rest of the afternoon dragged on remorselessly.

Cassie tried to act as normal as possible, which was
the most difficult of her tasks. Since dinner was early,
the children came to the table. Cassie had hoped to
avoid this. At best, she never felt comfortable with
Walter Summers. He was never unkind or mean to her,
but she knew her place with him. She was a Negress, a
servant. This she could have easily borne, but Danielle
insisted on elevating her status to nurse, even govern-
ess, insisting she eat with the family. Summers never
said anything, but Cassie knew her presence at the table
was at his sufferance, a humoring of his wife.

Danielle seemed more quiet and withdrawn than
usual. But this may only have been because her husband was in an expansive mood. He seemed preoccu-
pied with the children, asking them again about their
trip, how their grandma and great-grandma were, what-
all they had done. To Cassie, it was inevitable that she
be asked her impressions of Maryland. She answered
that it was beautiful, and spoke of the differences in
climate and terrain from South Carolina. Summers
pressed for details. What had she done to amuse herself? She gave hesitant, noncommittal answers about
long walks, a pleasant row on the river. It seemed they
did so little, yet time passed so quickly. He seemed to
accept her answer, and changed the subject. Silently,
Cassie sighed with relief. She had glanced at Danielle,
fearful she would speak of her and Morgan. She had
not.

The evening wore on. The children were read to,
then bathed and put to bed. Cassie came downstairs to
say goodnight to Danielle.

"Do you mind, Cassie? I just don't feel like being
alone tonight. Could we—oh, I don't know, talk or
something? Or how about a game of cards?"

Thus, for a couple of hours, two young women, both
lonely and troubled, amused themselves, or tried to,
at gin rummy. Neither spoke much during the game,
and not at all about their real worries. It was the first
time they had consciously avoided sharing information
with each other. Both knew their troubles were to be

borne alone. Eventually, bedtime came. Cassie helped Danielle to undress and spent the usual time with her hair. After goodnights and a silent embrace, which was perhaps a bit more lingering than usual, each got into her own bed, neither to sleep.

Danielle's mind was weary from her turmoil. For hours—the card game was the poorest of distractions —she had been absorbed in a mental tug of war. She was being silly, a suspicious wife, creating distrust where there should not be any. She had no right to know everything her husband did. On the contrary, he had a right to his privacy, his freedom of action. If a wedge entered their marriage, it would be her fault. She was the distrusting, questioning one.

Yet, she could not escape knowledge of his lie. She was willing to accept the words, "Does she know?" as referring to his going out tonight with the Red Shirts. But even that seemed strange. Why was the question asked? What business was it of anyone else what his wife knew or did not know? The question was an invasion of family privacy. And what had Walt replied? Yes? No? I'll tell her later? It's none of your business what I tell my wife? Why did those three words hurt so?

But it was the other comments she had overheard that really disturbed her. Someone had got away, but was possibly shot. Carley had seen blood. Who was shot, and for what reason? Who had done the shooting? And why was the information being imparted to her husband, outside, away from the house so she could not hear? Why would he care? What difference could this information possibly make to him? She was not a fool. Nor was she blind to the world. This area, this state, was a cauldron of violence. Men rode by night—men of both races—beating other men, intimidating them, sometimes shooting, lynching, burning out their homes. All men were not created equal. All men were not to vote. The gun and the lynch rope were more powerful than the ballot box. Her husband had been out till four in the morning last night. He had returned smelling of whiskey and smoke. Coon-hunting, he had said. She believed him them. Did she now? Yes, yes. Her husband was not a nightrider, a murderer. She would not believe it of him—never. Was he a liar? From the past came memories: the garret, the masked man, British, horribly scarred . . . so many lies. Over the years it had become amusing, their private joke. But now there was no escape for Danielle. Walter Summers could be an adept liar when he chose to be.

He came home and she was awake to hear him, speak to him.

"I'm sorry I'm late. I guess we went too far and talked too late at the last place."

"It's all right. You're home now. Did your meetings go well?"

"Yes. Everyone listened. It was time well-spent." She did not reply.

"Let me wash the dust off, then I'll be with you."

It was not at all an unusual invitation. They made love with great frequency. Several nights in a row was not uncommon. They were still in love. He was young, virile. She was willing, receptive. She removed her nightgown and waited for him. Yes, they needed to make love, this night of all nights. His embrace, their passions, would wipe away her fears, doubts, the distrust. Always, it was so.

"Is something the matter?" he asked.

"No, not really. I guess last night was enough to last a while. You go ahead. I'll enjoy it."

She turned her mouth to his, felt his deeper, faster thrusts, the tensing of his muscles, his shuddering release within her. She heard his groans of pleasure, then felt him roll off her. Just before he fell asleep, he said he loved her. She lay staring into the darkness. It had been the first time since she had known him, since long ago in the garret in London, that she had not responded to him.

Chapter 16

Cassie knew she must wait until Walter Summers came home, then a bit longer to be sure that he and Danielle were asleep. She would need a light to tend to the wounded man, and it would be visible in the attic window.

When she decided it was safe to go, she arose, put on her robe, but no slippers. Bare feet would be quieter. Everything was prepared, a pitcher of water, a basin, an old muslin sheet, a candle and matches. Not until she was on the upper floor, at the door to the attic, did she risk lighting the candle. The strike of the match, the rasp of the key in the lock, were horrendous noises to her, making her heart pound.

He had moved a little, but that was the only change. She set the candle on top of a wooden crate, and poured water into the basin. Ought to be warm water, she knew, but that was impossible. She turned to him, staring at the wound. She couldn't. The blood was everywhere, black, horrible. His shirt was caked with it. But she must. It was the only way.

Suddenly, his hand moved, startling her. She looked at his face. His eyes were open, full of suffering, but she could tell he was lucid and trying to remove the gag. She bent to do it for him, untying the knot, removing the slimy ball of cotton from his mouth. His lips, dry and cracked, moved, but no sound came out. Then she knew. He was trying to ask for water.

From somewhere came knowledge she was unaware she had. "Your stomach," she whispered. "Should you drink?"

Again, the lips moved, asking for water. He must know. She turned to the pitcher, then realized she had no glass or cup. Dipping her fingers into the pitcher, she wet his lips, then cupped her hands into a scoop, carried the liquid to his open mouth and slowly dropped a little inside. He closed his mouth and swallowed.

"Thank you." He swallowed again. "More."

She repeated the process, managing to get more water into him this time.

"Awful. I couldn't swallow, talk. So dry. More."

"I don't think you should drink too much." But she dutifully gave him more liquid, watching him swallow, then wipe his lips with his hands.

"I came to clean your wound."

"Yes, go on."

She glanced at the black mass. "I'm afraid. Your shirt—it's full of blood. You'll start bleeding again."

"Go on, do it."

Still she stared at his midsection. "I—I wish I had scissors."

"Tear it, go on."

Timorously, fingers trembling, she pulled the tail of his shirt from his trousers, then began to unbutton it from the bottom. The right side of his shirt fell open, revealing his bare, black skin. But the left side of the shirt was caked to him. "I can't," she whispered. "It's stuck."

He brought his left hand to his waist, gripped the shirt and, with one savage movement, tore it away from his skin. She nearly screamed as she saw the black hole, blood now oozing from it.

"It's all right now. Wash."

Swallowing hard, breathing deeply to settle her nerves, she began her task, ripping off a piece of the sheet, dipping it in the basin of water, washing him.

It was easier than she had figured, for most of the caked blood was removed with the shirt.

The wound, she now saw, was not in his abdomen, but more to the side, in the fleshy part beneath his ribs. Gingerly, she wiped at the skin around the area, frequently sponging the rivulet of blood that flowed from the hole.

"Clean the wound."

She looked at him, wide-eyed with fear. "I can't."

"Do it."

When she had rinsed out the cloth, she timidly brought it back toward the hole. He grabbed her hand that held the rag and clamped it over the wound. She could feel him wincing, breathing hard from pain.

"Hold it there . . . to stop the bleeding."

She did as he showed her, pressing against the wound. "Is that too hard?"

"No. What's your name?"

"Cassie. Cassie Brown."

"You're very beautiful."

She looked at him. Despite his condition, he was a handsome man, virile, powerful, and possessing an intriguing spiritual quality as well. "Please, I just want to get you out of here. I'm terrified . . . someone will find you." She saw him smile, a feeble smile that quickly faded into a grimace of pain. "I shouldn't help you. I was a fool. I have everything to lose."

"But you did."

"Who are you?"

"Josh Calhoun."

The name meant nothing to her, but he seemed to say it with pride. "Am I supposed to know you?"

Again, the smile, the flash of white teeth. Yes, he had a definite magnetism. "I guess a house nigger like you wouldn't have heard of me."

Her anger flared and, forgetting her task, she stood up straight. "Don't talk to me that way."

Again, the teeth. "Has the bleeding stopped?"

She looked at the wound. "Mostly."

"Then help me." He was trying to roll over. "It came out the back."

She helped him, pushing, lifting him to his right side. When he tore back his shirt, she gasped at the sight of a second hole, now also bleeding.

"Clean it."

She bent to her former task, which came easier now as she washed away the caked blood and pressed on the wound to curb the bleeding.

"Why did you come here?"

"It was the safest thing to do."

"What d'you mean?"

"Nobody'd think I'd come here."

"I don't understand."

"No one looks for the fox in the hunter's yard."

"Please, I don't understand. Talk sense."

"It was Summers who shot me, you fool—at least he was the leader of the gang that did."

"No! He couldn't."

"If you know so much, why did you ask?"

"No, Walter Summers is—"

"Walter Summers is a pig of a slaver. He's a house-burning murderer."

Again, she stood up, moved away from him, removing her pressure from the wound. "No, I won't hear it."

"Can't believe ill of your master, eh, nigger?"

"Stop it! I won't hear it." In her agitation, she almost forgot to whisper.

He smiled ironically. "Has the bleeding stopped?"

"I don't care. I don't care about anything except getting you out of here."

"Really love him, do ya?"

"Please, you have no idea what you're saying, what you're doing. Just go. Please go."

He looked at her. "All right, I'll go. But not tonight. I'll never make it."

"When?"

"When I can."

"Listen to me, please. You may think you're so smart coming here, but you're not. Anyone can come up here at any time. You're anything but safe here. Believe me and go, just go."

His eyes were sharp, questioning as he looked at her. "All right. Tomorrow. I'll go tomorrow night. Now bandage me up."

She looked at the pair of holes in his side. "I—I should get alcohol, salve or something."

"No, just wrap me up."

As she tore the sheet into strips and began to bandage him, sliding the strip beneath his back, winding the muslin all the way around him, they talked, still in breathy whispers.

"Why did they shoot you?"

"You mean Summers."

"Don't say that. I won't hear it. Just tell me why you were shot."

Again his belligerent smile. "There is only one way to fight these people—with their own weapons, their own methods. Fire with fire, bullets with bullets. It's the only language they understand. A life for a life. Gabriel Prosser knew it in Virginia. Denmark Vesey knew it here in Charleston. Nat Turner knew it. And I know it. Kill, kill, kill—it's the only solution."

"No!"

"Yes! It's the docile ones like you, the passive, white niggers, waiting for a crumb to fall from the table —instead of taking the table—who enslave us. We got no one to blame but ourselves."

"Stop it!" If a whisper could be a scream, hers was.

"They always want the beautiful ones, like you. You bear their kids, you—"

"Stop it, I say! He hasn't—I haven't—"

"Well, well, will wonders never cease? But he will. You won't have to wait long."

Kneeling beside the cot, she covered her face with her hands, trying to blot out the sight of him, his ugly words, get control of herself. He said no more, and she finally regained her composure.

Able to look at him again, she said, "Why do you say these things to me?"

"To make you mad, to make you fight."

No more was said, and in silence she finished bandaging him. When she stood up, she could see the fabric already turning red with blood.

"I need food. I'm starved."

She sighed. "All right. I'll get what I can."

Silently, stopping frequently to listen but hearing only her own pounding pulse, she made her way in darkness down to the kitchen. For a moment, she stood there, gripping the edge of the table, breathing hard, head whirling, desperately trying to control herself and her near terror. Finally, she gathered some bread, a few pieces of meat. It would have to do. She remembered a cup. She'd leave him the water.

He was sitting on the edge of the cot when she arrived back in the attic. The red stains on his bandage had stopped spreading. Handing him the food, she watched as he stuffed it into his mouth with both hands. "You'll leave tomorrow night?" Chewing vigorously, he nodded.

She waited a moment, watching him eat. "How do you know about Walter Summers?"

He chewed a minute more, swallowing hard, then drank from the cup she'd given him, dipping it back into the pitcher to refill it. "Because I do, that's how. He's the leader of a band called the Red Knights. Real nice fellas. Usually, they specialize in women and children, house-burnings. Now they've sworn to get me. Hunted me for days. But they won't get me. Never." He looked at her sharply. "Unless you tell him."

"I won't. I just want you gone."

"Tomorrow night."

She filled his cup with water, then picked up the pitcher and the basin. "I've got to take the candle."

"Take it."

"Do you want the gag?"

"No, I'll be all right now."

She watched him a moment, then left the attic. At her last sight of him, he was stuffing his mouth with bread. Locking the door, she blew out the candle, waited a moment for her eyes to adjust, then went to her room. As she lay in bed in the darkness, a single thought pounded through her brain. Never, but never, must Danielle learn about her husband. Never. . . .

The next morning after breakfast, as she, Danielle and Esther were in the kitchen, Cassie heard Josh cry out—a sound that stabbed into her like a saber.

"What was that?"

"It sounded like one of the dogs."

"That was no dog. It sounded like it came from up-stairs."

Cassie looked at Danielle, forcing a smile, hoping she was being natural. "Well, I'll go check, but I'm sure it's nothing."

Out of their sight, she took the stairs two at a time, frantically opening the attic and rushing inside. She reached him just as he was about to scream again, muzzling the sound with her hand. Quickly, she shoved the gag into his mouth, binding it with the rag around his head. But she already knew the worst. He was delirious, burning up with fever. He would be going no-where this night. As a final precaution, she pulled and lifted him from the bed to the floor, to avoid the noise of his falling out.

Downstairs, she forced a smile. ".There's not a soul but ghosts upstairs. It had to be the dogs."

"I guess it must have been."

Chapter 17

At midmorning, Danielle left for Charleston in a rig. Supplies were needed and she did purchase them, but her trip had a more important purpose. The best solution to her doubts about her husband was to obtain more information. And she knew just where to get it.

Thus, in the early afternoon, she entered army headquarters and asked for Major Bertram Lennon. Within moments, she was greeted by a tall, slender man in his forties, with dark hair and a fine, full mustache. His brown eyes were bright as he spoke. "My dear Mrs. Summers, what a pleasant surprise to see you."

She smiled her best. "One I share, major—although it is not a surprise. I was hoping to find you with a few minutes to spare."

"Indeed, I have some time, Mrs. Summers. And I can think of no better use for it than to chat with you."

She was ushered into his office, and a few minutes were expended in serving coffee and answering inquiries about health and families and recent activities. "You must have enjoyed your trip to Yankeeland, Danielle." In the privacy of his office, they became Danielle and Bert, for if not old friends, they were friendly acquaintances, members of a small coterie of "Yankees" in a hostile land. Lennon's wife, Emily, had invited Danielle to teas and other social events. A natural community of interests and values had drawn them together.

"Yes, I did enjoy myself. It was a good trip."

"And now, being back, how does it seem to you?"

Danielle was not about to be disloyal to her husband. She was determined to say nothing of her doubts about him. At the same time, she hoped for information that would dispel them. She sighed. "Oh, Bert, you know how it is. It's sometimes like living in a foreign country. All this violence. I don't understand it."

He nodded sympathetically. "I know."

"It seems to have got so much worse in the short time I was gone. I don't understand why. I was hoping you could tell me."

"It will only worsen, Danielle, as the election draws closer." She looked at him expectantly, inviting him to continue. "I suppose this election of eighteen seventy-six will be looked on one day as the most pivotal in the history of South Carolina. We—I should say the Republicans—are determined to hold on to power in the state. The Democrats are equally determined to wrest it away."

"I think you oversimplify, Bert. This is no ordinary political campaign."

"Of course it isn't. You know the situation as well as I do. South Carolina, along with Louisiana and Florida, are the three unreconstructed states from the rebellion. My very presence here, wearing this blue uniform, attests to the failure of the Carolinians to resolve their problems." He saw her nod. "Eleven years after the war, and this state is still under martial law."

"I thought Governor Chamberlain ruled the state. Was he not elected?"

"He was and he does. The question is whether he would have been elected in a fair vote. We think not. The franchise is new to the freedmen. They would have been intimidated or cheated out of their vote. The army's job has been to try to ensure their right to vote."

"And they outnumber the whites?"

"Yes. We believe the fact Governor Chamberlain sits in the State House is proof we have done a reason-

ably good job of supervising elections in the past." He
smiled. "How well we do this year remains to be seen."

"How good a governor has Chamberlain been?"

He sighed. "I'd like to give you an impartial answer,
but I doubt if I, or anyone else, can—not for a long
time, perhaps never. There has been without doubt
wholesale corruption and mismanagement. Some of our
Yankee friends—" his voice dripped sarcasm, "—the
celebrated carpetbaggers, have looked upon the public
treasury as their personal purse. Bribery has been a
way of life. Railroads and other corporations have been
given land grants and financial benefits that are embarrassing—to put it mildly. Yet, the person who uses
only a black brush to paint this picture does a dis-
service. Some good has come. The state constitution
of eighteen sixty-eight is, despite flaws, a good one.
Representation is based on population. Each county
has a senator. Imprisonment for debt has been abol-
ished—and many a white planter must be grateful for
that, these days. Women are allowed to own property.
Public education has been improved." Again, he sighed.
"I don't know what to tell you. An impartial evaluation
of Chamberlain, indeed of all of Reconstruction, is
impossible. It all depends on where you sit, on which
side of the Mason-Dixon line you come from."

She pursed her lips. "I see."

"If you do, you're ahead of me." He laughed.
"Political corruption is not exclusive to South Carolina.
Consider the Tweed ring in New York, for instance."

"Yes, I had personal knowledge of that."

"I remember your telling me, yes. Dishonesty, corruption, greed, all have swept the nation since the war.
Everyone is out for himself. I wonder if it doesn't happen after every war."

"Do you think Governor Chamberlain should be
reelected?"

"If I were a Negro living in South Carolina I would.
The whites, the former Confederate officers who once
held sway here, hate the army, the carpetbaggers, the
scalawag Southerners who hold power now and in

many cases abuse it, heaven knows, but the true hatred is for the former slaves now in power."

"And hatred is based on fear?"

"Yes."

"Have they been so bad?"

He shrugged. "Again, impartiality is impossible. Considering the illiteracy, the lack of political experience, the answer is probably no. Given time and more experienced and honest leadership, I, for one, think the freedmen would do fine. And there are now many fine men of color in government. F. L. Cardozo, who has served as secretary of state and treasurer, is an Edinburgh graduate. A fine, intelligent man. There are others."

"What of this General Hampton, who is running against Chamberlain?"

"Wade Hampton is a good man." He laughed. "And that's high praise from a Union officer. Many think that if he is elected there will be a bloodbath in South Carolina. I think not. He is a moderate, a gentleman, trying to win this election fairly. I think, I hope, that if elected, he might help to unify this state. I've heard him say he has no intention of disenfranchising the Negro. He says he plans to give the freedmen a role in his administration. I believe he means it. Unfortunately—" he sighed, "—there are others around him who are not so moderate, so restrained, nor so dedicated to fair play and honest elections."

Danielle was aware that her attention, which had lagged, was now focused on the army major. "Who do you mean?"

"If you want a name, then it's General Martin W. Gary. 'Mart' Gary heads what I guess you could call the militant wing of the Democratic party. Where Hampton is trying to woo the freedmen into party ranks, Gary and his people are attempting to force them in—or worse, shoot them to keep them from voting Republican. Much of the violence can be laid at the feet of Gary and his men."

She could feel her heartbeat quickening. "His men? Who are they?"

"Oh, ex-Confederate officers and soldiers, planters, farmers, those who distrust democracy as too slow, or believe violent times require violent actions—something like that."

Danielle swallowed with difficulty. "Have you heard of an organization called the Red Shirts?"

"Of course, Garibaldi's men."

"Who is Garibaldi?"

He smiled. "Garibaldi is an Italian—in Italy. He is a bit of a hero there, trying to unify that country. To do so, he organized bands of men called 'Red Shirts' to scour the countryside, enlisting support for his cause. The Red Shirts hereabouts are doing much the same, riding throughout the state, enlisting every possible white man to vote for Wade Hampton."

Her eyes widened. "Then they *are* just a political organization?"

"Yes, I guess you could say that."

"They are not violent?"

"That depends. They have a bad habit of walking into Republican rallies wearing their red shirts. They just stand there, saying nothing, but it's a form of intimidation to black voters. A threat is implied. But no, in the main, they are not violent."

Danielle looked down at her hands, enjoying the first feeling of inner relief she had known in over a day. "Then these are Gary's men you speak of?"

"Some. I'm afraid Gary is addicted to more direct action—like burning people out, shooting, lynching. The fear he seeks to engender is real. It goes far beyond intimidation. You've heard the term *nightriders?*"

"Yes."

"It's apt—armed men, often ghoulishly masked, riding by night. The masks, the hoods, the costumes, are to protect their identity, to be sure, but also to add a ghostly flavor. They hope to sweep down like apparitions, feeding a certain amount of superstition and the fear which follows." He laughed. "It sounds silly when you talk about it. One organization called the Ku Klux Klan wears what I swear are bed sheets. Another, the Red Knights—well, they are a bit fancier. They wear a bright red hood and a red satin cloak. You wouldn't catch me dead in such a getup." He laughed again, but his laughter faded quickly. "But it really isn't funny— unless arson and murder are amusing."

She shuddered. "Not hardly."

He hesitated, looking at her, idly tapping the top of his desk. "Look, Danielle, I don't want to give you a one-sided view of this. There is plenty of violence on the other side. The Negroes have guns and know how to use them. They are not about to take this lying down. They want to hold onto their political gains. And they are fighting back, an eye for an eye, that sort of thing, conducting their own raids. The bullet and the torch don't know the color of the hand that uses them. For example, there is one young Negro firebrand named Josh Calhoun. Made a couple of raids we know of. Supposed to be a stemwinding orator. Gets the people all stirred up. And his message is violence—fight back with the same methods the white man uses."

Danielle nodded her head sadly. "I suppose it is inevitable."

"It does make it difficult for us to control—impossible, really. The Red Knights have sworn to get Calhoun. We hear they almost caught him a couple nights ago. Big shootout. Calhoun's band was dispersed, but we hear Calhoun got away."

His words seemed to tear into Danielle like barbs. "Was he shot?"

"We hear he was, but that doesn't mean anything. Every one of these Johnny Rebs thinks he's a direct descendant of Daniel Boone and can't miss. Half of 'em can't hit the side of a barn. Until somebody finds Calhoun and there's a bullet hole in him, I, for one, think they missed him. All I can tell you is that the army is sending out patrols day and night. We're trying to find him and lock him up, before the Red Knights get him."

She sat there a moment, nearly unable to bear her

sinking feelings of despair. Then she stood up, forcing a smile. "I thank you, Bert. I fear I've taken more than a few minutes of your time."

He rose also. "You know it's a pleasure to see you, Danielle. I'll tell Emily of your visit."

"Please do, and give her my love."

He nodded. "Danielle, if I may, is there some particular reason for your questions?"

She paused, then forced another smile. "You must know. It's always easier to cope with . . . with things, when you understand them."

He came around his desk, showing her to the door. "Yes. I hope I've helped."

Danielle raced the horse and rig toward Seasons, her mind a roiling pit of emotions, her mind devoid of coherent thought. But with time and distance, the wind in her face, the strain of holding the reins, the discomfort of the lurching wagon, all brought physical awareness to her body, and she took the conscious action of slowing down. The reduced speed calmed her, and she was able to think.

She still did not know anything for certain. Walt was a Red Shirt, but the Red Shirts were not violent. They were a political organization, getting out the vote. She could not visualize her husband standing stony-faced in a church or meeting hall intimidating Negroes by his presence. And she had no reason to believe he did that.

Nor could she accuse him of belonging to the Red Knights. Walters, the fellow referred to as Carley, those other men out front surely did. But they may only have been reporting some news to him. She forced herself to remember the exact words. *He got clean away, Walt, but I think we winged him. Carley here saw some blood.* Yes, those men could just have been reporting news. Apparently, the whole countryside was buzzing about the shootout with Calhoun. When they said *we*, it did not necessarily include Walt. *We* could have been the

other men. And they did not have to be referring to
Calhoun. But she was certain that was who they meant.

She really didn't know anything. If she were judge
and jury deciding the case of Walter Summers, she
could not convict. And she was not his judge, his jury.
She was his wife, sworn to love, honor and obey him.
Surely, he deserved the benefit of every doubt. Surely,
he was innocent till proven guilty. Surely, he had a
right to defend himself. She must stop it. Ruin lay ahead
if she did not. She must put it out of her mind, keep
busy, think of her duties, not dwell on what would
destroy her marriage.

She drove the rig behind the house, and with the help
of Cassie and Esther unloaded the parcels from the
wagon. "Where is Mr. Summers?"

Esther answered. "He and a couple men are beyond
the far pasture, clearing stumps."

"I see, thank you." She looked at Cassie. "And the
children?"

"Napping."

She walked the horse and wagon to the barn. Many
times, she would have left this task to another, but
keeping busy would keep her mind from dwelling on
painful thoughts. She was quite capable of tending to
the animals. She unharnessed the horse and led it to a
stall, giving it some hay and a little water. As she
turned to go, she saw the lather on its flanks. She had
run it hard. The least she could do was curry it a little.
Besides, it would keep her busy.

She looked around for a brush, but none was in
sight. Walt Summers was nothing if not neat. A place
for everything and everything in its place. But where
did he keep the brushes? Crossing to his workbench on
the far side of the barn, she opened a drawer, then a
second, finding the currying brushes neatly arranged inside. She selected one. Surely, Walt was the neatest man.
He certainly did set an example for her as a housewife.
Almost idly, she opened another drawer, a cabinet or
two.

Wives should not inspect their husband's things.
Wives should tend to their own affairs. In a cabinet,
she found the rifle and holstered revolver he had carried years ago out West. And, on hooks, were a hood
and cloak, both made of brilliant red satin.

Chapter 18

Cassie spent the day in a state of physical and emotional exhaustion. She had slept little in two nights, and
weariness lay on her like a weight. Yet, she hardly noticed it in her preoccupation with the man in the attic
and the assorted fears he caused.

With Danielle gone a good part of the day, Cassie
was able to make several trips to the attic. Josh Calhoun seemed a cinder, literally consumed by an inner
fire. Each time she touched him, she was sure the fire
would have burned out, that he would be cold now in
death. That he was going to die was inevitable to her.
No man could live with such a fever. And she had no
idea what to do. She thought of changing his bandage,
but what good would that do? The bleeding had
stopped. A new dressing would hardly help him.

Nor was Cassie able to decipher her own feelings
about her mysterious patient. Surely, she was afraid
of him. He posed a terrible threat to her and to this
whole family. Walter Summers would drive her from
the house if he ever found out she had harbored a
Negro fugitive under his roof. This she was sure of.

And if Calhoun's accusations against Walter Summers ever became known to Danielle—for reasons she could not fathom, Cassie knew that what Calhoun said was true—the life and happiness of her dearest friend would be destroyed. This must never happen.

Once, Cassie wished Calhoun would die. The problems of removing a lifeless body from the attic were nothing compared to the damage he might do in life, threatening, even killing Summers, confronting him with accusations within the hearing of Danielle. But to wish someone dead—anyone—was horrifying to Cassie, and she quickly drove the thought from her mind, never letting it enter again. She had to hope Calhoun would recover, and soon leave Seasons and not return. But as she touched his forehead, felt his inner heat, she knew the hope was faint.

In this fashion, Cassie got through the day, doing her chores, trying to distract herself with the children, encouraging Esther to chatter away, forcing herself to listen. When Danielle returned from Charleston, she tried to rouse herself. Perhaps Cassie's only real distraction came when Danielle returned from the barn. There was a ghastly pallor to her face, and she seemed unsteady on her feet.

"Danny, what's the matter? What's wrong?"

Danielle had a vacant expression in her eyes. It was as though she didn't recognize her, or had suddenly lost her faculties.

"Are you ill?"

A moment longer, Danielle looked at her, eyes probing through her, unseeing. "Yes, I mean no. I . . . I'm going to . . . lie down."

"Do you need help?"

"No . . . I'll be all right. I—I'm going . . . to my room."

Cassie watched her take a few steps across the kitchen. She seemed dizzy, unsteady on her feet. "I'd better call Mr. Summers."

Danielle wheeled. "No! I don't want to see him."

The late afternoon and early evening wore on. Walter

Summers came in from the fields and went to Danielle's room. He came down to report she was all right, just a headache. She was resting. He showered and put on clean clothes. Dinner was served and consumed, mostly in silence. Walt announced he was going out for the evening again. Danielle would know where and what he was doing. Cassie helped with the dishes, took the children for a walk, read to them, gave them baths. Finally, they were in bed, accepting the explanation their mother wasn't feeling well. Yes, she'd be fine in the morning.

At the tag end of the purple twilight, Cassie went up to Danielle's room, expecting to find her in bed, sleeping. She was doing neither, but rather standing, fully-dressed, staring out the window into near darkness. She did not turn around as Cassie entered with the coal-oil lamp.

"Are you feeling better, Danny? Is your headache gone? Do you want some dinner?"

Each question seemed to lie there in the stifling air of the room, unheard, unanswered, unreacted to. Finally, Cassie put down the lamp and went to Danielle, putting her arm around her. "Is there anything I can do?"

Slowly, Danielle turned from the window to look at her. There was, Cassie saw, anguish on her face, a mixture of shock, fear, great inner pain. Slowly, she shook her head negatively.

"Whatever it is, would it help to talk about it?"

Still Danielle stared at her, unblinking. Cassie wondered if the lovely blue eyes were seeing her. Finally, her mouth came open, then closed, no sound having come out. Again, it happened. Finally, the words: "I can't."

Cassie nodded, as though understanding, then with her hands turned Danielle from the window and took her in her arms, resting the beautiful face with the onyx hair against her shoulder. She patted her back. So tiny, so delicate she seemed, so very vulnerable. "You have comforted me when I needed it. I don't know what else to do for you now."

It seemed to Cassie that she held Danielle for the longest time, standing there, patting and rubbing her back. Then she was aware of a movement, a gentle trembling. Danielle was crying, not in sobs, without hysteria, but gently, sorrowfully. She held her a moment, then led her to the edge of the bed and sat with her, still holding her trembling head on her shoulder.

Muffled sounds were heard, distorted by her shoulder. At first, Cassie didn't understand, then the meaning stabbed into her, making her body rigid. "My husband is a murderer." *Calhoun was dead. Danielle had gone to the attic and found him.*

Cassie pulled her head back, unaware of her own wide eyes as she looked into the now-streaming blue ones. She saw the head nod. "It's true. My husband ... is a ... a murderer."

Completely misunderstanding, Cassie said, "No, he didn't. I—"

"It's true, Cassie, it's true. Ohh. . . ."

Danielle tried to return her head to her friend's shoulder, but Cassie wouldn't let her. "He didn't kill him. He—"

"Don't defend him. I know the truth. In ... the barn, I found. . . ." She swallowed hard, struggling for air. "I found ... that horrible hood ... the cloak."

Awareness came slowly to Cassie. "What are you talking about?"

"Walt's para ... paraphernalia ... in the barn. He's a ... a *Red Knight*."

She hadn't been to the attic. She didn't know. This was something else. "What hood? What cloak?"

"Hidden in the barn ... red satin hood and cloak. The Red Knights wear them ... burning and murdering. That's ... where ... Walter is now." A great wail came from her, and Cassie let her collapse to her shoulder, patting her back, trying to think.

Danielle didn't know about Calhoun. But she had found out about Summers and the Red Knights some other way.

"I suspected ... those men who ... came the other

day. I heard . . . what they said. I didn't believe . . . didn't want to . . . couldn't be true. I—I went . . . to Charleston . . . talked to Major Lennon. The Red Knights . . . horrible. I—I still didn't . . . believe. Then . . . in the barn . . . I found. . . ." She was sobbing now, her whole upper body convulsing.

Cassie held her, trying to think. Danny knew. She had discovered the truth on her own. Yet, Cassie's reaction was to protect her friend from her own knowledge. "No, Danny, you're mistaken. It can't be."

"No, I'm not mistaken. My husband is . . . is a murderer. I can't . . . I can't live . . . with him, look at . . . him . . . let him . . . touch me. I can't."

Cassie swallowed hard, trying to quell her own rising panic. "It's not true, Danny. He wouldn't, couldn't."

"It's true. I know it. He's a . . . a Southerner, a . . . Confederate officer. He . . . he believes he's doing . . . right." Another great sob came from her. "But he's wrong . . . so wrong. I can't . . . I won't. . . ."

"I don't believe it."

Danielle sat up sharply, anger that her friend wouldn't believe her overriding her tears. "It's true, all true. Why won't you believe me? There's a man . . . named Calhoun, a colored man. The Red Knights . . . have sworn to kill him. He was . . . shot the other night . . . got away. That's where Walt is now . . . hunting him. I know it . . . hunting him down like a dog . . . to kill him."

Cassie got up from the bed, leaving Danielle sitting alone, and walked across the room, clenching, clasping, twisting her hands, unaware she was doing it. Her back to Danielle, she said, "He's here—in this house."

There was no reply, until Cassie finally turned to look at her. "What are you saying?" Danielle stared at her blankly.

"Josh Calhoun. He's upstairs in the attic."

Danielle seemed unable to register the meaning of the words. "I don't understand."

"The other night—two nights ago—I couldn't sleep. I—I went downstairs to make a cup of tea. He . . .

came to the door—Josh Calhoun. He was wounded, shot. He begged me to hide him. I—I didn't know what to do. I couldn't think. I—I . . . I took him up to the attic. He's there now—more dead than alive."

Danielle could only stare at her, eyes wide in disbelief.

"I'm sorry. I shouldn't have. It was a mistake."

Slowly, Danielle stood up, still staring at Cassie. Then she blinked, which seemed to instill understanding and resolve into her. "Take me to him."

"No, I . . . ."

"I said *take me to him.*" Strength seemed to come to her. She strode to the table and picked up the lamp. "We must go to him."

Cassie hesitated a moment longer, then led Danielle out of the room and up to the attic.

Danielle leaned over him, felt his forehead. "God, he's burning up with fever."

"I know. He seemed better last night. I put the bandage on. He was going to leave tonight. Then, this morning, he was like this, burning up."

"Why the gag?"

"I—I put it in . . . to keep him from crying out . . . being heard."

"Take it out."

As she bent to the task, Cassie heard, "We've got to get liquids into him, lots of liquids. And bathe him. We must bring that fever down, or he'll die. Help me lift him to the bed, then bring water, Cassie, cold water, lots of it."

For the next hour, the two women worked on him, repeatedly forcing water down his throat. At Danielle's instruction, Cassie cut the remainder of Calhoun's clothing off, and they bathed his body over and over with cold cloths.

"He seems cooler now, but we must keep it up till the fever breaks."

"Yes."

"All night, if necessary. Can you stay with him, Cassie?"

She started to say she could, then looked up and to her left. "The window. Mr. Summers will see the light."

"I'll fix it." Danielle left the attic, returning with a hammer to tack a piece of heavy black wool over the window. "That should do it."

Cassie wet and applied a cloth to Calhoun, then looked up at Danielle. "What's going to happen to him?"

"He's going to get well. We're going to get him out of here—as you wanted to do." There was resolve, determination in her voice.

"Danny, I . . . I'm so sorry."

"No, you did right. You couldn't let him die. You did all there was to do."

"But. . . ." Suddenly, she felt utterly tired, defeated. "What are *you* going to do, Danny?" The words were little more than audible.

"I'm going to leave my husband—go back to Aurial with the children, with you, if you'll come. But not until this man is well and gone from here. This is one murder I won't have on my husband's hands."

"Oh, Danny, he's not a nice person. He says terrible things."

"I don't care. He's a human being."

When Walter Summers came home, Danielle feigned sleep. He crawled in beside her, but made no effort to touch her. Later, she arose and relieved Cassie in the attic, so she could get some rest.

The next afternoon, Cassie reported the fever had broken and Calhoun was awake.

"Get as much of this broth into him as you can, and let him sleep."

Cassie looked at the steaming bowl. "Esther?"

"She doesn't know. I'll take care of her. You look after him."

That day, Danielle found resources within herself she didn't know she had. She realized she was being fueled by a simmering anger that left her cold, bitter. She disliked the feeling of callousness, lifelessness, yet she was able to function. She was under control, able to look at her husband, meet his gaze, say what needed to be said. Joylessly, she watched him with the children and was able to restrain herself from snatching them away from him. One day, she would try to explain to them. But at least they would not grow up under his influence.

She knew he sensed the difference in her, but she made no attempt to clarify her behavior. Walt was, in fact, unusually solicitous, repeatedly asking her if she felt all right, was her headache better? Yes, yes, she was fine, just tired. He even helped her clear the supper dishes, knowing something was wrong, but unable to detect what it was.

"I was going out tonight, but if you'd rather I stayed home. . . . ?"

"No, not if you believe what you're doing is important."

"It is, of course, but—"

"By all means, do what you must."

As he was leaving, he embraced her. Woodenly, she endured, but when he tried to kiss her, she turned away. "I'm coming down with something. I'd better not give it to you."

"Tonight," he whispered. "I want to. We both need to."

She swallowed and said nothing, just looked at him.

"What's wrong, Danny?"

She forced a sort of smile. "Nothing." He left her then.

After the children were asleep, Danielle accompanied Cassie to the attic. Calhoun was awake, though obviously sick and still weak. Surprise and fright mingled in his eyes when he saw Danielle.

"I am Danielle Summers. You are a guest in my home."

He glared at Cassie. "Damn you, you told, you—"

"My husband knows nothing, nor will he."

"This bitch will turn me in, she'll—"

Cassie endeavored to shut him up. "You owe your life to her, so be quiet. You were burning up. I didn't know what to do. She did. You wouldn't be alive, except for her."

Danielle saw him look at her, eyes hostile. "How are you feeling, Mr. Calhoun?"

"*Mister* Calhoun, is it?"

"Unless there is something else you'd prefer to be called?"

"How about *nigger*—or *boy?*"

"God, Josh, please. She's not that way. You don't know her."

"I know she's the wife of a murdering—"

"I know all about my husband. I'm here to . . . to try to save your life—make amends, if I can."

He looked at her a long moment. "You talk funny."

She smiled wanly. "I was born in Maryland, reared in London."

"England?" He saw her nod. "Then you're not. . . ?"

"No, I'm not."

"Then how did you . . . ?"

"Marry my husband?" Again, the slight smile. "It's a long story, Mr. Calhoun, and I don't believe any of us have time to recount our lives. The important thing is to get you well and out of here—safely." She watched his eyes, his expression. She was getting through to him. "Unfortunately, you are a very sick man, and likely to remain so for several days. You will be a while in recovering your strength."

"I'm fine. I'll leave."

He made an effort to rise, but groaned and fell back even before the women reached him.

"Lie still, Josh. Have some of this." Cassie began to spoon some broth into his mouth.

Danielle watched a moment, then said, "Keeping you here poses great risks, to Cassie, to me—most especially to you. Have you somewhere safe to go?"

"Yes, over by the swamp—a friend. I got lots of friends. You may find it hard to believe, but people look up to me. I'm a leader."

Danielle heard the pride in his voice. A leader. She knew what kind of a leader he was. She wanted to cry out that he was not one whit better than her husband. But there was no point to it. "Yes, I know of your reputation, Mr. Calhoun. Your friend's house—would it be possible for Cassie and me to take you there by wagon?"

He pushed away the spoonful of broth Cassie held out to him, spilling it on the sheet. "You would do that?"

Danielle again smiled wanly. "I assure you, Mr. Calhoun, I would do absolutely anything in this world to get you out of this house."

He stared at her. "There's a road—sort of. It would be possible, but not at night . . . two women."

Cassie saw Danielle glance at her in amusement, then heard, "You would be surprised, Mr. Calhoun, at our resourcefulness." She brought the spoon back to his lips, watched him take it, swallow.

Danielle looked down at him. "Mr. Calhoun, you need as much of that broth inside you as you can swallow, other food, too, lots of liquids. And you need to rest. Get as much sleep as you can. You are young, strong. Hopefully, by this time tomorrow night, you will be able, with our help, to make it down those stairs and out of this house. We will take you by wagon wherever you wish to go. Do you think you can manage that?"

"Yes. I'll be ready."

"Good. I hope so."

On impulse, she pulled back the sheet to look at his bandage. His hands leaped downward, grabbing the sheet to protect his nakedness. Despite herself, Danielle had to suppress a laugh. "I think his bandage ought to be changed, Cassie. Can you manage, or do you need help?"

"I can do it, Danny."

"Use some of that special ointment. It will burn, but disinfect. You know the bottle I mean." She saw her friend nod. "Mr. Calhoun, Cassie will stay with you for now, and I'll come—"

"I won't need anyone. I'll be all right."

"Are you sure?"

"Yes, I'm sure."

She looked at Cassie, nodding, half-smiling. "I know of two women who are grateful for that. Neither of us has broken any records for sleep lately."

"You've done all this for me? Why?" He spoke to both of them.

"I told you. I want you out of this house—we both do." She saw Cassie nodding agreement even as she turned to descend from the attic.

To Danielle's surprise, she fell asleep almost the moment her head reached the pillow. Yet, she was awake to hear Summer's horse riding up, going to the barn. It was not difficult for her to imagine him removing the cloak, the hood, hiding it away. Or did he remove them some distance from the house, carrying them in his saddlebags?

When he entered the bedroom, she faked several coughs, a couple of sneezes. It worked.

"Where on earth did you get a summer cold, Danny?"

With any luck, by this time tomorrow night, she would already have left him. He would return from his nightriding to find his family gone.

Chapter 19

For a time, Danielle thought her husband was not going out the next evening. He worked late in the fields and supper was at the usual time. When she asked if he was staying home, he said he was, to look after her. He apologized for neglecting her in recent evenings. Danielle was disappointed. She wanted to get all this over with, very much so, yet realized another day of rest would be good for Calhoun.

But Walter Summers seemed so restless, fidgety, Danielle said, "You needn't stay home on my account."

"But I want to."

"I know, but I'm all right, really." Actually, her throat was a trifle raspy from all the forced coughing.

"Are you sure?"

"Yes, very."

He remained reluctant, but ultimately he did ride off into the night. At once, Danielle went to join Cassie in the attic. Everything was ready. Danielle had spoken to Esther, telling her that no matter what happened, what sounds she heard, she was to remain in her room. Then, when the house was quiet, she was to watch the children.

When she arrived in the attic, Cassie looked at her questioningly, and Calhoun asked, "He's gone?"

She nodded. "Mr. Calhoun, do you feel strong enough for this? Or should we wait another day?"

"Let's do it now."

She looked at him carefully. He was lying down now,
but obviously he had been sitting up, even standing,
for he was dressed in an old shirt and trousers of
Walt's that Danielle had provided. She could tell he
was terribly weak, but he had made a surprising recovery. She sensed he had the strength to make it
downstairs, at least.

"All right. I'm going now to bring the wagon. You
rest till I return." Halfway to the door, she turned back
to him. "Are you sure, Mr. Calhoun? It will not be
an easy trip in the back of a wagon."

"I said to do it."

In the kitchen Danielle picked up several blankets
and a basket of food that had been prepared. He might
need it in the next few days. She went to the barn and
spread the blankets in the wagon as a sort of mattress,
then hitched up the horse and brought the rig to the
kitchen door.

The trip downstairs and out to the wagon was slow
and painful, with Calhoun leaning heavily on the
shoulders of the two women. Cassie was appalled at
the noise they made, for she was accustomed to whispering. But Danielle spoke in normal tones, and their shoes
made a fearful racket. She could only guess that Danielle had spoken to Esther. Calhoun was in great pain.
He did not complain or even groan, but his labored
breathing told of his suffering. Cassie's admiration for
Danielle was boundless. She must be as afraid as Cassie
herself was. She must be suffering from her terrible
knowledge about her husband. Yet, she remained outwardly calm, purposeful, thinking of everything. Cassie
knew she could never have done this without her.

They stopped to rest in the kitchen, sitting Calhoun
in a chair, His wound had started to bleed again, the
red stain spreading even to his shirt.

"Do you think you can go on, Mr. Calhoun?"

"Yes. I've lost . . . so much blood—" He winced.
"—a little more won't matter."

A few minutes later, he was lying in the back of the

wagon, covered with a blanket. Danielle and Cassie climbed to the seat and Danielle took the reins. They rattled off into the darkness.

They rode in silence mostly. Once, Danielle spoke. "We sure could use some of that moonlight you and Morgan enjoyed at Aurial."

Morgan. Cassie had not thought of him in days, her desires, her vision of the future lost in the immediacy of fear, worry and fatigue. Morgan, blessed Morgan. Soon she would be back at Aurial and in his arms, this nightmare ended. She had hardly thought of what she had come here for. Now the matter was being settled for her. It was just as well. "Danny, will we be leaving tonight?"

"Yes. As soon as we return to Seasons, I want you to pack a few things for yourself, the children. Just enough for a couple of days. Then we will carry the children out, and in this very wagon take them to Charleston. We will go to Major Lennon's home. He and his wife, Emily, will protect us until we can go to Aurial."

Cassie stared off into the darkness, barely able to make out the forms of the trotting horses. "Are you sure, Danny?"

"Yes. I've never been more sure of anything."

It seemed to Cassie there was a trifle of hesitancy in her reply, but her voice was firm as she spoke.

For over an hour, they rode. Danielle had a rough idea where they were heading, and counted on the horses to follow the road. She was uncertain, however, where to turn off to cross the swamp. But they stopped and questioned Calhoun, who knew.

Walter Summers had agreed reluctantly to one more attempt to find the fugitive Calhoun. His personal opinion was that either Calhoun was dead, had fled the area, or was hiding out in the swamp where they'd never find him, at night, especially. He couldn't go to the authorities, who wanted him almost as badly as they did. And if somebody was hiding him, they were doing a damn good job of it. For three nights, they had scoured a twenty-mile radius. They had forced their way into nigger homes, searched barns, threatened and terrorized the Negro community. But Calhoun could not be found.

It was, in truth, distasteful work for Walt. He was not a personally violent man, and he knew the colored people would one day be needed if South Carolina was to rebuild and prosper. But it was a job that had to be done. It was vital that Wade Hampton be elected, and any means toward that end was justified. Mart Gary had talked to him personally, asking him to head the Red Knights. At first, he had demurred, saying there were others who really enjoyed that sort of thing. Gary had insisted. He didn't want a hothead, a damn fool. As an officer of the Confederacy, it was Walt's duty to lead these men. Duty. Walt had accepted it, but that didn't mean he liked it. He was dead tired from lack of sleep. His nerves were raw from the strain of lying to Danielle. She must never find out. Whatever happened, he must never lose her. No damn Negro fugitive, no Wade Hampton or Mart Gary, no damn election, nothing, was worth the loss of Danielle.

He and his men stood at the shallows where the swamp could be crossed. There were only six of them now, where once there had been over twenty. He was not the only one with faint heart for this business. And this was to be the last of it. They would wait here a bit longer, in case Calhoun or someone who knew him emerged from the swamp. If not, then he was personally going to pack it in. He was so tired he was ready to fall out of the saddle.

"Douse that light, damn you!"

It was Walters's voice, his second in command, a former sergeant who had a real thirst for blood. They stood in darkness, torches out, the shades down on the two lanterns, waiting—waiting for what?—peering into the darkness, listening for any meaningful sound, swatting mosquitoes.

Danielle had been acting strange lately. Her failure

the other night was the first since he'd known her, and it had surprised, even stunned him. And since? All right, he was willing to believe she didn't feel well, the summer cold and all. Yet, something was wrong, he knew. Could she suspect something? No, he was sure she didn't. He had been too careful. Probably neglect. He had been out every night since she came home. What wife wouldn't feel put out? Yes, this damn Calhoun business would end tonight. Then he was going to stay home for a while, repair any damage. Danielle was too important to be risked.

"What's that noise?"

Twelve ears were cocked, intent on the sound.

"There's a wagon coming."

As the wagon approached the swamp crossing, Danielle knew her arms were tired, but she was determined to push ahead and deliver Calhoun to safety. But so hard was she concentrating on the approaching crossing, she had no sense of the men lurking in the darkness, until the horses suddenly stopped and a pair of lights shone in her eyes. She saw a man on horseback dressed in a red hood and cloak bending over, holding the bridle of the lead horse. Then she heard a single word: "Danny!"

She shielded her eyes from the lights with her hand, trying to see. "Walt? Is that you?"

"What're you doing here, Danny?"

She bristled. "It's none of your affair, Walt. Let me pass." She snapped the reins, but the horse, held at the mouth, didn't move.

"What've you got in the wagon, Mrs. Summers?"

She recognized the voice of Walters, now holding the horse. "Let me pass, I say."

"In a minute. Carley, see what's in the wagon."

Torches were lit, extending the area of light. Danielle could see all the men now, their hideous costumes. She knew which one was her husband. "Walt, don't let them do this."

"What have you got in the wagon, Danny?"

"Goddamn, it's the nigger Calhoun. Been shot. I knew I winged him!"

There was a moment suspended in surprise, then horrid words. "Thank you, Mrs. Summers. We'll take care of him now. Somebody get the rope." Walters turned his horse, releasing Danielle's animal. "We need a limb. Shine that light up in the trees."

It all seemed to happen as one movement, the spot-lanterns pointing upwards, Calhoun kicking at Carley as he climbed into the wagon, rising over the seat, grabbing the reins from Danielle and knocking her to the ground, the horse and wagon bolting forward into the water.

Surprise was a factor. A second, perhaps two were lost before someone screamed, "He's getting away," and the lights were lowered. Even then, the wagon was midway through the water, almost beyond the light.

Walt was the one man in a position to shoot. Surprised at confronting his wife, he still held his rifle at ready. The others were looking upwards, reaching for rope, their minds on another task. Even as Danielle got to her feet, she saw Walt raise his rifle, aim.

She lunged. *"No!* You'll hit Cassie." Her words were lost in the crack of the gun, but she grabbed at the barrel just in time to deflect his arm. She clutched the rifle, pulling it downward toward herself. "Shoot me if you must—not them." But these words were lost, too, in a barrage of gunfire. The bullets were fired randomly into the darkness. The racing wagon could not be seen.

"Hold your fire, men."

Danielle, still holding the rifle barrel, saw her husband, his face hooded in red, looking down at her. Then he raised his free hand, and swept the mask from his head. In his eyes, she saw fear, anger, surprise.

Another shot rang out. He turned. "I said hold your fire. That's my best damn team of horses out there." He looked down at Danielle, trying to wrest the rifle from her. But she held on.

"Shoot me, Walt. Me—not them."

They were staring at each other in a test of wills, when Walters shouted, "After them, men! They can't get far."

"No!" Walt turned to his men barking the order. "They'll go right for the swamp. We'll never find them at night."

"We can't let them get away, Walt."

"I know. We won't. We'll find them tomorrow—when it's light." He looked around at his men. "Let's go home—get some sleep."

"But, Walt—"

"I mean it, Walters. I'm in command here, not you."

Arms extended, clutching the rifle barrel, Danielle watched her husband's face, sensing his battle of wills with the men. It seemed to stretch endlessly, hanging there in the night air.

"I guess you're right, Walt."

Walters would not give up. "But he's got the wagon. He'll head for Timbuktu."

"No he won't. The swamp is his only chance. He's wounded. We'll get him tomorrow—easy."

Turning her head to look at Walters, Danielle sensed that behind the hood he was hesitating, wavering, then relenting. He pulled on the reins of his horse to turn it. "I guess you're right. But as soon as it's light—"

"Yes. We'll get an early start. Meet here an hour after sunup."

Danielle watched the men turn their horses, kick their flanks, ride off. Again, she felt the tug of the rifle in her hands, and this time she released it. There was a terrible coldness in Walt's eyes as he looked down at her. Then he bent down and lifted, pulled her into the saddle in front of himself. He discarded his torch, then rode off in darkness with her, toward Seasons.

Chapter 20

She jumped down from the horse at the barn and ran to the house. Esther met her in the kitchen. "What happened, Miss Danielle? Where's Cassie?"

"I can't explain now, Esther. Just go to your room. No matter what happens, stay there."

She bolted past the old woman and up the stairs to her room. She was throwing garments into a suitcase, when he entered.

"What're you doing, Danny?"

The suitcase was on the bed. Without looking at him, she turned from it and strode back to the bureau, opening a drawer. "I'm taking the children and leaving you, Walt—this very night."

"No, you're not."

She heard the steel in his voice, but, strangely calm, she neither reacted to it nor looked at him. "I'm not one of your Red Knights, Walt. You'll not issue orders to me."

"What were you doing with Calhoun?"

"What did it look like I was doing? I was hiding him from you."

"How did you know about him?"

"The whole county—the whole state—knows about you and Calhoun."

"How did you happen to be with him?"

She made a trip back to the suitcase, haphazardly

shoving her undergarments into it. "It's simple, Walt. You'll be surprised to know he's been upstairs in the attic for three days."

"Here?"

"Yes. You'll be even more surprised to know that just because a man's skin is black, it doesn't make him dumb. After you shot him, he came here, made Cassie hide him. He told her the hunter never looks for the fox in his own yard. Clever of him, don't you think?"

There was silence for a moment, as she crossed again to the bureau, dipping into another drawer.

"Don't leave me, Danny—please."

The command was gone from his voice, replaced by pleading. She was not affected by either. "I am. I cannot remain here, knowing what I do now."

"What d'you know?"

"That you command the infamous Red Knights, that you're a nightrider, a burning, murdering, terrorizing nightrider."

He sighed. "When did you find out?"

"I guess when your *friends*—" she made the word drip sarcasm, "—came to the door the other day. I was certain when I found your costume in the barn. I wish I could say you look good in red, but you don't—not to me."

She turned back to the suitcase. She still did not even glance at him, nonetheless she sensed his discomfort.

"I can explain, Danny."

"Don't bother. I don't want to know."

"Danny, I'm not a murderer, a lyncher. You must know that. But it's a . . . a job that has to be done. This election is vital. This state is being destroyed by corruption, by carpetbaggers and nig—and colored folks who don't know what they're doing. Look at us, the way we live. We're practically paupers, groveling in the dirt, no money, hardly enough food. I love you, Danny. I want only the best for you, the children. The only way is to return this state to its rightful leaders. Can't you understand that?"

She went to the chifferobe, opened it, extracted a dress. "I understand, all right."

"I'm not the only one, Danny. Our people have been murdered, kidnapped. The army turns a blind eye to that."

"I understand that, too."

He watched her fold the dress, lay it in the suitcase. "Then why are you doing this—packing?"

"To leave you. Didn't you hear me?"

"But why? God, Danny, I love you—only you."

"But you're a murderer. I can't live with a murderer."

"Danny, listen to me. I—I don't know that I've killed anyone."

She turned, looked at him for the first time, her eyes hard, mocking. "You mean you don't know if the actual bullet from your gun took the life. Does it matter? You shot."

"Yes, it matters."

She turned away from him, back for another dress. "To you, perhaps, not to me. You raised your rifle and shot tonight. You would have killed Calhoun or Cassie, if I hadn't stopped you." She sensed him coming toward her and turned, facing him down with her eyes, her voice. "Don't touch me, Walt. I won't be touched by a murderer."

He stopped, dropping his hands, shaking his head in frustration. "Danny, you're being foolish. I killed men in the war. Does that make me a murderer?"

"Perhaps. I don't know and I don't care." She jerked a gown from a hanger, and twisted past him to the suitcase. "I suggest you go downstairs, leave me alone. I'll be gone in a few minutes."

A new argument came to him. "Did it ever occur to you that I might be helping you, your mother, your family? Tilden's a Democrat, on the ticket with General Hampton. I'm helping to elect Tilden. Your stepfather will get a big job in—"

"That's a low point, even for you, Walt. I don't want to hear it. Just leave me alone."

As she folded the dress into the suitcase, she sensed him standing there helplessly. Then he turned and went out of the room. She was nearly finished with the packing when he returned, a large glass of brandy in his hand. It seemed a long time before he spoke, his voice wan, defeated. "Where will you go?"

"To Aurial."

His sigh was deep, prolonged. "They're my children, too, Danny."

"I know. Believe me, they're a major reason for my leaving. I won't have them growing up . . . in this atmosphere, knowing about you."

"I have a right to see them."

"Yes. We'll work out something."

Again, he sighed. "Danny, is it really over between us? Are you never coming back?"

She glanced at him, but only fleetingly. "I don't know. I only know I'm going now."

"God, Danny, I love you—so much. Doesn't that mean anything to you?"

"Yes." She closed the lid on the suitcase. "And I love you—or did."

"Not . . . anymore?" He could hardly get the words out.

"I don't know, Walt. That's why I'm going to Aurial —to think." She fastened the clasps, then stood erect and looked at him, a slight smile on her face. "Life's funny, Walt. Morgan and Cassie are in love—want to get married." She saw that fact register on his face. "I can imagine how that news affects you. What's the word? Oh, yes, miscegnation. Cassie came here to think about it, mull over the problems, ramifications. Now I'm going back to Aurial to do much the same thing— only in reverse."

Their eyes met, great distance between them. "Is there someone else?"

"That isn't worth answering, Walt."

Suddenly, emotion surged through him. "God, Danny, I love you. I can't live if I lose you."

"You should have thought of that earlier."

"I've loved you since the first moment I saw you on the street in London. Don't our years together mean anything? I loved you enough to abduct you, take you to that garret, make love to you. I followed you across the ocean, halfway across the continent, rescued you from that cabin, when you were sick and nearly dead. Twice I rescued you. I went to jail, was almost hung for you. Doesn't it mean anything?"

She looked at him, feeling a lump in her throat, but did not speak.

"I fathered your children, Danny. That has to mean something to you."

"It does."

"God, Danny, what will I do without you? The way we make love—there's no one like you. And only I know how to please you. What will you do without me?"

She shuddered, couldn't help it. "It is something I'll learn to live with. My mother did."

"You can't leave me, Danny. It'll never work—not for you, not for me."

Even as he spoke, he went to his stand beside the bed, put down his empty brandy glass and opened a drawer. When he again faced her, he held a small bottle of clear liquid in his hand. He was unscrewing the cap.

"No!" It was the aphrodisiac from India.

"Yes. You can't go. I won't let you. I'll prove to you, you can't leave me."

She tried to run, but was too slow. In two strides, he grabbed her, pinioning her arms to her sides with his left hand, raising the bottle in his right. "No, I won't!" she screamed. It was a mistake. He inserted the bottle into her open mouth and poured the thick, sweet liquid inside. The speed of his movement surprised her. She tried not to swallow, but he dropped the bottle and clasped her chin in his hand, holding her mouth shut. She tried to struggle, to shake her head free of him. But he was too strong. In moments, she had no choice but to swallow the unwanted fluid.

"Now I'll show you why you can't leave me."

There began for Danielle a time she would never forget, a time that would affect her whole life. He had poured down her throat all his remaining store of liquid, far more than was necessary. It was as if she had consumed liquid fire, burning all the way down, exploding in her stomach, spreading flame throughout her body, heating her to a point she could barely withstand. Her mind knew what was happening and opposed him. She called him "assassin," "murderer," every vile name she could think of. But her body went out of control, reacting in a way she had never dreamed possible. All her senses became enormously magnified, until her own racing heartbeat sounded like thunder, her rapid breathing the accompanying storm. The candlelight in the room became blinding, and when he touched her, torrents of sensation tore through her body. It was unbearable. She screamed. To keep her from waking the children, he covered her mouth. She bit his fingers till they bled.

When he had first given her the potion in the garret in London, a much smaller amount, she had felt hot all over. His hands had been cooling, and she had ached for his touch. His every caress created what seemed like lightning, striking again and again in what she thought of in her innocence as her "woman's place," creating heat, igniting her, spreading into an inner conflagration. It was much the same this time, only everything was much more intensified, much more rapid. Her need to be filled was far greater, and when she was, she felt she was bursting. The fire exploding upwards was a holocaust consuming her, and the violent spasms that convulsed her body seemed to disintegrate her, yet they offered no release, brought no fulfillment. And there was no love in it. She loathed him even as he was doing it. Yet, she was powerless to stop him—or herself.

Danielle had no consciousness of it ending, only of awakening. She was in bed naked, he asleep beside her. Her entire body ached and she felt too exhausted to move. But she did, willing herself to her feet. Somehow, she dressed and went to the nursery, packing a suitcase for the children, awakening them, dressing them. Carrying both suitcases, she led Stephanie and Andrew to the barn, begging them to be quiet, not to ask questions. She loaded everything into the gig, then, nearly collapsing with fatigue, harnessed Mask, Walt's horse, to it.

She remained a week with the Lennons in Charleston. They did not ask, nor did she offer to explain, why she had left Walt Summers. He might be a murderer and now a rapist—hadn't it really been rape long ago in the garret, anyway?—but she would not see him imprisoned. The first day, she was certain Cassie would come to the Lennons, where she knew she would be. On the second day, she was positive. But assurance gradually gave way to hope, then an act of willing her arrival. It was with despair for her friend that she finally boarded the train with the children for Washington and Aurial.

PART III

Miriam

Chapter 21

Pierre Chambeau's gown was delivered to Miriam late Saturday afternoon. Indeed, she had decided it wasn't coming and had made up her mind to wear something else, when there it was. She opened the box excitedly, but when she held it in front of her, she was seized by dismay. When she timorously put it on, she felt singed with humiliation.

Pierre Chambeau had played a private joke on her. *You should go naked, chérie.* She had wondered why there had been no further fittings. Now she knew. The garment he had designed for her was not a gown at all, but a nightdress, an expensive, white chemise. It made the wearer a walking advertisement that she was going to bed.

She stared at her image in the mirror in utter shock. The gown had practically no bodice, just wisps of sheer silk shielding her nipples, held up by tiny, puffed sleeves at her shoulders. There were no stays, no reinforcement of any kind; indeed, very little sewing had been done. If she bent over, she would fall out, she was certain. Her every step, every movement of her arms, was reflected in her breasts. She was all but naked. She was on her way to bed. Horrid man. How could he do this to her?

Actually, the gown was artfully made. The transparent muslin of the bodice—what bodice?—was draped cleverly over her waist and hips, falling to the side to reveal the shimmering slip of white satinet. It came to a short train in back. The matching bow that bound the draped muslin gave the appearance of a bustle. The effect of the gown was of simplicity, softness, utter femininity and—Miriam could not escape it—nakedness. She recognized for just a moment that she might have adored the gown had it not been for her conversation with Chambeau. *You should go naked, chérie.* He was laughing at her with this dress. He was making fun of her, humiliating her. Suddenly, she hated his effete face and disdainful eyes. He did not dress women to make them beautiful, but to make fools of them. He hated women, despised them.

She was unfair. She had demanded a bold, daring gown from him, and he had merely provided it. His disinterestedness was entirely sincere. He wanted only to create innovative fashions to enhance his reputation. In truth, he was ahead of his time. His enormous prices reflected the fact that few women had the courage to wear his creations, although a reasonable number would have liked to, if they had the figure or their husbands would permit it. The gown he made for Miriam was indeed beautiful. Only a girl as young and beautiful and innocent as she could wear it—or so he had thought.

Miriam's pique at the gown was a product of her mounting apprehension over the evening. If three nights before, as she intended, Blakeley had taken her to his bedchamber, her anger at Morgan Kingston, her newfound resolve would have accompanied her there. But two days of waiting and wondering had diminished her anger, weakened her resolve. Oh, it had not disappeared, but it was now more contrived. She had to tell herself, repeatedly, how angry she was at Morgan, how much more she wanted money than love, how she would use her beauty and body to restore the Prentiss wealth. She would be a courtesan. Yes, that was her destiny. The day after tomorrow, tomorrow, this night would begin it. Miriam was tough-minded. She could force her thoughts to obey her will, and her will was strong. Yet, by Saturday night, her anger cooled, her momentary brittleness dissolved, her zest for the role she had elected to play had vanished. Shoved aside, submerged, was the knowledge that she was scared to death.

"My dear, such an exquisite gown."

In the mirror, Miriam saw her grandmother entering the bedroom, delight—or was it surprise?—registering on her wrinkled face. "Do you think so, grandmama?"

In truth, Edith Prentiss was stunned, utterly disconcerted. At her age and with her upbringing, she could not help it. The girl was nearly naked. No proper young woman would ever appear in such a garment. It was unthinkable. But such was Edith Prentiss's financial desperation, she could not admit any of this. Miriam Hodges must this night give herself to Peter Blakeley, or it was the poorhouse for her. The day Miriam left for Maryland, Blakeley had come to her, angrily denouncing her and her granddaughter. He did not like being made a fool of. If this girl did not return and do what was expected of her, the deal was off. He would bother with her no longer. Now, looking at Miriam, whom she really did love, she saw the gown, so revealing, so disreputable, as a savior. Peter Blakeley would be so enflamed by her, she would have no chance but to give in at last.

"It is truly lovely, my dear. Peter will just adore it—and you."

Wandering in the corridors of Miriam's mind, all but unrecognized, was the knowledge that if her grandmother said a single word, cast a solitary doubt, she would remove the gown, wear something else. "Are you sure, grandmama?"

"I've never been more sure of anything in my life, my dear."

Again, Miriam studied herself in the mirror. It really was a lovely gown. And she was really not any more revealed than in the marine-blue satin she had worn so often. If only there were some stays, some support.

She raised her arm to touch the back of her coiffure
and witnessed the echoing movement of her breasts.
You should go naked, chérie. For a moment more, she
dwelled on her anger at Pierre Chambeau, then willed
it aside. More, she willed herself to elevate her spirits.
This dress would serve its intended purpose—serve
very well. Yes, she would go through with it. After all,
Morgan didn't want her. Gone was her reckless in-
souciance, but in its place was a new motive—despair.

What did it matter, anyway? She would have to go
through with this some time, Peter Blakeley would do as
well as another. All men were the same, no comfort
could be expected from any of them, only material
gain. Thus, Miriam attempted to steel herself against
imminent trauma. But something in her young soul
rebelled against this cynicism and disillusion. She hadn't
the martyr's nature, she must find something to look
forward to, hope for. And so, she reverted to an earlier
fantasy.

In the days when Peter Blakeley had been absent,
Miriam had imagined her own seduction, rehearsing in
her mind what it would be like, what she would do,
until, particularly in her bed at night, she felt a flush
invade her body. In her mind, she reenacted her visit
to Aurial, substituting Blakeley for Morgan Kingston.
She wore her blue gown, her most revealing. Blakeley
sent his carriage, brought her to his home for a quiet
supper. His eyes devoured her, his hands leaped for
her, but she laughed, kept him away, yet enflamed. He
offered champagne. She wanted brandy. She could still
remember the heat of it suffusing her body. They went
to dinner. She insisted on filling his plate, bending over
him, laughing as she tormented him. He became too
enflamed to eat and she fed him, licking his lips with
her tongue. She leaned against the table, facing him,
making him eat—so he would be strong. Yes, that was
the way it would be. She would be warm, giddy. Yes,
she would be ready then, ready to enjoy, ready to begin the rest of her life. His hands would reach for her

bodice. She would not stop him, nor want to. She would feel—

"There's the doorbell. I told Hannah I'd get it."

Her grandmother's words brought her back to the present. "Yes, grandmama. Tell the driver I'll be there in a moment."

Again, she studied her image. Her dismay had lessened, if not entirely disappeared. This gown would serve extremely well.

None of what she had imagined was to be. Peter Blakeley did not send for her. He came himself. He was standing in the foyer, wearing evening clothes. She saw him from the top of the stairs, and was surprised, flustered. As she descended the stairs, carrying a small cape and purse, she was suddenly conscious of the exaggerated movement of her breasts with each downward step she took—and that he was watching. She tried to hold her body still, but with no chemise, no corset, no restraint of any kind, there was nothing she could do except endure the eyes she knew were on her. The staircase might have descended to Hades, so long did it take.

"My dear, I've never seen you lovelier."

She had to look at him, the blue-gray eyes, so often lusterless, now shining. "Thank you, Peter."

"The Frenchman has exceeded himself."

She handed the cape to him, then turned—anything to turn away—for him to drape it around her shoulders.

"I thought we might dine at Delmonico's first."

The name buffeted her. She couldn't go there dressed like this. She had not thought they might be seen in public. But, will of iron, she said, "That will be nice, Peter."

They left the house, entering the carriage, a landau. He told the driver "Delmonico's," then settled into the seat beside her. "These two days have been an eternity, my darling."

"Yes."

Suddenly, he swept her into his arms, kissing her

urgently, passion flowing out of his mouth. She had not expected it and was not ready. The moist lips, the probing tongue, the excess of passion, overwhelmed her. She wanted to pull away, stop him. She knew she was shaking, but it was not from desire.

"God, but you excite me."

He needn't have said it. It was clearly so. His hand shook as he opened her cape, reached her breasts, stroking, kneading. His mouth returned to hers and she became his captive, his tongue lascivious, penetrating, his fingers at her risen nipples, tormenting. Yes, all was torment to her. She was not prepared. It was an assault of sensation, an aggression to her senses. And, in his passion, he did not realize that in the darkened landau her hands were still in her lap, clenched until the knuckles were white.

"I can wait no longer. I must have you." He rapped with his cane to the driver. "Take us home."

When he turned back to her, it was to bend to her breast, sweeping her inside him, mouthing, biting. She winced from pain, and involuntarily raised her hand to push him away. But she stopped herself in time. This had to be. Money, not love. There was no other way. It was the beginning of her new life. Will of iron. But as she held his head and turned her body, more to gain relief from discomfort than to enlarge sensation, she remembered another head she had held like this. That had brought pleasure. This. . . . Endure. It must be.

He led her into the house, past a surprised Hadley with the admonishment, "See that we are not disturbed," and up the stairs so fast she thought her breasts were going to bounce out of the dress. Closing the door, he again swept her into an embrace, his mouth ravenous on hers, his body pressed against her, his hips pulsing against hers in a movement the meaning of which she did not fully understand. Still at her mouth, he released her and slid her tiny sleeves from her shoulders, then bent to her, pressing her breasts together, sweeping his face from one rosy nipple to the other, moaning with passion. Sensation swept her, but none of it was pleasant. She was frightened.

He left her standing there, naked nearly to the waist, as he quickly, almost frantically, took off his jacket, his tie, studs, links, shirt. She watched, wide-eyed. It was happening, really happening. All her wondering and, yes, wanting, and it was finally happening. If she had not been so young, innocent and frightened, she might have felt pride that by her person alone, having taken no overt action herself, she had so aroused a grown, experienced man that he was virtually tearing off his clothes. If she were already the woman of experience, the courtesan she was determind to become, she might have known how to restrain him, tease him, delay him until he aroused her. But she knew none of this. She knew only fear.

Numbly, she looked around her. Could she find an escape? There was none. It was a bedroom, a single locked door, a bed, high, large, demanding, already turned down, masculine furniture. She looked back at him. He was kicking off shoes, sliding trousers down over bent knees, hurrying, frantic. Money, not love. Will of iron. It was what she had come for. It had to be. Slowly, she reached behind her back, slid the tiny buttons from their loops. There were not very many of them in Pierre Chambeau's latest creation.

"Lord, but you're beautiful."

There were other words of praise for her body, but they were lost in skin against skin, hardness pressing against her thighs, mouth devouring mouth, and everywhere hands, hands, hands. She was taken to the bed to lie on her back and there was more, a very little more, wet mouth, hands, hands, hands, then he was over her, spreading her thighs. A moment was thrown away to eternity, then came probing, pressure—*God, no!*

It was all a huge mistake. At best, Peter Blakeley was not the most empathetic of men. Indeed, he could be downright insensitive in business dealings, a point of pride with him. But in his urgency, which she had brought on herself by repeated coquetry, he mistook her trembling for desire, her moaning for readiness, her screams for ecstasy, her tears, which came as she lay beside him, for joy.

She had no idea why she wept. She had screamed, not so much from pain as to make him stop his violent plunging, the assault both on her body and on her person. If ever she had felt a deep, instinctive antipathy, it was toward Peter Blakeley. It was too high a price. She couldn't pay it. But she did. The transaction was underway. She could not halt it. Money, not love. Will of iron. Why did she cry? In relief that it was at last over. For lost innocence? Because of the greatest disappointment she had ever known? Because she had been violated, negated, because she suddenly understood, in body and soul, how foolish, how unrealistic, all her daydreams and fantasies had been?

Albeit belatedly, some sensitivity came to him. "Those are tears of joy, aren't they, my darling?"

Wiping her cheeks with her fingertips, she nodded. "Yes."

"Didn't I tell you it would be like this?"

Again, she nodded, but did not speak.

The worst was yet to come. He almost leaped from the bed, ebullient. "Now, on to Delmonico's."

She stared at him in horror. "You can't mean that."

"But of course." He laughed. "You must be starved. I know I am."

Still she gaped. "But . . . but, I can't. I'm a mess, my hair."

"Don't be silly. You look lovely."

There was nothing else but to get up, put on the lascivious gown, accompany him to the famous restaurant. She had time to wash her face and apply powder from her compact. She tried to repair her coiffure, patting and smoothing it, but she knew it was ghastly. As they entered Delmonico's and he slid the cape from her shoulders to show off his companion, she was aware of a trickle of fluid down her inner thighs. No one had ever told her what to do about that. As she followed the maître d', Blakeley a stride behind her, she saw heads turn and heard gasps. She kept her face a mask, but bitterly asked herself who could blame them. Here was a woman wearing a nightdress in public, not signaling that she was going to bed with her escort, but that she had already done so. Damn Pierre Chambeau. Damn Peter Blakeley. Damn everyone, the whole hateful world.

Among those observing her entrance was an older couple with a distant connection to Miriam Hodges. Glenna Morgan Fairchild's normal aplomb deserted her, and her mouth fell open in surprise. She gasped.

Franklin Fairchild turned, following her gaze, his masculine interest registering more pleasure in the girl and her figure than dismay. "Isn't that your—"

"Yes, it is."

"That's some dress she's wearing."

"Isn't it? And please turn around, Franklin. There's quite enough spectacle already."

He obeyed. "But what's she doing—"

"I don't know what she's doing here, or where she got that gown."

"I don't mean that. What's she doing with Blakeley?"

"Who's Blakeley?"

"You know, the Shylock of the East." He saw her lack of understanding, and in a few words enlightened her. His description of Blakeley's business dealings and his social reputation was hardly charitable.

Glenna listened, her distress deepened by her surprise at seeing Miriam. Something was terribly amiss. She didn't know what.

"Isn't she awfully young to go out with him, dressed like that?"

"Yes."

"What are you going to do about it?"

"Nothing, Franklin, nothing." She saw his surprise and smiled. "I don't know about you, dear, but I've lived long enough and raised enough daughters and granddaughters to have learned to mind my own business."

"Aren't you at least going to speak to her?"

"Not if I can help it. Unless they will let us out through the kitchen, you and I are going to spend a long time lingering over dessert and brandy."

Miriam hoped, as she had hoped for few things in her life, that nothing showed, that she looked as poised and unruffled as she had the last time she dined at Delmonico's. Rigid with tension, she hid behind the menu as long as she could, then told Blakeley to order for her. She would be unable to eat, anyway. When the waiter came to take their order, she tried to sip from her goblet of water, hoping the action would distract her from the knowledge of what the waiter was looking at. But, as she extended her gloved hand, she knew it was trembling too much for her to risk raising the glass. She would spill water down her cleavage.

"You seem tense, my darling. Don't be. There's no reason for it."

She forced a smile, but through her teeth hissed, "Isn't there? Everyone is staring."

"Only because you are the loveliest, most elegantly-gowned woman in all New York."

"I'm sure they have other reasons for staring."

He laughed. "That's why I like you. How innocent you are."

"Not anymore."

"In your innocence, you think it shows. I assure you, it doesn't. You are utterly lovely."

She let it go. The subject was distasteful to her.

"I think, my darling, know, in fact, that you have made me the happiest, proudest man in this city."

She looked at him. Happiness? Pride?

"You are everything I've ever wanted, hoped for. I want to shower you with gifts, buy you everything, the whole city. What would you like?"

She opened her mouth to speak, but he gave her no time.

"That Frenchie. He's making you more gowns?"

She nodded.

"Good. And they'd better be as beautiful as this one.

I'll buy you anything you want, dresses from Paris, furs, jewels. Name it and it's yours."

He prattled on. She would move into his home immediately. He'd hire whatever maid she desired. He'd redecorate a room to her taste—the whole house if she liked. He knew a splendid pair of matched bays that were for sale. He'd buy them—and also a fine carriage for her. She would set New York—the whole East Coast—agog.

She only half-listened, for she was immensely uncomfortable. She was smarting and burning a little, and fearful of a stain on her skirt when she stood up. Worse were the eyes, thousands of them. She felt she was being smothered by eyes. All she wanted was for this to end, but it would not, not for a long time, an eternity.

She was determined to go home to her own bed. It was not to be. "Don't be silly. The evening's young."

Yes, young. They returned to his house. Now came the champagne that might have helped her earlier. She asked for brandy. It didn't help now. In the bedroom, he was less urgent, more tender and patient, more romantic in his words and caresses. It was too late, her aversion was too deep. For her, it only took longer to achieve the same result.

Before falling asleep, Blakeley made a mental note. He must send those promissory notes to Mrs. Prentiss. He had made a good deal, most satisfactory, indeed.

Not too many blocks away, Glenna Morgan Fairchild sat at her vanity, brushing her silver hair. It was uncomfortable, and made her arms ache. Usually, Jessie did it, but because the hour was late, Glenna had told her servant to get her rest. None of them were young anymore. Glenna knew she would not have to brush much longer. Franklin would be entering in a moment. She would welcome him. She always did.

She was not disappointed, smiling as he entered, wearing his robe, standing behind her. He offered to brush her hair, and she gratefully accepted. He performed a few strokes; then, hands on her shoulders, he bent to kiss her cheek. "Have I told you lately of the happiness you've brought me? I was so lonely so long."

She raised her hand to his cheek. "I'm just glad we've both had this chance for happiness."

She felt the gentle upward pressure on her shoulders, rose in obedience, turned, stepped from behind the stool and embraced her husband, feeling his ardor. In time, she untied her robe, grateful that her figure could still enflame a man, and that she could still respond. When he led her to the bed, she was grateful that she could still know these joys.

They lay in silence for a time afterwards, both with private thoughts. She soon let him know hers. "You say that Blakeley is an awful person?"

"What a thing to think of at a time like this."

"I've already thought all those other thoughts." She raised her head and kissed his cheek. "I just wonder how Miriam knows him?"

"A vulture like Blakeley always finds the vulnerable."

She continued to think of Miriam, shaking her head slowly as she remembered that shocking gown she had worn, her general dishevelment. The poor child.

All this was characteristic of Glenna. She was a master at seeming to do nothing while accomplishing a great deal, particularly in affairs of the heart. She had done it with Moira when she was an impetuous girl, and with Danielle when she was confused, misguided. "Could you find out?"

"Find out what?"

"How Miriam knows this Blakeley?"

"What's to find out? I probably know already. Edith Prentiss is her grandmother, isn't she?"

"Yes."

"Then she, doubtlessly, introduced the girl to him."

"I don't understand. How would—"

"Edith Prentiss has run through most of the money her husband left her—or so I hear. She's likely been selling off antiques, jewels, paintings and such. I'm sure Blakeley showed up to offer her the lowest conceivable prices."

"Why wouldn't she hold an auction, get a good price?"

"Pride. She wouldn't want people to know. And, she'd wait until other creditors were hounding her before parting with anything. That's a situation made to order for the Shylock of the East."

"I see." She thought a moment. "Franklin, would you find out for sure? You *are* just guessing about that man and Edith Prentiss."

He sighed. "All right—if you promise I can get some sleep now."

Chapter 22

Miriam lay in the darkness like a wounded child. Without willing it, she had pulled up her knees and lay in the fetal position, her back to the sleeping Blakeley, as though trying to protect her body from further harm. Tears rolled silently from beneath her eyelids, down her cheeks, dampening the pillow.

She was weeping, not from physical pain, although she was terribly sore, but from mental anguish. She felt violated, mind and body, and in a state of impotent revulsion. The things he had done. The places he had touched her. And she couldn't stop him. Mother of God, was that always the way it was? She had thought of it so much, dreamed of it, wanted, believed it would be beautiful, fulfilling. God, it was so ugly, repugnant, full of intrusions, invasions, to be endured without protest.

Awful. Terrible. The whole evening had been an un-
mitigated disaster. That dress. That vile gown. Delmonico's. People staring, knowing. Images of herself
at the restaurant sped across her mind. She knew what
the others, seated amid their elegance and luxury, saw
when she entered, and she shuddered. Then came the
cruelest whiplash of all. She was a fool, all kinds of
fool, to think she could be that kind of a woman, to
wear such a gown, to be seen with such a man, to let
him. . . .

Full of revulsion, self-loathing and sudden panic,
she almost leaped from the bed, unmindful of awakening Blakeley. She wanted to scream, run, but she managed to control her instincts enough to wait and listen.
He was sleeping. Now was her chance to escape. She
wouldn't stay in this house another minute.

In the darkness, she found her dress where he had
slid it from her to the floor. But she could not find
her other apparel or shoes. Rather than risk waking
him, she stepped into the gown, forcing herself to take
time to button the back; then, on bare feet, crept from
the bedroom. There was some light in the foyer from
low-burning gas lamps, and she was able to move rapidly down the stairs. Yes, she would go home, to her
grandmother's. She would be safe there. She would
never have to come back here.

Moving quickly, nearly running, she crossed the foyer
to the front door, grasping the brass knob, turning,
pulling. It didn't budge. She pulled harder. Nothing. It
must be bolted. Frantic now, she looked for the bolt,
but there was none. She tried the knob again, jerking
on it as hard as she could. She almost screamed. The
door was locked with a key from the inside. And she
didn't have the key.

Panicking, she ran to the drawing room, which
fronted on the street. She'd climb out a window. Pulling back the heavy drapes, she peered out. Gaslights
illuminated the street, but she saw only the ornate,
wrought-iron bars over the windows. She leaped to a
second and third window. All barred. Then she remem-

bered. He had bragged that his home was a fortress.
He kept money in a safe, but he never worried. His
house was safer than any bank. You could get neither
in nor out. God! It couldn't be. There had to be a way.
Running now, she went to the kitchen. There had to
be a rear door. There was. It was also heavy, and securely locked. Panting for breath, shaking, more desperate than she had ever been in her life, she slowly
padded back to the foyer.

"What are you doing up, my darling? You need your
beauty sleep."

He was descending the stairs toward her, wearing a
light blue robe of silk.

"Come back to bed."

She watched him, open-mouthed. "I—I want to go
home."

"But that's impossible, Miriam. It's the middle of the
night."

"I don't care. I—I want to go home."

He had reached the bottom now, and was coming to
her, smiling. "There's nothing to be afraid of." He put
his arm around her shoulders. "Why, you're trembling."

"Yes, I'm frightened. I want to go home."

He held her more snugly. "How thoughtless of me.
I should have realized, a strange house and the room
dark. Of course, you're afraid." The pressure moving
her toward the stairs was gentle but firm. "There really
is nothing to be scared of. Come back to bed. I'll hold
you till you go to sleep."

"No, I—"

"And I'll leave a nightlight on. Then you won't be
frightened."

She was led back up the stairs, unable to prevent it
from happening, and back into the bedroom. As promised, he turned up the gas. "There. You won't be
frightened now. Just crawl into bed."

She stared at him a moment but obeyed, raising one
knee to the mattress. She heard him laugh. "You can't
wear your beautiful gown to bed, darling. You'll wrinkle
it beyond redemption."

She looked down at herself, confused, uncertain. He came to her, deftly unfastened the buttons in back and slid the gown from her. "There. That's much better. The dress will look nice to go to your grandmother's tomorow to pick up your things."

If only to hide her nakedness, she climbed into bed and pulled up the sheet. As he got in beside her, she turned her back to him in the fetal position, trying to protect herself from what he might do. But he slid against her, his knees bent companionably to hers. His arms came around her and he cupped her breasts.

"Are you still afraid?"

"No." She felt the movement of his hand, the caress of her nipple. "I'm going to sleep now."

The movement of his fingers quickened. "Are you sure?"

"Yes. I—I'm very tired."

His fingers toyed with her a moment more, then became still. "Yes. I'll just hold you till you sleep."

She forced herself then to endure his arm around her, his skin pressed against hers. She felt utterly trapped, a prisoner, but her fear of what he might do next made her lie very still. She concentrated on her breathing, keeping it regular and shallow so he would think she was sleeping. To her surprise, she did fall asleep.

She was awakened in the morning by the door opening, a rattling noise. Then she saw Blakeley and Hadley entering, wheeling a small table laden with dishes and food.

"I hoped you'd be awake by now. I don't know about you, but I'm famished." He smiled at her. "Do you want a tray in bed? Or would you prefer to sit at the table?"

She stared at him. "I—I'll get up."

"Good. I always find it uncomfortable to try to eat in bed."

He waited while Hadley brought in two chairs and finished preparing the table. When he left the room, Blakeley came to her, pulling back the sheet, extending his hand to help her up. She rose, if only to avoid the

bright look in his eyes. "May I say, my darling, you
are lovely in the morning—as I knew you would be.
You truly are a beauty."

She had to face him, look at those glittering eyes. He
clasped her shoulders, then bent, brushing her cheek.
"Good morning, my darling."

"Good morning."

He kissed her neck, her shoulders. "Now let's eat. I'm
starved."

"I—I have nothing to wear."

He laughed. "I'm sorry. I'll fetch one of my robes
for you." He went across the room through a door to
what was apparently an adjoining bedroom, returning in
a moment with another silk robe, this one maroon-
colored, holding it out for her. She slid her arms into
the sleeves, then felt him turning her. He bent and
lightly kissed a rosy nipple, then closed and fastened
the robe, guiding her to the table and seating her. It
was he, not she, who poured the coffee and dished eggs
and bacon, far more than she could eat, onto her
plate.

She poked at her food, swallowing a couple of
mouthfuls, as he ate with gusto. He seemed full of
energy and enthusiasm, prattling on about what a
pleasure it was to have breakfast with a beautiful
woman and how happy she made him.

"Are you still frightened?"

She was, but she shook her head no.

"Good. I knew you were just having nerves—the
dark and all. A little later on, we'll go to your grandmother's house for your things."

She brightened at his words. Yes. She would get
away from him there.

"It's only temporary, mind you. I'm buying you all
new things, the finest dresses in the city. You're going
to have such fun shopping. I want you to have everything you've ever wanted, ever dreamed of owning."

Yes. Her grandmother would protect her, not make
her come back here. That knowledge reassured her,
and she even managed a sort of smile. "That will be

nice, Peter. I like to shop." A thought came to her. "You needn't come along to my home. I can just run over there by myself."

"Don't be silly, darling. It's Sunday. I'm looking forward to spending every moment of it with you."

The morning dragged intolerably to Miriam, but at midday, wearing her evening gown and accompanied by a still ebullient Blakeley, she arrived at the Prentiss house. The woman who opened the door might be old and wrinkled, but to Miriam she was the most beautiful creature she had ever seen, an angel of mercy. "Oh, grandmama," she cried, hugging her close. Against her ear, she whispered, "Help me, please."

But Blakeley was there to be greeted and received. Edith Prentiss seemed confused, looking at him warily. She didn't know whether to remain with him or not.

"We just came to get my things, grandmama." She pulled on the old woman's hand. "Come upstairs and help me."

"But, Mr. Blakeley, he's—"

"Nonsense, Mrs. Prentiss. By all means, assist Miriam. I'll be fine."

"Yes, we'll only be a minute." She left her grandmother and showed him to the small parlor. "You can wait in here, if you like." He seemed amused as she ran from the parlor and led her grandmother up the stairs far more rapidly than she wanted to go.

The door to her bedroom was hardly closed, when Miriam threw her arms around the old woman. "Help me, grandmama! I can't go back there. I *won't*."

Almost as an involuntary gesture, Edith Prentiss patted her back. "What happened, child?"

Her head against her grandmother's shoulder, Miriam blurted out a torrent of words. "It was so . . . so awful. The things he . . . oh, grandmama, I couldn't stand it, but he . . . he wouldn't stop, he made me . . . go to bed and he . . . he . . . oh, it was so awful. . . ."

Edith Prentiss held her truly close then, not to comfort her, but to hide her own elation. So, it had happened—at last. The specter of the poorhouse was re-

moved from her. Praise the Lord! When her eyes filled
with tears, it was not from sympathy for Miriam, or even
gratitude for what she had done, but from pure, simple
and, to her, most blessed relief.

"He made me go to . . . to Delmonico's. People . . .
stared at me. It was so . . . so awful. . . .".

"There, there, dear. I know you're upset, but—"

"Then he . . . he took me to his house and made
me—" a strange sound came from her, as she sup-
pressed a wail, "—*again.*"

Behind her back, Edith Prentiss smiled. Twice. He
could not complain he didn't get his money's worth.
Then she felt the first sympathy for Miriam. Poor child.
He must have been rough, demanding. The poor darling must have been scared to death. Memories of her
own wedding night came to her. Barton Prentiss had
been drunk, cruel. It had been insufferable. But she
had endured, that night and many nights thereafter. It
was a woman's lot.

"I know, dear, it can be unpleasant. But it's something you learn to accept, get used to. It'll be easier
when—"

"No! I won't." She pulled away from her grandmother, looking at her with tear-filled eyes. "I'll never
go back. I'll never let him touch me again."

"You're upset. I can understand, but—"

"You don't understand at all, grandmama. I won't
go back there. I tried to run away last night, come
here, but I couldn't get out. The house is locked from
the inside. This is my only chance. I know it. You've
got to protect me, hide me. I can't go back with him."

Edith heard the urgency in Miriam's voice, but it
only confused her. To give herself time to think, she
again hugged Miriam, patting her back and saying sooth-
ing words, while her mind grappled with the problem.
Peter Blakeley was downstairs. She had made a bargain
with him. It had been fulfilled last night, more than
fulfilled. He must return the notes. If he did not. . . .
Yes. Miriam was frightened of him, didn't want to return. Yes. That was the way.

"Don't make me go back, grandmama. Please help me."

"Yes, dear, I shall." She released Miriam and guided her to the bed. "You just sit here and calm yourself. I'll speak to him at once."

Miriam looked at her, eyes brightening with hope. "You'll tell him I'm not going back . . . I'm staying here?"

"I'll say whatever is necessary, my dear." She marched resolutely toward the door.

Miriam watched her leave, suddenly feeling great relief. She had escaped him. Grandmama would get rid of him. She was safe now. She tried to visualize the scene downstairs. He would be angry, imperious, but grandmama would stand up to him. He could say what he wanted, but it would do him no good. And let him think what he wanted. It was all over now. Thanks be to God!

She wiped the tears from her cheeks with her fingers, then arose from the bed. Almost as an involuntary action, she went to her vanity to examine her face. She saw her image. The dress. The horrid dress. Imagine wearing it in public. She had been foolish, stupid, dressing up in such a costume, going out with a man old enough to be her father, yes, her father, letting him. . . . She shuddered from the memory. Never again. She had learned her lesson. She was Miriam Hodges, nineteen years old. She was going to act her age—not try to be some . . . some femme fatale. She would go to cotillions, meet young people. Morgan Kingston crossed her mind. If he had, she wouldn't have. . . . No, it wasn't his fault. He couldn't help it, he didn't love her. *A colored girl!* No, she cared nothing about Morgan Kingston. He really was a hick, a farmer. There were plenty of young men in New York, lots of them wealthy.

Suddenly, she knew. The way to help her grandmother, rebuild the Prentiss fortune, was through a proper, respectable marriage. She was young, beautiful, came from a good family. She could have a splendid marriage, pick and choose whom she wanted. She didn't need Peter Blakeley. How could she have been so stupid? But never again. It was not too late to start over, begin a better life.

Even as Miriam planned her future upstairs, it was in reality being determined for her downstairs. In the small parlor, Blakeley looked at Edith Prentiss expectantly. "Is she almost ready?"

She rendered a small smile. "I fear not, Mr. Blakeley."

"What d'you mean?"

"I mean my granddaughter is upset, quite inconsolable, crying, sobbing, really."

"But why?"

She detected a slight defensiveness in his eyes, and recognized it for an advantage she would not surrender lightly. "I believe you know, Mr. Blakeley. My granddaughter is a young, sensitive girl, extremely well brought up, sheltered her whole life. She is unaccustomed to . . . to *harsher* treatment."

Blakeley looked at her, his gaze level, a little hard. He now understood what this old hag was up to. It was suddenly a business transaction, one of thousands he had conducted. His lips spread into a slight smile. "I assure you, Mrs. Prentiss, your granddaughter has been treated with the utmost solicitude. I'm sure it is only that she is young and away from her family for the first time that upsets her."

She was about to argue with him, but did not when she saw him reach inside his coat and extract some papers. She recognized them at once.

"I believe I am to return these to you?"

Her eyes widened. "Yes." She reached out a gnarled hand to take them. It was shaking.

Again, he produced a stretched smile, as he placed part of the papers in her hand. "I was rushed this morning. Miriam was so eager to come here and pick up her things. I fear I've had time to sign only half these papers."

She gaped at him. He might have struck her.

His smile broadened. "While you go upstairs and hurry Miriam along, I'll sign the rest of these notes."

She grabbed for the remaining papers, but he deftly pulled them away. "You can't do this. We have a bargain."

"I am a businessman, Mrs. Prentiss, not a fool. Your granddaughter pleases me a great deal, but a single . . . evening hardly qualifies as an equitable bargain."

She stared at him in loathing, filled with anger that he was doing this to her. But such pique was a luxury. Old age, the desperation of helplessness, had taught her well. There were other methods. She turned from him, as though looking around the room. Actually, she was trying to think. "Would you care for a sherry, Mr. Blakeley?"

"What I want is for you to go upstairs and bring down your granddaughter."

Suddenly, she knew, and that knowledge made her smile. "I cannot tell you, Mr. Blakeley, how it pleases me to witness your . . . your attachment to Miriam. She *is* a charming young woman." She saw him hesitate. She noted the momentary confusion in his eyes. "And I am likewise pleased that a man of your tastes, your sophistication, finds her—" Words dropped through her mind, *pleasing, desirable.* "—interesting."

She had prompted him. "Yes, I do find her—you might say I am fond of her, extremely fond. She has brought me much pride and happiness. I find her enchanting and look forward to greater happiness with her."

The fool. He was smitten, and he would pay and pay to have her. "Yes, Miriam is a sweet girl—very affectionate, very outgoing, if only. . . ."

"I have assured you of my regard for her, Mrs. Prentiss."

"And I am sure of it, too, Mr. Blakeley. But it is just that she is so very upset."

"A mere whim. It will pass with proper . . . treatment." He smiled. "I'm sure if you go upstairs, talk with her while I—" He gestured with the unsigned notes. "—affix my signature to these, she will want to . . . to share in the many *advantages* I can offer her."

The gaze of Edith Prentiss lingered a moment on the pieces of paper. She rendered a minuscule smile, nodded and took her leave, mounting the stairs in a state of jubilation. Miriam was standing before the mirror, brushing her hair.

"How did it go, grandmama?"

"Splendidly, my dear. He is most upset. Why, the poor man is positively despondent to think that he—"

"I won't see him, grandmama. I never want to see him again."

Edith Prentiss took her hand and led her to the side of the bed, sitting beside her, patting her hand, a beatific expression on her face. "You poor child. If only your mother were here to talk to you about these things. Just answer me one question. Was he cruel to you? Did he hit you or beat you?"

"No."

The old woman both patted and smiled. "Well, then." In those two words she managed to dismiss all Miriam's feelings, as of utter unimportance.

Disbelief welled within Miriam. "Grandmama, I couldn't *bear* what he did to me, having him . . . touch me, put his hands . . . on my—"

"I know, dear."

"H—He hurt me . . . when he. . . ."

"I know that, too, dear. I am a woman and a mother. I'm sure it was difficult for you—the first time. Mr. Blakeley is so in love with you—quite enraptured, really. I'm sure he was impetuous and, well, demanding. But it is something a woman learns to accept—and take pride in." She managed a small smile. "You are a most beautiful young woman, Miriam—highly desirable to men. You wouldn't want them not to be *interested* in you?"

Miriam stared at her, trying to fathom the meaning of all this.

"It is not important that you enjoy it, believe me. I

never did. Oh, I became . . . *accustomed* to it. I took pride in *doing my duty* . . . for your grandfather. But I can't say I ever *enjoyed* it or looked *forward* to it." She smiled. "Now your mother always said she . . . well, liked it. I never could understand that. Perhaps you are more like me in that regard."

Miriam no longer wondered about her grandmother's meaning, although she clung to her disbelief a little longer. Finally, she said, quiet determination in her voice, "Grandmama, if you are asking me to go back with Peter Blakeley, the answer is no."

The old woman heard the obstinacy in her voice. "My dear child, you are too young to realize what you are saying."

"I'm saying I will *not*."

"Miriam, you are a Prentiss, a Prentiss woman, your mother's child. You have a duty to your name, this family, your future."

"Grandmama, it won't work. I've heard it too many times before." There was a cutting edge to the words, which wounded Edith Prentiss. "Grandmama, I love you very much. I wouldn't hurt you for anything. But you are old and foolish, living in the past. You have . . . no right to : . . to try to live my life for me."

Edith Prentiss stood up, looking away from her, anger flaring. "Impertinence!"

"I'm sorry, grandmama, but I have—"

"Will you be sorry when I'm in the poorhouse?"

"Oh, grandmama, you're not going to any poorhouse. I'll look after you."

The old woman looked at her now, eyes cold. "And when will that start, exactly?"

Miriam rose from the bed, trying to hug her grandmother, but she backed away.

"The man downstairs waiting for you. He—he holds notes. I owe him a . . . a great deal of money. He can take this house, everything I own. He can do it this very minute."

Miriam stared at her wide-eyed, trying to decipher

this. It came to her slowly, an unfolding horror. "Then that's why you . . . ?"

"Of course."

A time longer, Miriam stared at her. Hope died slowly. Then, nausea rolling her stomach, she turned away from her, walking across the room to a window. She forced herself to breathe deeply, struggling for self-control. "All right. You did what you did. But I'm still not going back to Peter Blakeley. I'll borrow the money. I'll—"

"Borrow! Where will you borrow it?" Edith Prentiss's voice dripped scorn.

"From my father, the Kingstons. I'll pay them back when—"

"With what, child? *Think,* if not of me, of yourself, your future."

Miriam turned to look at her, away from the window. "That's exactly what I am doing. There are many fine young men of well-to-do families in this city. I don't have to settle for Peter Blakeley."

"Oh, but you do, you most definitely do—either Peter Blakeley or someone very much like him—maybe infinitely worse."

There was a chill to her words. Miriam shivered. "What are you saying?"

"I'm saying that none of those fine, decent young swains from the better, well-to-do families will have you now."

Miriam could feel her whole body shaking, but was powerless to control it.

"The so-called better people—the ones who thought I wasn't good enough to be a Prentiss, that I was a . . . a social climber—they're the ones who have made an outcast of Peter Blakeley. He's a pariah. No one will be seen with him. He is not good enough to invite to their homes. But—"

"Please, I don't want to hear any more." The words came out of her as though she were extremely weary.

"He loans them money when . . . when they are foolish. They need him, and that is why they hate him."

She looked at Miriam, seeing the pain on her face. "But he is not a bad man, dear. He adores you. He really does. He'll be good to you. I know it. He'll give you—"

"I don't want to hear it."

"You will have a good life. You will be *envied,* for your beauty, your mind, your wealth. Peter Blakeley will be the first of—"

"STOP IT, I SAY! STOP IT THIS INSTANT!"

She screamed the words at the top of her lungs, covering her ears as she did so. Nevertheless, she heard her grandmother say, "You will thank me one day. Of that, I'm sure."

She watched as the old woman went to the closet, extracted a suitcase, opened it on the bed and began to fill it.

"What are you doing?"

Her things were going into the bag, her undergarments and cosmetics, a pair of her shoes, the blue satin gown, an afternoon dress. "I'm doing what is best for you, Miriam."

"No! You can't."

"You won't be sorry, Miriam. He's a good man." She threw other items into the suitcase, then closed and fastened it. "I'm doing this for you, Miriam, only you. All I care about is you, your future. You're all I have left."

It was unreal to Miriam, like a painting etched sharply into her mind: her grandmother by the bed, suitcase in hand, the door opening, Peter Blakeley standing there. His voice seemd to rumble, as though very loud, and yet far away. "I heard a scream. I thought someone might be hurt." He was looking at her. "Are you ready now, Miriam? We really must be going."

He was striding to her, taking her hand, leading her out the door, down the stairs, her grandmother following. .He stopped and took the suitcase from her. "I'm sorry, that's a bit heavy for you."

"You are so thoughtful, Mr. Blakeley."

She saw all, heard all, but as if in a dream, a nightmare she was powerless to wake from. She even saw him stop in the doorway, reach into his pocket and hand some papers to Edith Prentiss. "I believe these are for you," he said.

Chapter 23

Cassie had to blink her eyes twice to be sure they were open. Yes, they were open, but there was nothing to see. She was in utter darkness, an experience she had never had in her life. She had a moment of disorientation and panic, then her other senses detected the odors of dampness, mustiness, the feel of straw beneath her body and she remembered.

Cassie had screamed, or thought she had, as the wagon, Josh Calhoun at the reins, lurched forward into the swamp, racing out of the rim of light created by the lanterns and torches of the Red Knights. She had heard the gunfire behind her and felt, she was sure, the wind of death close by.

By instinct, she held to the side of the seat as the wagon pitched and lurched through the deep water of the crossing, up the shallow bank on the far side, then left along the edge of the swamp. Against the night sky, she sensed trees racing by overhead.

"Stop, let me go!" She screamed it, but he seemed not to hear her over the noise of the wagon. "Let me go, I say!" Still the wagon raced on through the night.

She reached to seize the reins from him, but felt nothing. She reached with both hands. "Holy Mother of God!" He had collapsed over the back of the seat, dropping the reins. The horses were running wild.

Frantically, she bent down, groping in the darkness, nearly falling from her seat, then she found the reins loose on the floor boards, grabbed them and pulled. Her action had no effect at first; then, gradually, she felt the frightened horses slowing. "Whoa, boy, whoa. It's all right now." Within a hundred yards, she managed to bring the animals to an uncertain halt.

She sat in the darkness, shaking from her effort, breathing disordered, not knowing where she was, uncertain what to do.

"You can go now."

She turned to him, sensing he was on his knees, leaning over the seat. He had aroused himself enough to raise his head. The whites of his eyes were visible in the darkness. "Yes, I'll go now."

"Just . . . help me . . . out of the wagon. Then . . . you can go." His difficulty in speaking told of his pain. "You can . . . take . . . the wagon back."

She stood up, touching his shoulder. "What're you going to do?"

"The swamp."

"You can't go there. You'll die."

"I'll be . . . all right."

"No. Water mocassins will get you. And you have an open wound. You can't go in the swamp.'"

"I don't die . . . easy."

"But—"

"Do as I say. Help me." The words were said sharply, obviously costing him great effort. Slowly, she climbed over the back of the seat into the wagon. Supporting him with her arms, she helped him to his feet and started toward the back of the wagon. "Wait here. I'll let down the back."

She had just jumped to the ground and was unfastening the tailgate, when she sensed she was not alone. Turning, she screamed. There were men there, several of them. Against the night sky, she could see heads and shoulders, something sticking up. Guns. They were armed.

"Don't be ascared."

The deep voice hardly reassured her. "Who are you?"

"Who're you?"

She couldn't speak, her eyes, her mind fixed only on the outline of the guns. She saw them lower toward her, then heard, "Answer me."

"Cassie Brown." Her mouth was so dry she could hardly speak.

"Hector . . . is that you?"

"Josh?"

"Yes."

"We figured you dead."

When no reply came from Calhoun, Cassie said, "He almost is. He was shot. He's badly hurt."

"Where he shot?"

"In the side. It came out the back. He's lost lots of blood."

A moment of indecision came then, but it was brief. "Get in de wagon. Look after him."

"But, I—"

"Do like I tell you, woman."

She heard the gruffness of the order, and had no choice but to obey. She climbed over the wheel and back into the wagon.

"Lay him down, stay wif him."

Again, she did as she was told, helping Calhoun to the blankets and sitting beside him, holding his head in her lap. She felt men mount the seat, and heard them flick the reins at the horses.

There began then a slow procession through the night, the horses moving at a walk, as though being led. Other men were walking beside the wagon.

Cassie lost all track of time, but the swaying of the creaking wagon seemed to go on endlessly. No words were spoken by anyone. Touching Calhoun's face, she realized he was asleep or passed out, possibly even dead. She fought against a wave of vertigo, and realized

she was near exhaustion herself. Twice, her head fell
forward and she dozed off, lulled by the motions of
the vehicle.

She was nodding when the wagon suddenly stopped.
She snapped awake and looked around. Against the
sky, she could see the roof of a small shack. A door to
it was opened and an elongated rectangle of light
marked the ground and lit the wagon. She saw men
letting down the tailgate and climbing up. Calhoun was
taken from her and carried inside. She followed, entering a small, bare, sparsely-furnished hut with a single
room, a former slave quarters, obviously. Calhoun was
lying on a small bed. One of the men and an older
woman were leaning over him.

"Is he alive?"

"Yes, but not by much," the woman answered.

Cassie looked at the man called Hector. He was
short, stocky and powerfully built. On his squarish face
was a black, brush mustache, but the head of curly
hair was nearly white. He had to be in his late fifties,
Cassie realized, even sixties, for the deeply-lined brown
face held within it the wisdom and fearlessness of a
man who had endured much. He leaned his rifle against
a chair.

"You the girl from the Summers' place?"

"Yes."

"How come you with Josh?"

"He came there . . . after he was shot. Wanted me to
hide him. Said it was safest for him."

The leathery face broke into a smile, showing broken,
yellowed teeth. "Yeah, Josh he do dat. He's a fox."

"That's what he said, the fox—"

"Go on. What happen den?"

"I hid him in the attic, tried to take care of him.
Dan—Mrs. Summers and I both did."

"The Yankee lady? She knows?"

"Yes." From his expression, Cassie knew she was to
go on. "We had to get him out of there, away from
Seasons. He said he knew a safe place. We were taking
him in the wagon, when we were stopped by the . . .

the Red Knights." She saw him nod. "They were going to lynch him, but he grabbed the reins, raced across the swamp to where . . . where you found us."

He looked at her a long moment, as though appraising both her and her story. "Why you wif Josh?"

"I couldn't get away. It happened so fast . . . when he grabbed the reins."

A bit longer he studied her, finally nodding and turning to one of his men. "Isaiah, you take de wagon back beyond de crossing. Leave it pointin' d' odder way. Make it look like Josh went in de swamp."

Cassie saw the man named Isaiah move toward the door. "Take me with you. I've got to get back."

Hector looked at her sharply. "No. You stay wif Josh, look after him."

"No, please. I've got to get home. I live there. I've got to—"

"I said you stay, woman."

"Oh, please, you don't know what you're saying." She felt no tears, yet the words came out of her in a sob.

"You stay now. Later, you go."

She looked at him in horror. What he was saying was like a sentence, an execution. Her mouth came open to protest, but no words would come out, for her knees were already buckling and she was collapsing to the floor. And then, she lost all consciousness. . . .

Now, lying in the pitch blackness, she remembered. They had brought her to, and she had watched as boards were lifted from the floor of the shack. Calhoun was carried down a ladder, then she was helped to descend. It was a cell dug into the earth, perhaps five or six feet on all sides. She shuddered, both from the icy dampness and the awareness she was in a tomb big enough for two coffins. Calhoun lay unconscious on a bed of straw under a blanket. She was instructed to lie beside him. She did as she was told. There was no other choice. Then the men left, taking the candle. In the blackness, exhaustion won out over fear, and she slept.

Awake now, unaware how long she had slept, she struggled with her panic, forcing herself to lie still in the darkness. But she couldn't keep from shuddering. A tomb. It had been like entering a grave.

She forced her mind to think of something else. Danny. Pushed from the wagon to the ground. Had she been hurt? Probably not. But she was there, surrounded by those men. Hideous hoods, like hangmen. One her husband. He would have taken her home. But would she be able to get away from him? Yes, she would try to get away. Danny couldn't live with him now. She would leave, take the children with her. She was going to an army officer's. What was his name? Lennon, Major Lennon. Then to Aurial. Cassie clenched her fists. She had to get away from here, just had to. Danny couldn't go without her. *Oh, Morgan, Morgan, help me.*

In what seemed a few minutes, she heard footsteps above, and the sound of the boards being lifted. Then came a shaft of light that momentarily blinded her. She was still blinking against it when she saw Hector descend into the cellar. He looked at her, then leaned over her to place his hand on Calhoun's forehead, nodding approval. When he glanced at her again, he said, "Come."

She arose from the straw and followed him up the ladder, watching as he replaced the boards. He was alone in the shack except for the old woman who was placing food on the table: cornbread, a plate of beans.

"Eat."

"What time is it?"

"De sun is half-high."

Of course. He would have no clock, probably couldn't tell time. Half-high. He must mean morning.

"Eat. You need strength."

"Please. I don't want food. Just let me go."

"No. You stay, look after Josh."

"I can't. I don't know what to do for him."

"Doctor come soon. He show you."

"Oh, please. I can't stay here. I have to get back. Danny—my mistress needs me."

"You stay. Josh more important."

"Oh, God." She clenched her fists, desperate to make him understand. "You don't need me." She looked at the old woman. "She can look after him."

"No. Ida's old. She can't climb de ladder." He motioned to the table. "Eat."

She stared at him in frustration, shaking her head, then went to the table. Suddenly, she was ravenous. She couldn't remember when she had eaten last. Between mouthfuls, her strength increasing rapidly, she tried to explain why she had to leave, but he would listen to none of it. Finally, in desperation, she blurted out, "But it's no use. He's going to die anyway."

"Josh won't die. De doctor come soon."

"Oh, God, why is he so important? He's not worth all this."

The old man stared at her, clearly disbelieving what he'd just heard. Finally, he said, "Your skin is colored, but you is not. You have lived too long wif white folks." He looked to the old woman, his wife, for approval. Cassie saw her nod agreement.

"Oh, please, I don't know what you're saying." She pleaded to the old woman with her eyes.

Finally, she answered, her toothless mouth making her words mushy, distorted. "Girl, a man like Josh Calhoun comes once in a lifetime—no, once in a hunnert years—if we is lucky. He cannot die young."

"Please, I don't understand." Again she appealed to the old woman with her eyes, but when there was no response, she turned to Hector. "I want to know. Tell me."

"Josh Calhoun is the wise one, the leader." He looked at his wife for approval, and received her nod.

She spoke. "He is the savior."

"The one who'll lead us. He cannot die."

Cassie was still trying to understand, when the door opened and three men entered. She recognized two from the previous night, one of them as Isaiah. With them was a wizened little man in a torn frockcoat and a battered hat. He carried a black bag and was, without doubt, the doctor.

No word was spoken as the floor boards were removed. Isaiah carried a candle and led the doctor below. In a moment, he emerged. "Build up de fire," he commanded.

She sensed what was to happen and it filled her with horror. In macabre fascination, she tried to follow the men outside, but she was stopped. She had to remain inside in daylight. No one must see her. A few minutes later, she was told to descend the ladder. She huddled in the corner under the ladder as the two men descended, the doctor bearing a red-hot poker.

"Hol' 'im fast."

Isaiah gripped Calhoun's shoulders and arms, the other man his feet, and he was turned to his side. The doctor lifted up the shirt, and in one movement ripped away the bandage, then quickly applied the poker to the wound, first to the back, then to the front.

The screams that came from Calhoun were of primeval agony. Cassie screamed, too, biting her knuckles in horror at what she was witnessing and hearing. The odor of burnt flesh assaulted her until she nearly fainted.

Isaiah and the other men released Calhoun, who had again passed out, and promptly mounted the ladder. The doctor looked at her. "He live now. You bandage. He sleep."

During the next several days, it seemed to Cassie that the doctor's confidence was entirely unfounded. The poker stopped the bleeding all right, but the blackened wound began to fester with infection, and the horror of the cauterization was repeated. Calhoun lay in the subterranean tomb more dead than alive, racked with both fever and chills, often delirious. When he was hot, she applied cold cloths to cool him. When he shivered uncontrollably in the damp room, she sought to warm him with her own body, even removing her clothes so more of her body heat would be passed to him.

It was a purgatory on earth. She was trapped with him, for hours at a time, in the hole in the ground, so claustrophobic she had to bite her knuckles to keep from screaming. She climbed up and down the ladder so often, carrying water, broth, cold cloths, it seemed to her the ladder became the rungs of hell. Her only surcease came when she slept, or during the few minutes at night when she was allowed to go outside. She would gulp in fresh, warm air, and under the stars and beneath the setting quarter-moon, she would pray for release from all this. But she knew it would come only with his death or with his recovery. And it would be too late. Danielle had surely returned to Aurial by now —Aurial and Morgan Kingston.

Chapter 24

Danielle was indeed at Aurial. Her return was not nearly so happy as the last time, especially when she had to endure the expression on Morgan's face as she told him what had happened and that Cassie was lost.

"Believe me, Morgan, no one feels worse about it than I do." She cringed at his reply.

"I know someone who feels much worse." He turned on his heel to leave her.

"Morgan, where are you going?"

"I'm going to find her, bring her back." He spoke while going away from her.

He had come in from the fields when he learned she had returned, and they had spoken in the kitchen. He was now at the bottom of the back stairway. "Wait, Morgan, please." She saw him pause, a foot on the first step. He turned his head to look at her. "Your going won't do any good, Morgan. It won't help."

"That's for me to decide."

"Listen to me. You'll never find her. It's a terrible swamp. Runs for I don't know how many miles."

"I'll find her—if she's there."

"What are you saying?"

He looked at her, anger, bitterness in his eyes, and when he spoke his voice was hard. "You said shots were fired after the wagon. She may be hurt. She may be lying dead someplace. In either case, there's no one to look after her. You left, remember?"

Danielle's eyes quickly filled with tears. "Oh, Morgan, that's hateful. You know I love Cassie. All right, you love her more, but she's my dearest friend. I—I practically raised her."

"Then why'd you leave her?"

She raised clenched fists, as though trying to hit out at something. "I *couldn't* stay, Morgan. I had to think of the children. And there was nothing I could do."

"You could have looked for her—" he hurled the words at her, "—like I'm going to do."

He started up the stairs, but she ran the remaining steps to him, grabbing his arm. "Hate me if you want, Morgan, but for God's sake listen to me. It's a terrible swamp. There are thousands of places to hide. You'll never find her if she doesn't want to be found."

"What're you talking about? She'll want me to find her."

"But she's with Calhoun." Frantic now, her voice rising in pitch, she said, "He's a fugitive, Morgan. The army hunts him by day, the nightriders by dark. He can't let her be found, for then he will be, too."

"Nonsense. She'll get away from him. She's probably wandering around by herself—or dead."

"No. Morgan. Major Lennon took special pains to find her. That's why I stayed the week. She could not be found. Nor her body, either. She's alive, Morgan, I'm sure of it. She's been forced into hiding by Calhoun."

"Okay, then I'll find her."

He pulled his arm from her and started up the stairs. She let him go a few steps, then said, "If the army can't find her, what makes you think you can?" It was the first telling point she had made with him. He stopped halfway up the stairs, but did not turn around. "It's an awful place, Morgan, full of snakes and alligators. You don't know the swamp, you don't know the area, you don't know the people. There's terrible violence, Morgan—everywhere shooting and killing. You'll get yourself lost or killed, Morgan, and you'll have accomplished nothing. You'll not have helped Cassie. You'll only have made matters worse, believe me."

She stared at his motionless back for what seemed a long time. Then he slowly turned to look at her, pain showing in his face. "Danny, I can't just stay here and wait, knowing Cassie is. . . ."

"I know, Morgan. Waiting and wondering is a woman's lot. The man in you wants to charge in, take risks, force a result by sheer determination. I understand that, Morgan." She was pleading with him now. "But just this once, honey, don't. No matter how hard it is, control it. Cassie will find her way back to you . . . to us, if we just give her a little time."

"You don't know that."

"Of course not. No one ever knows anything for certain. But I do know she's strong and resourceful. And I know she loves you very much. She wants to come back to you. She'll find a way."

"How can she?"

"She knows I was going to Major Lennon's in Charleston. She will find her way there, and he'll put her on the first train to Washington. Believe me, that's exactly what will happen. You will not find her if you go down there. All that will happen is that you'll be lost or hurt down there while she's up here." She smiled. "Then we'll have to send somebody to find you."

He looked at her forlornly, and she knew she'd won. Slowly, she extended her hand, beckoning him to come to her. His surrender came with effort, but finally he descended the stairs. She embraced him fervently. "Oh, Morgan, please, don't hate me. I know you expected me to look after her, but—"

"It's not your fault, sis. I guess it just couldn't be helped."

"Any other person would have turned Calhoun away at the door, refusing to help him. But Cassie is too kind, too loving. She'll make you a wonderful wife, Morgan."

Her head was against his chest, under his chin. Above her, she felt him nodding. "It must be so. I can't live without her."

Moira returned from Chicago the day after Danielle arrived at Aurial, and there was another report to be made. Danielle told her everything, the men coming to the door, what she'd overheard, her suspicions, the chat with Lennon, finding the Red Knight costume, Cassie's sequestering of Calhoun, the confrontation at the swamp, Cassie's abduction. She even related the scene in the bedroom, including the potion and Walt's assault upon her.

Moira listened, wide-eyed with shock. "God, Danny, I can't believe it."

"It's true, mother, all of it."

They were in Moira's bedroom, Danielle sitting on the bed, Moira, at her daughter's insistence, in a chair. Now she got up and walked to the window, looking out, seeing nothing. "I believe you, Danny. Of course I do. I just can't believe it all happened, that Walt would. . . ."

"Mother, I saw the costume. Walt was there at the crossing. He—"

"You needn't repeat it." She looked at her daughter.

"I don't doubt you. It's just so . . . so incredible, so shocking that—oh Danny, Walt loves you so."

"I think he loves South Carolina and the unrepentant Confederacy more." She watched Moira slowly nod her head. "Did I do wrong in leaving him, mother?"

Moira shrugged and sighed. "I don't know. I've never had your experiences."

"Mother, I couldn't let him touch me. I hated it when he did the last time, only I couldn't help myself. I couldn't stay there, knowing . . . having my children grow up . . . learning from him . . . becoming. . . ."

"Do the children know?"

"No. They think they're just visiting grandma again." She sighed. "I'll tell them—someday, when I can, when I have to."

"You're not going back?"

"I don't see how I can—not for a long time, not until conditions change, not until . . . I forget."

"Do you love him, Danny?"

The question was asked softly, little above a whisper. Danielle let it lie there for a time. When she answered, her own voice was low. She spoke as though very weary. "I don't know. I did once. I loved him very much. Only a few days ago, I was madly in love with him—the day I returned to Seasons. Then. . . ." She paused for a time, thinking, remembering. "I don't know whether I love him now. I think I must. I once did. Can love die, mother?" She saw Moira shaking her red hair. "Tell me, does love ever die?"

"I don't know, Danny. I have no way to know that."

"Did I do wrong in leaving him?"

"I don't know that, either. If you want absolution from me, I can't give it, Danny. I know there are problems in every marriage. Mostly they work themselves out, with time, if the two love each other and try to save the marriage."

"Then you think I should have stayed?"

"No, I'm not saying that. Perhaps a separation is the best thing. It'll give you both a chance to think." Moira looked at her a moment, then came to sit be-

side her on the bed. "You're my child, Danielle, but
you're a grown woman. Only you can decide what is
best."

"Was it, mother? I don't know."

"Let me finish. You made a decision—a decision to
get away, take time to think. I believe that was wise.
Nothing permanent has been decided, has it?"

"No."

Moira smiled and put her arm around her. "Then
abide by your decision. Besides, I'm glad to have you
here—and my grandchildren. Your first visit wasn't
long enough."

The two women talked a bit then about Cassie,
agreeing they should give Morgan all the comfort and
support they could.

Within her first week back at Aurial, Danielle received a visitor, Benjamin Fairchild. He said he was
in Washington on business and came to Aurial to visit
Morgan and Moira, if she were there. He seemed as
surprised to encounter Danielle as she was to see him.
Moira encouraged him to stay for supper, then to spend
the night. He could stay to eat, but he had to return
to his hotel. He had an early appointment the next day.

Danielle could not decipher her own feelings at seeing Benjamin. She remembered the kiss in the moonlight, her own unexpected response. *Is there someone
else?* Briefly, she forced herself to consider if she had
been treacherous toward her husband. Yet, Benjamin's
surprise at seeing her was unfeigned. She believed he
had not come as a vulture, picking the bones of a
wounded marriage. He was a friend. His conduct was
impeccable, the conversation at dinner irreproachable.

She accompanied him to his carriage to say goodbye,
thanking him for coming, saying she was glad to see
him again. She offered her hand in farewell.

"I can't tell you how surprised and delighted I am
to see you again—so soon. Could I take you out to
dinner? Washington has some fine restaurants, I'm
told."

She looked at him in the twilight, blinking, conscious of his cool hand enveloping hers. "Benjamin, I. . . ."

"Just as a friend, Danielle, I promise. I have no right to more."

She searched his face a moment and removed her hand from his. "'As you say, you have no right." She smiled. "And I have no right to refuse a friend. I'd love to have dinner with you."

All the following day, Danielle had misgivings about her acceptance. She had been impetuous again. Was it becoming a habit? Or had she always had the trait? She even asked Moira whether she should go.

"I see nothing wrong with it, dear. Benjamin is an old friend, practically family." She smiled. "Besides, I think you could use a little diversion. Do you good. It is possible to worry over a problem too much."

Danielle remained unconvinced. Her anxiety was not lessened when Benjamin took her to the Willard for dinner. It was a haunted hotel for her. She had stayed here with Hamilton Garth, as his mistress. She had worn a wicked dress created by Pierre Chambeau. Black satin, as she remembered. Whatever had become of poor Pierre? He had so wanted her to be a courtesan. She took comfort both in the fact that she was not and that the gown she now wore, while stylish, was demure and conventional.

Unconsciously, Danielle began to study Benjamin, measuring and approving his ease in his surroundings, the confidence with which he ordered the best foods and wines, his poise and sophistication, his sense of command over waiters, the business of dining in an elegant restaurant. Benjamin had certainly matured in the six years since they had dined at Delmonico's.

He told amusing stories about the treasury secretary, the senators and congressmen he had met that day, reporting to her the nature of his business in Washington. There was a short discussion of the forthcoming election and what it would be like to have her stepfather working in the White House close to Samuel

Tilden. None of it worked. Danielle remained as tight as a drumhead.

"I fear I am not showing you a very good time."

She smiled wanly at him across the table. "I'm sorry, Benjamin, but I'm afraid I'm not very good company. I shouldn't have come."

"Please, at least let me decide that. Personally, I'm having a wonderful time, just sitting here looking at the most beautiful woman I know." He saw her purse her lips. "I guess that was the wrong thing to say. Do you want to talk about what's bothering you?"

"No." She sighed. "Yes, I might as well tell you. You'll find out soon, in any event." A hesitation. "I . . . I've . . . left Walt."

"I'm sorry."

His reply surprised her. She remembered his words from the garden. *If anything ever happens, I'll try to be waiting.* She had expected him to be elated. He seemed not to be.

He laughed. "You expected me to have another reaction. I'll have it, all right. Later, when I'm alone, I may even jump up and down, turn a few cartwheels in my room."

She had to smile. The image was outrageous.

"I am sorry, Danielle. It must be difficult for you."

She looked at him, blinking hard. "Yes, it is."

"Do you want to talk about it?"

"No, I can't—and shouldn't."

"Was it the political situation down there? I hear there's a lot of conflict between the colored folks and the whites."

"Yes, that was a factor. But I really don't want to talk about it, Benjamin."

"Of course."

They spoke of other things during the remainder of dinner, although the forbidden subject hung over them like a cloud. After dinner, she said she would return to Aurial alone, but he insisted on accompanying her in his rig rented from a livery.

They rode in silence for a time, perhaps half the

twenty miles to Aurial. Then he spoke. "Is it irreconcilable?"

"Walt and I?"

"Yes."

"I don't know."

There was a certain finality in her voice, and he made no reply. They rode in silence behind the walking horse for several minutes.

"Dare I hope?"

The reply was so long in coming, he was certain there was not going to be one. Indeed, he had accepted her silence as an answer, and was trying to interpret its meaning, when he felt her bare hand on his as he held the reins. Her touch was like a bolt of lightning, electrifying his whole body.

"I'm so tired of saying I don't know. Benjamin Fairchild, you are a good person and a true friend. I suspect this has been an important evening. I guess I needed to feel attractive, wanted."

"You are, Danielle—by me, by many men, no doubt."

She took her hand away, to his regret, and they rode in silence for another interval.

"I can offer you no hope, Benjamin. I'm too . . . too confused. Everything has happened so quickly. I—I don't know myself—let alone know what to say to you."

"May I just wait? I fear I'm awfully good at that. Be supportive, give counsel, hopefully not unwise, be a friend when you need one?"

"Thank you, Benjamin. I'd appreciate that."

Chapter 25

Miriam was being held prisoner by Peter Blakeley. Of that she had no doubt. The house was securely locked and barred at all times. When she did leave it, which was often, she was always accompanied by Blakeley or the ever-watchful Hadley. When she suggested she could go shopping alone, Blakeley said there were many dangers in the city and a beautiful young woman needed "protection."

Dimly, Miriam realized that her grandmother was to blame for her captivity. Edith Prentiss had the capacity to take her granddaughter away from all this, but she simply did not. Miriam did not hate her for it. She told herself she was helping her grandmother, restoring the Prentiss fortune, but as the days went by Miriam felt less affection for the old woman, and even occasional bitterness.

In reality, Miriam was her own jailer. Her certain conviction that she was ruined, devoid of a future, was the chain that bound her. There were many times, in stores, restaurants or on the street, when escape was possible. She could have run and jumped in a cab. She could have appealed to a police officer or even a passerby for help. But she was kept from such actions by the knowledge of who she was and what she had become. It would do no good to escape. *It is either Peter Blakeley—or someone infinitely worse.* Yes, worse.

That knowledge, the fear of a bleak future, was the stick that made her obedient to her confinement.

Peter provided the carrot. Hers was a gilded cage, Peter Blakeley a most indulgent warden. He spent money lavishly to make her happy. She had everything she had ever dreamed of. Her closet brimmed with beautiful gowns, many in the height of fashion. Others, by Pierre Chambeau, were exotic and daring, so much so that she created a sensation wherever she went. She was the talk of New York. And it was not just gowns he purchased, but hats and shoes, so many of them, and everything else she needed. She had fur wraps if the night turned cool, and she sometimes wore them even if it didn't. And she sparkled with diamonds given her by her doting and generous companion. There was a sapphire to match her eyes and, after Chambeau concocted a red gown for her, a ruby on a pendant.

True to his word, Blakeley hired a French maid, Mimi, to look after her. She was in her late twenties and highly professional, a genius at coiffures and makeup. Her talents made Miriam look older, more beautiful and far more sophisticated. When Mimi first came, Miriam hoped she might offer some companionship, but this was not to be. Mimi knew hardly any English beyond, "Is bootiful, *oui*" and "luffly, *mais si*," and Miriam knew absolutely no French. Thus, communication and companionship between them remained virtually nonexistent.

Peter's other promises were kept, too. He acquired the matched bays and a splendid victoria, considered the foremost showcase for feminine elegance of the day. When she rode in it during the afternoon carriage parade on Fifth Avenue, she could hear the excited "oohs" and "aahs" from the throng lining the street. He had not yet redone her bedroom to her liking, but at least the decorators had visited to discuss the process. He denied her nothing material; her slightest whim was indulged. Even a casual mention of some item frequently led to its delivery in a day or so. If she had no money, hardly more than change in her purse, she had no need for it. Everything was charged. And when she returned with Hadley from a shopping expedition, Blakeley seemed more pleased by her acquisitions than she was.

Spending his money became for her a sort of balm, applied to a wound that would not heal. Over and over, she told herself that if she had lost her independence, self-respect and happiness, she at least had possessions to show for it. But the bulging closet, the gradually-filling jewelry box, her increasing celebrity status, none of these brought her any lasting pleasure. She was discovering at a young age what money would not buy.

In truth, she was costing Peter Blakeley far more than she realized. Edith Prentiss, quite aware Miriam was underage and could be snatched from Blakeley's home in an instant, wasted no time in obtaining various emoluments from him. Her haste was engendered by awareness that Lawrence Hodges would sooner or later learn what had happened to his daughter and storm up to New York to recover her. Thus, Mrs. Prentiss quickly suggested certain antiques, sacrificed earlier to Blakeley, which ought to be returned, as well as various "improvements" that needed to be made in the house. Her daily requests were a nuisance to Blakeley, but the sums were not excessive to him. He considered it a fair price, a sort of dowry. If the old hag's demands got out of hand, he would simply pay her off and marry the girl.

He truly delighted in Miriam. Once or twice, he wondered why he hadn't done this years before, then admitted he had never found a girl as pliable as this one. He found great pleasure in owning her and showing her off in public. Having this gorgeous creature on his arm, knowing people were staring at them, cleansed away years of slights and snickers. He had, in effect, purchased her. So what? Hadn't Jim Fisk bought the celebrated Josie Mansfield?

Miriam brought him many private pleasures, too. He enjoyed simply looking at her, particularly when she was beautifully and revealingly gowned. He wanted her with him. Indeed, he began conducting more of his business from his home, at which times he wanted her to enter, be introduced, serve drinks, remain for the conference. It pleased him to see how ill at ease she made his "guests." But even more, he enjoyed being alone with her. When they came home at night, he would routinely dismiss the maid. He loved to undress Miriam, savoring every stitch he removed, thrilling at her figure, the softness of her skin. Then he would help her into a filmy negligée and stand behind her, brushing her hair. When he took her to bed, he was already in a high state of arousal. Oh, how she enflamed him! Never had he made love so often or felt so potent. If she was not as responsive as he might like, she had ceased her efforts to deny him. Not that he had minded them. In fact, he had rather enjoyed overpowering her. But he was not worried. She was still afraid. Clearly, she had led a sheltered life. But she would come around with proper "treatment." Thus, he spent most nights in her bed, clutching her with a viselike grip. They breakfasted in the morning, spent much of the day together. Indeed, it surprised him that he had not tired of her. His continuing delight in her told him what a treasure he had found.

For Miriam, it was an unending nightmare. More than his possession, she was his plaything, his toy, his human doll to be dressed and undressed, played with and fondled, sometimes roughly. She thought of suicide, but lacked the courage, and besides, it was a terrible sin. The thought of being buried in unconsecrated ground—perhaps even a potter's field—was horrible to her. Strange that she should care what happened to her body after death, but she did. At heart, Miriam was completely conventional and, in death as in life, longed for all the proprieties. And so, she continued in living death, dejection alternating with anger. She remembered her grandmother insisting that Peter was a good man, and tried to believe it. But she knew he wasn't. It wasn't so much that he was evil as inhuman. In his

business dealings, she knew, he contributed to an increase in human suffering, and it made her vaguely
uncomfortable to be associated so intimately with such
a man. While Miriam herself felt no personal call to
altruistic activity, she was not a malicious person, and
her religious upbringing had given her a sense of the
evil in deliberately causing harm to another human
being. Yet, Peter Blakeley had accumulated his fortune
by willfully causing the ruination of others, Lord knew
how many. Even more keenly, she felt a personal sense
of humiliation and dehumanization by her relationship
with the man. That fishy gaze, those cold, perfectly-
manicured hands, the lipless mouth, his implacable
will . . . he was like some bizarre, fiendishly-constructed
machine, and he made her feel like a machine—his
personal pleasure-machine—as well.

All casualness went out of her life. Gone were the
days when she could just be by herself, relax, let down
her hair, snuggle into a robe and curl up with a good
book. She was to be beautiful every waking hour,
coiffed, made up, perfumed, beautifully gowned. And
she was. He showered her with compliments, again
and again calling her "enchanting," until she felt she
would scream if she heard the word again. Always, she
was on display. Her evening gowns were stunning, but
so revealing it took all her resolve to wear them. Pierre
Chambeau seemed obsessed with nakedness. Even when
her flesh was concealed, the effect was of nudity, leaving little doubt of what lay beneath the fabric and the
purpose for which it was used. There were times when
it took all her will to walk into a public place. Often,
her whole body seemed to blush. Nor was there much
relief at home. He insisted she wear negligées when not
otherwise dressed, even at breakfast or when Hadley
entered the room. She protested, but Blakeley only
laughed, saying Hadley didn't even notice such things.
On one occasion, he even had her serve drinks to his
guests while so-attired. It was the ultimate humiliation.
But wasn't it what she deserved?

If she was his plaything, his pet, she was also his

concubine. He was, as near as she could detect, in a
state of nearly constant arousal. He had become a satyr
to her. At first, she assumed, fervently hoped, he would
tire of her. But it never happened. Her attire, her
constant display of herself, the dressing and undressing
of her was, she now knew, a device for his own excitement. At first, she tried to refuse, making excuses,
flirting with him about "later," but the ruses never
worked. She was trapped. He was convinced she
"enjoyed" it and he was "pleasing" her. Always, it was
on the basis of what *he* was doing for *her*. And fighting
him only increased his ardor. He never really hurt her,
but he enjoyed mastering her. She quickly decided
resistance was self-defeating.

The pretense was the hardest part for her—that and
enduring. She learned to moan and roll her head, the
sooner the better, for the plain fact was that she could
scarcely bear his mouth, his touch, his violation of her
body. But even as she feigned passion, she worried—
about becoming pregnant, about what was wrong with
her that she didn't like what he was doing or respond
to it, about what was happening to her. He was leading
her deeper and deeper into what she thought of as per-
versions, bending her body into strange positions,
performing acts that she did not know occurred between a man and a woman.

Then came the complete loss of herself. Only a few
minutes before, he had spread her thighs and bent his
head to her. Sensation such as she had never known
tore through her. She tried to push and kick him away,
but he was too strong. She could only endure pleasures
she didn't want to know from him, the sharp rise of
tensions, the sudden, cataclysmic spasms within her
body and, worse, his joy in having done it. He didn't
really care about her pleasure; he only wanted to make
himself feel more powerful. She lay beside him now,
weeping silently. He had forced her to finally give herself to him, had exerted his complete control of her
body. All these times she had held back from it, clinging to the one small facet of her life that no man can

compel a woman to surrender—or so she had believed. But he had. There was nothing left of her now. She should have felt pleasure in the sensations, in the knowledge of her womanliness but, as she lay in the semi-darkness, she felt only desolation.

Her future seemed absolutely bleak to her. How had it happened? Only yesterday, it seemed, she had been happy, a young girl going off to spend the summer with her grandmother. No, not yesterday, an eon ago. She thought of Aurial, the majestic, white-stone house nestled amid the trees, the rolling, green land stretching in the distance, the timeless Patuxent lapping at its banks. She loved it, truly she did. She had been happy there, safe, secure, life so uncomplicated. No, it wasn't so. She had hated it there. There was nothing to do. She was stifled, her life wasted amid dirt, tobacco plants and boredom. And she had hated the Kingstons, their success, their happiness, their beauty. They had seemed so superior, and she had wanted only to hurt them, in some way punish them for being happy.

She thought of her stepmother, the usurper of her mother's place, so beautiful, so sensuous with her red hair and rich figure, making her father so happy. She held a moment to a vision of her father standing with his arm around Moira, both of them smiling, happy, her turning her face to kiss her father on the lips so affectionately. Once, that image had burned Miriam. Now her eyes burned with hot tears. Of course they were happy. They were man and wife, living respectably, building a future together. When her stepmother lay in bed, it was beside her husband, a man she loved and respected, a man she could give herself to wholly, without fear or restraint. She was a good woman, a kind woman. She had tried to be nice to Miriam, had suffered numerous rebuffs, yet tried again and again. Miriam was stung with remorse. Oh, what she wouldn't give now for a tender, loving mother. Moira would never have sold her to Peter Blakeley.

Morgan? The mere thought of him made her sob until she shoved her knuckle into her mouth, biting

down to suppress the noise that might awaken Blakeley. This was her private grief. Morgan. She loved
him. She knew she did—now. He was all she wanted
in life. And she could have had him. He couldn't
marry a colored girl. She shouldn't have run off. She
should have stayed and fought for him—for the man
she loved. He wanted her. She had seen it in his eyes,
his hands that reached out for her. He was like all
men, so stupid about women and whom they really
loved. No, *she* was stupid, stupid to have become angry,
stupid to have run off, stupid to give up the one person
who mattered. Oh, how she regretted her folly and
vanity.

"Are you crying, darling?"

She swallowed hard. "No, I'm fine—just going to
sleep."

"Then goodnight."

She felt him roll against her, his arm around her,
clutching her breasts. She lay there rigid, trying not to
tremble, feeling utterly trapped, imprisoned, desolate.

Glenna knew she was imposing terribly on her husband. Poor Franklin. He so needed his rest at his age,
but here she was dragging him out nearly every evening, to Delmonico's, the Hoffman House, the Fifth
Avenue Hotel, the opera, theaters. She would deserve
it if he became angry with her and refused. But he was
understanding, if not entirely sympathetic to her desire
to run into Miriam Hodges casually.

"If you are so worried about her, my dear Glenna,
why don't you take yourself over to that man Blakeley's
house and ask to see her?"

"No, I don't want to do that."

Her efforts to encounter Miriam had been rewarded
with partial success. She had seen Miriam at the Standard Theater on Thirty-third Street during a perfor-
mance of *Trial by Jury* by Gilbert and Sullivan, the
new sensations of both London and New York. Miriam
was standing perhaps twenty feet away, with Blakeley.
Glenna almost didn't know her, so lovely and sophis-

ticated did she look, her hair so artfully done, her
makeup so expertly applied. And the gown. It was
clearly intended to have a Grecian effect. Made of
soft, clinging muslin, it was draped about her body and
wound over her right shoulder. Her left shoulder and
most of her left breast were bare. The gown was shocking, but sensuous. Glenna noticed the gown before she
recognized the wearer.

Startled, Glenna raised her hand to motion to her,
then stepped forward to speak to her. But she stopped.
Miriam had seen her. What halted Glenna was the look
in the child's eyes: fear, panic, pain. The eyes of a
wounded animal. And Miriam had given a quick, short,
nearly imperceptible shake of her head. She was telling
her not to come. Glenna had stared a moment, then
turned away to speak to her husband.

That single encounter left an indelible impression
on Glenna. Miriam, so beautiful, was rigid with tension. And that look in her eyes. Yes, it had been fear.
That girl was terribly afraid of something. But why the
headshake? Why did she not want to talk to her? It was
baffling to Glenna, and she realized she really didn't
know her stepgranddaughter very well. Oh, she knew
her and knew of her, but she spent much of the year
in New York, while Miriam resided in Maryland with
Moira and Larry. And when Glenna did visit Aurial,
her efforts to get better acquainted with Miriam were
rebuffed. The girl was aloof and hostile. Glenna knew
Moira had been having a difficult time with her all
during her marriage. Miriam was far from a bad girl,
but there was a streak of rebelliousness and impulsive-
ness in her that had mystified and alienated Moira. Yet
now she seemed so vulnerable, so defeated.

Glenna had stayed out of it, and now wished she
hadn't. What had that single movement of Miriam's
head meant? A denial, certainly, but a denial of what?
She hadn't wanted to have her approach, speak to her.
Why not? She didn't want to have to introduce her
stepgrandmother to Blakeley? Or didn't she want him
to know about her? Or, perhaps, she didn't want

Glenna to know about him? Could there have been other meanings? Don't tell my father? I don't want him to know what I'm doing? That was certainly understandable. Larry Hodges would have a fit if he knew Miriam was dressed like that, living with Blakeley, becoming the scandal of New York. Fear of what he might do certainly could account for that expression in her eyes. Or was she afraid, not for herself, but for the family? Was she trying to protect them from knowing about her and her notoriety? Glenna simply could not decide, and this fueled her desire to see Miriam again. She would not hesitate this time, but would go straight up to her and speak.

"I'm glad you don't want to go to that jackal's house. But why don't you simply write to her father or her stepmother? She is your granddaughter, after all."

"I don't want to do that either, Franklin."

"May I ask why? It seems to me it is your duty to report—"

"I know it seems that way." She sighed. "And it may not be right, but I have the strongest hunch that I should mind my own business."

"Then I wish you would. Anything would be better than dragging your husband out to Delmonico's—again."

She smiled. "I'm sorry, Franklin. Running into them is like finding—" Suddenly, she stopped. "Why on earth didn't I think of that before?"

"What now?" His voice was pure resignation.

"If you can't go to the mountain, bring the mountain to you. Why don't we have a small dinner party and invite Blakeley and Miriam?"

"Over my dead body!"

"He'll come. I know he will. You told me he's dying to be accepted socially. We'll—"

"That man is not entering my house, Glenna. I absolutely forbid it."

But to Glenna, his words constituted virtual acquiescence, and the next afternoon she was struggling with a guest list. It was a problem, a far greater one than convincing her husband to host the party. She had to find just the right people to be at least halfway decent to Blakeley, while not being too offended to be sitting to dinner with him.

Her ruminations were interrupted by Joe. "There is a gentleman to see you, madam."

Joe was in his butler's uniform, which often made him playful. She saw his exaggerated bow, his dreadful sobriety. Calling her "madam" was too much. She liked it better when he called her "missy" in the jungle. "I'm very busy just now, Joe—too busy for your hijinks, I might say. Who is it?"

Again, he rendered a mockery of a bow. "Someone you know, madam. A Mr. Thomas Hodges."

Glenna's spirits leaped at the name. "Why didn't you say so, instead of . . . of all this tomfoolery. Bring him right in."

Chapter 26

Just about the last thing Thomas Hodges wanted to do was visit his sister. He was still uncertain why he had to, or how he had got roped into doing it.

His month at Atlantic City had been grand. He and his friend from school, Bertie Slocum, had larked about, swimming every day, running on the beach. They had traipsed up and down the boardwalk, managing to stay out of serious trouble. The big adventure had been getting Marylee and Penelope St. Clair to sneak out of the house one night and have a wienie roast on the beach. Marylee was a nice girl, even if she did giggle too much.

He and Bertie had returned to New York in the dregs of summer. Without permission, Thomas had stayed a couple of days with the Slocums at their house off Madison Square. Anything was better than staying with Grandma Prentiss in her mausoleum. He had calculated it carefully. He could pay a duty call on the old lady, then say he had to catch the train for Maryland and school.

He knew about Miriam, of course. He had seen her name in the papers, and Mr. Slocum asked him point-blank if she were any relation. After only a trifling hesitation, he denied his sister. Why should be allow her to wreck his social opportunities? His sister was an embarrassment. No way out of that. But he didn't need to shout their relationship from the rooftops. What she did was her affair. He and Miriam might have the same father, but that was about as far as it went. She considered herself the reigning beauty of the family, heir apparent to their mother. As far as he was concerned, his sister was nothing special. And the way she treated their stepmother was . . . well, he liked Moira Hodges. She was a nice lady, good to him. He didn't care what his sister thought. And if Miriam were taking up with some older guy who had a lot of money, that was her fish to fry. Sister or no, he really couldn't care less. He and Miriam had always been cut from different ends of the loaf.

His duty call on his grandmother Prentiss went better than he had hoped. The simple fact was that he could never warm up to her. Kissing her on the cheek was an odious duty, to be performed as quickly as possible. To him she was a cold, conniving old woman living in the past, doting on misspent pride. Her protestations of affection for him were just empty words. He felt a little guilt that he didn't love her more, but he couldn't. He was his father's son. Long ago, he had

made his choice, accepting the love and warmth offered by his father and the Kingstons.

He arranged to make his visit with Edith Prentiss
mercifully brief, telling a little white lie about how
soon he had to catch the train for Washington. And
he got the impression she would not be sorry to be rid
of him. She did look better than earlier in the summer.
She had a new dress, and she had had her hair done.
The whole house seemed brighter and more cheerful.
He noticed that the Chippendale china closet was back
in the dining room. When he remarked on it—it was
just something to say to her—she said it had been out
for repairs. It looked just the same to him, but then,
that was probably the way with antiques. She also had
a new servant named Zelda, who served tea. Anybody
was better than Hannah.

The subject of Miriam was unavoidable. "How is
she?"

"Oh, she's fine, Thomas, just fine. You'll hardly
know her. She's become very beautiful this summer.
Seems it often happens with young women."

"Yes." He had already decided to wallow in ig-
norance. "Is she staying here with you?"

"Oh, yes. As you perhaps know, she's been seeing a
very fine gentleman, a Mr. Peter Blakeley, one of our
better citizens. I believe he's taking her on the carriage
parade this afternoon, then the promenade at the Central Park Mall. I understand the Wednesday evening
concerts are quite lovely. The best people are there."

He let it go. "Yes, I went once."

He finished his tea, telling hyperbolic stories of his
good times on the boardwalk, then took his leave,
pleading an intransigent railway timetable. When he
kissed her withered cheek, he felt a momentary wave
of compassion for this old, fraudulent woman.

Out of the house, in a cab with time to kill, he
decided to visit his other grandmother, Glenna Morgan
Fairchild. It would be a more enjoyable experience.
She might be white-haired, about as old, and probably
just as conniving as Grandma Prentiss, but she was the

genuine article. What the hell, she loved him. He felt far more comfortable with her.

He was ushered into her parlor, and she arose from her writing desk, coming to him, greeting him fondly, kissing his cheek, saying how privileged she was to have him call on her. She was, despite her age, extraordinarily beautiful, so warm, so feminine—and real. Such a difference in a few blocks. He was so pleased to have his grandmother Glenna for even a half-relative. A celebrity, she even gave him bragging rights.

"How marvelous you look, Tom." It was the truth. He seemed to her to have filled out in the chest and shoulders, become more muscular. He was not the tallest of young men—a fact she knew disturbed him, particularly when he stood beside Morgan. Nor was he graced with particular handsomeness; just plain brown hair, brown eyes, a roundish face. Yet, there was an openness to that face, an integrity—it was indeed a mirror to his emotions—which had its own appeal. Seventeen, not quite eighteen, he was on the verge of manhood, quite a good manhood, she felt. "You look so tanned. Tell me about your summer in the sun."

He did, regaling her with stories. He even told her about Marylee St. Clair, something he thought he'd never tell anyone.

"She's a lucky girl, to be kissed in the moonlight by you."

"It wasn't much of a kiss. She was more scared than I was, I think."

"I've an idea she'll remember it always." Her smile lasted a while, then slowly faded. "Tom, do you know about Miriam?"

He shrugged. "What's to know?"

"She's—"

"I know all that. I mean, what difference does it make?"

"A lot, I think. She's your sister."

He looked down at his hands, then studied his feet. "Grandma Glenna, we're all family." He shrugged

again. "Miriam and I are—well, Miriam and I. Do I
have to explain?"

"No." She did understand. These two children had
come from the same mother's womb, but they were two
different individuals. Close they were not. Moira and
Andrew, while very different, had been confidants.
Morgan and Danielle loved each other dearly. These
two Hodges children were something else. Perhaps it
was because their parents had been so at odds. "Tom,
she needs help."

"Miriam? Help? I think not."

In five words, he had spoken five volumes. He had
summarized her own feelings about Miriam. Yes. . . .

"Tom, she's very young."

"Miriam was born old."

Again, in cryptic words, he had said a great deal.
Miriam *was* old, in her flirtations, in her manipulation
of people. "Tom, I've seen Miriam, twice in fact. Oh,
not to speak to, though I'd very much like to." She
hesitated, trying to find words. "She's scared, Tom,
frightened to death. Of what, I'm not sure." She told
him, or tried to, of seeing Miriam at the Standard
Theater, the look in her eyes, the enigmatic shake of
her head, the denial it implied. She told him of Blakeley's reputation, described him, said he was too old
for her.

"I don't know what this has to do with me. Sounds
to me like what she'd want."

"Perhaps it is—though I find that hard to believe,
the way she looked at me. She was a hunted animal,
Tom, cornered, looking for escape." She saw him
shrug his indifference. "I just think someone ought to
see her, try to talk to her. If I'm wrong and she's
happy, doing what she wants, then so be it. If—"

"Grandma Glenna, isn't it a little late? I've only
been in the city a couple of days, and my sister is about
all I hear discussed. She's living openly with this
Blakeley, who isn't at the top of everyone's popularity
list, I gather. She's his mistress. That pretty well finishes
her, if you ask me."

Glenna smiled. "Youth can be so censorious. Tom, when she finds the man who loves her, none of her past will matter."

"But that's a rather large when, isn't it?"

"Tom, when I was Miriam's age, I'd lived in a sultan's harem and been captured by a jungle tribe." She swallowed hard, struggling against the memories. "There was no woman more damaged than I. Yet, in my lifetime, I've been loved, deeply loved, by three marvelous men, my husbands. My past has not denied me happiness."

"All right, that's you, but—"

"It's every woman, if she wants it to be. Your stepmother—well, I won't go into the details, but she found love, including your father's, despite a past one might say was checkered. Danielle lived with a man here in New York—quite a cad, actually. The circumstances were not much different than Miriam's, I suspect. Yet, Danielle is happily married today, a mother." She saw him weakening. "Tom, if you loved a girl—" she smiled, "—your Marylee you kissed in the moonlight, say, and—"

"That's silly."

"You never can tell. My point is, that if you truly loved her, could it matter what mistakes, what misadventures she had had in the past?"

He sighed and clenched his teeth into an expression of resignation. "I gather you want me to talk to her."

"Yes, at least try. I'd go myself, but I have a feeling I wouldn't be effective. I don't know her very well, for one thing. I'm not close to her."

"Why don't we just tell father or Grandmother Prentiss, let them. . . ."

She sighed and rose from her chair to walk away a few steps, turning her back, struggling for words. Finally, she spoke. "When you've reached my age, Tom, and lived through all I have, there are things you know but can't explain. You sense what must be done. You sort of feel your way, particularly when it involves people. They are not always rational. Everything can-

not be ordered, explained, justified. . . . Oh, I'm not
saying it very well, am I?"

"I think you're saying it too well." He stood up.
"I'll go over there now, try to see her—but I can't
imagine it doing a particle of good."

It was deepening twilight when Thomas Hodges
dropped the brass knocker on the door to Peter Blakeley's house. It seemed a prolonged interval before he
heard the sound of a key rattling a lock, then the
door was opened by a tall, burly man in a butler's
uniform. He offered no word of greeting.

"I wonder if Miss Miriam Hodges is in and if I might
speak to her?" This got no response, either. The butler
just looked at him, his eyes noncommittal. Simple
courtesy was in short supply with this fellow. "My
name is Thomas Hodges. Miriam is my sister. I'm passing through town and thought I might inquire how she
is."

A moment longer the level gaze held him, then came
two words. "Wait here."

The door was shut and the lock rattled again.
Thomas gave his characteristic shrug and waited on the
stoop, examining the front of the house. Bars on the
windows. He looked up. The upper floors, too. Now
that was unusual. And the front door was windowless,
locked from the inside. The place was a fortress.

Ultimately, the door opened again, this time by a
smaller, slenderer man with strange gray eyes. He wore
evening clothes. "May I help you? I'm Peter Blakeley."

"How do you do?" Tom offered his hand, but it was
not accepted. "I'm Thomas Hodges. Miriam is my
sister. I hoped to speak to her."

"What did you want to speak to her about?"

Thomas's instinct was to say it was none of his business. But he saw the wariness in Blakeley's eyes, a hint
of defensiveness. He smiled. "Nothing in particular,
Mr. Blakeley. I'm passing through town. I've got to
catch a train, very soon in fact. I thought I'd just say
hello to her. She is my sister, after all."

Blakeley made a quick appraisal. Her brother. Miriam had mentioned a brother Thomas at Delmonico's that first night. He supposed this young man could be that brother. Awfully young. He disliked the whole idea of Miriam having a family, but there was nothing to be done about it. Yes, terribly young. He could pose no threat. Best not to antagonize him, if he didn't have to. "Miss Hodges and I were just going out for the evening, but perhaps a few minutes won't matter." He opened the door wider, admitting Thomas. "I'll tell your sister you're here. Hadley will show you to the drawing room."

At that very moment, Miriam was upstairs in her bedroom wanting to scream. Indeed, she was quivering from the effort to restrain herself. Pierre Chambeau had created another monstrous gown, another of his exercises in public nakedness. This one was made of pale bluish-gray satinet. Indeed, Chambeau had obviously had his little joke, for the color almost precisely matched Blakeley's eyes, as if all this display was for his eyes alone, or the person who looked at her was to see what he saw. It was a monstrous humiliation to Miriam. She looked like a harlot, and felt like one. Actually, the gown was extremely beautiful, proof once again how much of a trend-setter Pierre Chambeau really was. One day, all women would delight in such a garment, but not in 1876. The skirt was cut extremely narrow, but gave an illusion of fullness because it was gathered in back to form a significant bustle and train. All Miriam could see, however, was the outline of her thighs and hips against the thin fabric, the tight waist and her near nakedness above. There was virtually no bodice, just minuscule wells in which her breasts, raised up, pushed together, nestled.

In truth, except for the narrowness of the skirt, which forced her to take small, mincing steps, the gown was no more revealing than others she had worn. But her reaction to her image in the mirror reflected her state of mind. She was falling apart, and knew it. She felt her nerves were scraped raw, and all day she had been on the verge of both tears and screams. Blakeley was insufferable. He had insisted on having her in the morning, not out of physical need, but out of a desire to amuse himself. For her, it was an agonizing prolongation of being fondled, petted, licked and physically explored, all in the misbelief that she was enjoying it. She tried to get him to get it over with, but he apparently only wanted to play with her. Then a batch of new gowns was delivered. He insisted on dressing and undressing her "to see how they looked." Unable to escape him the whole day, she had been reduced to a quivering mass of nerves. She was desperate for some privacy, some sense of herself, for escape from him. But there was to be none. She was to wear this gown in public. Again, she looked at herself, fighting back tears. She couldn't wear this. She couldn't go on. It was too much to ask of her.

Blakeley entered her room. She couldn't bring herself to look at him.

"Do you have a brother Thomas?"

Now she did look at him. "Yes."

"Is he about my height, brown hair and eyes, quite young?"

"Yes. Thomas is seventeen. Why?"

"He's downstairs asking to see you."

It seemed to Miriam that her heart skipped a beat. "Thomas? Here?" She could feel her eyes starting to fill.

"Do you want to see him?"

"Oh, yes, please."

He watched her warily for a moment. "All right, but keep it brief. Just tell him you're fine—everything is fine."

Thomas Hodges almost didn't recognize the girl who accompanied Blakeley into the drawing room, a girl with blonde hair intricately wound atop her head and wearing a gown that made him blanch with astonishment. Why, she was almost naked to the waist! He saw blue eyes, now bright and liquid, heard a cry, part-gasp, part-sob, and she was running toward him, arms outstretched, taking short steps. It seemed to him her breasts were going to bounce right out of the dress. He hadn't realized his sister had such a figure. Then she was in his arms, kissing his face, wetting him with her tears, and saying his name over and over. "Oh, Tom, Tom, it's so good to see you." Then other words were lost in sobs as she clutched him, her head against his shoulders. She was crying uncontrollably.

Of all the greetings he had imagined from his sister, this was not one of them. He and Miriam had never been affectionate. He had always been the little brother to her, a nuisance, and in recent years their relationship had been reduced to mere tolerance. To have her show up looking as she did, wearing such a dress, then throw herself into his arms and weep nonplussed him.

Blakeley came over, put his hands on her shoulders and tenderly pulled her away. "My dear, my dear, control yourself."

"I'm . . . sorry." She managed those two words.

"I had no idea you were so fond of your brother."

"Ohh, yes." The words came out as a wail, and she again clutched at Thomas, holding him close.

He looked at Blakeley over her shoulder. Her paramour seemed ill at ease, disconcerted.

"How enchanting to have a brother and sister so fond of each other." Blakeley sounded anything but enchanted.

Thomas looked down at his sister's shoulder, then back at Blakeley. "Yes, we've always been very close."

Blakeley pulled her away again, and helped her to sit in a small settee. He gave her his handkerchief, remonstrating with her in a low voice to control herself.

She wiped at her eyes, blew her nose and managed to say, "I'm sorry, very sorry." When she raised her head to look at Tom, she was more composed, although her eyes still brimmed with tears. "Oh, Tom, I'm so glad to see you." She patted the seat. "Please, sit beside me."

Mystified, flabbergasted, he obeyed. As he approached, she reached out for his hand, then held it as he sat beside her, gripping it so tightly her knuckles were white. She would not let go of him.

Blakeley tried to gain control of the situation. With unaccustomed heartiness, he said, "I'm afraid Hadley here has been remiss. Would you like a sherry, Thomas, perhaps a whiskey?"

Thomas looked at him. "I can't stay long, but, yes, I'll have a small sherry."

"Yes, you did say you have to catch a train."

Miriam picked up the cue. "Train? You can't stay?"

"No, I'm on my way to Maryland."

"To see mother."

He looked at her sharply. "You mean Moira?"

"Yes, mother."

Never in his life had he heard his sister use the word in referring to their stepmother. She had adamantly refused. Her mother was dead. This woman was not her mother, never would be. The closest she came to the word was "MaMa," but it was said in derision.

"She's been ill, you know."

"Ill?"

"Yes, didn't you get my telegram?"

Again, he looked at her. There was appeal in her eyes. He felt her fingers grip his hand more tightly. "Oh, yes, the telegram. . . ."

"I was down to see her. She seems better. But she'll be so glad to see you."

"Yes."

"And give her my love, all my love." She swallowed hard. "Tell her I miss her and think of her all the time."

Again, the eyes, the hand. "Yes, I—I'll be . . . sure to tell her."

Hadley came with sherries for them both. Thomas tried to free his hand to take the glass, but she wouldn't let him. He used his other hand.

"I must say it is nice to see such affection within a family." Blakeley was smiling, his voice expansive.

"Yes," Thomas said, "we've always been close."

Blakeley sat opposite them, raising his glass in a

salute. All of them sipped. "This place you're going in Maryland. Exactly where is it?"

"It's in southern Maryland, sir, much closer to Washington than Baltimore."

"Oh, it's the most wonderful place, Peter. The house is so beautiful. It lies on a triangle of high ground between the Patuxent River and. . . ."

Thomas listened as Miriam began a lengthy and glowing description of Aurial and the joys of living there. This was nothing less than remarkable. She had always detested the place and considered it boring. Her pet word was "stifling." Strange, all very strange. As she talked, Thomas looked over at her. Suddenly, he was embarrassed. God, she was naked. The way she sat, bent forward a little, leaning on her leg, he could even see the pink edge of her nipple. How could she go out in public dressed like this?

Her animated description ended. Blakeley said, "Yes, life in the country has its attractions, I'm told."

Silence followed, uncomfortable, unfilled for a time. Thomas glanced at his sister, met her gaze. She smiled, but only with her teeth. Her eyes were saying something far different to him. *Save me. Oh, God, please, save me.*

"I—I went to see Grandmother Prentiss today. She seemed well. Have you seen her lately?"

"Not for a few days." There was a coldness, a distance in her voice. Miriam normally adored the old woman as a "real" Prentiss.

"I also went to see Grandmother Glenna."

"Did you? How is she?" Her voice was much brighter.

"Fine, just fine, beautiful as always."

Miriam turned to Peter. "You should see her, Peter, sixty-five if she's a day, and still absolutely gorgeous. You've probably heard of her, the celebrated Glenna Morgan. She's the wife of Franklin Fairchild, the banker."

Blakeley's interest immediately focused on the name of the financier. "She's your grandmother?"

"Not exactly. She's really our stepgrandmother."

Thomas interjected, "Our stepmother is her daughter."

"And we both simply adore her, don't we, Tom?" The pressure on his fingers became fierce. "Tell her I'm sorry I haven't been to see her. Tell her I will as soon as I can . . . can get away."

He wouldn't have believed his sister's fingers were so strong. "Yes, I'll tell her." He saw Blakeley getting out his watch. "I'm afraid I have to be going."

"Do you have to? So soon? You just got here."

"I know. But I hear they're running the trains on time these days." He got to his feet, pulling Miriam up after him. He held both her hands now, looking at her as they stood apart. Grandma Glenna had been right—she was like a wounded animal. He felt a flood of compassion for this stranger, his sister. "I must say, you sure are a stunner, sis. That's some dress."

He felt her wince, saw pain in her eyes. "Peter helps me pick them out."

The older man laughed. "I fear I can't claim credit, but she does look lovely, doesn't she?"

"Yes, very lovely." He smiled at her, warmly. "I really have to go, sis."

He saw her bite her lips and nod. For a moment, he thought she was going to cry, then, impulsively, she embraced him, kissing him on the lips. In his surprise, he recognized that as another first. She clung to him, standing on tiptoe, her cheek against his cheek. He held her, patting her shoulders, then behind her back he extended his hand to Blakeley. "Thank you for letting me see her."

"Happy to do it." He smiled. "If you are ever in town again, drop in." He didn't mean a word of it, but it was something to say.

Thomas had intended to return to Glenna and give her a report. Instead, he went directly to the train station. Father had to be told, and as soon as possible. He considered wiring him, but it was too difficult to explain in a telegram. He'd rush to Aurial, tell father, and bring him back to get Miriam out of that house.

There was no doubt in his mind that was what she wanted. It wasn't her strange behavior, her crying and smothering him with kisses, her protestations of love for Moira and Glenna, or even her clue—"when I can get away"—which told him. As she had embraced him in farewell, she had said into his ear, more air than sound, "Help me."

Chapter 27

Cassie stood in the shadows waiting for the Charleston street to clear, her eyes fixed on the house across the street. She had been waiting a long time. There was some kind of a party going on four houses down the street, with lots of carriages and people coming and going. But she felt she couldn't risk being seen, so there was nothing to do but wait. Now the party seemed to be breaking up, the last of the revelers leaving. But the lights had already gone on in the upstairs window of the house she watched. After all she had been through, was she going to be too late?

Minutes more, she waited. Finally, the last carriage rattled off. She hesitated, perusing the street in both directions, then covered her head with a shawl and crossed the gaslit street. It seemed strangely bright. She would surely be seen. But she forced herself to walk normally, approach the door, rap the knocker. She waited, then rapped again. Finally, a light came on

downstairs and the door was opened by an elderly
Negress, a servant.

"What you want at dis hour, child?"

"I have to talk to Major Lennon."

"De majer and de missus is asleep in bed, like you
should be."

"I—I have to speak to him. It's . . . terribly important."

"Whasso important?"

"I—I can't tell you. It's . . . private."

"Lookee here, I ain't gonna wake up de majer jus'
cause some slip o' girl wants—"

"FloraMae, who's at the door?"

Cassie heard the male voice from the top of the
stairs. Quickly, she said, "Tell him Cassie Brown is
here."

Josh Calhoun's recovery had been painfully slow,
studded with relapses, and still far from complete.
Cassie knew he would never get well as long as he
remained in that damp hole in the ground. He needed
fresh air and sunshine, far better food that he had
here, and time to rest and recuperate. But at least his
fever was gone, or seemed to be, and he had stopped
hallucinating and re-injuring himself when he thrashed
around on the straw bed. He was able to sit up, take
some food, and talk lucidly. Indeed, he had assumed
control of his destiny. She no longer dealt only with
Hector and the others.

His first lucid moment had come a few days earlier
and had taken her by surprise. She was lying on the
bed beside him in the darkness, when she felt his hand
on her thigh, then his words, "Are you still here?"

"Yes."

"Why?"

"I was given no choice." She sat up, groping in the
blackness for the candle and matches. It was a risk to
light the darkness, but a small one. The army and a
succession of nightriders had been to the shack. They
had not been found. The searchers were unlikely to

come again soon. The matches were damp, but finally one caught. Squinting, she touched the flame to the wick and turned to look at him. He was terribly thin, his cheeks shrunken, his eyes deep in his skull. "Can I get you anything? Food, water?"

"What time is it?"

"I don't know. It's the middle of the night."

He seemed to digest that information slowly. "How long have I been out?"

"I don't know. I've lost count of days." She poured water into a cup from a jug and brought it to him, raising his head to drink. "Will this do for now? I really shouldn't go upstairs till daylight." She saw him nod. "Do you know where you are?"

His eyes searched the tomb. "Yes, I know. Hector's." He coughed a little, then winced with pain. "They used to hide runaway slaves here. It's where I intended to come." He looked back at her. "You didn't tell me why you're still here. It wasn't . . . part of the bargain."

"I said I had no choice."

"Hector?"

She nodded. "I'm going to put the light out. You go back to sleep."

"Yes."

She reached for the candle, but his hand came out to touch her wrist. "I remember someone . . . in bed with me . . . naked . . . a woman. Or was I dreaming?"

"No."

"Why'd you do it?"

"You were cold. I had no other way to keep you warm." He was still looking at her as she wet her fingers and snuffed out the candle.

His strength began to return more quickly after that, as she plied him with liquids and warm food. But his wound remained ugly-looking, and he was far from himself. That's when she told him he would never get well down in this hole. He needed air and sunshine. Finally, he agreed to risk going out of the tomb. He made it, with her help, and in the dead of night, after the moon had set, they sat together on the ground, leaning against the side of the shack.

He was silent for a time, breathing heavily from his exertions. She sensed he was in pain. Finally, he said, "God, it's lovely. I never thought I'd see stars again, feel a warm breeze."

"Yes."

Again, he was silent for a time, looking upward. Then he said, "I'll never get used to these Southern skies. The stars are so different up North."

"Is that where you're from?"

"Yes, Boston."

"What're you doing down here?"

"Oh some people asked me to come down here, help out."

"What people?"

"People I know. Frederick Douglass, for one."

She knew him, of course, former slave, friend of Lincoln, the great leader. He had done more to free the slaves than any man. "Why did Mr. Douglass want you to come here?"

"He didn't say here, this place particularly, but to come South. I was born and raised in the North, my father and his father before him. Douglass felt I should know what life is like here. He felt I could . . . do some good."

"Violence is good? Killing is good?"

"You know about that, do you?"

"Yes."

He sighed, then was silent for a moment. "All right, I know the violence is no good. But you've got to understand. Our people here have been enslaved for two hundred and fifty years. They're docile, afraid. They've got to learn to stand up for their rights, to fight for what's theirs, or ought to be theirs. That's all I'm trying to do—put some fight into them, show them their power."

She made no reply, none at all, until, finally, he prompted her. Then she said, "I don't know. I don't know any of it."

"You don't know what?"

"What you're talking about." She sighed. "I've lived here all my life, and I still don't know. I was born a slave—or so they tell me. I still don't know."

"You've lived in that house too long."

"I don't know that, either."

"You always live there?"

"An army post first—in Charleston. All I really know is that those men, Northerners, treated me well. Then I went to live with Danny—Mrs. Summers. All I know is, she's my dearest friend, and I want to be with her."

"Oh, yes, Captain Summers's good wife," he said sardonically.

"You owe your life to her. You wouldn't be here without her. She risked everything for you, her home, her marriage, her happiness. And all you give back is hate—just because her skin is white."

He was silent so long, she finally said, "We'd better go back inside."

"Do you ever look in a mirror—see that beautiful brown skin of yours?"

"Of course."

"You can't escape it, Cassie, not in this country, no matter how hard you try."

She felt him move beside her and thought he was getting up. Instead, he leaned toward her. When she realized what he was going to do, it was too late. Her "No, please" was futile. Perhaps it was the lingering residue of his fever that made his mouth so hot on hers. Heat passed from her lips throughout her body. It was as though she were receiving a contagion.

"That's for keeping me warm."

"Please. You don't know what you're doing."

"Oh, yes, I do."

His mouth, soft, moving, scalding with heat, came to hers again. She felt as though she were being baked from the inside. She tried to fight him, pushing against him, but it was to no avail. He held her head fast within the crook of his arm, and her struggles were useless.

Perhaps if she had pushed harder, perhaps if she had actually struck with the fists she raised, but she didn't, then she couldn't. The heat from him seemed to melt her resistance, then her will. She heard him speak. "God, such lips." Then he was electrifying her with tender little kisses, nibbles, licks at the corners of her mouth, the insides of her lips, along her teeth, her tongue, melting all. She felt him fumbling with the front of her dress, unbuttoning, then his hand, like soft fire, at her breasts.

She hungered for it. There was no escape from her own desire, her great need. Perhaps it was the soft night, the sense of freedom in being out of that hole that sheltered them, her loneliness, despair, her simple human need to reach out and touch another human being. Whatever the reason, she wanted what happened to her, the warmth and tender caresses, the sense of being beautiful, desirable and womanly, the surrendering, if only for a moment, to forces too powerful to struggle against. Yes, she was so weary of struggling against circumstances, against all the dangers that lay around them. She longed for tenderness and oblivion —and he offered it. Her moment of passion and fulfillment there on the warm soil of South Carolina was, more than anything else, simple surcease from fear, a moment for herself amid a million moments given to others. Perhaps because it was dark, she had no sense of being with Calhoun, indeed with anyone. Hers was almost disembodied pleasure. It was a force more than a person that entered her and propelled her past knowledge or even awareness.

Reality had to come sometime. They were back in the hole. By the light of the candle, she looked at him. "Why did you do that?"

He smiled. "Again, I ask if you've looked in a mirror? You're so beautiful, Cassie."

She said nothing. No words would form in her mind.

"And we're tired and lonely, sick in body and in spirit, two hunted animals living in a hole in the ground.

God gave us this to use when there is nothing left for two human beings."

She stared at him. "God? You believe in God?"

"I'm an ordained minister, Cassie—Baptist."

"Then pray for me. I love another."

Her decision to go to Major Lennon was made at that precise moment. As she lay in the darkness, she worked out how to do it. She would simply tell Calhoun he didn't need her any longer. He was well enough for her to leave, and she would leave.

Major Lennon and his wife Emily both got up, welcoming her, insisting she have tea. Pressed for details —"We thought you were dead"—Cassie told the truth. "Josh Calhoun and I have been in hiding. I was forced to stay with him till he recovered from his wounds."

"You poor child."

"Where is the blackguard? We've looked everywhere for him."

"I won't tell you that, major. There's no point in killing him."

"He won't be killed, but he'll be locked up so he won't do any more damage. Where is he?"

"I can't tell you."

The army officer's voice took on an edge. "Miss Brown, I understand you've been through a lot. But you must tell me where Calhoun is."

"Bert, please, don't badger the child."

He turned to his wife. "I'm not badgering her, Emily. I'm just trying to explain to her how important it is that I find Calhoun." He turned back to Cassie. "The situation is a powder keg here. The army is just trying to maintain the peace, permit honest elections to occur. Locking up Calhoun will defuse the situation."

"Do you have to lock him up?"

"We certainly can't permit him to run around the countryside stirring up these people."

Cassie hesitated, biting her lower lip. This was what she had come for. "What if he just left the area?"

Lennon looked at her sharply. "What're you saying?"

"Suppose he left this area, went North. Wouldn't that solve your problem?"

"You want me to let him escape?"

"Yes."

"Never. I have a sworn duty."

There was dreadful finality to his words. She knew she was wasting her time. Rising from her chair, she said, "I should not have come. I'm sorry to have awakened you."

Emily Lennon was aghast. "You can't just leave, child."

"I've no choice, Mrs. Lennon. I thank you for the tea."

"But where will you go?"

"Back to Calhoun. I'll have to think of something else."

"But you can't. We promised to send you to Danielle as soon as we found you."

"I know that, too, Mrs. Lennon. But I can't go alone. I—I had hoped. . . ." Again, she bit at her lip. "Calhoun is still a very sick man. He will never get well where he is now. I want to take him to Maryland, to Aurial. He'll recover there. And he'll be safe." She looked at Major Lennon. "I had hoped you would send us both, but I see that is impossible. I'll just have to find another way."

"Good heavens, why do you care so much about him. He's a—"

"I know exactly what he is, major. And I'm not doing this because I care about him, but because other people do. Joshua Calhoun is from Boston, major, a Baptist minister. Frederick Douglass asked him to come down here, organize the freedmen, help them fight for their rights. You and I may not approve of his methods, but—"

"I should say not."

"But lots of people do. He is called the leader—savior, even, a man in a century. I was forced to stay with him because he could not be allowed to die."

"And you believe that—"

"It doesn't matter what I believe. I—I can't let him die—not after all that's happened." She turned to Emily Lennon. "Thank you again. I must go now."

She was halfway to the front door when she heard, "Wait. At leave give a body a moment to think." She stopped and slowly turned back to face the army officer.

"I gather you want safe conduct to Maryland?"

"Yes."

"That's not easy. He is a wanted man, well-known. Any of my men will arrest him on sight. I needn't tell you how many people will shoot him if they see him."

"I know that."

He began to pace the floor, deep in thought. Finally, he said, "Is he well enough to travel?"

"Not very far. He doesn't have much strength."

He smiled. "Good. It's better that way."

"What're you going to do?"

"I'll make some arrangements tomorrow. You remain here tonight." He saw her hesitate. "Miss Brown, if you're not going to trust me, then we might as well forget the whole thing."

It was difficult for Cassie to return to the shack and re-enter the cellar. But it was infinitely harder to convince Josh Calhoun of the wisdom of her plan.

"You went to the *army!*"

"There was nothing else to do."

"There was *everything* else to do. You could have just gone as you said you were going. You didn't have to turn me in."

"I didn't turn you in. They don't know where you are. I didn't tell them."

"I'll bet."

"Oh, God, Josh, don't be so stubborn. I didn't talk to anyone but Major Lennon. He's a nice man. He agrees there is no point in killing you or locking you up. Getting you out of this area will serve the same purpose.

"Oh, sure, I can see him now." He lowered the pitch of his voice, mocking an army commander. "All right, men, I've got this darky girl bringing in Calhoun. Shoot first, and ask questions later."

"It wasn't that way at all. You've got to trust somebody sometime."

"I trusted you."

"And I haven't betrayed you, honey. You don't hear footsteps upstairs do you, men beating down the door to get to you, do you?"

He was staring at her. She believed she was finally getting to him. Then he smiled. "You called me honey."

"I did not."

"I wasn't shot in the ear. My hearing's fine."

She was exasperated by this sudden change of subject. "What does it matter what I called you? What you really are is ridiculously stubborn. Somebody wants to save your life, and you won't let them."

"Look, Cassie, I'm not going anywhere. My work is here."

"What work? Holding up six feet of earth? Even if you recover, which is unlikely in this hellhole, you're as good as dead. If the nightriders don't get you, the army will. You're finished here. You're a dead man, Josh."

Now he really did look at her, eyes squinting a little. "You really care, don't you?"

"Yes, I care. Look at all I've gone through to keep you alive."

"I mean, you care . . . yourself."

"No, I don't care myself. But those people upstairs do. They think you're some kind of great leader. But what they don't know is you really are a stubborn, self-centered *nigger*."

His laugh swept over her. "So you finally learned to use that word."

Now it was she who stared at him, surprised at herself, her speech, the change in her attitudes. "Oh, Josh, you can do so much—but not here. Come up to Aurial with me, get well, regain your strength. Then you can go where you want, do what you want. Living is the first thing. Everything else is second."

There was silence between them for a moment, then he slowly held out his hand, beckoning her. She knew what he wanted and what would happen. She shook her head against it.

"Yes. Come here."

She held out a moment longer, then slowly made the single step to sit on the edge of the bed. He put his hands on her shoulders and kissed her gently.

"Who is this other you love?"

She had no time to answer, as his mouth returned to hers, hot, open, demanding. At some point, she managed to say, "I don't understand how you can do this, when you haven't the strength to walk a hundred yards."

The plan devised by Major Lennon was relatively simple, yet extremely risky. Calhoun was to board a train in Charleston in broad daylight. When Lennon first suggested it, Cassie gasped in astonishment, but relented when she realized there was no other choice.

Thus, Cassie helped to dress Calhoun in an army private's uniform, which Lennon had given her. Using bandages supplied by Lennon, she wrapped him as though he had received a head wound, covering his hair, forehead and half his face. Only one eye, his nostrils and one side of his mouth were visible. Then, for good measure, his left foot was heavily bandaged to explain why he couldn't walk.

In the dead of night, he was placed in the back of a wagon. Cassie lay down beside him and they were covered with hay. It seemed to her the circuitous journey to Charleston took an eternity, for the greatest risk in the plan was their discovery by nightriders. If the wagon were stopped and searched, there was no way to save him. Their only protection was the appearance of innocence, old Hector transporting a load of hay to the city. Beneath the hay, Cassie could only lie still, enduring the discomfort of the ride, straining her ears for the sounds of horses or voices above the rattle of the wagon. She gripped Calhoun's hand to support both him and herself.

Finally, the wagon stopped and the hay was pulled away from them. Cassie sat up. It was dawn and they were inside the army compound. She could see the parade ground, the outline of barracks and other buildings. She felt Calhoun start to sit up beside her.

"Lie still, soldier. You're badly wounded, remember?"

She turned. It was Major Lennon. Beside him was a man in a long white coat.

"This is Doctor Josephson. He's in charge of the patient."

Suddenly, Cassie reacted with fear. She had delivered Calhoun into the hands of the army. What a fool she was.

"Climb up on the seat next to your father."

He motioned toward Hector, and she obeyed, turning, watching as Major Lennon and the doctor climbed into the back of the wagon. The rest of the straw was pushed aside and Calhoun revealed. She saw the wild fear in his uncovered eye. He started to get up.

Lennon shoved him down. "I told you to lie still, soldier."

Cassie's own fear matched Calhoun's as she watched him being placed on a stretcher and carried from the wagon to be put inside a military ambulance. Doctor Josephson climbed in with him and the door was closed. For Cassie, it was a moment of panic. Had she delivered him to his enemies?

In a louder voice, Lennon said, "Old man, take that hay over to the stables, then go to the quartermaster. He'll give you your money."

The next two hours of waiting were hell for Cassie. She stayed with the wagon at the stables while the hay was unloaded. She waited in front of the headquarters building for Hector to come out with his money. She tried to find some irony in the army actually paying out money while Calhoun escaped, but she could not.

Was Josh escaping? The ambulance had been moved. She had no idea where he was. Had he been locked in the stockade? Had all she accomplished been a betrayal of him? *You must have faith in someone.*

When Hector came out with his money and climbed to the seat of the wagon, Major Lennon came by and spoke to them.

"He is Trooper Henry Brady, wounded last night in a scuffle with nightriders. The train leaves in a half-hour. He'll be transferred from the ambulance and put into a Pullman sleeper. You're going along with him as his wife—to look after him. Got it?"

"Yes. Is he all right?"

Lennon smiled. "Badly wounded, I'm afraid. Got to get him North for immediate medical attention."

Hector drove her to the train station, and she alighted from the wagon. She paused a moment, looking up at the old man. How involved she had become with him. They looked at each other, then he slowly nodded his head. There were no words to be said.

She waited on the platform beside the train, her nerves ragged with fear. Then she saw the ambulance approach and stop. Two soldiers climbed down and opened the back. Dr. Josephson climbed out and beckoned her. As she approached, she saw the stretcher being carried out. For a moment, she thought it wasn't Calhoun. The bandages had been changed, and they were now stained with what looked like blood. Then, with a second glance, she saw it was Calhoun.

"Mrs. Brady, you know what to do. Keep him as warm as possible. Try to move him as little as you can. You won't need to change the dressings until he is transferred to the army hospital in Washington."

Unable to speak, she nodded.

He smiled at her. "Goodbye and good luck." He extended his hand to her. Timorously, rigid with fear, she took his hand. Within his grasp, she felt him transfer a piece of paper to her hand.

The two medics were carrying the stretcher to the

Pullman, carefully raising it up the steps. Cassie followed, waited for the steps to clear, then reached for the handle to mount the train herself.

"Cassie! What are you doing here?"

She turned, startled. Striding rapidly toward her was Walter Summers. Mouth open, she looked as though fear had turned her to stone.

"I thought that was you. Where've you been?"

"I—I—"

"I've looked all over for you."

She saw then how terrible he looked, haggard, unshaven, his clothes wrinkled and unclean. She had the impression he had been drinking heavily.

"What happened to you?"

"I—I've been . . . with Major Lennon and his wife." It was a poor effort, but lies came dear in her state of mind.

"Where's Calhoun?"

"I—I don't know where he is."

"But you got away from him. Good." Then, suddenly, he seemed to become aware of where he was, the train, her starting to board it. "Are you . . . going to Danny now?"

She nodded. "Yes."

An expression of sheer agony seemed to enter his eyes. "Tell her. . . ." He couldn't deliver the message. Instead, he fumbled in his pockets, pulled out some crumpled bills. "Here. Give her this. She may need it."

She took the money. "All right. I will." She held his gaze a moment, compassion momentarily overriding her fear, then she turned and began to climb the steps.

"Cassie."

She turned back to him.

"Tell her . . . tell her I love her." He swallowed hard, struggling against tears. "Tell her I'm coming . . . to see her as soon as—" He looked down at his clothing and felt his whiskered chin. "—as soon as I can."

"I'll tell her." Then she climbed inside the car and went to where Calhoun lay. As soon as the train was out of the station, she read the note Dr. Josephson had handed her:

> *Just before you get to Washington, remove the bandages and disappear in the crowd. You're on your own then. Good luck.*

It was unsigned, but she knew it was from Major Lennon.

Chapter 28

Moira's reaction to her stepson's story was mostly resignation. Nothing Miriam Hodges might do could surprise her.

"We've got to get her out of there. I just wish father were here."

"Well, I'm glad he's not. He'd probably have the same reaction as you. And believe me, it is precisely the wrong thing to do."

"How can you say that, mother? She asked Thomas to help her."

Moira looked at Danielle. "It seems to me that you, of all people, ought to know better."

"What do you mean?"

Moira looked at her daughter levelly. "Doesn't this situation sound familiar to you?" She saw remembrance and recognition come to Danielle. "When you had . . . taken up with Garth, I did not march over there and snatch you away—and believe me, I wanted to. My mother didn't do it to me when I was . . . foolish. She allowed me to come to my senses on my own. I did the same with you." She turned to Thomas. "However hard it may be, waiting is the only way. Miriam will be all right."

"Then why did Grandmother Glenna send me over there? I didn't want to go, but she insisted. There was something terribly wrong, she said. Miriam was in trouble and needed help. And she was right, I know she was."

Moira hesitated. Her mother's actions were surely uncharacteristic of her. Indeed, Moira had learned this whole attitude of restraint, letting a child work out her own problems, from her mother.

Danielle moved to widen the breach in her mother's resistance. "If GlennaMa is worried, then I think we should be, too."

Morgan joined her. "If Mirry asked her brother for help, then that's what she needs. We can't deny it."

Feeling badgered, Moira bristled. "If she doesn't want to be with this Blakeley, whoever he is, all she has to do is walk away."

"But I told you, the house is a fortress, mother." Thomas spoke with great intensity. "There are bars on all the windows. The front door is heavy and locked from the inside. I don't think she can just walk out of the house."

"But you said she was going out with him, wearing some scandalous gown. She doesn't sound like a prisoner to me."

"How do you know, mother?" The voice of Morgan Kingston had a hard edge to it. "I don't mean to be impertinent, mother, but you really don't know what is going on up there, what her real situation may be. The important thing is that she asked for help. There's no choice in the matter."

"She could have meant anything by asking for help."

Thomas Hodges stood up, staring at his stepmother.

"I can't believe what I'm hearing. I'm going to wire father."

"No, Tom, don't." She looked at him. "I'm sorry. I guess I'm wrong." She smiled wanly. "I'm certainly outvoted." She rose from her chair and embraced her stepson. "Your father is busy, and what he's doing is important. There's no emergency here that you and I can't handle. We'll leave for New York at once." She was smiling as she kissed his cheek.

"I'll go, too. If she really is locked up in that house, you may need an extra body."

Danielle looked at her brother quizzically. "Are you sure, Morgan? What if Cassie comes?"

"We'll only be gone a day or so. You'll be here if she comes." He wasn't quite sure why, but he felt a sense of personal responsibility toward Miriam.

Late that night, following a long train ride to New York, a strategy session was held at the Fairchild home. Moira, who still harbored doubts about the wisdom of "rescuing" Miriam, had them shattered by Glenna.

"From what Tom says, I'm sure we're doing the right thing."

Moira stared at her mother. "I said I'd go along with this, and I will. But, mother, I just can't believe you. Have you suddenly developed two heads? You're the one who let me go off with . . . you know who, and didn't interfere. You're the one who kept me from barging over to bring Danny home. What's happening now?"

"Different situations call for different actions."

"What's different about this?"

Morgan interrupted. "God, mother, I thought we'd ended the argument. If you're not going along, why did you come all the way to New York?"

"I came here to do what must be done, Morgan. This is just a private discussion between your grandmother and me. I'm trying to understand something." She looked at Glenna, demanding an answer to her question.

"I just don't think Miriam went of her own free will,

Moira. If she had, I wouldn't interfere. But—" She hesitated, then plunged ahead. "I asked Franklin to make some inquiries. He says Edith Prentiss has gone through all her money—foolishly, bad investments trying to rebuild the fortune. Actually, most of the money was spent by her husband before he died. In any event, Edith Prentiss is in difficult straits. She sold off some antiques and heirlooms—to Peter Blakeley, the worst sort of man to deal with. I'm sure he gave her only a fraction of their true worth. But, in her pride, she didn't want anyone to know what she was doing. She even allowed Blakeley to loan her money, using her house as collateral."

"How did Franklin find this out?"

"I don't know, Tom." She sighed. "I didn't ask. All I know is bankers have a way of finding out anything they want to know, especially if it involves money." Glenna turned back to Moira. "You know how fond Miriam has always been of her grandmother Prentiss."

"Yes."

"I just feel that if Miriam knew of that old woman's difficulties, she'd do whatever she could to help her."

Moira was aghast. "You're not suggesting. . . . ?"

"I am. I just don't believe Miriam is in that house of her own free will. I hear this Blakeley character is parading her around town, half-dressed, like a possession, some sort of living doll he owns. People say he's trying to gain social respect by showing off a girl from one of the finer families."

Her mouth firm, all resistance gone, Moira said, "It's settled then. How are we going to get her out of that house?"

"I've been thinking about it," Thomas said, "and I think we should go there first thing in the morning." He went on to detail what he had in mind.

Moira listened, then said, "It doesn't sound like much, Thomas, but as you say, if they are surprised and we're determined, it might work. If it doesn't, we'll just have to get a lawyer."

Glenna said, "I'm sure it'll work. And while you're

doing that, I'm going to visit Edith Prentiss. It's time we two old women had a little chat."

For Miriam, the last two nights had turned into a nightmare. In part, it was her own frame of mind. Her reaction to knowing Thomas was in the house had surprised her. Her frantic signaling to him, her whispered words of desperation in his ear, had been impulsive acts. But, having done them, she now wanted escape more than she had ever wanted anything in her life. It seemed to her she was counting minutes, hoping amid despair, that he had heard her and understood. But what could he do? Send for father? Yes, someone had to come and help her. But as the hours dragged by and nothing happened, she increasingly surrendered to despair.

Far worse was the change in Blakeley. The coming of Thomas Hodges had upset him. Miriam's behavior with her brother was extremely strange, and Blakeley was suspicious. He refused to take her out the night after Thomas came, all the next day, and even the next night. He questioned her about her brother, her family, the involved relationships, her attitudes. Miriam lied repeatedly, desperate to allay his suspicions, convince him she was there of her own choice, that she liked being his mistress. Her best chance for escape, she believed, would come when she was out of the house. Clearly, he was not going to let her set foot out the door.

She paid a high price for her efforts to disarm his suspicions. His own fears of losing her aroused him, and she had no choice but to pretend and pretend, anything to borrow time. Time for what? No help was coming.

They sat at breakfast in her room. She wore a sheer black negligée, he his robe. He seemed once again expansive, kissing her affectionately, fondling her breasts after he held her chair for her.

"I have good news for you this morning, my darling, the best possible news."

"Yes?"

"There is a boat leaving for London tomorrow. We're going to be on it."

The words fell on her like blows. She could hardly breathe.

"Aren't you happy? I was sure you would be."

"Of course, but . . . it's so sudden."

He laughed. "Oh, yes, it is a bit. But I like to be impulsive sometimes. Adds spice to life."

"But why? I thought—"

"Aren't you just thrilled? London, Paris, all those exotic places you've always wanted to see." He reached across the table and clasped her limp hand. "And I promise you shall see them all, every one. Isn't it wonderful?"

She looked at him in horror, couldn't help it. He was doing this deliberately, taking her away so she couldn't. . . .

"I've saved the best news till last, my darling. We'll have the captain marry us on board ship. Won't that be romantic?"

As she looked at him, he suddenly began to swim in her vision. All was lost. She couldn't hold back the tears.

"I knew you'd be happy." He laughed. "I even knew you'd cry, my darling."

"Why . . . why . . . are you doing this . . . now? Because my . . . brother came?"

"The thought had occurred to me that he, your father, someone in your family might come, try to ruin our happiness. I can't let that happen."

Choked with tears, she did not hear the first sounds from downstairs. And when the shouting began, it had no meaning for her. Peter Blakeley was not nearly so slow. He leaped from his chair, knocking it over backwards. "Damn you," he said. "I knew they'd come for you." In an instant, he was at the door. "They'll not have you." When he went out the door, he snatched up the key, and quickly locked her inside.

Thomas's plan to gain entry was to exploit the weakness of the front door. In its massiveness, it was blind to the street. It had to be opened for anyone to see who was there. The instant Hadley turned the lock and the latch, Morgan and Thomas simply shoved it open with their shoulders and burst inside, bowling over an unprepared Hadley. Moira entered imperiously to stand over him.

"I am Moira Hodges, and I demand to see my daughter at once." When there was no answer, they all began to holler for Miriam. It was this noise that alerted Blakeley.

Moira saw him at the top of the stairs in his robe. "I demand to see my daughter this instant."

"You will demand nothing, madam. You and these two men will leave my home at once, or I will call the police."

"Is Miriam Hodges here? I demand to see her."

Blakeley began descending the stairs slowly. "Hadley, get Karl and throw these people out." Karl was the footman, and nearly of a size with Hadley.

Morgan was not about to be cowed. "She's upstairs somewhere, Tom. Let's find her." But they had not yet reached the bottom stair when they stopped. From the pocket of his robe, Blakeley had taken a small, silver pistol.

"I recommend that you two come no further. I have every legal right to shoot you."

Morgan stared at the pistol. Then he saw Hadley entering with another man. It was now three against two, and one of them had a gun. His shoulders slumped visibly in surrender, and he sighed deeply. "Okay, I can tell when it's no use." He turned to his stepbrother. "We'd better go, Tom. No sense in getting shot." Together, they strode to the door. "Come, mother. This isn't going to work."

At the open doorway, he seemed to turn around in dejection. "May I just ask one question, Mr. Blakeley? Is my sister happy?"

"Yes, very."

Blakeley had descended the stairs and was coming toward them, gun in hand.

"I'm sorry, sir, I didn't hear what you said."

"I said Miss Hodges is extremely happy. She is exactly where she wants to be."

Blakeley was closer now, only a couple of strides away.

"You seem like a nice man." Morgan extended his hand to him. "I'm sorry we broke into your house this way."

The gesture of friendship, seemingly so open and naïve, flustered Blakeley for just a second. It was long enough. Morgan grabbed the gun-hand. He hoped to press Blakeley's finger against the grip so he couldn't fire, but he failed in that. The gun went off, but harmlessly, into the floor. Then Blakeley could fire no more, as Morgan's big fist pounded into his jaw, knocking him senseless. The other two were no particular problem, and Morgan and Thomas would later declare what great fun it was. Morgan was extremely strong from his labors at Aurial, and Thomas was in good shape from his summer in the sun. Despite their size, Hadley and Karl were no real match for them. Morgan and Tom came away with sore jaws and scraped knuckles. Not too much furniture was smashed in the scuffling. It was over in a couple of minutes.

Both young men took the stairs three at a time then, confronting a screaming and jabbering Mimi. There was no need for her to tell them where Miriam was. They could hear her pounding on the inside of the door.

"Miriam, move back from the door." Still, she pounded. "Miriam, listen to me. It's Morgan. Move back from the door."

Finally, her pounding and screaming stopped, and two shoulders rammed against the wooden door, splintering it like matchwood. Thomas tripped and stumbled to the floor, but Morgan managed to lurch inside, still on his feet. He saw Miriam, her face contorted with hysteria, then she was running into his arms.

"Oh, Morgan, Morgan, I knew you'd come."

Morgan had two quick impressions. First, she had nothing on beneath the filmy garment, and second, the kisses she was smothering him with were not very sisterly—nor his reaction to them very brotherly.

"Come on, hurry. Let's get out of here before they come to."

Morgan pulled away from her. "Yes, let's go."

Moira spoke from the wrecked doorway. "She can't go out in the street like that."

Several pairs of eyes, including Miriam's, examined her near nudity with dismay. An amused Moira was the least dumbfounded. "Where's your closet, Miriam? I'll find something for you to put on." She went to where Miriam pointed and extracted a full-length silver fox fur.

Meanwhile, a few blocks away, Glenna Morgan Fairchild was paying her morning visit to Edith Prentiss. Glenna was her charming best, dressed in the height of fashion, her silver hair coiffed, her sapphire eyes even more brilliant because she was performing a task she enjoyed. She looked years younger than sixty-five, particularly when contrasted with the woman who received her.

"I think it's past time we met, don't you, Mrs. Prentiss? After all, the lives of our grandchildren are intertwined. We are almost family."

There was nothing for Edith Prentiss to do but say "yes" and admit her visitor. They sat in the small parlor, rather stiffly. Tea was served, then pleasantries exchanged.

Then Glenna, after a suitable lull in the conversation, dropped her bombshell. "I really did want to meet you, Mrs. Prentiss. It is long overdue."

"Yes."

"But I also came to report some news. Even as we sit here, Miriam is being rescued from the home of one Peter Blakeley by her brother, my daughter and grandson. She will be taken home to Aurial, where she belongs." Glenna watched the eyes of Edith Prentiss. She was startled at first, then wary, finally fearful. "I don't believe I have to tell you how despicably you have acted in this matter."

Edith Prentiss surprised Glenna. The fear remained
in her eyes a moment, then was replaced by something
else. Glenna was uncertain what it was, until she spoke.
"Yes, I know." A moment later, she was looking down
at her hands, her frail shoulders shaking with sobs.

Glenna had expected any reaction but this. She
would have thought anger, denials, challenges. But
tears? A wave of compassion swept Glenna, but she
denied it. "I wish I could feel pity for you, Mrs. Prentiss, but under the circumstances I hardly feel it war-
ranted." Other words, much rehearsed, formed in her
mind. *To use your granddaughter this way, ruining her
life for. . . .* But she did not utter them. There was no
need. Weeping, Edith Prentiss was already nodding her
head in agreement. She was a broken woman. There
was no point in badgering her further.

Glenna let her cry a moment, but made no effort to
comfort her. Then she heard broken words. "Take . . .
good care . . . of her. I—I . . . do . . . love her."

Glenna bit back angry words. *You have a fine way
of showing it.* "I assure you Miriam will receive the
best possible care." Again, she waited for a few moments. "Perhaps some good will come of this. Perhaps
she will now be able to accept the affection of her stepmother."

Edith Prentiss nodded.

"This episode will be forgotten. Miriam will meet
some young man who loves her. None of this will
matter. It is always so."

"Yes."

Glenna was thinking about leaving, when she remembered something else to be said. "I assume that
through Miriam's . . . efforts, you have erased your
indebtedness to this . . . this Blakeley?"

"Yes."

"May I suggest an alternative course of action to
you, Mrs. Prentiss, one less destructive to the lives of
other people." Immediately, Glenna wished she had
not said those unkind words. "My husband is Franklin

Fairchild. I'm sure that if you went to him, or one of the other officers of his bank, some more suitable arrangements could be made to resolve your financial difficulties. Will you do that?" She saw the old woman nod. "At our age, Edith, pride is a foolish luxury."

Chapter 29

Glenna was prophetic. Miriam's greatest joy was in loving her stepmother. She hugged Moira repeatedly, clinging to her, crying out her pain, fear, gratitude, telling over and over of her sorrow for the way she had treated her all these years.

"If I can now love you as my daughter," Moira said, "all this was worth it." She smiled. "Or almost worth it." And Moira did enjoy mothering her, comforting her, fussing over her. She insisted that Miriam take a hot bath, then go to bed to rest, even though it was daylight. She stayed with her till she slept, then went out to buy her clothes for the trip to Aurial. That negligée and fur coat would never do.

Mostly, Moira listened, letting Miriam cry out her pain and shame. Perhaps the most revealing moment came when Miriam was tucked into bed for her nap. Moira was sitting on the edge of the bed, wiping away a new outpouring of tears.

"It was so awful, mother."

That word alone touched Moira deeply. She was filled with happiness to at last be recognized as this

child's mother. It made all her years of effort and longing worthwhile. Mother. Yes, Miriam needed a mother,
always had. In her mind, Moira thanked the Blessed
Virgin Mary for delivering this child to her care at
last.

"It's over now, Miriam, dearest. You'll forget it
soon."

"I couldn't bear to have him touch me, mother. His
hands . . . they were so awful." Fresh tears rolled
down her cheeks. "And when he. . . ."

"Don't think about it, darling. It's over now."

"I—I thought . . . I couldn't . . . bear it."

"I know, dear. But it's over now—all over." She let
Miriam cry a moment, wiping her cheeks with the edge
of the sheet. Then she realized Miriam was trying to
control herself. There was something she wanted to say.

"I . . . I hated it, mother. I—I never . . . enjoyed it.
I thought . . . I would. I—I wanted to—at first. But I
—I . . . never did. Not once."

"I know, dear."

"Is . . . is there . . . something wrong with me?"

Moira smiled. "Not at all, darling. You just didn't
love him. You were frightened. When you are in love
. . . and loved, it will be just fine for you. There's nothing wrong with you, darling, believe me."

"Are you sure?"

"Yes, very sure. Believe me, I know." Miriam seemed
to take comfort from the reassurance, and Moira again
wiped her cheeks. How long had she waited for this
girl to let her touch her? "Try to sleep now. You'll
feel better if you rest."

Miriam closed her eyes. "Yes." Then she opened
them. "Stay with me?"

"Yes. I'll be right here till you sleep."

Moira sat there, holding her stepdaughter's hand.
It seemed to her she was relaxing a little, sliding toward
sleep. Then she heard words. "Will anyone love me now
. . . after . . . ?"

"Oh, yes, Miriam—many men will love you. You are
so beautiful. You will choose the man of your dreams."

Moira was tempted to suggest she had an idea there was someone who already loved her, then thought better of it. "Just go to sleep. You're home now, safe, and loved very much." The pressure on her fingers told Moira her love was reciprocated. Few things in her life had ever pleased or relieved her so much.

If Moira brought joy to Miriam, Morgan Kingston did not. She had fallen asleep thinking of him, how handsome he looked, how powerful he was as he burst through the door to rescue her, and she remembered the passion of his kisses as he embraced her. But when she awoke, all had changed. She fussed with her hair and makeup and put on the new dress Moira had bought. It was a pretty blue that enhanced her eyes. But all was to no avail. Through dinner, the whole evening, the long train ride back to Aurial, Morgan seemed distant, distracted, even irritable. He had not wanted to spend the night in New York, but rather to return to Aurial immediately. Cassie might return. He wanted to be there. He gave in to his mother's demand that they wait one more day, give Miriam a chance to rest, but he was visibly put out. Oh, he was not unkind to Miriam. He was worse. When she went up to him to thank him one more time for rescuing her, he was *brotherly,* kidding her about being a damsel in distress.

The worst came when they arrived at Aurial. Cassie Brown was there. Miriam could only watch as Morgan gasped, cried out and ran to her, sweeping her into his arms, devouring her brown face with kisses. She had lost him. Clearly, he loved another. So intent was she on what she was witnessing, she was unaware that her stepmother was looking at her closely.

Cassie could not guess what her reaction would be when she saw Morgan. She and Calhoun had arrived yesterday. She was disappointed that Morgan was not there, but had no time to dwell on it. Calhoun's fever had risen during the trip, and he was hardly able to walk through Union Station in Washington or sit up during the long taxi ride to Aurial.

With Danny's help, she put him to bed immediately. The doctor came. He said Calhoun would need a long period of rest to overcome his lingering infection and recover his strength. The wound was still nasty, but, yes, he would recover with proper care. Both Cassie and Danielle took elaborate pains to reassure Calhoun that he was welcome at Aurial and would be safe there.

Danielle smiled at him. "Besides, Mr. Calhoun, I don't think you have much choice in the matter, do you?"

"No." He looked at her, hard, as though studying her face. "I am grateful, Mrs. Summers—truly I am."

She smiled again. "That's a great deal of progress, Mr. Calhoun."

"And I'm sorry about you and Mr.—your husband."

Danielle glanced at Cassie, wishing she hadn't told him. But it couldn't be helped. "Yes, thank you."

The two dear friends spent the afternoon, evening, well into the night, hugging each other and relating all that had happened. Cassie told everything, or nearly so, the wagon rattling into the night, the endless days in the cellar beneath the shack, going to Major Lennon, the rescue. Finally, she told of seeing Walter Summers at the train. She delivered his message.

Danielle seemed to have no reaction, except a slight firming of her mouth. She merely said, "Thank you."

"He looked ghastly, Danny. I think he'd been drinking."

The firmness of her mouth increased. "I guess I'm not surprised."

"He—he said he's coming to see you."

"I've been expecting it."

"What will you do? Have you thought about it, decided anything?"

"Of course, I've thought about it, but decided—no. I think I'll know when he comes." She smiled warmly at her friend. "But enough of that. I want to know why you stayed with Calhoun so long. Couldn't you get away?"

"I couldn't at first, then . . . I didn't want to." She

saw Danielle's left eyebrow rise in a gesture of surprise. "He's a good man, Danny, a man of God, a Baptist minister from Boston. Frederick Douglass sent him down there to help organize the freedmen. He was hoping to teach them about freedom, their rights, fighting for them."

"You mean kill for them, don't you?"

She sighed. "I know. He said the former slaves were too docile. They need to learn to fight back."

"Perhaps. But I still don't understand why you—"

"The people down there call him a leader. They say he's one in a century, a man who will help them find the way. He's a sort of younger Frederick Douglass, I guess you might say."

"And?"

"I—I couldn't let him die, Danny—or be killed. I had to bring him here where he could be safe. I hope you don't mind."

"Of course I don't. He's welcome here." She smiled. "So, I guess under all his nastiness lies a. . . ."

"He's really not a bad man, Danny. He wants to do good." She smiled. "I'm talking to him about staying around here. He can do more good in Washington, talking to congressmen and such. I think he may do it."

Danielle was extremely tempted to ask if there was another reason for her friend staying with Calhoun, but she decided not to. It would all come out, eventually. Instead, she looked at the clock. "I guess they're not coming tonight. Morgan will hate not being here when you arrived."

"How is he, Danny?"

"Just the same—very much in love, very worried about you. It was all I could do to keep him from rushing down to Charleston to search for you."

Cassie spent the night in the same bed in the same room next to the nursery where Morgan had come to her in passion. She remembered, but could not escape the feeling of distance from it. She told herself she was eager to see Morgan again. But she knew she was filled with apprehension.

She was waiting in the middle of the foyer, when the carriage drove up. She saw him alight—how handsome he was—and help a young, blonde girl down from the carriage. That must be Miriam Hodges. Then she heard Danielle say, "Cassie's here." He turned, saw her, registered surprise, then ran up the steps and across the veranda.

He hesitated a moment in the doorway. "Oh, Cassie, thank God you're safe." Then he was coming to her, she to him, and all impressions were lost in his embrace, his mouth on hers. She felt tiny within his arms, comforted by his words. "Oh, Cassie, Cassie, I love you. Thank God you're here."

It seemed to go on for a long time, the two of them clutching at each other in reunion. Then, Cassie was aware of silence around them. She turned away from him, pushing against his shoulder a little, and looked at the others standing by the door. Most were smiling at her. "I'm sorry," she said. "I'm so embarrassed."

Moira came to her and hugged her. "About what, my dear? We're all so glad you're home." The hug ended and Moira turned her. "I don't think you know my son, Thomas Hodges, my daughter, Miriam Hodges."

Cassie smiled and nodded to Thomas, but looked deeply at Miriam. When she had turned in embarrassment from Morgan's embrace, the first face she saw was Miriam's, unsmiling, an expression of torment in her eyes. She went to her now, and smiling, took her hands in hers. "I'm so glad to meet you at last—and know that you're safe, too."

Miriam looked down at the brown hands holding hers, then back at the beautiful brown face. "Thank you, Cassie." For reasons she could not fathom, she suddenly found herself smiling at her, then hugging her warmly.

The afternoon was given to the telling of tales. Cassie gave a carefully-edited version of her misadventures and escape, leading up to the fact Josh Calhoun was upstairs in bed.

"Here?"

"I hope it's all right, Morgan. He—he had no place else to go."

She saw him hesitate. "Of course, it's all right. I'm just—surprised, that's all."

Moira already knew about Calhoun, Danielle having whispered it to her. Now she moved to fill an awkward moment. "Well, where is our guest? Can he come down?"

Danielle answered, "The doctor said strict bed-rest. But maybe we can go up and visit him. Why don't you see if he's awake, Cassie?"

"Yes." She stood up. "I fear I'm the world's worst nurse."

"You're nursing him?"

Danielle answered that, too. "Somebody has to, Morgan. You're being absolutely insufferable."

He laughed then. "I hardly sound like I'm offering a big welcome to him, do I?" He stood up. "C'mon, Cassie, I'll go up with you and tell him he's got a home here as long as he wants."

When they were alone in the upstairs hallway, he embraced her again, kissing her deeply. "God, darling, I missed you so."

"And I missed you, Morgan."

"I'm never going to let you out of my sight again. I don't care what anyone says."

"Yes."

Again, he embraced her, pressing her lithe body hard against himself. Finally, she was able to say, "We'd better go, hadn't we?"

"I want to see you tonight. I've got to be alone with you."

"Yes, we will."

There was another quick kiss, then she led him down the hallway, greatly disturbed. The first greeting, seeing him, being swept into his arms had been all she had expected or wanted, greatly reassuring. This one had made her uncomfortable. She had endured. Why was this so? Why didn't she want his arm around her now?

At the doorway to Calhoun's room, she smiled and, extricating herself from Morgan's arms, opened the door, gently guiding him in first. She hesitated momentarily, to see which side of the bed he chose, then deliberately took the other. Calhoun was awake. "Josh, this is Morgan Kingston. I guess you could say he's your host."

The two men eyed each other, one seeing, especially from his angle, a very tall, ruggedly-built and handsome white man, the other seeing a black face, shrunken and hollow-eyed against the pillow.

Calhoun spoke first. "I want to thank you, Mr. Kingston."

"Morgan, please." He smiled and extended his hand. "I want you to know you're welcome here as long as you need to stay or want to."

Calhoun hesitated, then pulled his hand from under the covers and shook the white hand. "I'll try to get well soon."

"We'll all help you."

"Again, I can only thank you."

Morgan laughed. "It's I who must thank you. After all, you brought my girl back to me."

The words stabbed at Cassie and she shuddered, couldn't help it, especially when Calhoun glanced at her, quick, hard, hatefully.

"Well, I guess we'd better let you get some rest. We'll have to get you out in the sun as soon as we can." He saw Calhoun look at him and nod. Morgan turned toward the door. "Coming, Cassie?" He extended his hand to her from the foot of the bed.

"Could she stay a moment? I think I need her."

Morgan smiled. "Sure. I'll see you downstairs, honey."

She was shaking as she looked down at Calhoun, seeing his eyes, so dark, so full of rage. His words came out in a hiss. "So, it's him, is it? I knew it would be a white man. I just guessed the wrong one."

Again, she trembled.

"Is he the one?"

She sighed. "Yes."

"You love *him?*"

"I—I—"

"Get out. Get out of here—out of my life."

She stood there a long moment looking down at him, seeing his anger and hurt. Then, she smiled. "I'm afraid I can't do that." She paused, mostly for effect. "You see, I think I'm carrying your child."

She told Morgan that evening. They went for a walk under a setting quarter-moon, hand in hand, then arms around each other. She was really amazed at herself. When she realized what she had to do, she expected to react with dread. She even tried to conjure up the feeling, but simply could not do it. An inner peace had come to her, a contentment. She was happy, and knew it.

She really didn't know for sure she was pregnant. It was too soon for that. But she had the strongest feeling she was, and that conviction would do for now. There, in the bedroom, amid Josh's anger and hateful words, she had realized she loved him best. She really couldn't understand it, but it was somehow born of need, his need for her, and, yes, her need for him. Something about him called to her. It felt right. It brought this inner peace.

As she and Morgan walked along, mostly silent, through the early darkness, she knew where they were heading, Kingston, the study. There would be difficulties. He was going to be hurt. But, somehow, in her contentment, she couldn't worry. Everything was going to work out all right.

Arms still around each other, they approached the study. He unlocked the door, led her inside, lit the light, then he embraced her. She did not fight him or his kiss, just enjoyed the feeling of being tiny, comfortable.

"What's the matter, Cassie? Today, upstairs in the hall, now again. What's wrong?"

"I'm sorry, Morgan."

He embraced her again, searching her mouth, seeking reassurance. He found none.

"Don't you love me?"

"Oh, yes, Morgan, very much. I'll always love you."

"Then . . . ?" Awareness came to him then, recognition, shock, disbelief. "I thought you loved me. I thought we—"

"I do, Morgan, so much. I always will. You were my first love, my first . . . everything." Biblical words came to her. "You're my Alpha and Omega."

He looked down at her. "Calhoun?"

"Yes. I'm sorry."

He stared at her in disbelief, then, as though in slow motion, pushed her away and turned, walking away, his back to her. Over and over, he said a single word, "God," as if it were a talisman to instill belief, understanding. Finally, he could ask, "How can you love him?"

"We were together a lot in that cold, damp tomb, in so much danger. There was need, closeness. I really don't know, Morgan. Who can explain love?"

He turned to face her, pain showing in his eyes. "You love him, yet you say you love me."

"I do, Morgan. I will always love you. I just can't be your wife."

"Why not?"

"Oh, Morgan, don't be angry. It would never work, you and me. I wouldn't be any good as mistress of Aurial."

"You would so—if you tried."

"Oh, Morgan, my place is not here, with you. It's with him. He needs me."

His face contorted. He was near tears. "God, Cassie, I need you, too."

"But not like he does, Morgan. He wants to live nearby and work in Washington, try to help our people from there."

He stared at her. *"Our* people?"

"Yes, Morgan." She bit at her lower lip, trying to

reach out to him with her eyes for understanding. "It's where I belong."

"No, never. I won't let it happen." He came to her, pulling her into his arms, kissing her, hard, as though commanding her body to do what her mind wouldn't.

She did not resist. Finally, he stopped, looking down at her in frustration. "I think I'm having his child, Morgan."

"So that's the reason."

"No. All it's done is help me to know what I want."

Those words did it, finished him. He slowly turned from her to sit on the couch, the same place where they had consummated their passion.

"It's better this way, Morgan. Our love for each other will remain, always. Nothing will ever spoil it. But if I'd married you, it would have been ruined. I know that." She looked at him, but he just sat there, dumbly, staring at his boot crooked over the top of his knee. "I'm not the one for you, Morgan, believe me. I'm not the one to make you happy, the one to make Aurial shine with happy laughter." She smiled. "But I know someone who is—someone who loves you very much."

He looked at her, his expression quizzical, disbelieving.

"Miriam Hodges."

He finally spoke. "For Christ's sake, she's my little sister."

Chapter 30

Once again, Moira sat in the gazebo, watching a rowboat slide from view on the river, once again worrying about what might be happening to one of her children.

"It's broad daylight, Moira. I think you're being terribly silly."

Moira turned to look at Glenna. "Am I?"

"Danielle is a mature woman. You must know that."

Moira nodded, but there was no special conviction in the gesture. Once more, she looked at the water, as though the rolling stream could deliver a message. "I just wish you and Mr. Fairchild hadn't brought Benjamin here."

"I didn't bring him, Moira. He came. I couldn't very well stop it."

Moira sighed. "I know."

"I think you worry needlessly, Moira. There is no reason to believe Danielle and Walter won't patch up their marriage."

"Oh, but there is." There was fear, a little bitterness in her voice, as she said, "It just went downriver with my daughter."

"Benjamin? Surely, you joke, Moira. Benjamin is—"

"I know exactly what he is, mother." She turned from the river to face her mother. "He's a very attractive man who is madly in love with Danielle—has been for years."

"Surely, you aren't suspicious enough to believe he and Danielle have—"

"I don't, of course I don't. But that isn't necessary. Benjamin's mere presence is a great threat to Danielle, her marriage and her happiness. I don't think I need to mention the children." She saw the doubt in Glenna's face. "You must see it. Benjamin is an alternative, a most attractive alternative. She cannot possibly deal wisely with her marriage if someone else is waiting in the wings, hoping."

"I credit Danielle with more sense, more virtue, than you do."

"It is not a case of sense or virtue, mother. I think I know my daughter. She is too beautiful, much too beautiful, too fragile, too vulnerable, too everything. Above all, she is much too . . . too passionate."

"I know, Moira, you believe Danielle has your . . . nature, but—"

"I *know* it is so. With my red hair, this body, I've always looked the part. I know Danielle doesn't. But believe me, beneath that snowy skin, that cool exterior, she is her mother's daughter." Moira's eyes began to burn. "I worry about her terribly."

"Surely not with Benjamin?"

Moira's eyes were filling with tears now. "If she does not save her marriage to Walt, she will . . . will go from . . . from man to man—lead a most unhappy life. That is my worry."

Glenna clasped Moira's hand, squeezing it. "I think you're wrong on several counts, darling. You forget she looks like me. When I look at her, I'm seeing myself at her age. It's uncanny. I think there is ample reason to believe she has more my nature than yours." She smiled at her daughter. "I truly think you worry needlessly."

Moira nodded, wanting to believe. "I hope so, mother. I hope so."

Danielle told Benjamin to row to shore. "There's a beautiful spot over there. I haven't seen it in years."

She accepted his hand to step ashore, then held it, leading him along the path toward the copse. Now, amid
the shimmering leaves, she said, "There. Isn't Aurial
beautiful?" It was, so quiet and majestic in its blanket
of green. In the distance, she could pick out the forms
of her mother and grandmother, still sitting in the
gazebo where they had left them.

"Yes, Danny, it is indeed very beautiful."

She took his arm and turned him. "And over there
is Kingston, my other grandfather's home." She studied
the view a moment, then turned back to Benjamin. She
smiled. "You weren't looking."

His eyes were like brown fire, warm, holding her.
She felt suspended. Her smile, unwilled, was actually a
nervous reflex. He was bending to her. Too close. She
closed her eyes against the distortion of her vision.

The kiss galvanized her. It was as if their mouths
had become separate from their bodies, filled with sensation, brimming with passion. She did not resist or
struggle, but rather leaned weakly against him, absorb-
ing the sensations into her body. Nor did she end it.
He did.

"I love you, Danny. I can't help it." He moved away
from her, holding her shoulders. "But I can help this.
I love you enough to protect your honor."

She looked at him, nodding. "I know."

She leaned toward him, he toward her, and they
truly embraced this time, she on tiptoe, crushed against
him, enveloped within his arms, feeling his manhood
against her thigh, welcoming the desires that flooded
her.

Again, he stopped it. "Danny—" His voice was
quivering. "This doesn't make it any easier for me. I
don't want—"

She put her fingers to his lips to silence him. "I
know, and I'm sorry." She brought her fingers away,
touching her own lips with them. "I'm being selfish. I
wanted to know. . . ." She smiled. "What every woman
wonders about, I guess."

"And?"

Her smile broadened. "I needn't have wondered." She laughed lightly then, to break the spell, and turned him back to look at the view of Aurial. Their moment of passion was ended.

He would not quite let go of it. "Dare I hope, Danny?"

She was looking at Aurial, still feeling the passion he had ignited—or had she done it?—wondering what to reply. Then, as though in a dream, she saw a carriage drive up in the distance, stop, a man alight, her mother and grandmother walk from the gazebo to greet him. He doffed his hat. Yellow hair.

"I think you'll have your answer soon, Benjamin."

He followed her gaze. "Your husband?"

She turned to Benjamin. "Do you mind if I row back by myself?"

"Of course not. I understand."

She was turning to leave. "Take the long way back, Benjamin. Be a long time returning."

She invited Walt inside. He refused. "Is there someplace private where we can talk?" He saw the gazebo. "Over there, perhaps?"

"If you like."

They sat opposite each other on the swing, only a few feet apart, but it seemed to Danielle a great distance separated them. She looked at him carefully, trying to detect the haggardness Cassie had mentioned. She saw none. He looked the same.

"You look lovely, Danny—as always."

"Thank you."

"Have you been well?"

"Yes, I'm fine."

"The children?"

"Fine, too, both of them. They're napping now."

"Perhaps I can see them later?"

"Of course."

Awkwardness filled the space between them. He looked down at his hat, as though it were a curiosity, slowly revolving the wide brim between his fingers.

Then he stopped that motion. "I've missed you, Danny. It's been hell for me." When there was no reply, he looked up at her. "Did Cassie come?"

"Yes."

"Did she give you my message?" He saw her nod. "It meant nothing to you?"

"Of course it meant something." She hesitated. "She said you looked like you'd been drinking."

"I was. That's over now." He looked at her, pain, remorse, on his face. "I'm sorry, Danny, sorry for everything, sorry for that last night. I didn't mean . . . I was just hoping—"

"You needn't explain. I know what you were doing."

"Can you forgive me?"

"Forgive? Yes. Forgetting may be something else." She saw the line of his mouth harden. "I can only hope that potion is all gone now."

"Yes. There'll be no more of that, I promise."

"It was hardly the action of a loving husband." There was a hardness to her tone, a tinge of bitterness.

"I said I'm sorry."

She let it go then. She watched him, sitting there, toying with his hat, so big, so powerful, now helpless and miserable. She could not feel one shred of compassion. "How's the nightriding going?" She saw him look at her, detected his surge of anger. It matched her own. "Your hood and cloak must need cleaning—to wash the blood off."

Walter Summers had a temper, and she had goaded him terribly. She saw his anger rise, but as quickly saw him tamp it down, shaking a little from the effort.

"So, this is still what this is all about?"

"Of course."

He sighed. "Danny, I've killed no one."

"Not that you know of."

He bolted to his feet, his head almost banging the top of the gazebo. "You're being unreasonable, Danny. I can't help what I am. A white man, a landowner deprived of my livelihood, my birthright. I am a Southerner. I must do what I must."

"And so you have."

He looked down at her, furious, shaking with frustration. "Does it have to matter so much? Isn't it enough that I love you, that I've always loved you, that we were happy together? I'm the same man who loved you in London, rescued you twice. I'm the same man whom you once loved, and gave yourself to for all time. I haven't changed. Have you?"

"I don't know."

"Doesn't everything we were, everything we had together, our love, our children, mean anything to you?"

She stared at him, sapphire-blue eyes meeting brown. He had put her on the defensive. Somehow, all this was now her fault. Once again, her anger flared. "Josh Calhoun is upstairs in bed. He's sick. Now's your chance to kill him."

He raised his hand to her. She did not wince or blink or even look at it, though she readied herself for the blow.

It didn't come. Slowly, he dropped the hand, struggling visibly against his rage. Finally, he said, "Is it over between us?"

"I don't know. It doesn't look very good at the moment, does it?"

"I just wish I understood *why*."

"I think you do, Walt. You're doing what you feel you must. It's just intolerable to me. It's that simple."

"Doesn't love mean anything?"

She paused. The words that came out of her mouth just happened. It seemed to her they were not preceded by conscious thought. "Love can die, Walt. It may survive an isolated incident or two, but not a series of hurtful transgressions. Love cannot endure *all*."

He looked at her a long moment. She found it impossible to read his mind. Anger, frustration, resignation, longing, desperation, sorrow—all were there in his eyes. He looked away, toward the rig he had come in.

"Is there someone else?"

She hesitated, willing herself not to look away, even

blink, keep her voice level. "There may be. I'm not sure."

He looked at her, but said nothing, only wheeled on his heel, put on his hat and stalked to the rig, climbed in and flicked the reins hard. She did not look after him, but she heard him drive away. She sat there, looking down at her hands, hoping that one day she would forget his last, recriminating glance at her.

Moira watched it all from an upstairs window, hoping, wanting so much. Then, when her son-in-law stalked to his rig and drove away, she gasped in horror and cried out for him to stop. Then she began to weep, couldn't help it.

Danielle was still sitting in the gazebo, when Benjamin returned. He went to her, standing in the entrance, leaning against the doorjamb. "It didn't go well?"

She sighed. "Not very."

"I'm sorry."

She looked at him. *"You're* sorry? I thought you wanted hope."

"Not at the price of your unhappiness."

She let that soak in a moment, then smiled lamely. "I'll be all right, Benjamin. It just takes a little getting used to, I guess."

His smile was broader. "I'm an expert."

"At what? Hardly the break-up of marriages."

"Waiting."

She looked down at her hands then. "Good, for I fear that's what's going to be in store for you."

"I know. I'm very patient."

She raised her head and looked at him, her lips spreading into the slightest of smiles. "It may take a long time, Benjamin."

Truly happy, unable to hide it, he grinned. "You'll forgive me if I try to turn the clock ahead from time to time?"

Chapter 31

Morgan Kingston knew only one cure for his ailment —work. Spurned by Cassie Brown, he turned for solace to the one continuing love of his life, Aurial. Tending the fields, the animals, keeping books, was already a full-time job, and he gave himself to it wholly. But it was not enough, so he undertook the laborous job of replacing a large section of the three-tiered white fence that surrounded the estate. He kept busy from dawn till dark, until he rolled into bed exhausted.

When Glenna, the Fairchilds, Joe and Jessie came down from New York, he welcomed the excuse to move out to Kingston. With Calhoun there, every bedroom at Aurial was full. At Kingston, it was easier to avoid seeing anyone. He had become antisocial, a hermit.

All this Miriam knew, understood, sympathized with and welcomed as her opportunity. Her "new" mother urged her on. "Why don't you take Morgan's lunch out to him, dear? The poor boy has to eat."

"Should I?"

Moira laughed conspiratorially. "I can't think of a single reason why not. And if you should happen to become interested in the propagation and cultivation of tobacco plants, or whatever ridiculous thing he is doing today, then you might find it—well, educational."

"All right, but I don't think he'll want to see me."

"I'm sure he won't. Right now he's wallowing in

self-pity so much, he wouldn't notice a visit from the
Virgin Mary Herself. But go anyway."

She rode out on horseback, carrying the basket of
food. When she reined beside him, he looked up, glar-
ing at her. "Mother says you have to eat." She held the
basket out to him. "It's awfully heavy. I wish you'd
take it." He wavered a moment. It seemed to her she
could almost see his hunger winning out over his
petulance.

"I guess I am hungry."

But when he took the basket, it snagged on her
skirt. He fumbled with it a minute. "If you help me
down, it'll come loose easier." And so, he had no
choice, since the basket was in his one hand, but to
put his arm around her waist to lift her down. She may
have had a choice, but she leaned heavily against his
shoulder and chest with her hips, then took all the
time she reasonably could in sliding her body slowly
down his frame till her feet touched the ground. Only
then did she bend and deftly unsnag the basket. There
was a small hole in her new skirt—all her clothes were
new and decidedly modest—but she considered it
worth it.

She smiled at him. "There's enough for two—unless
you're *that* starved." She saw him glower and looked
away. "Over there, under that tree, will be nice."
Abruptly, she picked up the basket and strode toward
the shade, laying out the cloth and the food.

They ate mostly in silence. What words there were
had to do with food, and how good it was, and would
he pass the salad, and why didn't he eat the last sand-
wich? No sense in taking it back to the house.

"Anything I can do to help you, Morgan?"

"No."

"But I want to. I'm tired of being cooped up in-
doors. You know I like to be outside." She saw him
glare again. "I know. I'll hoe corn—over there."

"It doesn't need hoeing."

"Corn always needs hoeing."

Two hours later, she thought it all a huge mistake.

Her arms were ready to fall off, and her hands had three blisters each. Then she saw him striding toward her.

"Had enough?"

She smiled. "Oh, this is great fun, Morgan."

"I'll bet." He took her hands and looked at the palms. "C'mon. I'll get something to put on these."

He walked so fast toward the barn, she had to half-run to keep up with him. Then he rubbed an ointment on her hands. It felt cool and hot at the same time.

"This'll toughen them up."

"Just what a girl needs, tough hands."

"I didn't ask you to hoe."

"I know." Under his tutelage, she began to rub her hands together, smoothing the ointment into the skin. "You're being beastly to Cassie, you know—staying away, not seeing her, not speaking." He had already turned away, putting the ointment back into a drawer. "She's a nice girl, Morgan. She couldn't help . . . what she did . . . how she feels."

He said two words. "Drop it."

A visit to the fields became a daily event in her life. She progressed from hoeing corn to helping him lay fence. She held the posts while he swung the heavy maul, and the sideboards while he nailed them to the posts. It was hard work, particularly when he swung the heavy hammer. Each blow felt like it was breaking her arms. And her hands, her hands! They went from blisters to splinters and calluses. Her reward was his acceptance of her, a few words of appreciation, and the knowledge she was at least staying near him—as well as having him hold her hand to remove a splinter.

Every evening, so tired sometimes she could hardly fall asleep, she despaired of her quest. Only Moira's bemused encouragement kept her going.

"Didn't you tell me how sorry you were that you didn't stay and fight for him when you thought he loved Cassie?"

"I don't think he'll ever get over her, mother."

She smiled. "Oh, yes, he will. Just be patient."

"All right—if I survive."

Moira laughed. "You poor dear. Let me massage your shoulders."

Miriam gratefully turned her back and let her mother knead the aching muscles. After a time, she said, "Is he right, mother? Are we brother and sister?"

"Stepbrother and stepsister. You are no blood relation."

"But we were raised together."

"He was already grown, a man, when you came to live with us."

Miriam sighed. "But would it be wrong for us to. . . . Maybe he's right."

"All he is is a stubborn mule—and a blind one, to boot."

Morgan's avoidance of the family became an increasing embarrassment, but at Moira's urging, they all contrived to ignore it. Cassie offered to leave with Calhoun, but Moira would not hear of it. "My son is embarrassing me enough already, Cassie. I'll not let him make it worse by driving you away."

It was a very difficult time for Cassie. She felt responsible, but didn't know what to do about it. She tried several times to talk to Morgan, but each time he walked away from her without answering. Finally, she cornered him in the kitchen when he was having his usual late, cold supper.

"I asked to leave, but your mother won't let me."

There was no reply from him.

"Is this the way it is to end, Morgan, with you hating me?"

He looked at her finally, saw her eyes filled with tears. "I don't hate you, Cassie."

"No? It sure does seem as if. I mean, if you like me, you have a strange way of showing it."

He turned back to his plate, stabbing a cold, boiled potato with his fork. "There's nothing strange about a farmer working his fields."

She sighed. "Have it your way, Morgan." She turned to leave him.

"Cassie." He saw her stop, turn. He forced himself to voice the question. "How's Calhoun?"

"Improving. We'll be able to leave in a few days."

"I didn't mean *that*. Cassie, does it help if I say I'm sorry—that I'm trying to get over it?"

She smiled. "The way you've been acting, anything would help." She saw him grin sheepishly. She came to him and, hands on his shoulders, bent and kissed his cheek, whispering, "We just weren't meant to be, Morgan. Recognize and accept what is—before you lose her." Then she was gone.

Miriam detected a change in Morgan the next day. Oh, it was hardly earthshaking. She just caught him looking at her a couple of times, a puzzled look on his face. It was almost as though he were looking at a stranger. She decided that about summed up what she was to him—a stranger.

When Morgan did not come to Aurial for supper, even well after dark, Moira suggested that Miriam take it to him. "I'm sure he's down at Kingston working on his books. He hasn't enough sense to eat."

"Should I?"

Moira smiled. "At this point, you've got nothing to lose, have you?"

"Hardly."

He was working at his desk when she arrived in the study with the basket of food. "If Mohammed won't come to the mountain, the mountain comes to him."

He actually smiled. "Thank God. I'm famished. I just wanted to finish this first."

"Go right ahead. I'll lay out your dinner." She delved into the basket, bringing out a tablecloth, silverware, plate. "Maryland fried chicken, I see, potato salad, baked beans. A veritable feast." She glanced at him. "Are you finished? Can I lay out your dinner on the desk?"

He was staring at her, eyes squinting a little. "Didn't you do this once before?"

"Yes." She laughed. "You don't remember, do you?"

"No."

"I'm not surprised. You were awfully tipsy."

"What happened?"

"Nothing very much." She motioned for him to move his ledger book, then spread the cloth on his desk, laid out his plate, napkin, knife and fork.

"I'm sorry, I just don't remember."

She laughed. "I'm not, not sorry at all." She forked a chicken leg and thigh to his plate, then spooned out salad and beans.

"You won't tell me what happened?"

"Oh, no. I think I'd better not."

"But I want to know. It's bothered me all this time —not knowing, not being sure."

She finished serving his dinner, then looked at him, smiling. "All right. It wasn't much, really. Nothing terrible happened. I came in with a basket of food, and laid it out on the desk like this." She laughed, sounding a bit nervous, high-pitched. "Actually, it was just about the same food. You were sitting there like you are now." She laughed again. "You were awfully drunk, Morgan."

"I remember. You were wearing—"

"I was afraid you might remember that. It was awful."

"No, you looked nice. I remember."

"What else do you remember?"

"I'm not sure. I. . . ."

She moved around the desk, leaning against it, half-sitting, facing him as she had before. "You were so drunk, Morgan, you couldn't even eat. I had to feed you."

"You're kidding."

"No, I'm not." She picked up the chicken leg and put it sideways into his open mouth. She watched him bite and begin to chew. Then, as before, eyes laughing, she began to lick the grease from her fingers, slowly, one at a time, making little smacking noises. She saw him react.

"You did that?"

"And more." She took the chicken leg from him and

rubbed it across his lips, then bent and began to lick off
the grease with her tongue. She felt him gasp, then
shudder, and in one movement he came to his feet and
pulled her hard against him, and she was being kissed as
she longed to be, as he had when he broke into her
room at Blakeley's. She surrendered to him, to her longing, to the knowledge she had won, won at last.

He pushed her away, staring at her in shock, disbelief. She smiled. "That's exactly what happened,
Morgan."

"It couldn't have."

Still she smiled, "But it did. I wouldn't lie."

"God, Mirry, it couldn't. You're . . . you're my
sister. What will people think?"

He might have slapped her. Her anger flared. "The
same thing they'd think if they knew you pulled down
my dress and had at my breasts."

"God, Mirry, that's awful. You're my sister. People
would—"

"Oh, shut up, Morgan Kingston." She wheeled away
from him toward the door, more angry than she'd ever
been in her life. "I'm sick of you, just sick of you,
mooning over a colored girl you wanted to marry. Oh,
that was all right. It didn't matter *what* people thought
then. But love a girl who grew up in the same house
with you, a girl who's not really any relation—why,
that's just terrible, unthinkable. Goodbye, Morgan."
She punctuated her farewell by slamming the door
behind her.

She was still fuming when she arrived back at Aurial
and reached her room. She had her suitcase open and
was packing, when Moira entered.

"Going somewhere?"

"I can't stay here, not with him."

Moira smiled. "I gather it didn't go well?"

"Not hardly." She sighed, visibly controlling herself.
"I don't mean to take it out on you, mother, but he's
impossible, just unbelievable. I'm his sister, and that's
all there is to it. I give up. I can't stay here with him."

"What happened?"

"Please, I don't want to talk about it."

"All right." She took one of Miriam's new dresses from her and began to fold it into the suitcase. "Where will you go?"

"Grandmother Glenna is going back to New York in the morning. I thought maybe she'd take me in for a while."

"I'm sure she'd love to have you. But what then?"

"I don't know. Maybe I'll go to school in the fall."

Moira smiled. "A good idea. Education is always useful."

Moments later, Morgan opened the door without knocking. He was panting heavily. Obviously, he'd run all the way from Kingston.

"Get out, Morgan, I'm finished with you. I've got blisters, splinters, calluses. I can't take any more. I'm through—forever."

"You didn't finish your story. What happened after I . . . ?"

"You came up here for that?"

"Dammit, I wanna know."

"Ohhh." It was a sound of total exasperation, half-growl, half-wail. "You fell asleep, you dummy. Nothing happened."

"Thank God!"

"I knew you'd feel that way. Now just leave me alone. You've had your bedtime story for tonight." She turned away from him, back to the suitcase.

"Where're you going?"

"To New York, that's where."

"Again?"

"Yes, again. What's it matter to you?"

"I'm tired of busting down doors. My shoulder still hurts."

She turned, saw him grinning. He continued to look at her, but spoke to his mother. "Are you sure she's not my sister?"

"That, young man, is a gross impertinence."

"I don't seem able to do anything right these days."

He came to Miriam, touching her shoulder. "Is it too late for me to try?"

"Try what?"

"This." He kissed her, and it was not at all brotherly.

"I've been such a fool, Mirry."

"My name is Miriam, and I don't like to be called Mirry."

He smiled. "Isn't it better than sis?"

TAKE ADVANTAGE OF THIS SPECIAL DISCOUNT OFFER!

ANY TWO TITLES-ONLY $5.<u>00</u>